Put your sword in its place, for all who take the sword will perish by the sword.
<u>Matt 26 vs 52.</u>

THE JOCKEY'S WIFE

WIFE

A DCI BUCHANAN MYSTERY

BY

ALEX WILLIS

Books by Alex Willis
Non-Fiction
Step by Step Guitar Making 1st and 2nd editions
Standalone fiction
The Penitent Heart
The Falcon, The Search for Horus.
The Road Home
Crichtons End

DCI Buchanan Series

Book 1   The Bodies in the Marina
Book 2   The Laminated man
Book 3   The Mystery of Cabin 312
Book 4   The Reluctant Jockey
Book 5   The Missing Heiress
Book 6   The Jockey's Wife
Book 7   Death on the Cart
Book 8   Death Stalks at Night
Book 9   Death Sleeps Late
Book 10

Published by Mount Pleasant Publishing 13-02-2022

The story contained between the covers of this book is a work of fiction, sweat, and perseverance over many months. Characters, place names, locations, and incidents are either the product of the author's imagination or are used fictitiously. Any resemblance to actual persons, living or dead, or locals is entirely coincidental.

ISBN-13: 978-1-913471-22-4

Text set in Garamond 12 point.

This book is dedicated to every Pevensey Starbuck's barista who has or will serve me my coffee. Thanks, you really do make my day. ☺☺☺

1

Flying Golfs

Sunday dawned, as Sunday will,
to find Buchanan standing still,
in front of the window, cup in hand,
thinking of the goodness of the land.

Today he would be clearing the last of the brambles and repairing the greenhouse on his recently acquired allotment.

'My Adonis, with coffee cup,' said Karen, as she opened her eyes. 'Why are you up so early? Come back to bed, it's Sunday.'

'Can't sleep, too much to do today.'

'Ah, your allotment,' she said, looking at the time on her phone. 'Surely you're not going over this early?'

'No. I'm going down to the newsagent's first to see what gardening magazines they have.'

'Well, if you are determined. Pass me my dressing gown, please,' she said, sitting up. 'I'll have your breakfast ready when you return, so don't be too long.'

'Aren't you going to church today?'

'No. If you remember we have Jill, Stephen, Poppy and Harry coming to celebrate Jill's three-month scan this evening, I'll watch the service online in the kitchen.'

'How could I be so forgetful? This time next year I'll be a grandfather!'

'Are you going to drive down to the village?'

'No. I'm going to walk, it'll do me good, get the oxygen flowing through my blood. Won't be long.'

Towards the east in the morning sky, the sun hung low. Above, the azure sky interspersed with billowing clouds caused Buchanan to smile at a distant memory. It was of a day, many years prior, which he'd spent with his grandfather. They'd planted potatoes in a deep trench on top of grass clippings.

'That will keep them warm as they get growing,' his grandfather had said. It was just one of those obscure memories he cherished of his grandfather.

In the distance, over Beachy Head, the drone of a WW2 Spitfire caught his attention. He watched as it re-enacted an arial ballet of loops, dives, and rolls, just like the WW2 pilots had done seventy years previously. Many of those pilots had not yet begun to shave, yet each had fought ferociously for air superiority, later referred to as 'Their Finest Hour' in the speech by Winston Churchill.

Buchanan stood and watched till the Spitfire came out of a final loop, climbed skywards, and disappeared into the clouds, leaving only the diminishing sound of the mighty Merlin engine that seemed to be saying *'Remember us, we died fighting tyranny so you would have freedom'*.

Today, no matter what, it was going to be a good day at the allotment. A gentle breeze ruffled Buchanan's hair and, with the warmth of the rising sun on his face, he continued his walk down Rattle Road towards the newsagents.

As he walked past The Heron pub, he looked across at Kendals coffee shop and thought he'd pick up a slice of cake for a tea break later in the day.

He entered the newsagent's, selected his copy of the *Herald* for Monday morning reading, two gardening magazines and a copy of the *Sunday Telegraph*.

As he exited the newsagents he met Dave, one of his allotment neighbours.

'Morning, Jack, lovely day. I see you're really getting involved,' he said, nodding at the gardening magazines under Buchanan's arm.

'In for a penny, in for a pound, Dave. Besides, I hear you grow super-sized potatoes and I fancy having a go at knocking you off that pedestal.'

'You're welcome to try. Going down this morning?'

'Yes. After breakfast, I'm eager to check out the greenhouse and see if it survived yesterday's storm.'

'Let me know if you need any glass. I have a stack of old panes from an abandoned plot.'

'Thanks, I may take you up on that.'

'Are you going to Kendal's for coffee?' asked Dave, as Buchanan stopped at the pedestrian crossing.

'No, not this morning. Karen is making breakfast for us. I just thought I'd see what cakes they have. Be nice to have a slice of homemade cake later with my cup of tea.'

'Kendals should do well being so close to the school. The perfect location for mothers to congregate after dropping off their little ones in the morning,' added Dave, as they crossed the High Street.

A slice of coffee and walnut cake for later, Buchanan and Dave stopped on the edge of the pavement and waited for traffic to pass.

'The railway crossing must have just opened,' said Dave, as they waited for a steady stream of traffic coming from their left. The last car passed and, as Buchanan stepped out into the road, Dave grabbed his elbow and pulled him back.

'Stupid shite!' yelled Buchanan, at the disappearing brake lights of a speeding Golf GTi.

'That was a close call! Are you OK?'

'Yes, I'm fine, thanks.'

'Are you sure? You're shaking a bit.'

'No, really, I'm fine. I of all people should have remembered my green-cross code.'

'Look right, look left and look right again before crossing?'

'That's the one. Wonder if it's still taught to schoolchildren?'

'Who knows what they teach children these days?'

'New maths, do you remember that farce?'

'Years ago. Tried to help my son figure it out. I complained to the school about them trying to mess with children's minds with new age thinking.'

'What did they say?'

'Eventually the school saw sense and went back to teaching basics. Talking of basics, Westham High Street is a thirty zone, that car must have been doing close to sixty. I wonder what possessed him to drive like that. Did you get its registration?'

'Yes, and if it was up to me, he'd be arrested and jailed for that sort of driving.'

'I saw him parked outside the church earlier, I assumed he was waiting for someone. I've been on at the council for months now to get speed cameras installed, we need a twenty-mile an hour speed limit in this village. What mayhem that kind irresponsible driving could cause during the week, with the village school only a few yards further along the High Street.'

Buchanan took out his phone and, using its notepad, wrote down the make and licence number of the car.

'That kind of driving should be reported,' said Dave.

'Don't you worry, I'll report the driver when I get to work tomorrow morning.'

◆

'What will be the first thing you do at the allotment?' asked Karen.

He held up a substantial padlock. 'Fit this to the shed door, can't afford to have someone pinch my new tools.'

'What about the greenhouse? You will be careful with the broken glass?'

He smiled at her. 'I'll wear gloves and be careful.'

'Now you're making fun of me.'

'Sorry.'

'I know you are. You're just excited about getting your hands proper dirty. You want to scratch in the dirt and sing to yourself without a care in the world.'

'Have I been talking in my sleep?'

'No, my dear. After thirty-five years of marriage, I know how you think.'

'Oh.'

'Would you like me to bring you a piece when I come down?'

Buchanan looked at his wife. 'My we are regressing. The last time I heard someone ask me that, was when I was at school and my mother brought me a jelly sandwich for lunch.'

'Glad you still remember her. When was the last time you called your parents?'

'I'll give them a call this evening.'

'I'm sure they'll appreciate hearing from you. How about your brother Matthew?'

'The last time I talked to him we ended up arguing about some point of law. You know what he said?'

'No, because you were so wound up, I decided not to ask.'

'I'll tell you then. He thinks criminals should be treated as though they weren't responsible for what they do, it's society that should be in jail.'

'He does have a point, doesn't he?'

'Perhaps, but don't you dare tell him I said so.'

'As you wish, cheese and pickle do?'

'Yes, that would be lovely.'

'Morning all, what would be lovely?' said Poppy, as she wandered into the kitchen dressed in jeans and long-sleeved blouse with a light jacket draped over her arm.'

'Good morning, Poppy,' said Karen. 'I'm making sandwiches for Jack's lunch. Shall I make some for you as well?'

'No thanks, Harry is picking me up in a few minutes, we're off to London for the day. He's taking me to the Victoria and Albert Museum, whatever that is.'

'Oh, you'll enjoy that, it has a bit of everything,' said Karen, picking up her phone. 'It's the world's leading museum of art and design, housing a permanent collection of over 2.3 million objects that span over five-thousand years of human creativity. It holds many of the UK's national collections and houses some of the greatest resources for the study of architecture, furniture, fashion, textiles, photography, sculpture, painting, jewellery, glass, ceramics, book arts, Asian art and design, theatre and performance.'

'Gosh, you are well informed.'

'No, not really, I just googled the museum website.'

'Sounds like I'm going to have a busy day, thanks.'

'Have you settled into university life?' asked Buchanan.

'Yes, but it's so different here in England from the university I was going to in Dallas.'

'Is that an issue?' asked Karen.

'No, it's kind of quaint, I'm still trying to get used to the different accents.'

'Well, I'm sure that when you and Harry get married and you move back to be with your folks in Dallas, life will return to normal for you.'

'I'm not sure if I want to go back. You and Jack have sort of become family while I'm here.'

'Thank you, we've tried to make your stay as comfortable as we can.'

'And you have. I'll always cherish the memories of my stay.'

'That's nice,' said Karen.

'If you two ladies will excuse me,' said Buchanan, 'the weeds won't pull themselves. Hope you and Harry have a nice day.'

'You won't be late home from the allotment, Jack?' said Karen. 'Remember Jill and Stephen will be here with Harry and Poppy for dinner.'

'How could I forget?'

◆

Buchanan returned from the allotment, showered, and came down the stairs in time to let Poppy and Harry in the door.

'How was the museum?'

'Fantastic. I think you need at least a week to see everything. Where's Karen?'

'The kitchen.'

'Are Jill and Stephen here yet?'

'No, not yet.'

'Fine. I think I'll go see if Karen needs help.'

'What about me?' asked Harry.

'How about you and I have a drink?' said Buchanan.

'That suits me fine. A cold beer would be great if there are any.'

'I'm sure I could find one. Why don't you go through to the sitting room, and I'll bring you your beer?'

♦

Buchanan and Harry were chatting in the sitting room when Jill and Stephen arrived.

'Sorry we're late,' said Jill, 'but someone forgot we needed petrol for the car.'

Stephen, looking rather sheepish, said, 'We did have enough to get here, it was the getting home I was concerned about.'

'Well, we're all here now,' said Karen, 'why don't we sit down, and Poppy and I will bring dinner through?'

♦

'When are you and Harry getting married?' asked Jill.

'Not till next year,' replied Poppy. 'We're going to wait till I complete university. I do hope you and Jack will be able to come to our wedding, Karen?'

'I'm sure we will make the time, Poppy. Yours will be the third wedding Jack and I will be going to in the next twelve months.'

'Oh, who else is getting married?' asked Jill.

'Two couples that Jack met during cases.'

'Do I know them?' asked Jill.

'Do you remember the female suspect in the Dutch canal murder?'

'Yes.'

'She's getting married to the Dutch policeman who helped in the investigation. The second is closer to home. Cynthia Mountjoy, remember her?'

'Who could forget Cynthia?'

'Who is Cynthia?' asked Poppy.

'The wife of a very nasty person called Victor Mountjoy. Jack will be giving her away when she marries Pat, her stable jockey,' said Karen.

'Do you remember the Castlewood Cup race?' asked Buchanan.

'Of course, I do, that's where I met my lovely hubby to be, Harry.'

Buchanan smiled at the memory. 'Cynthia was a competitor, along with her husband, Victor

'Oh, that's right, my dad came third, and I think you came in fourth, Jack?'

'I believe I did.'

'Wait a minute, if Cynthia is still married to Victor, how come she is going to marry her jockey, Pat? How can you be giving her away?

'It's a long story, Poppy. I'll try and be brief.'

'Before you start, Jack,' said Karen, 'anyone for coffee, tea?'

Teas and coffees served; Buchanan continued with his story about Cynthia Mountjoy.

'Cynthia was married to Victor, a colonel in the Army. Apparently, he was more interested in making money through various criminal activities than being an attentive husband. Being a hot-blooded woman, Cynthia struck up a friendship with their jockey, Pat McCall. This friendship, in absence of attention from Victor, developed into a full-blown relationship.'

'My dad says that happens all too often,' said Poppy.

'As I said, Victor was involved in many criminal activities and had decided to have a final fling at raising funds before he and his co-conspirator did a disappearing act. They had planned to fly out directly after the Castlewood Cup race.'

'But where did you meet Cynthia?'

'I met Cynthia at Castlewood Country Club the weekend of the race.'

'Cynthia was flirting with Jack,' said Karen.

'Really?'

'It wasn't like that, Poppy,' said Buchanan. 'Cynthia is a much-misunderstood lady. Her husband ignored her, and it was inevitable she would stray and seek out someone who could love her back, and that was when Pat came into her life.'

'That happens, but there's something I don't understand,' said Poppy, 'didn't you say she is married to this Victor chap?'

'*Was* married. As part of his get rich scheme, he and his cohorts were supposed to fly off to France at the end of the Castlewood Cup race, but the plane ran out of fuel over the English Channel and he and the other passengers are presumed drowned.'

'Does she still have the horses?'

'Yes, at her stables. They're not far from here in Kent.'

'Sounds an ideal situation.'

'Pat, her intended, is a professional jump jockey and Cynthia teaches stable management, dressage and show jumping.'

'Quite a lady, I'd like to meet her.'

'You probably will at the wedding. I suppose you and Harry will get an invitation along with Jill and Stephen.'

'More coffee anyone?' asked Karen.

2

Mucking Out

'Are you going to the office this morning?' asked Karen, as she came out of the bathroom.

Buchanan pulled the bedclothes off his head, squinted at the bedside clock, and pulled them back again.

'Jack, you have a job to go to. You'll be late.'

'I have a headache.'

'That's nobody's fault but yours. You should have thought of that before you and Stephen had the nightcap.'

Buchanan squinted and tried to focus his eyes on his wife. 'I only had a wee one. Just to celebrate Jill's news.'

'Is that what you remember? You've forgotten you and Stephen finished the second bottle of red, then went on to the whisky? What Poppy and Harry thought about you two, I don't know!'

'Ach, it was a special occasion. It's not every day a man is able to celebrate he's going to be a grandfather.'

'Well, as long as you don't make a habit of it – *are* you going to work today?'

Buchanan nodded then grimaced.

'You get up and dressed and I'll get you some water and paracetamol. Do you want breakfast?'

'Please.'

◆

'Feeling better?' asked Karen, as Buchanan spread marmalade on his toast.

'Yes, thanks. It's been years since I was hung over. Did I really drink that much?'

Karen nodded.

'What about Stephen?'

'Jill drove him home.'

'And Harry and Poppy?'

'I think they thought it funny when you and Stephen started singing.'

'Oh dear! How will I ever live that down?'

'I wouldn't let it worry you.'

'Where's Poppy? She'll be late for her train.'

'She left half an hour ago, while you were getting dressed. Now, are you going to work today? It's already eight-fifteen.'

'Yes, I've got the paperwork on the Barazani case to finish for the coroner's court. Thankfully it should be a quiet day for Jill and me.'

'Jack, you of all people should know you shouldn't say things like that – you'll jinx the day!'

'Ach, that's just superstition.'

♦

Buchanan looked at the wall clock as he entered his office and smiled; eight-forty and he was first in. He placed his coffee and pastry on his desk, removed his jacket and draped it over the back of his chair. Picking up the remote control for the air conditioning he pressed the on button; today was going to be a hot one.

He contemplated whether to read the paper first or get down to work. Even though the *Eastbourne Herald* was published on Friday, he didn't like to spoil the weekend with the local goings on, so it was his habit to put off reading it till Monday morning.

He decided work first. He reached over his pastry, clicked on his computer, and logged in. Picking up his coffee and as he moused over to the Barazani file, he caught sight of an article in his news feed. The article was about a money-launderer in northern England who, under the Proceeds of Crime Act, had been ordered to surrender around ten million pounds of cash and properties consisting of apartments and houses. All of which he was unable to show how he earned the money to pay for them.

By now he had momentarily lost interest in the Barazani file and picked up his copy of the *Herald*. Page eight had him shaking his head. It wasn't just the north of the country having issues with gangsters and their ill-gotten gains. The article in the upper left corner of the page said that a local gang of people traffickers had been found guilty and sentenced to various terms in prison. As well as the prison terms, under the Proceeds of Crime Act, the gang members had been ordered to repay hundreds of thousands of pounds.

A paragraph on page seven caused him to pause and think. A small section of an unidentified aeroplane wing had been found on Shoreham beach. He put his coffee down, wondering if the section of wing could have come from the plane that Victor Mountjoy had been a passenger in when it ran out of fuel?

He continued with the article and read that fishing boats working in that area of the channel had been warned of the possibility of damage to nets if encountering the wreck.

Putting the paper down, he looked up at the office clock. It was now nine-twenty and still no sign of Jill. He shrugged and realised this was probably what was to be the norm over the next few months till she went off on maternity leave.

He reached for the weekend incident report and saw that early on Saturday morning a carpenter had died as a result from falling off a ladder while working on an oak-framed barn. The report went on to say that he'd fallen fifteen feet and accidentally stabbed himself in the chest with a chisel. His co-worker had gone outside for a cigarette and, when he returned, he found his unfortunate colleague lying on the ground in a pool of blood. By the time the ambulance arrived, he'd lost so much blood they were unable to save him. The HSE were investigating to see if there had been any breaches of the safety at work regulations. One less incident for Buchanan.

He went back to the *Herald* and read an article about the increasing volume of bicycles being stolen in the area. It had him reminiscing about the time when car radios were the item of choice. On a happier note, he saw that Eastbourne town ranked as the sixth best place for holidaymakers to go, alongside destinations like Brighton, Bournemouth, and Southend-on-Sea.

The sound of footsteps had him glancing at the office door and the arrival of his co-worker, Detective Sergeant Jill Street, now Hunter since her marriage to Constable Stephen Hunter. Though happily married, she chose to continue to use her maiden name: Jill Street. After all, wasn't she was half of the Buchanan and Street duo and the butt of many good-natured jokes about the main shopping street in Glasgow and even a few about her being Buchanan's bag lady? There were also murmured recitations of the children's nursery rhyme about their first names: Jack and Jill.

'Sorry I'm late.'

Buchanan shrugged and smiled. 'How are you this morning?'

'I'm fine, it's Stephen that's not. Unfortunately, he can't mix his drinks like you can; red wine and whisky is a bit much for his system.'

'How is he?'

'Fine now. He was up and down like a yoyo most of the night, but I suppose it was a bit of a practice run for when the baby's born.'

'Never having had the pleasure of that experience, I'll have to leave it for you two to discover.'

'Thanks,' she said, as she hung her coat on the coat hook behind the door. 'What do we have on for today?'

'A good question. Apart from completing the Barazani file there's not a lot to do.'

'In that case I'll follow up on the recent cases of van break-ins. I was looking at the list from the past three months and there seems to be a pattern showing up. Though robbery division told me, with the car-boot markets ending soon for summer, they expect the break-ins to tail off.'

'What do you think?'

'Unlikely. I think the proceeds of these burglaries are exported to the continent. Who's going to ask questions of a builder crossing the channel at the end of the week with his tools in the back of his van?'

'There's logic in that.'

'That's what I thought. Oh, Karen mentioned you two are going to a wedding next weekend and that you are giving the bride away. Is that Pat and Cynthia's wedding?'

'That's the one.'

'I seem to remember last night you said her husband died when the plane he was a passenger in crashed in the Channel?'

'Yes, that's what we think. Cynthia wrote to me a couple of weeks ago and said she'd received a certificate of presumption of death from the coroner, so they are going ahead with the wedding. While we were at Castlewood, she jokingly asked me to give her away.'

'You don't think she had anything to do with the plane crash, do you?'

'No, definitely not Cynthia,'

'The reason I mentioned it was there was a case a couple of years ago about a husband who tried unsuccessfully to kill his wife by tampering with her parachute.'

'I doubt Cynthia had anything to do with the crash unless you blame her for blocking Victor's credit cards. I think the plane simply ran out of fuel.'

'And the wedding is the week after next?'

'Yes, a week on Saturday.'

'That's cutting it a bit fine.'

'I think they are quite eager to make it official, also I think it might have something to do with the stables and ownership of the horses. Or maybe she wants to start a family. I don't think her time with her first husband was a happy or productive one. If I have time today, I will go to see her and discuss the arrangements.'

'Where do they live?'

'The stables are near the town of Paddock Wood.'

'Has the plane been found?'

'Not yet. Initially the coastguard made a search of the crash scene, but only found an oil slick. By now, with the currents in that part of the Channel, the plane could be miles away.'

'So, do you think the coroner's court will reconvene any time soon?'

'Unlikely, the wreck of the plane would need to be recovered first, complete with the bodies of those on board. Otherwise, the coroner will wait the requisite number of years then declare Victor to be legally dead.'

'So, three weddings in twelve months; let's hope there are no funerals.'

'That only happens in movies and the *Midsomer Murders* television series.'

'Have you ever wondered who would play you if our working life was made into a television show? For you, I reckon Roger Allam would suit the bill.'

Buchanan looked at Street, thought for a minute, then smiled, 'for you, I could see Keira Knightley.'

'Really, you think so?'

Buchanan nodded.

'Thanks. Stephen will have a good laugh over that.'

'You're welcome.'

'Cynthia Mountjoy must have had money of her own if what you told me about her husband losing everything in his fraudulent schemes is true. I imagine it takes quite a bit of cash to feed and care for horses. Is she rich?'

'I don't think she is particularly wealthy, especially since she said they had to remortgage the farm. Apparently, her late husband, Victor, almost bankrupted them with his get-rich-quick scheme,' said Buchanan, as he returned to the incident sheet. He scanned the first two pages, put it back in his in-tray and glanced at his emails.

'Remind me, what was Victor Mountjoy's scheme? Remember I was off with Karen visiting your mother-in-law during the week.'

'He entered two horses in the Castlewood Cup and, using hair dye, he swapped their identities, pretending that the faster of the two was the slow one, and vice versa. He then bet heavily on the one everyone thought was the slower one.'

'That's fraudulent.'

'Absolutely, but thankfully we found out before the race and switched the horses back.'

'I bet he was angry.'

'He was livid!'

'What did he do about it?'

'As soon she realised his fraud had been discovered, he and his partner-in-crime took off in the plane and attempted to fly to France. If his attempt at defrauding the bookmakers wasn't bad enough, he and his henchmen abducted Harry and intended to shut him up for good.'

'You mean kill him?'

'Yes. Victor Mountjoy and Du Marchon were also working other schemes that since they are no longer with us will have to be left to conjecture.'

'Didn't you and Travis rescue Harry?'

'If we hadn't, Harry might not be with us today.'

'So that's why Victor had to disappear.'

'Yes, but in doing so he perished in the English Channel.'

'Quite a character, I'll bet Cynthia is glad to have him out of her life.'

'I do believe you have expressed her sentiments correctly.'

'What do you know about her intended – Pat?'

'Not much. Cynthia told me Pat had been a promising jockey, but when his parents became invalided at home, he put his ambition of being a jump jockey on hold to stay at home to look after them. When they died, he started looking for work in the horse-racing field. He saw an advertisement in the horse-racing press for a riding jockey at the Mountjoy stables, applied and was duly accepted. Getting the job as jockey to the

Mountjoys was his way of getting back in the saddle, so to speak.'

'My, you do know a lot about the Mountjoys! But tell me, what is a riding jockey? Don't they all have to ride?'

'I should know about the Mountjoys, I spent a week with them at Castlewood, and I think the term *riding jockey* is given to jockeys who ride and exercise the horses at the stables.'

'Quite a tale, shall we get to work? Anything of interest on the weekend incident sheet?'

'Oh, just remembered something.'

'What's that?'

'Could you run a plate for me?'

'Sure, what is it?'

Buchanan flicked through his phone screen to the note app and read off the licence plate for the car that almost ran him down.

'Are you sure you wrote down the number correctly?' asked Street. 'What kind of car was it?'

''09 Golf GTi.'

'And you're sure of that?'

'Yes, why?'

'That reg does match an 09 Golf GTi, sounds like a cut and shut deal. The car was written off two years ago.'

'So, why was it doing sixty miles an hour down Westham High Street, and why be in so much of a hurry and attract attention to himself, especially since there weren't any police in the area?'

'You were there.'

'Nah,' he shook his head. 'I was in my allotment clothes; no way could the driver know I was a policeman.'

'There's a traffic report, 'said Street, staring at her screen, 'about the car being seen on the A22 by a patrol car late last night. They got a hit on the ANPR and when they tried to stop the car, it sped off. At one point it was clocked doing ninety-five. As they approached the Hailsham exit roundabout they were slowed by a farm tractor and momentarily lost sight of the GTi. They picked it up again just before the brow of the hill and caught sight of the Golf as it turned off onto the Arlington Road. They were close behind when the driver turned left at the junction and headed towards Bushy Woods. Unfortunately, the GTi swerved to avoid a car coming out of the Old Oak Inn and ran off the road. By the time the police caught up with the accident, the driver had done a runner into the woods.'

'Did they get the eyes-in-the-sky up?'

'No. The helicopter was working a case on the Kent border.'

'Hmm. Well, I suppose we can let traffic follow up on that one, it's out of our remit.'

'Anything else of interest in the weekend incident report?'

Buchanan returned to the incident sheet and read, 'Officers from the Neighbourhood Policing Team and the Roads Policing Unit joined forces to patrol hotspot areas for noisy and anti-social driving. There was one arrest for a driver being in possession of class A drugs, another for having no insurance and a third for being under the influence. There was a separate incident where a patrol car tried to pull over a speeding Audi. It went out of control at a roundabout and rammed a house. The passenger was arrested but the driver ran off before the patrol car could get there. The house was deemed unsafe, and the householders had to spend the night in a hotel.'

'At least there haven't been any suspicious deaths - the town is getting a reputation. Anything else?'

'Ah, this might interest you: a long-wheelbase VW Crafter van with French plates was stopped on the A259 for non-functioning turn signals. Due to the driver acting suspiciously, the vehicle was searched. A substantial quantity of expensive bicycles were found, with an estimated value of thirty thousand pounds. The driver was unable to give a credible reason for having so many and was arrested for being in possession of goods with no means of proving ownership. The cycles were confiscated pending the driver providing proof of ownership.'

'Does it say who's investigating?'

'DC Ambrose. Know him?'

'I've just signed up for an antenatal class with his wife, Grace. I'll get in touch with Lazarus and see how far he's got with his investigation.'

'Fine, if you're going to do that, I'll get back to the Barazani paperwork. Thankfully I'm almost done with the report, which only leaves the coroner's court to attend.'

'OK. I'll go and have a chat with Lazarus, see you later.'

♦

Buchanan closed the Barazani file and looked up at the clock on the wall: five past eleven. Good, time for a coffee, and to make a call. He picked up his mobile and scrolled through the phone directory till he got to Cynthia Mountjoy's number.

He pressed the dial button and listened to the ringing. He was getting ready to leave a message when the call was answered by a man's voice.

'Hello, Cynthia's phone.'

'Is this Pat?'

'Yes, who's this?'

'Pat, it's Jack Buchanan. I just wondered if you two would be in this afternoon?'

'We will be, why?'

'Just thought I'd pop over and go through the details about the wedding, if that's all right.'

'What time were you thinking about? Cynthia has students till four. Then we start evening stables.'

'How about I get there for four o'clock, will that work for you?'

'I guess so.'

'Great. The address is still Appleton Equestrian Centre in Tudeley Brook?'

'It was when I got out of bed this morning.'

'OK, see you at four.'

The thought of instant coffee from the canteen didn't appeal to him, so he wrote a note for Street to say she could find him at Starbucks.

◆

He was busy looking at the assortment of pastries and cakes when a familiar voice distracted him. It was Sam Richmond from the HSE.

'Hi Sam, haven't seen you in here before.'

'Unlike you guys, we have to work for a living.'

'Very funny. Want company?'

'Yes, we're over by the window.'

'OK, let me get my coffee and I'll join you.'

'Good morning, Jack. The usual?' asked the barista.

'Yes please, Molly. And could I have a piece of choc chip shortbread as well?'

'Certainly.'

Buchanan collected his coffee and choc-chip shortbread and joined Sam and his assistant by the window.

'Jack, this is Abbey, we work together.'

'Morning, Abbey. So why are you two here?'

'Just about to wrap up an on-the-job accident out at Rickney.'

'Is that the carpenter who managed to stab himself with a chisel?'

'Yes.'

'Was it an accident?'

'Always the policeman. Yes, it was an accident.'

'I read an account this morning. Just seems a bit odd to me that an experienced carpenter should accidentally stab himself in the chest with a chisel.'

'Jack, you're like a dog after a bone. Why don't we finish our coffees and I'll show you the scene? We've still got a couple of items to wrap up, that should put your mind at rest.'

◆

Buchanan followed Sam as he turned right out of the garage, then left onto Rickney Lane. As he drove, he wound down his window and let the warmth of the late summer air spill into the car. Not for the first time during the last months, he thought how fortunate they were to be living in such a beautiful part of the country.

He was brought out of his daydream when Sam slowed to navigate a sharp left-hand bend onto a short track that led across a field. It was a typical Sussex barn; the walls were constructed of flint with a peg-tiled roof which sagged at one end. The whole exterior of the barn was encased in scaffolding. A hanging sign said it was erected by Koly Scaffolding Services.

Sam waited for Buchanan to park his car, then walk over to the closed barn doors.

'No lock on the door,' said Buchanan, as Sam opened a small side door.

'Not necessary, the barn is empty and, before you say anything, it isn't a crime scene.'

'Where did it happen?'

'Over there, at the far end of the barn. The carpenter was chiselling out a socket in readiness to fit that cross beam,' said Sam, pointing to a short substantial piece of oak resting on two sawhorses.

'And that is the ladder he was working from?'

'Yes.'

Buchanan walked over to the ladder and stopped four feet away. He looked at the ground beneath the beam where the carpenter had fallen.

'You say he fell from the top of the ladder and landed there?' He said, pointing at what was left of the bloodstains in the dirt.

'Yes, we are surmising he fell off the ladder, landed on the chisel then dragged himself over to the door to call for help.'

'He was alone? I thought he had a mate.'

'Yes, and that's the only part of this tragic accident that bothers me.'

'Why would that bother you?'

'He's disappeared.'

'Can you expand upon that statement?'

'When the carpenter fell from the ladder, he managed to get to the door and call his mate. It was he who called the emergency services. When they arrived, the mate explained what had happened, said he tried to help but was unable to do much as the carpenter was bleeding too badly. He was taken away in the ambulance and that was the last anyone has seen of the mate.'

'When was this?'

'Early Saturday morning.'

'Do you have an address for the mate?'

'Yes, but when we went to interview him, the landlady said he had paid the bill, stayed on Saturday night, then left early Sunday morning.'

'Did she say where he was going?'

'No. She assumed since his boss had died, he'd have to go and find work somewhere else.'

'Were they both staying at the same address?'

'Yes.'

'Did you ask her if she knew where somewhere else might be?'

'She said she'd heard them mention Glasgow. So, it would likely have been back there.'

'And you're sure it was an accident?'

'Unless there is any other evidence to prove otherwise, that's how the incident will be reported.'

'Did you take photos of the scene?'

'Yes, want me to send you copies?'

'Please.'

'Anything else?'

'Does he have a name?'

'Yes, though not much else. His driving licence has him as a Jackson Hardcastle. Want to have a root around, see if there are any more bodies?'

'No, that won't be necessary, I've seen enough. Oh, you could let me have the landlady's address, just in case?'

'I'll email the photos and the address when we get back to our office.'

'That will be fine. In the meantime, I'm off to see a man about a horse.'

♦

After the last few days of being overcast and damp, this Monday afternoon the sun shone brightly and the temperature at two-fifteen in the afternoon was just into the low teens. The drive from East Sussex to Kent took Buchanan past Herstmonceux Castle, the Observatory and on through the town of Battle – where nearby in October 1066 there had been a battle between William, Duke of Normandy, and King Harold Godwinson, which began the Norman conquest of England. Buchanan exited Battle, drove over the Hastings to London railway line, passed the largest gypsum mine in the UK and on to the A21.

As he left the London Road, he wound down the windows and breathed deeply, reminiscing about the smells of autumn, and thought back to the time he had first met Cynthia Mountjoy. He had been on leave and staying at Castlewood Country Club. Karen and Jill had gone to France for the week to visit his mother-in-law and he was at Castlewood for a week of relaxing, reading, riding, and sipping on his favourite Scottish malt.

He had been relaxing in the Castlewood library when Cynthia walked in, talking on her phone. As soon as she saw Buchanan she hung up and walked over to him. Although she was married to Victor, and involved in an affair with her jockey, she was quite obviously in a cheeky mood as she pretended to flirt with Buchanan. He gently rebuffed her advances and by the end of the week she and Pat had become friends with Buchanan to the point of her asking him to give her away, should she ever become divorced from Victor.

He left Paddock Wood behind, drove up over the main railway line and on to Whetsted Road and Appleton Equestrian

Centre. He wasn't quite sure what to expect. Would it be a grand edifice like that of Castlewood, or a caravan in a field with a collection of wooden stable boxes with a rope and pole exercise ring?

Buchanan almost missed the entrance to the stables. The high hedge – being close to the road – made it almost inevitable that unless you were aware of the entrance you might go sailing on by.

He stopped abruptly and backed up, thinking it was fortunate there wasn't anyone close behind. He turned onto a gravelled driveway that led off to the right and presumably the house and stables.

He drove slowly in and parked in front of the main entrance, away from a dark green Land Rover Discovery, attached to a double-width horse trailer. The trailer doors were clipped back and the ramp down. Buchanan got out of his car and walked round to the rear of the trailer. There were no signs of horses or people. He stepped back and looked at the house in front of him and was immediately confronted by an Alsatian. It did not bark but stood there eyeing him up.

'Hello,' said Buchanan, crouching down and offering the back of his hand. The dog came slowly forward, head down, hackles up and sniffing the air. It came close enough to sniff his hand then stepped back, relaxed, and walked off.

The house was a typical example of an eighteenth-century building. Built from London stock bricks with a peg-tiled roof, it looked like at one time it had been a modest country house suitable for a London banker or similar profession. Over the years it had been extended to the right and now had almost doubled in size by the addition of what would be, anywhere else, a two-storey bungalow.

Just in view behind the house was the end of the barn. As he walked towards it, he could see a high hedge with a gate in the middle separating the working stables from what he assumed was the domestic tranquillity of the house.

Mucking Out

Buchanan continued round the end of the house and saw a low-level structure attached to the end of the barn, the office he assumed. On closer inspection he saw a weathered sign that confirmed his suspicion. It said *Office* with a large, faded arrow indicating the end of the barn.

Walking towards it, he saw to his right a wide farm gate leading out to Whetsted Road, the probable stables entrance. He could hear the muffled sound of voices and clattering hooves. The voices became clearer and, as he turned the corner, he could make out the unmistakeable form of Cynthia and sitting patiently beside her was the Alsatian he'd met earlier. Cynthia was talking to another rider.

'That's right, Marjorie, the vet said to keep Rocky rugged when he's out, and make sure he gets plenty of water – oh – Jack. Marjorie, this is my boyfriend, Jack.'

Buchanan looked at Marjorie's face, it was one of bewilderment.

'Just kidding, Marjorie. Jack is going to be giving me away when Pat and I get married the week after next.'

'Oh, I'm glad to hear that, you had me quite confused for a moment.'

'Sorry, Marjorie, I was just winding you up. Jack and I met a few months ago at Castlewood. He came fourth in the Castlewood Cup.'

Marjorie looked at Buchanan, and said, 'I seem to recall seeing you being mentioned in the racing press. Something about being a jockey to watch in the future.'

'I'm surprised to hear that; I only ride for pleasure.'

'Oh. What do you do?'

'I'm a policeman.'

'Pity you weren't around to catch Victor.'

'Marjorie was one of Victor's victims,' explained Cynthia.

'Almost screwed us out of thousands, the shit. If it were not for Cynthia telling us to stick with backing Turpin, we'd have lost a fortune.'

'That was Jack's doing, Marjorie. He found out about Victor's scheme and warned us in time.'

Marjorie turned back to Buchanan and said, 'I take it you are not just an ordinary policeman?'

'I'm not sure what you mean by ordinary, Marjorie. I just do my job.'

'Well, thank you anyway.'

'What's the dog's name?' said Buchanan, as he crouched down to scratch the dog's head.

'His kennel club name is quite unpronounceable, so we just call him Major, and even though a Major is a junior rank to that of a Colonel,' she said, with a mischievous smile on her face, 'in our hearts Major outranks Victor any day.'

Buchanan thought that was interesting – even the stable dog outranked Victor!

'If you'll excuse me,' said Marjorie, 'I need to get Rocky back home.'

'I'll give you a hand, Marjorie,' said Cynthia, pointing to a door on the side of the barn. 'Oh, Pat's in the office, Jack. I'll be with you after I help Marjorie.'

'Thanks.'

Buchanan watched as Cynthia, with Marjorie, and her horse Rocky, walked off round the corner of the stables. Cynthia certainly was in her element he thought as he crunched his way across the yard.

The office consisted of a large oak-framed extension jutting out from the side of the barn. On the left wall, sitting neatly between some small bushes. was an air-conditioning unit exhausting the heat of what probably was a busy stable office. The entrance to the office was through a set of tinted double-glazed doors.

Quietly closing the office doors behind him, Buchanan walked across a polished oak floor to where Pat was sitting behind a desk.

He was talking on the phone and nodded at Buchanan to sit on one of the two empty chairs in front of him. It was a one-sided conversation with a supplier, and Pat was winning. Finally, with a nod of agreement, Pat put down the receiver.

'Did you see Cynthia? She's out in the yard with Marjorie.'

'Yes, she said to come in and wait for her, she's walking them back to the trailer.'

'So, how are you?'

'Fine.'

'Been doing any riding?'

'No, been too busy for that.'

'Pity, you're quite good at it, another twenty furlongs and you and I would be fighting for the lead.'

'Never, I'm a complete amateur.'

'So was I when I started. One thing I've learned these past years is, it's never too late to try something new.'

Buchanan shook his head. 'Maybe when I was sixteen, but I've jumped too many hurdles in my life for me to change horses now.'

'A man of metaphors,' said Cynthia, as she entered the office with Major walking by her side. 'How are you, Jack?'

Buchanan stood and faced her. 'I'm fine, thank you, and yourself?'

'What do you think? Victor dead and gone, the stables starting to pay for themselves, and Pat and I shortly getting married.'

'I'm glad to hear it.'

'You want a coffee, Jack?' said Pat. 'We usually have one at this time of day before we start evening stables.'

'Yes please, I have time,' he said, looking at the clock. 'I was having a quiet day so thought I'd pop over and talk about next week's arrangements.'

'Oh, we can do that over dinner,' said Cynthia. 'You are staying for dinner, aren't you?'

'I hadn't planned to.'

'Nonsense, you've got to stay. There's three lovely fillet steaks in the fridge that need to be eaten; you can help with evening stables.'

'Well, if you insist, I'll give Karen a call and let her know I'll be late.'

'Great, you can use Victor's overalls and wellies. They may be little loose on you but should keep your clothes clean while you muck out.'

Buchanan was about to say something then thought it might be fun to do some mucking out.

'OK. How many horses do you have here at the stables?'

'The three that you know and four other boarders. Don't look at me like that, we should be done by six. Then we can relax and have an enjoyable evening. C'mon, let's get started. This way.'

Instead of going out the main office door, Buchanan followed Pat and Cynthia through a door behind Pat's desk leading into the tack room and horse stalls beyond where he was to spend the remainder of the afternoon mucking out.

The sweet-sour smell of the barn had him thinking back to his childhood and Jock's stables in Busby. It was a pity that memories were all he had and all he probably would have. He'd crossed that bridge from childhood and could never return. As a youngster he'd spent many happy hours after school helping with mucking out in exchange for an occasional ride. Sadly, there would be no riding today, just hard work and an enjoyable dinner to follow.

The interior was quite different from what Buchanan remembered of Castlewood. There the stables were laid out in three-sided blocks. Each block was connected by a wide internal corridor containing twelve stalls. Here at Appleton, all the stalls were in one barn with eight stalls against the back wall and three stalls each side of the barn doors on the front wall. The feed store was in the middle of the far wall, and the tack room was in the middle of the wall he'd just walked through.

Mucking Out

'A bit different from Sir Nathan's at Castlewood, Jack?' said Cynthia, as she saw the quizzical look on Buchanan's face.

'It is well laid out,' said Buchanan. 'And I see you have room for a few more guests.'

'Thanks, that's the results of Cynthia's teaching,' said Pat. 'A few months ago, we had only our three horses, and now the barn is filling nicely. A big difference from Castlewood, there they have a permanent crew managing the cleaning of the stalls and feeding and exercising the horses. Here at Appleton, it's just me and Cynthia to feed, clean and exercise the horses. It's a full-time job.'

'Sometimes we get local youngsters helping out in exchange for free lessons,' added Cynthia.

'I don't know how you two manage to find the time to do all this every day,' said Buchanan, as he parked the wheelbarrow beside the barn door and glanced into one of the empty horse stalls. The bedding straw was at least a foot thick and spread out in readiness for its occupant to return from the exercise ring.

'We start at six in the morning,' said Pat, as he removed the halter from a horse that had been waiting to come in from the yard. 'We are usually done by eight. Then we have breakfast and begin the exercising – and lessons if there are any students.'

'We are looking for a stable lad to do some of the day-to-day work,' said Cynthia, with a wry smile on her face as she fastened a hay net to the outside of Turpin's stall. 'Would you be interested in the position?'

Buchanan shook his head and wondered what Karen would say if he went home and said he'd got a new job as a stable lad!

'Sorry, I already have a job.'

'I didn't think you would be interested. Pat does the cross-country training,' said Cynthia, 'I do the dressage and show-jumping lessons. We share managing the business.'

'What's up there?' said Buchanan, pointing to a narrow wooden staircase in the far corner above the door to the office.

'That leads up to what will be the stable lad's flat,' said Cynthia. 'It has a small kitchen, bathroom and bedroom. We use it for storage at the moment. You wouldn't want to live there just now, it's quite a tip. C'mon, let's get finished, those steaks won't cook themselves.'

♦

Buchanan shook off the borrowed wellies, peeled off his borrowed overalls, put his shoes back on then followed Pat and Cynthia out of the barn. They walked across the yard, and through a gate in the hedge which opened out onto an expanse of lawn, flower beds and fruit trees.

'You like what you see, Jack?' said Cynthia.

'This I did not expect.'

'It was what enticed us to buy it,' said Cynthia, as they walked across the lawn past a huge climbing frame for a child.

The house from the back bore little resemblance to the front. Whereas the front had all the marks of a typical eighteenth-century Kent country house, the rear displayed the work of many hands down through the years.

The ground floor had been extended out at the back with each window sporting a box festooned with flowers. On the right there was a large outdoor barbeque area under a rose-strewn pergola. Under the pergola there were painted wicker basket chairs arranged around a low wicker table.

In the middle of the upper floor, on the corner of the original house, there was a protruding window giving views over the garden and stables. It looked every bit like the quarter galley of an 18th century man-o'-war.

'You like the windows?' said Cynthia, pointing up at the bedroom window.

'Yes, looks quite interesting.'

'The previous owner was a retired Royal Naval commodore. I think he was a bit of a history buff. When we cleared out the back bedroom, we found stacks of old naval charts from all over the world.'

Buchanan followed Cynthia and Pat into the kitchen.

'You two go through to the sitting room, I'll call you when dinner's ready,' said Cynthia.

Buchanan accompanied Pat through the dining room and on to the sitting room. 'Would you like a drink while we wait for dinner? We have wine, or would you like something a bit stronger?' said Pat.

Buchanan looked at the time and nodded. 'Could I have whisky and water, please?'

'My pleasure,' said Pat.

'Pat,' said Buchanan, 'what was the outcome of the situation about the money Victor had swindled from the investors?'

'We had to remortage the farm to pay everyone back.'

'And you never found the money?'

'No. The money Victor stole has never been recovered. I suppose since we have paid everyone back the money – if ever found –would now rightfully be ours.'

'Do you have any idea how much was involved?'

'In all, we paid out three hundred and fifty thousand pounds to the syndicate to keep everyone satisfied,' said Pat.

'That's why we had to remortage the stables,' said Cynthia. 'Dinner's ready.'

'Be right there. I've been looking forward to this dinner all afternoon,' said Pat, as they walked through to the dining room. 'It wasn't all cash to syndicate investors though, part of the pay-out was to a group of people who'd invested in a property deal Victor was working on.'

'What was that?' asked Buchanan.

'We're not sure, we've not been able to find any of the paperwork for the deal,' said Cynthia.

♦

Cooking was a side of Cynthia that Buchanan had never imagined. He'd expected a plate with a steak and maybe a potato and a couple of leaves of lettuce, instead it looked like she was entertaining royalty.

'Pat's forever on a diet,' she said, 'so it's wonderful to have someone to dinner that I can cook for.'

Buchanan glanced at Pat's plate and the steak and baked potato.

'I have to watch what I eat,' said Pat, 'but am allowed red meat a couple of times a week.'

'I see. How did you get involved in horse racing, Pat?'

'Back home on the farm in Derry, we never had anything you would call a horse. The only four-legged one we had around was a pony, but it was so old and sway-backed it looked like every day would be its last. It showed up in the front of the house one morning, I guess whoever owned it didn't want it anymore and just untied it and sent it on its way.

'My dad was dead against putting animals down, so he gave him to Seán, my younger brother, and me to look after. To me at eight years old it was all my Christmases rolled into one. I made a stall for it in one of the old sheds at the back of the farmhouse. It must have really been abused by the previous owner as it tried to kick and bite anyone who tried to get close to it. Eventually as it learned to trust me, I could brush it without it trying to do me an injury. With gentle care and feeding, eventually I was able to get on his back and ride him round the small field in front of the house.'

'And he still has the touch with horses,' said Cynthia. 'Anytime a horse acts up, all Pat has to do is to stroke its head and talk quietly to it then it settles down and behaves.'

'Thanks for the testimonial, Cynthia,' said Pat, as he cut a tomato in half. 'When I was ten years old, one of my dad's friends saw me riding and suggested I get proper riding lessons. I was fifteen when I went to work at Seán Lennox's racing stables. I wasn't employed, the deal was I could help two to three days a week plus holidays in exchange for being allowed to ride out with the horses on their morning gallop. It soon became apparent to those around me that I had a bit of talent and much to my father's delight I was put on the amateur jockey scheme. I'd been there for about four months when one of the jockeys fell and broke his shoulder. He was scheduled to ride that following Saturday, so Seán, in one of his rare benevolent moods and not expecting me to even stay on the horse gave me the ride. Much to his disbelief, I came second, so from there on I got more and more rides with several credible first and second places.'

'I seem to remember you had an interruption to your career?' said Buchanan.

'Yes. My parents became invalided at home and being the oldest child, I felt it was my duty to stay home and look after them. I was nineteen and only weighed five stone three pounds.'

'That must have been really tough on you, and right at the beginning of your career as a jump jockey.'

'My parents always said family comes first. I could never have looked at myself in a mirror if I hadn't taken the time out to nurse them, Seán, my brother was too young to look after them. It was a wonderful time for me, a blessing I will always treasure. Most people only get to know their parents as just that, parents. I was the lucky one, my parents in their final years became my best friends.'

'Now you can see why I love Pat,' said Cynthia.

'I jobbed around for a few years till I saw Victor's ad in the racing press, and that was when life changed for me, for the better I might add,' said Pat. 'I came to work for Victor and fell in love with his wife.'

'One thing about Victor was,' said Cynthia, 'he could see potential in horses, pity he could never see it in people.'

'Talking about people, how many are invited to the wedding and where do I fit in?' asked Buchanan.

'It will be a small affair,' said Cynthia. 'The actual exchange of vows will be at the registry office in the Bishop's Palace at Maidstone — don't look so worried, it's only ten miles away. With you driving we will be there and back within the hour.

'After the registry office, there will be a blessing in a marquee that will be setup on the lawn here at the stables. That way all our friends will be able to share in the excitement of the day. Oh, just realised, the seats in the marquee will need to be reset after the blessing.

'After the blessing, there will be dinner and dancing. Your main job will consist of giving me away at the registry office, then walking me down the aisle and once again giving me away here at the stables.'

'Will there be a rehearsal for the blessing?'

'Yes, and also a short one at the registry office on Friday, then the marriage for real on Saturday before the blessing later at the stables. I do hope people will have time to come to the blessing ceremony.'

'Have you sent out the invitations yet?'

'With Victor only now being declared dead, the invitations just went out a couple of days ago. Oh, I don't have your daughter's address, would you mind giving her the invitation? It's a bit late to post it now.'

'No problem, I'll pass it on to her when I see her.'

'The actual wedding at the registry will be just a bit of a formality, but after the sham marriage with Victor, I want the blessing to be a day that I remember till the day I die. There will be invited neighbours, friends in the horse world, which includes our dear friends Nathan and Susan, and his stable manager, Harry.'

'Harry is now engaged.'

'Then he must bring his fiancée. Who is she? Does she like horses?'

'Her father came third in the Castlewood Cup.'

'Oh, I remember him, bit of a John Wayne character if I remember.'

'An apt description, Pat. Cynthia, it has been a wonderful evening, but I do need to get home,' said Buchanan.

Mucking Out

'Must you go? There's still half a bottle of red open and Pat won't be drinking any of it.'

Buchanan shook his head, 'I have work in the morning.'

'Look, why don't you stay? We have two spare bedrooms, both with en-suite, though one of them is full of stuff for the wedding. Marjorie has been staying in the other while her horse was here being schooled. I've already changed the bed linen. We're always up at six. Have breakfast with us and still be on time for work.'

Buchanan smiled. 'OK, let me call Karen and let her know.'

'Fine. While you're doing that, I'll clear the table.'

'I'll close up the barn,' said Pat.

♦

'Hi, how was dinner? Did Cynthia behave herself?' asked Karen.

'Shush, she's in the kitchen, and yes, I've had a lovely evening.'

'I suppose this phone call is to say you won't be home this evening?'

'I shouldn't be driving.'

'An excellent thought.'

'Did we get an invitation for Cynthia's wedding?'

'As a matter of fact, we did, it was in today's post. She certainly is cutting it a bit fine.'

'I've got Jill and Stephen's invitation with me, would you give Jill a call and let her know. Poppy and Harry are also invited.'

'Certainly, Jill and Stephen will probably still be up, I'll let Poppy know when she comes in, she's gone out with Harry. Just wondering if Jill is needed tomorrow?'

'Why?'

'If we girls are going to a wedding, we need to get hats.'

'I believe Jill has some leave due to her.'

'Good. I can help her with maternity clothes at the same time, that's if she is interested.'

3

Marjorie

'How did you sleep?' asked Cynthia, as Buchanan pushed the kitchen door open.

'Slept like a log but had a strange dream. I was lying in a meadow and frogs came out of the stream, climbed onto me and went to sleep, croaking contentedly.'

'Ah, that would have been Pat, he snores like a frog.'

'That must have been it, but Cynthia, I do need to get on the road, I can't be late for work.'

'Not without a hearty breakfast, I've learned that from Pat. How about I make some cheesy scrambled eggs?'

'Sounds lovely.'

'Bacon to go with your eggs?'

'Sounds perfect.'

'How about tomatoes? Grilled or fried?'

'As they come. Is there any coffee?'

'In the cafetière, just made a fresh pot, sorry there's no lemon drizzle cake.'

'Lemon drizzle cake at breakfast?'

'It's a joke Pat and I have. We were in a tearoom a few months ago. It was full of senior citizens and at just about every table someone was having a slice of lemon drizzle cake with their tea. Newspaper is on the sideboard.'

'Thanks. You want a refill?'

'Yes please, my cup is over there,' she said, pointing to a large brown coffee cup with a Thelwell cartoon of a very overweight pony standing beside a dismounted rider. 'Do you want your eggs on toast?'

'On the side, please.'

As Buchanan was about to eat the last forkful of eggs, Pat walked into the kitchen. He went over to Cynthia, put his arms round her waist and pulled her towards him. Cynthia looked at Buchanan, smiled and said, 'Jack's almost finished his eggs, Pat.'

Pat let go of Cynthia and turned to Buchanan, an embarrassed look on his face.

'Oh, didn't see you there! Sleep well?'

'Yes, as a matter of fact I did.'

'Marjorie says the same thing,' said Cynthia. 'That's the room she always stays in when she is here.'

'On her own?'

'Yes. Her husband was in the Army, he was killed while serving in Afghanistan, we've sort of become family.'

'Sorry to hear that. Not the bit about being family, just the bit about her losing her husband.'

'Thanks, but she's not alone, she shares her house with Susan. They both lost their husbands in Afghanistan. They met at a memorial ceremony and decided to set up home together.'

'How did you come to know Marjorie?'

'Do you have time to listen to a story about how a little girl grew up?'

'I can make time if you don't mind raking up old memories.'

'I've heard it before,' said Pat. 'I'll go and start morning stables.

'Before I begin,' said Cynthia, 'Do you need a refill?'

Buchanan looked at his nearly empty cup. 'Yes please.'

'As you can probably tell, I have always been a bit wild,' she said as she filled Buchanan's cup.

'I would never have guessed if you hadn't told me that exciting bit of information!'

'You're funny. I was born in Hanningfield, a small village near Chelmsford. I was an unexpected addition to the family. My parents had been trying for years to have a child, then years after giving up hope of ever having a child, I turned up. For someone like me who loved the outdoors it was a fantastic place to spend childhood. There was the nearby Hanningfield Nature Park and the reservoir where my dad would take me fishing when he wasn't out on patrol.'

'Patrol?'

'He was a security guard for Rentokil. Used to do a lot of night patrols, till he had his heart attack, which sadly he never recovered from.'

'I'm sorry to hear that.'

'You weren't to know, but there was some good that came out of Dad's death.'

'Oh, what was that?'

'Major was Dad's patrol dog. He was mostly a one-man dog so when Dad passed away, the company asked Mum if we would like to look after him. He was only a year old at the time Dad died. Unfortunately, Major was too much for Mum to handle, so he came to stay with us.'

'That was very thoughtful of them.'

'We had a riding stable within a short bike ride of the house. Weekends and school holidays I volunteered to help round the stables with the cleaning of the horse boxes. I also groomed the horses in exchange for the occasional riding lesson.

'I did well at school and after getting the required GCSE's I moved on to King Edward the Sixth Grammar school. I wasn't a great academic and struggled with maths and the sciences but did enjoy the biology and art classes.

'I eventually graduated and to celebrate, Marjorie and I decided we'd go to Colchester for the weekend.'

'What did your mother think about that?'

'She was a bit nervous about me going away, especially with Dad not been gone long; but since it was only for the Saturday night, she gave in. I think her being on her own for the first time was what bothered her more than me being twenty miles away in a hotel.'

'Where did you and Marjorie meet?'

'We met in the bathrooms at school.'

Marjorie

'Wait, don't tell me, you'd sneaked out of class for a cigarette?'

'How did you know that?'

'Did it myself.'

'We'd each independently made an excuse to our teachers to leave the class to go to the toilet. Of course, you're right, we did go for a quick cigarette.'

Buchanan nodded. 'Like so many others.'

'I didn't know you smoked.'

'I don't anymore, these are now my cigarettes,' he said, holding up an open tube of fruit gums.'

'When my grandfather heard I was smoking he made a deal with me. He said if I gave up permanently, he would pay for my wedding, including the honeymoon.'

'That was quite an incentive.'

'Yes, it was, and I tell you, it wasn't easy. When did you give up?'

'A couple of years ago, and I now eat my way through tubes of Rowntree's fruit gums instead.'

'How about that, we actually have something in common.'

'And Victor, how did you come to meet him?'

'It was the Saturday Marjorie and I went to Colchester. At first it was just like any other night. To get the evening started, we stopped at a minimarket for a bottle of vodka to share. Don't look like that, we were teenagers, we couldn't afford to get drunk on club drinks. Then at eleven o'clock we went into the club feeling on top of the world. We even had enough money for a couple of rounds.'

'Not much has changed on that.'

'About two o'clock in the morning, we were tired and decided to return to the hotel. We were trying to avoid a group of lads that had been pestering us all night. Just when we thought things were getting awkward, Victor and his friend, Steve, showed up. They had been to a function and were returning to barracks.

'I tell you, it was as if the cavalry had just arrived. The lads that had been bothering us were too drunk to see sense and told Victor and his friend, in no uncertain words, to piss off, that Marjorie and I belonged to them.'

'What happened?'

'It was as though they waved a red flag at a bull. Even though there were five of them and there was only Victor and Steve, the lads were no match for two fit, battle-trained soldiers. If it hadn't had been for a police patrol showing up at that moment, I think Victor and Steve would have put all five of the lads in the A&E department. But there were no real injuries, so the police let everyone go on their way.'

'And Victor and Steve?'

'Marjorie and I were just teenagers and completely awestruck when we saw them in uniform; I'm a sucker for men in uniforms,' she said, smiling at Buchanan.

Buchanan smiled. 'That's OK then, I'm safe. I don't have a uniform.'

'It wouldn't matter if you did, I'm very much in love with Pat,' she said, turning and kissing Buchanan on the cheek.

'So, after the police left, what happened?'

'We went for a walk and fell in love. Victor and I married the following spring – Marjorie and Steve at Christmas the same year. Sadly, her marriage only lasted a year, Steve died in an explosion in Afghanistan.'

'What did your mother have to say about you getting married so soon after meeting Victor?'

'She wasn't very happy about it, and with Dad no longer around I think she felt abandoned. On top of that, Victor was C of E and *not one of us* she used to say. Despite that she learned to accept the situation and adopted cats from the Cats Protection Charity for company.'

'When you and Pat are away, you say Marjorie looks after the stables on her own?'

'Yes. Just the feeding and mucking out, it's usually only for a couple of nights. There are no lessons given when we are away. We do have a couple of local kids who come along and volunteer their services in exchange for an occasional ride.'

'So, there's always someone here in the house looking after the stables?'

'Twenty-four-seven, three-hundred and sixty-five days a year,' said Pat.

'That would worry me,' said Buchanan.

'I wouldn't let it,' said Cynthia. 'Marjorie can look after herself.'

'Well, in that case I need to be on the road. Thanks for the wonderful food and bed for the night.'

♦

Would this be what it would be like, thought Buchanan, as he looked across the office at Street's empty desk. How would he manage when she was off on maternity leave, who would he chat to and bounce ideas off?

He checked the time, eleven-thirty, too early to go to lunch. At least this time it would only be for today. He thought about Jill and Karen, mother and daughter going to Tunbridge Wells shopping for hats.

Bored and unable to concentrate he decided to go over to Tesco's for a sandwich. On returning to the office, he was stopped at the reception desk by the duty sergeant.

'Jack, you have a message.'

'What is it?'

'Not so much a message, Dan O'Shea from traffic division was looking for you.'

'Is he still here?'

'I believe so. I think he's booking someone in.'

'Fine. If he still wants to see me, I'll be in my office.'

Buchanan was reading his well-thumbed copy of the SIO handbook when there was a knock on his door.

'Inspector Buchanan?'

'Yes.'

'Dan O'Shea, traffic division.'

'Come in,' said Buchanan, gesturing towards a chair under the window.

'Thanks.'

'How can I help?'

'I understand you were interested in the outcome of a recent failure to stop and subsequent RTA?'

'Was that the Golf GTi?'

'Yes.'

'That pillock, he almost ended my career. What can you tell me about the car and driver?'

'The car had cloned plates, as I believe you already know, and the VIN showed it to be first registered in Glasgow,' said O'Shea, looking at his notebook.

'Wonder what it was doing down here?'

'We thought you might be able to shine a light on that.'

'Sorry, too much water has gone down the Clyde since I knew what went on in Glasgow. I assumed it was just another stolen car on false plates, and that you guys would follow up on it. Did you ever catch up with the driver?'

'No, but we did find out who he was.'

'Go on.'

'We found his hold-all and tool bag in the back of the car. Inside the glovebox we found a receipt from where he had been staying, it was–.'

'No, don't tell me, let me guess. The receipt was from the Wiseley B&B in Pevensey, am I right?'

'How on earth would you know that?'

'Some might say a lucky guess. I prefer to think of it being a skill I have birthed out of a lifetime of dedication to leaving no clue unchewed. I believe it was Professor James Burke who said that nothing happens in isolation, everything is connected, like links in a chain; one event leads to another.'

'So, what's the story?'

'Last Saturday morning I was nearly run down on Westham High Street by a Golf GTi bearing the plates we now know were cloned. Yesterday, I met with Sam Richmond; he's an investigator for the HSE. He was investigating an industrial accident on Saturday and gave me details about a carpenter who had fallen off his ladder and accidentally stabbed himself with his chisel. The carpenter and his lad were working on a barn restoration on Pevensey Levels when the accident happened. It was Sam who gave me the details of where the carpenter and mate were staying.'

'So, you are thinking it wasn't an accident? Are you connecting the carpenter's death with the disappearance of the mate?'

'No, not at this moment. It could simply be a case of the lad went into shock seeing his boss die in such a way and being in the possession of a car with cloned plates he simply got scared and did a runner.'

'Did the HSE investigator think the death was suspicious?'

'No. He said unless there was any further evidence to say otherwise, it was going to be recorded as a simple case of an accident brought about by the ladder the carpenter was working on not being secured properly.'

'Hmm.'

'And the car?'

'The plates were from a Golf that had been written off. The car had been stolen from King Street NCP Carpark, Glasgow,' said O'Shea, consulting his notebook.

'That's in the East End,' said Buchanan.

'Is that significant?'

'Maybe not. I seem to remember that the King Street Carpark is the largest in Glasgow.'

'Do you want the driver's name?'

'Yes, though like the car registration it's probably false.'

O'Shea smiled. 'We went through the hold-all and found his wallet. According to his driving licence he is called Andy Jameson. That name was also on the B&B receipt.'

'Do you have his age?'

'Twenty-seven.'

'Hmm. I used to know a Andy Jameson when I worked in Glasgow, but he'd be in his late fifties by now. I wonder if they are related?'

'Will you follow up on it?'

'I doubt it, the PCC doesn't appreciate it when I spend resources on events outside our control. I will call Glasgow CID and let them know that young Andy Jameson may be on his way home. Besides, cars get stolen every day, just like bicycles.'

'Bicycles?'

'Yes. According to my partner DS Street, we are having a mini-crimewave of bicycle thefts in Eastbourne, though a lot of them show up a couple of days later in a hedge somewhere.'

'Well, in that case, I'll leave you to spin your wheels.'

'Thanks.'

♦

Twenty minutes later Buchanan had become uneasy. Something just wasn't right, but he couldn't put his finger on what was causing his uneasiness. The name Andy Jameson worried him. He decided to call Dr Mansell.

'Dr Mansell.'

'Andrew, it's Jack. Do you still have the body of the carpenter who stabbed himself with a chisel?'

'Didn't take you long, did it?'

'What do you mean?'

'Your niggler, niggling?'

'What have you found?'

'Come over and you can tell me.'

'Have you completed the autopsy?'

'Yes.'

'Can you hold on to the body till I come over?'

'Sure, it's not going anywhere. When will you be here?'

'Thirty minutes.'

♦

With the area in front of the emergency department being full of ambulances, Buchanan reluctantly parked in the visitor carpark. He put on his mask and after identifying himself at the A&E reception, made his way down to the morgue and Dr Mansell.

'Afternoon, Jack.'

'Andrew.'

'Interesting one, this,' said Mansell, as he pulled out the drawer with the zipped-up body bag containing the lately departed Jackson Hardcastle.

'And what is your conclusion – in laymen's terms, please?'

'The chisel entered the body just below the left ribcage, travelled in an upward transvers direction to the right, missed the liver and pierced the heart. Unless the injury happened on the operating table, death was a certainty.'

Buchanan looked at the photos on his phone of the scene sent by Sam Richmond, then at Dr Mansell's photo of the carpenter's chest with the chisel sticking out.

'You say the carpenter was working at the top of a fifteen-foot ladder, fell off it and stabbed himself in the chest with his chisel?' said Mansell.

'That's what Sam Richardson, the HSE investigator, says in his report.'

'Do me a favour,' said Mansell, handing Buchanan a pencil and a half-eaten sandwich. 'Imagine for a moment you have a chisel in one hand, a mallet in the other and you are standing fifteen feet off the ground balanced on a ladder. You've been chiselling out a socket on an oak beam. The ladder moves, you lose your balance, fall to the ground and stab yourself in the chest.'

Buchanan was quiet for a few minutes then climbed up onto a chair beside the wall. With the pencil in his left hand,

Buchanan tapped it with the sandwich pretending to be chiselling a socket on a beam. Next, he jumped off the chair pretending to fall from the imaginary ladder.

Picking himself up of the floor, still holding the pencil, now in two pieces, he looked at Mansell.

'What do you think?'

'It might just work.'

Mansell shook his head.

'You knew what was going to happen. Now imagine the carpenter, fifteen feet in the air, concentrating hard at what he was doing, when suddenly, the ladder slips. What does he do?'

'He lets go of the chisel and mallet and grabs for the beam.'

'Precisely.'

'But – he could still have let go the chisel and fallen on it.'

'You don't believe that any more than I do.'

'You think he stabbed himself, Hari Kari sort of?'

'Hari Kari is self-disembowelment. What we have here is a chisel to the heart.'

'He's not Japanese.'

'Back to the imagination game,' said Mansell, handing Buchanan a banana. 'Try not to break this one, it's my lunch. Now, demonstrate to me how you might stab yourself in the heart with a chisel.'

Mansell stood back and watched Buchanan go through the motions of holding the banana in his right-hand and poking at his jacket.'

'Doesn't quite work, does it? Out of twenty attempts, one might almost be successful. Now think back to when you were on top of the imaginary ladder and chiselling, which hand were you holding the chisel with and how would you be holding it?'

Buchanan looked at his right hand and at the banana and nodded. 'Who would, in that situation, swap hands with a chisel, when in fact they would be grabbing for something to stop them from falling?'

'Precisely, I'd say there was no way he accidentally or deliberately stabbed himself in the heart with his chisel,' said Mansell.

'How about this scenario. He was done with his work and coming down the ladder. I see him on, say, the fourth rung, hands on the ladder above shoulder height, when someone standing on the ground to his left takes a chisel and rams it up into his body.

'And while the carpenter is lying on the ground bleeding to death, the murderer goes outside for a cigarette. Cigarette smoked, he returns to check that death is imminent and calls 999. While he waits, he goes round the barn to make sure there's no incriminating evidence.

'Then, when the ambulance gets there, he tells them about the terrible accident, great shame, such a fine carpenter, will be missed, etc. Waits for the ambulance to leave, picks up any tools lying around. He then goes to his B&B, tells landlady of accident, pays his bill and leaves town.'

'That works,' said Mansell. 'What will you do now?'

'I'm going to sit on it for just now. I want to see if we can catch up with the lad first and hear what he has to say about what happened.'

'Want to see the unfortunate carpenter?'

'May as well since I'm here.'

Mansell unzipped the body bag to reveal the cadaverous face of the carpenter.

Buchanan came round the side of the drawer and stared at the face. 'I know him, he's not Jackson Hardcastle. It's —it's Jamie Gallagher, or at least it's someone who looks just like him.'

'Could it be Jamie Gallagher?'

'No, Gallagher's dead, died in a car crash on the M8, burnt to a crisp when the fuel tank in his car exploded.'

'Whoever he is, he's definitely dead,' said Mansell, zipping up the body bag. 'But suppose it is this Gallagher chap, and he wasn't really dead, what was he doing working on a barn on Pevensey Levels?'

'Good question.'

'Who owns the barn?'

'It's inherited by someone called Hanson, a retired mechanic. He retired to Spain a few years and didn't want to have anything to do with it. He said he just wanted it fixed up and sold.'

'How did you get all that information?'

'Sam Richmond told me.'

'So, that does raise an interesting question. What's a Scottish carpenter doing restoring a barn on the Pevensey Levels?'

'A very good question which I hope I can get an answer to when I call Glasgow.'

'Seen enough?'

'Thanks, Andrew.'

♦

Back in his office, Buchanan dialed the number for his former office in Glasgow.

'Ferguson.'

'Gus, it's Jack.'

'No, it's not, Jack Buchanan died! How the hell are you, why so long no call?'

'Sorry, been a bit busy.'

'So, we've heard. Getting a bit of a reputation your town, Eastbourne. The Midsomer of the South Coast I hear.'

'Very funny.'

'Any chance of you coming back up here to Glasgow?'

'Not a chance. We've just bought a house and I've taken on an allotment.'

'You have gone soft. What happened to the hardnosed Glasgow cop I once walked the beat with?'

'He got smart and decided to let the youngsters take over.'

'Wish I could get away with doing that. How's Karen?'

'Fine. She and Jill have gone hat shopping.'

'Who is Jill? And why have the ladies gone hat shopping?'

Marjorie

'It's a long story. My partner here in CID is Jill Street. She has no family, and we have sort of adopted each other. The hat thing is I'm giving the bride away at a wedding next week.'

'OK. So, Jack, I assume you're not calling to invite us to the reception?'

'Sorry, no, maybe another time. The reason for my call is twofold. One is to let you know that a young lad by the name of Andy Jameson is on the loose and probably making his way back up to Glasgow. We want to talk to him with regards to a stabbing incident here in Eastbourne and driving a car with cloned plates.'

'And the other?'

'I've just seen the body of someone calling themselves Jackson Hardcastle, or should I say Jamie Gallagher?'

'Jamie Gallagher? He's dead, died in a car crash on the M8 about five years ago, body burned to a crisp.'

'That's what I thought.'

'What was the other name again?'

'Andy Jameson.'

'Want me to check up on him?'

'Yes, please. He was working as a carpenter's mate with Jackson Hardcastle. I can't find anything on the PNC for him, maybe someone in your shop will have heard of him.'

'And you think Andy Jameson stabbed Hardcastle?'

'It's a growing possibility.'

'OK. I'll get back to you as soon as I can, and Jack, don't be such a stranger. Give us a call sometime and let us know how you're getting on.'

'Will do.'

♦

'Evening, how did the hat chase go, were you able to find something suitable?'

'Yes, we did, and quite a surprise it was when I saw Jill in hers.'

'What do you mean?'

'It transformed her completely, she looked like one of those models in a fashion magazine.'

'How abouot the maternaty clothes, you said you'd help her look if she wanted.

Karen shook her head slowly. 'We went to a couple of shops bu settled on JoJo Maman Bébé'

'Sounds posh.'

'Not realy, and they do have some really lovely clohes for the mother to be.'

'I'm glad about that. Oh, I kept some dinner for you, it's warming in the oven.'

'Thanks.'

4

Up from the deep

Buchanan was surprised when he drove into the police compound; Street's car was already parked in its space.

'Good morning, Jill, you're early, is everything all right?'

'Yes, thanks. I had to follow Stephen into the garage. He said his car was making a strange knocking noise and we couldn't afford to have it break down at a critical moment.'

'His car?'

'Yes, mine is only a small runabout, we use his car as a family car, that's why he's insistent on keeping it in tip top shape.'

'Is that normal?'

'I don't know, I don't drive it very often.'

'That's not quite what I was getting at.'

'Oh, now I get you. You think it's the case of me being pregnant has got through those sleepy grey cells of his. He is making sure the car is serviced often, so when the time comes to go to the hospital it won't let us down?'

'Exactly, he's starting to realise what being a father is all about. Don't you just love that boy?'

'Of course, I do, I married him.'

'Of course, you did. Oh, how did you get on with Lazarus and the stolen bicycles?'

'That was an eye-opener. I never knew how much petty crime goes on under the radar. Lazarus said the seizing of the van is just part of a bigger operation. He is working with a team from the Police Nationale in France tracking a gang that they think is setting up a new way of financing international drug trafficking.'

'I can't see how a bunch of stolen bikes is going to finance international drug trafficking.'

'Neither did I till Lazarus explained it to me. He thinks it is a trial set up to see how bartering will work instead of cash. Items stolen in one country are bartered in another country and the credit is used to pay for the drugs.'

'Stealing a few bikes won't raise much cash.'

'Lazarus said he heard from a contact in London about a worrying trend in bike thefts.'

'Was that about scooter riders hijacking bikes?'

'Yes. He said London police have put out warnings to cyclists that thieves carrying machetes have been targeting cyclists in Richmond Park. During the past week there have been three high-end bike thefts.'

'And I thought Glasgow was bad for violence.'

'One cyclist was ambushed by four masked men who chased him down on two motorbikes, while another motorbike dragged him and the bike along the ground for a hundred metres. He said he was threatened with a machete, at which point he handed over his ten-thousand-pound bike. He had tried to escape the men, but they rode one of their motorbikes into him, knocking him to the ground.'

'A ten grand bike! Who pays that much?'

'You'd be surprised. I think some tour bikes cost more than fifteen thousand pounds.'

'Makes my old Raleigh sound like a toy. Anything else?'

'Yes. Police said they are linking that robbery to at least two more, including one on the previous Monday when man in his 30s was threatened with a machete and knocked off his bike by two men travelling on a moped. He suffered minor injuries. Then, on Wednesday, a man in his 20s was pushed off his bike by two men on electric scooters. He was left with minor injuries.

'Unfortunately, there have been no arrests and police have asked for anyone with information about the incidents to come forward.'

'Do you want to be excused to work with him?'

'No, I'd rather be working here with you.'

'Good. Well, I'll be a ...' said Buchanan.

'You'll be a what?' asked Street.

'A breaking news story from the BBC newsfeed on my phone. They've found the plane!'

'Which plane – hang on, do you mean the one Victor Mountjoy was in when it crashed into the Channel?'

'That's the one. I was just talking to Cynthia Mountjoy about it last night.'

'How do they know it's the plane he was in?'

'The plane's registration number is painted on the side of the fuselage.'

'Did they find Victor Mountjoy's body?'

'I'm not sure.'

'What does it say?'

'At three twenty-five this morning, the dredger *Myrtle Rose* snagged the end of the starboard wing of a twin-engine private plane. The registration confirms it to be the plane reported lost in the Channel three months prior. The plane was on course from Headcorn airfield in Kent to Fécamp in France when it apparently ran out of fuel. The body of the pilot still seated at the controls and a passenger seated in the rear were recovered. Police are yet to notify the next of kin.'

'Nothing more about the passenger, do you think it could be Victor Mountjoy?'

'It doesn't say, but I think I should give Cynthia a call to let her know before reporters start showing up at her door.'

'I wonder how she'll take the news?' mused Street, as Buchanan picked up the phone.

'Probably relieved to have something definite about her husband's disappearance.'

'A thought just struck me,' said Street.

'Oh?'

'You remember what happened a few a few months ago?'

'Do you have anything special in mind?'

'What I had in mind was the footballer Emiliano Sala. He died in a similar fashion when the plane he was in crashed in the

Channel. The only difference is in Sala's case there was no sign of the pilot, it was only the passenger found in the plane.'

♦

'Cynthia, it's Jack. Sorry to be the bringer of sad news, but a fishing boat has just dragged the plane Victor was flying in ashore at Shoreham. I wanted to let you know in case you get inundated by reporters – the report says the pilot, plus one passenger – I'll take care of it. I'll get back to you as soon as I have any more information – next Friday, yes, I haven't forgotten, it's in my diary – but won't you be busy getting ready for the wedding – oh, OK, that sounds great, I'll talk to you later.'

'She doesn't sound like she's a grieving widow. Do you think Pat will be able to deal with reporters?'

'Maybe he won't, but Major will.'

'Who is Major?'

'Their Alsatian, a retired service dog that belonged to her dad when he worked as a security guard. It's very friendly when it gets to know you as one of the family, but I pity any uninvited reporter who tries to step beyond the gate.'

'Next Friday?'

'Cynthia has invited Karen and I to stay the night. There's a rehearsal Friday afternoon, and besides, I think Cynthia could do with some feminine support.'

'I know that feeling.'

'Fancy a drive?'

'Where to?'

'My knower wants to know more about the crash. Shall we go and talk to the fishermen who found the plane?'

'Isn't that a job for the Air Accident Investigation Board?'

'Maybe, but since Victor Mountjoy is involved, it becomes our job as well.'

♦

They took the Shoreham exit from the A27, made their way through the busy shopping streets, then drove down to the harbour. Buchanan turned off Basin Road and into the Fish market carpark.

'I never knew this was here,' said Street. 'I've driven through Shoreham many times but have never come down here.'

'Well, we're here now, shall we go and see what we can find out? I think we'll start in the shop.'

They waited patiently in line for the customers to purchase their pieces of cod, haddock, scampi, lobsters and crab.

'Yes, sir, what can I help you with?'

'Can you tell me where I can find the master of the *Myrtle Rose*?'

'You from the press?'

'Not quite, Sussex Police.'

'You'll find the *Myrtle Rose* tied up down the harbour by the Fisheries patrol boat.'

'Thanks, where will I find the Fisheries patrol boat?'

'Are you driving?'

'Yes'

'Go left out of the gate, then left again at the mini roundabout. Stay on the road about a quarter of a mile and you'll see a bunch of offices for rent. Turn left there and you'll find the Fisheries patrol boat. The *Myrtle Rose* should still be tied up beside it.'

'Thanks for your help.'

'You're welcome.'

◆

Buchanan managed to park on the quayside between two remote broadcast television vans each with their reporters recording interviews for the early evening news.

'I see the *Myrtle Rose*,' said Street, 'but where is the plane?'

'Let's go and ask the master.'

They walked across the quayside to the *Myrtle Rose* and stopped at the gangway. There were two crew members scrubbing the filleting table.

'Excuse me,' said Buchanan, 'is the master on board?'

'Yes, but she's busy right now.'

'We won't keep her long.'

'Who wants to talk to her?'

'Detective Chief Inspector Buchanan and Detective Sergeant Street, Sussex Police.'

'Oh, why didn't you say so? Follow me, I'll take you to her.'

'You go first,' said Buchanan.

Buchanan followed Street down the gangway onto the deck of the *Myrtle Rose*. The deckhand went forward to the bridge structure and opened a steel door and beckoned them to follow. He led them down a short passageway, which ended at a set of steep steel steps that led up to the bridge.

'In here,' he said, pointing to a varnished mahogany door. 'Sal, there are two policemen here who want to talk to you.'

'Send them in.'

Buchanan stepped over the sill and into the captain's cabin. It was small but laid out efficiently. On the far bulkhead was a high bunk with drawers under, its mahogany leeboard varnished like the adjacent desk. There was a plethora of navigation instruments fastened to the bulkhead over the desk. Seated at the desk was the master of the *Myrtle Rose*.

'Sal Mahaney,' she said, 'Master of the *Myrtle Rose*. How can I help?'

'It's about the plane you snagged early this morning.'

'Cost me a good net, that did. I thought the French had dumped an old car to sabotage our fishing, turned out to be a plane. Almost cut it loose till we saw the windows and the outline of a body.'

'I thought you managed to bring the plane in to the harbour?'

'We did. Cut it loose on the banks of the Ardur, it was too big to bring through the locks.'

'Where is it now?'

'We left it on the riverbank. I was told it was going to be hauled out by a crane. If it's not there now, it's gone off to be examined somewhere.'

'Do you know where it will be taken to?'

'Nope, too busy working out how we are going to make up for a lost net and day's fishing.'

'What state was it in when you hauled it up?'

Sal shook her head. 'Pretty bad, the plane was flopping about like a bird with a broken wing, the port wing was almost completely off. If it wasn't for our nets the wing would still be on the bottom of the Channel.'

'Were you able to get the plane on board?'

'No, it was too heavy to bring on board, so we lashed it behind the transom and just towed it behind us. We cut it loose when we entered the river.'

'And you weren't able to see inside the cockpit?'

'Couldn't if we wanted to. It was green with algae and covered in seaweed. There was a heavy sea running and I had a two-ton deadweight hanging off the stern. No sir, we weren't about to risk life and limb to look in a coffin.'

'Where could we go to see where it was dropped?'

She thought for a minute. 'You could go back up on to the main road and head west for a bit then cross the river and take a left and work your way back to the river mouth.'

'Is there an easier way?'

'Yes, drive along the frontage road to the end, there's a carpark there. You can walk the rest. You'll be on the wrong side of the river, but if the plane is gone, you won't have wasted your time driving.'

'Thank you, Captain Mahaney.'

'You're welcome.'

♦

Buchanan drove slowly along the frontage road, watching for the speed bumps while keeping to the twenty mile an hour speed limit. When they reached the small carpark, Buchanan parked the car and they continued along the promenade on foot till they got to a high fence at the edge of the estuary. Looking across it, all that could be seen was a large crane in the process of being de-rigged.

'Looks like we are a bit too late,' said Street, as they walked back to the carpark.

'Jill, would you give control a call, see if they know what happened to the plane? While you are doing that, I need to spend a penny.'

♦

'Any luck?' asked Buchanan.

'The wreckage has been taken to Shoreham airport for inspection,' said Street. 'There were only two bodies in the plane and being in the water for so long makes immediate identification difficult. The bodies have been taken to the Brighton morgue.'

'Fancy something to eat. That café looks like a nice place for lunch.'

'How can you jump from the morgue to fancying something to eat?'

'I'm hungry.'

'Oh, I remember - you're hypoglycaemic. OK, I don't want to end up working with a grumpy bear.'

♦

'How was your burger?' asked Street.

'It was just right, said baby bear,' said Buchanan.

'Very funny. What's next?'

'I will call the morgue and see if they have been able to identify the bodies found in the plane.'

'Suppose it's not Mountjoy? Suppose the passenger was just some unlucky soul cadging a lift?'

'Then we have a problem.'

'In what way? Emiliano Sala's pilot was missing and will probably never be found. Why couldn't Victor Mountjoy's body be the same?'

'I'll answer that question when we have a look at the plane.'

'What do you expect to find out from seeing the plane? It's been on the seabed for months; it will be in a right mess now.'

'I'm a doubting Thomas on this. I need to see the plane to put my mind at rest.'

'The Boss might not like you spending resources on a closed case.'

'All the same my knower just won't go back to sleep.'

'What will you do?'

'I'll going to start by contacting the morgue and see what they can tell me about the bodies found in the plane.'

'While you do that, I'll go and powder my nose.'

♦

'What did they say?'

'Positive identification of Julian du Marchon. They found his driving licence and pilot licence. Unfortunately, his hands and fingers have decayed so much it is beyond their capabilities to get fingerprint details. They will try later with dental records for a positive ID.'

'And the passenger?'

'Described as a young male in his thirties, no identifying marks. Stocky build and five feet four in height.'

'So definitely not Victor Mountjoy?'

'Looks that way.'

'So, if that's not Mountjoy, what happened to him?'

'Maybe he survived the crash, and the plane had a life raft?'

'You think Mountjoy may have been able to make it to shore and escape?'

'It's a possibility. When I called the coroner's office, she said she would contact the crew that attended the scene. They'll be on a break in a few minutes, and she'll have one of them give me a call.'

'What would you expect to learn from talking to them?'

'I won't know until I hear their side of the operation.'

'So, I wonder who the unknown passenger is?'

'That's something for us to figure out – though another question arises, why is there is no grieving relative knocking on our door? Definitely something for us to ponder on.'

'In that case, would you like another coffee?'

'Yes, please.'

'Your wish is my command.'

Street returned with two cups of coffee as Buchanan picked up his ringing phone.

'Inspector Buchanan – yes, just a minute while I put you on the speaker. OK, I have DS Street with me. What can you tell us about what your findings in the wreckage?'

'Yes, I'm Sergeant Jones. Where do you want to start?'

'Was the plane out of the water when you arrived?'

'No, the divers were still attaching the lifting slings. It took them about another 40 minutes to rig it up before the crane was able to lift the plane out of the water.'

'What did it look like when you saw it out of the water?'

'Surprisingly quite normal, except for the left wing - it was hanging off.'

'No damage anywhere else?'

'None that we could see.'

'What did you do when the plane was secure on dry ground?'

'We approached it and were able to make out the outline of a body seated at the front on the left. When we looked inside, the person – we assumed to be the pilot – was seated, still seat-belted, at the left-hand controls.'

'Was there any sign of a passenger in the right-hand front seat?'

'No, we did look but the pilot was the only body at the front the plane, the passenger was seated in the rear.'

'Was there much water inside?'

'Not when we got to enter. The divers had opened the doors as the plane came to the surface to let the water drain slowly.'

'Did anything wash out as the water emptied?'

'We watched for that, but the divers had only opened the doors a crack, nothing other than water came out. By the time we got in most of the water had drained.'

'What did the interior of the cabin look like?'

'Like it had been at the bottom of the English Channel.'

'Did you check for luggage?'

'Not specifically, we were mainly concerned about the bodies.'

'Were any of the windows broken?'

'No, they were all intact.'

'So, do you think the plane floated when it landed?'

'Sorry, we work for the coroner's office, we don't have expertise in plane crashes.'

'So, what else was there inside the cabin?'

'We found three small suitcases and the pilot's chart case.'

'Anything else?'

'Just what looked like the remains of sandwich wrappers and six empty beer cans. Anything else we can help with?'

'Yes. Would you make sure I get a detailed list of the contents of the cabin?'

'Will do. Can I have your contact details, please?'

'Hang on, I'll WhatsApp them to you.'

'Is that it?'

'Yes, that will do for now. Thanks for the info, it's been very helpful.'

'What's next?' said Street, after Buchanan had hung up.

Buchanan looked at the time on his phone and said, 'I think a visit to Shoreham Airport is in order, we shouldn't be too late home.'

♦

'Have you and Stephen thought of how you'll manage with the baby?' said Buchanan, as they drove along the A259 towards the entrance for Shoreham Airport.

'We're going to cross that bridge when we get to it. In the meantime, Stephen and I have signed up for the ante-natal clinic. It takes place at the Kings Centre every Monday evening.'

'Isn't that where Karen goes to church?'

'The very same. Remember the last time we were here?' said Street, as they drove under the railway bridge and into Shoreham Airport.

'I believe it's now called Brighton City Airport,' said Buchanan, pointing to a welcome sign, 'and yes I do. I wonder if Harry or Jasmin are here today?'

'Must be nice to own your jet charter business.'

'I don't remember them flying jets, I think they had a couple of turbo-props.'

'I seem to remember you were offered a flight in one. Did you take it up?'

'No, been a bit too busy.'

'Would you still like to?'

'Yes, but I doubt the offer still stands.'

Buchanan turned off Cecil Pashley Way and into a private carpark. He parked between a green Aston Martin and a highly polished left-hand drive silver Maserati with a dent in the front offside wing. A painted sign on the grey steel door informed them that the office of *Carstair* was third door on the left at the top of the stairs.

Buchanan knocked and entered. The office was just as he remembered from their visit a few years previously: it was still a working office. There were three desks: the one that had been covered with piles of packages and papers on their last visit was now screened off. The two other desks were tidy, giving the impression the occupants had just popped out on an errand. One desk had a typical office chair, the other an empty aircraft ejector seat. The bent propeller blade still hung from the ceiling, and the smashed cockpit window was still fastened to the wall like a trophy. The far wall consisted of a full-width window, which looked down into a vast hangar. Buchanan walked over and saw it contained two executive turbo-props, both in the *Carstair* livery.

'They're at lunch,' said a voice from behind the screen.

Street went round the screen. Her search revealed a curvaceous brunette reclining in a seat from a first-class BA cabin. She had a large Starbucks coffee in one hand, a phone in the other and the left side of headphones pulled back revealing a diamond-studded earlobe.

'Oh, it's you, I suppose you're here about the plane?'

'We were in the area and thought we'd drop in on Harry and Jasmin, that's if they are around and not off flying to exotic places?' said Buchanan.

'They're at lunch. Their trailer is at the side of the hangar: out the door and turn right.'

'I remember,' said Buchanan.

'Still short on words, isn't she?' remarked Street, as they descended the stairs.

◆

Trailer' didn't really portray the magnificence of the Carstairs' residence.

Street opened the white picket gate for Buchanan. They climbed the steps to the front door. Buchanan pushed the doorbell and waited. The door was opened by a tall Asian woman.

'Well, this is a big surprise – Inspector Buchanan and Detective Sergeant Street! What brings you here?'

'We're in the area and I thought we'd stop by and say hello.'

'Well, come on in, Harry's on the veranda.'

They followed Jasmin through the spacious double-wide trailer, out of the cool and onto the veranda.

'Harry, guess who's come for a visit?'

Harry Carstairs took off his headphones, removed his Ray-Ban sunglasses and squinted as his eyes adjusted to the sunshine. 'Didn't think police budgets extended to hiring executive jets.

Welcome, Jack and Jill. How are you? Still looking for dead bodies?'

'Now that you should mention it…'

'Just joking, would either of you like something to drink? We've just finished lunch.'

'Jill?' asked Jasmin.

'Could I have a glass of water, please?'

'Jack?'

'Water sounds fine.'

'So, Jack, you're just in the area?'

'Not quite. You hear about the plane brought up in the Channel by a fishing boat this morning?'

'A Cessna 320?'

'Yes.'

'I do happen to have heard about it, and in fact I can take you to it.'

'That would be helpful. Where is it?'

'In the back of our hangar, I suppose you would like to look at it?'

'As long as we aren't breaking the rules.'

'No problem, finish your drinks and I'll take you over.'

'Thanks.'

'You chose an excellent time to visit,' said Harry. 'We're just about to leave for Nice on a six-day charter.'

'That sounds nice, getting away from this contrary weather and off to the sunshine,' said Street.

'I suppose it is,' said Jasmin. 'Someone is getting married, and they have booked a jazz quartet for the entertainment.'

'Anyone I might know?'

'The Dave Bennett Quartet.'

Street shook her head.

'They're actually very good,' said Harry, 'He does a very good impression of Benny Goodman.'

'That sounds more like my kind of music,' said Buchanan.

'I helped get the plane in to the hangar,' said Harry, as they walked towards it.

'We're keeping the doors shut to keep out prying eyes,' said Jasmin, as Harry beckoned them to follow him round the side of the hangar.

'I'll catch up with you later,' said Jasmin. 'I've got some bookings to arrange.'

◆

Harry Carstairs opened a small door on the side of the hangar, Street and Buchanan followed him in. The wreck of Du Marchon's Cessna 320, basked in floodlights, was sitting on jacks at the far end. The wheels hanging underneath gave the impression the plane was coming in for a landing. The port wing, also sitting on jacks, was positioned beside the fuselage as though nothing had happened to it.

'The plane almost looks normal,' said Street. 'It looks like all it needs is a good clean, especially the windows.'

Three white-overalled individuals were inspecting one of the engines. Buchanan and Street followed Harry through the hangar towards the nearest investigator.

'Excuse me,' said Buchanan. 'DCI Buchanan, Sussex Police. We're following up an earlier investigation about this plane.'

'How can I help?'

'Can you tell me what caused the crash?'

'Not sure.'

'How about fuel?'

'Depends on where it was going.'

'It left Headcorn heading for Fécamp on the north-west coast of France.'

'That's about, say, 150 nautical miles – that would be no problem with what fuel it had on board. These 320's have a range of just over 700 nautical miles when the tanks are full. When we emptied the tanks there were about 230 litres left, plenty of fuel for the journey.'

'So, it wasn't lack of fuel that caused the accident?'

'Doesn't look like it.'

'Then why backtrack to Headcorn?' said Street. 'Why not head straight out across the Channel?'

'Mountjoy was after his cash,' said Buchanan. 'That would make sense for them to fly to Headcorn instead of flying direct to France. Any other ideas?'

'Pilot error, maybe he fell asleep.'

'Thanks. Can you tell me how it impacted on the water? It doesn't look too badly damaged, other than the wing that tore off.'

'It wasn't an engine out landing, he must have had some control over the plane for a belly landing. Landing on water is always tricky. In this case I'd say when the wing caught the wave, it made the plane spin out of control, nearly ripping off the port wing.'

'Would the plane have floated for long?'

'That depends on several factors.'

'Such as?'

'Was the cabin door already open on landing, or did it fly open on impact?'

'What is your theory?'

'You said there were three in the plane?

'Yes.

'This is strictly conjecture on my part. The pilot had passed out and the front seat passenger panicked and fought for control of the aircraft causing it to spin on contact with the water. If the passenger wasn't seat-belted and close to the door, they may have been ejected on impact. With the door open, the sea rushed in and, as it did, it pushed the door shut again.'

'What about the pilot?'

'We checked with Brighton morgue; they said the pilot had a broken neck. Pretty straightforward, and without new evidence to contradict, that is what will be in our report.'

'Did the plane have a transponder or flight data recorder?'

'No flight data recorder, and the transponder was switched off, seems like they were trying to fly unobserved.'

'Satisfied?' asked Street, as they crawled along the A27 with commuter traffic.

'The evidence is convincing.'

'But you're not convinced?'

'It's been a long day, Jill, I'm tired.'

'But Victor Mountjoy is dead. You heard the accident investigator – He was sure Victor was thrown from the plane when it crashed.'

'But there is still no body. That bothers me.'

'Murderers are sometimes convicted without a body.'

'You're right there, it does happen, and too often some say.'

'What will you do?'

'I'll give Cynthia a call when I get home and update her on our discussions with the crash inspectors.'

'What do you think her reaction will be to the news?'

'I imagine she will be relieved. With her husband gone, she is free to start her new life with Pat.'

♦

'How was your day?' asked Karen, as Buchanan entered the kitchen.

'Fine.'

'Just fine? You look exhausted. Where have you been?'

'Jill and I went to Shoreham to see the plane Victor Mountjoy perished in when it crashed in the Channel.'

'What did it look like?'

'A bit of a mess. The port wing had almost been sheared off when the plane hit the water.'

'That should put Cynthia's mind at rest then, Victor finally accounted for.'

'Unfortunately, that's not going to be enough. The only bodies on the plane were that of Julian Du Marchon and a yet unidentified body of a young male.'

'No Victor Mountjoy?'

'Nope. The crash investigator said in their opinion Victor had struggled with Du Marchon when the plane was about to land in the water. The wingtip caught a wave and caused the plane to spin out of control and eject Victor out of the door.'

'So, Cynthia is now free?'

'It looks that way. Oh, we're invited to stay over next Friday after the civil ceremony and blessing rehearsal.'

'Oh, that changes things, I thought you'd be home Friday evening. I suppose I need to pack for an extra night. But won't Cynthia be getting ready for her guests?'

'As far as I know, it will only be us and Cynthia's friend, Marjorie. Besides I think Cynthia could do with some female company.'

Karen smiled and said, 'I hope you accepted.'

'Of course, I did.'

'You know, I still can't get over how much you have changed since we moved down here.'

'Changed? In what way?'

'I suppose it's how you relax more, you've stopped swearing at everything that annoys you, and you've stopped grinding your teeth when you sleep.'

'Really? I never knew I did that.'

'And you take time to listen to me when we talk.'

'Oh sorry, habit of a lifetime, but do I really not listen to you?'

'Uh huh, but I still love you all the same.'

'I never realised I did that to you, I am sorry.'

Karen leaned forward and kissed Buchanan. 'Go and call Cynthia with the news and I'll put dinner on the table.'

5

Ashley Dale

Buchanan looked out of the bedroom window. The rain had finally stopped, the wind had died to a murmur and the moon illuminated the results of the passing storm. It had left its impression in the form of broken branches from the apple tree and several broken panes of greenhouse glass on his neighbour's lawn.

Something was bothering him, he couldn't sleep, a bad dream, he thought he'd left them behind in childhood, except these dreams were different. Gone were the bears under the bed, tigers in the cupboard, and worst of all, snakes in the drains. Thankfully now these were mostly replaced by dreams of steam engines, railway tracks and bridges under construction.

He went quietly down to the kitchen, made himself a coffee and sat at the table to think. In the past he'd have a pack of cigarettes in front of him, a lit cigarette in his mouth and a coffee mug in his hand. Today it was a cup of coffee and a bowl of leftover rhubarb crumble. He was uneasy, something was brewing, his knower was doing cartwheels, but what was it?

It couldn't be Victor Mountjoy, he was probably fish food on the bottom of the English Channel, and Julian Du Marchon was in Brighton morgue. There were no pending cases that required his services, so just what was it? Then it dawned on him: this is what it would be like if he was retired. He shook his head and thought, 'You silly boy.'

He looked at the clock on the oven and saw it was time to make breakfast. Today would be a quiet one with finishing up his delayed report on the Barazani case, and if he had time, preparing a revised report on the Du Marchon case for the coroner.

'Why are you up so early?' asked Karen, from the kitchen door.

'Strange dreams about flying trains and bridge building.'

'Too much television before bed. Shall I make breakfast?'

'Poached eggs?'

'Your wish is my command. What have you got on today?'

'Just paperwork, nothing but paperwork. I don't know why I bother, maybe I should retire.'

Karen dropped the egg she was holding on the floor.

'You, retire? What would you do with your time?'

Buchanan thought of Mrs. Reynolds on allotment plot thirteen and his overgrown plot nearby. 'We could grow vegetables alongside Mrs. Reynolds' plot, have cups of tea and spend the day just watching the veg grow. Now what do you say to that?'

'I say you need more sleep,' said Karen, as she stood from cleaning up the dropped egg.

'We eat carrots, don't we?'

'Carrots, of course we do. Where are you?'

'I was just thinking, if I retired, we could grow our own veg – and we could keep chickens – then it wouldn't matter how many eggs get dropped. What do you think of that idea?' he said, with a schoolboy grin.

'I think you shouldn't sit up late watching television. What were you watching?'

'*The Night Manager*. It's a John Le Carré story – boy, he was fit.'

'Who was fit?'

'Tom Hiddleston, he played the part of Jonathan Pine, the night manager in a hotel. It's a young man's world, Karen.'

'What's got you so down? You're usually more cheerful than this.'

'I looked in the mirror this morning and saw my future.'

'And what was your future?'

'Us sitting in the kitchen eating breakfast, and you telling me about the grandkids and me reading the paper.'

'What's so bad about that?'

'It's just not me, I need a challenge to keep me going.'

'OK, how about this for a challenge. Think of three positive things.'

'Just three?' he said, smiling.

'Yes, just three.'

'Let me see,' he said, putting down his half-drunk coffee. 'Number one would have to be, we love each other, number two, we have a fantastic daughter.'

'And three?' said Karen, as she cleared away the table.

'I'm going to be a granddad.'

'See, life's not that bad, is it? Now if you are not going to be late for work, I suggest you go and get dressed.'

◆

Despite Karen's encouraging words and a cup of freshly-brewed Starbucks in his hand, he still couldn't shake off the feeling of melancholy. He climbed into his car, placed his coffee in the cup holder, did up his seatbelt and proceeded to wend his way slowly past the cars waiting to fuel.

He was about to turn left out of the garage and join the queue of traffic waiting to cross the A27 when a memory surfaced. An idea took hold of him. On impulse he squeezed through the stationary vehicles, turned right onto Wartling Road then left onto Rickney Lane, leaving the morning commuters to their bumper-to-bumper crawl into town. He stopped in at Chilley Farm Shop for two fillet steaks and some fresh veg for dinner.

As he left Chilley Farm Shop behind in the mirror, he wound the windows down and drove on slowly through the morning mist that clung to the edges of the lane. He set the cruise control at its lowest speed and pulled his knees up against the steering wheel. With a coffee in his right hand, cinnamon roll in the left and steering with his knees, he let the car walk along Rickney Lane at a sedate sixteen miles an hour.

Just before the road took a sharp bend to the left, he steered off the lane, stopped in front of a metal gate and turned off the engine. He took a final gulp of coffee, exhaled slowly, closed his eyes, and waited for his mind to come to rest. The gentle sound of the wind in the grass and the birdsongs had him imagining he was back on Eaglesham Moor.

The first thing that drifted into the quietness of his mind was, not retirement, but what to grow next season on his allotment. Agatha Christy had Poirot retiring to the country and attempting to grow marrows, unsuccessfully. Instead, he would start with potatoes, he would have a contest with Dave down at the allotment to see who could grow the largest.

He opened his eyes and looked out across the Pevensey Levels at a land where time has stood still and hadn't really changed much since the Romans landed two thousand years previously.

In the distance he could see the Herstmonceux observatory and. slightly to the left, the castle where he and Karen had watched the medieval pageant the previous summer. Above, he saw a pair of honey buzzards wheeling in the early-morning updraft.

His reverie was disturbed by the plaintive scream from a bird as a sparrow hawk seized its next meal. That brought him back to the job at hand: Pat and Cynthia's wedding the following weekend. He was expected to be there Friday afternoon for the rehearsal and, before he could relax into his duty as father of the bride, he still had the Barazani file to prepare for the coroner.

He started the engine and at the Rickney bridge turned left and up the hill to Hankham and passed the house where in 1990 the IRA assassinated Ian Gow, the local Member of Parliament.

◆

He shook his head, turned on his computer, and googled the Marshal seed catalogue; work could wait. He was looking at strawberry varieties when his phone rang.

'Buchanan – there was – when was this – last night – OK – what's the number – thanks, I'll give her a call.'

'Give who a call?' asked Street, who'd just entered the office.

'Someone called Ashley Dale. The desk said she rang the gate intercom last night saying she wanted to talk to someone about a plane that crashed in the Channel a few months ago. I wonder if she is referring to Du Marchon's plane?' said Buchanan.

'More likely someone trying to sell travel insurance or something similar.'

'I hate those type of calls, usually get them as we are sitting down for dinner. The latest are someone with an Indian accent trying to make me believe they are from the tax office, and I am about to be arrested for not paying my taxes and the police are on the way to arrest me.'

'What did you say?'

'I was about to say just what I was thinking when Karen gave me one of her looks, you know the one?'

Street nodded. 'Was it the *don't you dare,* one?'

Buchanan nodded as he picked up the phone to call Ashley Dale.'

'I wonder why she would be calling you, and how did she know you worked here?'

'Who knows?' said Buchanan, as he pressed the speaker button for Street to listen in on the call.

'Ashley Dale.'

'DCI Buchanan. You came by the station and left a message for me to call you?'

'Ah, yes, so I did.'

'How can I help?'

'I believe you've met Victor Mountjoy?'

'Our paths crossed, but that was a few months ago. What is it you have to tell me?'

'It's about Julian Du Marchon, Victor's business partner. I wonder if we could meet somewhere? I have something I need to show you.'

'I'm very busy. Can you give me an idea what it's about?'

'I have something I need to give you.'

'Can't you just put it in the post?'

'No, it's too big.'

'What sort of thing is it?'

'I'll show you when we meet.'

'OK, where do you want to meet?'

'Do you know The Beachdeck?'

'The café on the promenade?'

'That's the one. I'll meet you there in an hour.'

'Quite determined, isn't she?' remarked Street, as Buchanan hung up from the call. 'I wonder what it's all about?'

'Who knows? Probably nothing. At least it gets me out of the office.'

'Want me to tag along?'

'I thought you were chasing stolen bicycles?'

'No. Lazarus is looking after that, and besides, I want to see why this Ashley Dale is so keen to see you.'

'Fine, let's go.'

♦

'We've been in this situation before,' said Street, as Buchanan parked in the busy carpark beside The Beachdeck café.

'What do you mean?'

'Meeting lonely women, remember Mrs Price?'

'Yeah, sad case that. The world is full of lonely people with aspirations and secrets.'

'I wonder what secrets Ashley Dale will be sharing with us?' mused Street, as they walked up the ramp to the promenade and the entrance steps to the café.

'Do you have a reservation?' asked the café receptionist.

'No, we're meeting someone here,' explained Buchanan.

'Ah, that will be the lady at table thirteen. She said she was expecting someone to join her. If you'll follow me.'

'Ashley Dale?' asked Buchanan, of the occupant at table thirteen.

'Yes, thanks for coming to see me.'

'DCI Buchanan and DS Street. So, what can we help you with?'

'I saw a report on the morning TV news about a plane being found in the Channel and two unidentified bodies being found on board. I think my brother, Alan, may be one of the bodies.'

'Are you sure you are thinking about the correct plane?'

'How many planes crash in the English Channel?'

'There were many during WW2.'

'How about within the last three months?'

'Just the one we know about.'

'I thought so.'

'So, why do you think your brother was on the plane the night it crashed?'

'The morning of the day he disappeared I was in my bedroom – my bedroom is directly opposite his. I overheard a conversation he was having with Julian. I only heard one side of the conversation, you understand, but I got the impression it had something to do with them flying out of the country in Julian's plane.'

'Do you remember when this phone call was?'

'Not exactly, but I do remember him saying something about a horse race at a castle or something that Victor was riding in. I could check my diary for you, I had a hair appointment that day.'

'That won't be necessary, it was the day of the Castlewood Cup.'

'That's it.'

'Did you ask Alan what it was about, why they had to disappear?'

'I didn't have to. A short time later, while I was in the kitchen, Alan came in and handed me a slim briefcase and said to hold on to it.'

'Did you ask what was in the briefcase?'

'No, he said it would be better if I didn't. He said to keep it safe and not to look inside. When he saw the look on my face, he said not to worry. If I held on to the briefcase, he would be safe. It was his get-out-of-jail card. He went on to say he was going away for a while and was going to be well cared for.'

'What do you think he was afraid of?'

'That, I can't figure out. My brother had a rough time growing up. He struggled at school and subsequently he was bullied a lot. One day he announced he was fed up with how he was living and had applied to join the Army. He said his reasoning for joining the Army was that by becoming a soldier he could make a fresh start and joining the Army would make a man out of him.'

'And did it?'

'Boy, did it ever! The first time he came home on leave I almost didn't recognise him. He'd gone from being the typical wishy-washy weedy teenager to a sturdy, opinionated, young man who knew what he wanted from life. Though I could never figure out why he didn't stay in longer and make a career of the Army.'

'Did you ask him why?'

'Yes, but he just shrugged and said he'd had enough. Within a few months he'd reverted to his old ways, just drifting from one squat to another.'

'How did he come to be associated with Julian Du Marchon and Victor Mountjoy?'

'He met Victor at a party in the officer's mess. Alan and a friend had started a band and would be asked to play at Army functions. I think Julian befriended him one night when he was in Brighton. Despite how Julian and Victor treated him, Alan could take care of himself.'

'Where did your brother live?'

'After our parents died, Alan sort of came to live with me. We have no other family.'

'So, you and your brother were close?'

She smiled and nodded. 'We were the only family we had.'

'Can you explain what you mean by saying he came to live with you?'

'When I say he lived with me, what I mean was, he used my address to get his post and to doss down when he wasn't staying with friends. I was more of a landlady than his sister.'

'Do you know who his friends were?'

'The only ones I knew he talked about were Julian Du Marchon, and Victor Mountjoy when he was around.'

'Do you still have the briefcase Alan gave you to keep safe?'

'Yes, and that's the reason I wanted you to come here. I'm afraid of going outdoors with this,' she said, reaching under the table. She brought up a slim black and chrome briefcase and handed it to Buchanan. 'It's OK. Since Alan's no longer with us, you may as well open it – it's unlocked.'

'I'm confused,' said Street. 'If this briefcase and its contents are your brother's security, why are you giving it to us?'

'Why not? Since Alan is dead, there's no point in dragging it around. Besides, I'm curious to see what's inside.'

'So, if you were sure your brother was dead, why didn't you just open it?'

'I don't know, sort of felt I'd be betraying a trust.'

Buchanan sat the briefcase on the table, released the catches and opened the lid. Inside were various sheets of A4 paper, a couple of top-shelf magazines and underneath, a large manila envelope.

'Is this what you want to show us?' he said, holding up the envelope.

'I don't know, I've never seen inside the case.'

He closed the lid on the briefcase and placed the envelope on top. Taking one of the knives on the table he inserted it under the envelope flap. The glue had dried and as soon as Buchanan pushed in the knife in, the flap popped open. He reached in and extracted a manilla sleeve containing some documents and stack of certificates.

He flicked through the stack of certificates and saw they were gilts whose maturity date had passed four months previously. He looked at the stack in his hands and at the serial number on the first and last. He estimated there were about one hundred and forty of them, at ten thousand pounds each.

He put the gilts down on the table and picked up the accompanying documents. They were ownership documents registered in the name of Du Marchon's investment company, Sovereign Secure Investments.

Buchanan read the opening paragraphs and saw the documents were instructions to a London broker to sell the gilts when presented. He looked through the papers till he came to the page that dealt with the signatures and saw that Du Marchon had placed his signature in the relevant section. The line for Victor Mountjoy's signature was blank. Buchanan wondered with all this money available in gilts, why Du Marchon and Mountjoy needed to try the scam at the Castlewood Cup.

'Did Alan say anything else about Julian and Victor's plans?'

'He said he overheard Julian talking to Victor on the phone saying they were going to disappear with their winnings right after the race. The proceeds of the race and some cash were Victor's contribution, those gilts I presume were Julian's.'

'Did your brother say where Victor had hidden the cash?'

'No.'

'There's only one signature on the sales mandate page,' said Buchanan, showing it to Ashley.

'I don't think Victor trusted Julian, so he made him sign them,' she said, looking at the section requiring two signatures to cash the certificate. 'This looks like it will just require Victor's signature to turn the gilts into cash.'

'That's the way I see it. So, how did Alan come to be in possession of them?'

'That you would have to ask him, but since he's dead, I guess we will never know the answer.'

'Surely, as soon as Julian realised the envelope was missing, its disappearance would point to Alan, and it would have gone badly for him?'

'Alan called me late that Saturday afternoon and said not to worry about him, he had things fixed and under no circumstances was I to let anyone have the briefcase till he came for it.'

'And you were unaware of the contents of the briefcase?'

She nodded. 'He said when things settled down, he would contact me with instructions on what to do with the contents.'

'So, the tables had been turned. It looks like Alan was using the gilts as leverage to control Julian and Victor for a change,' said Street.

'It sounds that way.'

'Why have you waited so long to contact us?' said Buchanan.

'I didn't know he was dead until I heard the account on the radio of the plane being found.'

'You didn't realise he was gone?'

'I just assumed he'd gone off on a trip, he never was much good at staying in touch.'

'He'd done that before?'

'Alan was a law unto himself.'

'Why did you contact me especially?'

'A few weeks before Alan disappeared, he said if anything happened to him, I was to go straight to the police in Eastbourne and get someone to investigate Julian and Victor's nefarious activities.'

'So, how did you end up by contacting me?'

'I didn't. I just left a message with the reception. You know your police station isn't a very friendly place to visit. Makes me think you lot prefer to be behind bars while the criminals are running amok on the other side of locked steel gates.'

Buchanan smiled at her. 'You know we do have a drop-in police station on Grove Road in town?'

'No, I didn't know that. I was driving round to Sussex Bacon and saw the sign on the gate as I drove past, pity they've closed.'

'What's closed?'

'Sussex Bacon.'

'Oh. Do you know where Julian Du Marchon's flat in Eastbourne is?'

'Yes.'

'Do you happen to have a copy of the keys to the flat?'

'Yes, here,' she said, taking them out of her coat pocket. 'I figured you'd ask so I brought them with me. It's Carlton Road so we can walk. I need to have a look inside anyway. I had someone from the Real Estate office call me saying they wanted to relet the flat but couldn't until the personal effects had been removed.'

'Why would they call you if the flat was rented by Julian?'

'Apparently Julian put the rental agreement in Alan's name, and he gave mine as a reference.'

♦

'I wonder how much they want for the flat?' said Street, pointing at the For Sale sign. 'Do you know, Ashley?'

'No, and as soon as I've got Alan's personal effects out of there the happier, I'll be. My only interest is to see if he left anything behind that I should hold on to.'

'It looks like someone has been looking for something. This is a right mess,' said Street, as they entered the flat.

'It doesn't make sense. If Julian is dead, who's been in the flat?' said Ashley.

'Possibly the person from the Real Estate office?' said Street.

'Are you sure your brother was with Julian when his plane crashed?' said Buchanan.

'Of course, I am, where else could he be? If he were alive, he would have been in contact by now.'

'Could it be someone that Julian cheated looking for something?' said Street.

Ashley shrugged and thought for a moment. 'Who knows?'

'When was the last time you were here in this flat?'

'Months ago. I came over to drop off Alan's phone. He'd left it charging on the kitchen counter and gone off and left it.'

'Ashley, would you mind waiting while we have a look around the flat? We would also like to have a look in the room your brother used at your place, if you don't mind?'

'No, not at all.'

'For the purposes of identification, we would need something your brother, and only your brother, touched.'

'Checking for DNA?'

'Yes.'

'Would a toothbrush do? He left an old one at my place in the marina.'

'That would be perfect.'

'Will you be long here? I have a parcel to collect from the post office.'

'That depends on what we find, but probably not more than half an hour to forty-five minutes.'

'Good. I'll collect my package, then we can pop round to my place for the toothbrush. Meet you back here in about forty minutes.'

'Fine.'

Ashley Dale closed the door leaving Buchanan and Street to ponder the scene before them.

'First impressions?' said Buchanan.

'Doesn't look like the flat that someone as financially independent as Julian Du Marchon would call home.'

'That's also my impression, looks more like a typical hippy squat.'

'Du Marchon probably invested his money in his business, rather than accommodation for those who he permitted to associate with him.'

'Yes, I suppose his office was where he tried to impress his clients before he emptied their wallets.'

'Do we have an address for Du Marchon's office?'

'It will be in the files. But since he's been missing for several months. I imagine his office will have been cleared and rented out to a new client.'

'That makes sense. Now, this flat, how about you check the kitchen and I'll have a look in the bedrooms?'

'Find anything?' asked Street, as Buchanan walked into the kitchen.

He shook his head. 'Just an unmade bed and some clothes that haven't seen the inside of a washing machine in months. How about you?'

'Dirty dishes in the sink and the usual foodstuff in the fridge.'

'Oh.'

'But…'

'But? What have you found?'

'How long ago was your race at Castlewood?'

'That was back in August, why?'

'There's a carton of milk in the fridge that is three weeks out of date. If Alan Dale died in the plane crash two months ago, who's been sleeping in his bed and eating all his porridge?'

'So, you think baby bear is still alive? But if he wasn't on the plane when it crashed, whose body was found in the wreck with Julian Du Marchon?'

'A very good question, and even more reason for us to get a DNA sample of Alan Dale.'

'I wonder what's keeping her?' said Street. 'She said she was only going to collect a package from the Post Office.'

'I could make a comment,' said Buchanan, 'but for diplomacy's sake, I choose to remain silent.'

No sooner had he said that when the front door opened.

'Are you ready?' said Ashley, holding a plastic parcel displaying a John Lewis logo.

'Yes. I think we've seen all there is to see,' replied Buchanan.

'Good. My flat is in the marina, can I have a lift? I came here by taxi, and you still want something of Alan's to check his DNA, don't you?'

♦

'Quite a flat Ashley Dale lives in,' said Street, as they returned to their office.

'Is it the sort of place you'd want to live in?'

'Yes, I think it would be. The views out across the marina are fantastic. I could watch the boats going in and out of the locks all day,' she said, shaking her head slowly. 'It would be a fantastic area to raise children. And being so close to all those restaurants what else could you want? Pity she'd cleaned out Alan's bedroom, there wasn't much to tell he'd slept there.'

'Yes. Oh, I'll be late tomorrow morning, Jill,' said Buchanan.

'Coroner's court?'

'Yes. I'm hoping by lunchtime we will have a favourable judgement on the Barazani case, be good to wrap that one up and put it to bed.'

'How about the Victor Mountjoy case?'

'The coroner has already issued an interim judgement declaring Victor Mountjoy and Julian Du Marchon dead, but with the mystery body found in the crashed plane, I suspect the best we'll get is another postponement.'

'What about autopsy reports on the bodies found in the plane?'

'They' weren't complete the last time I checked. But what you ask makes me wonder if there is more to the plane crash than we first thought.'

'In that case I'd better get Alan Dale's toothbrush off for DNA matching, be back in a minute.'

'Good, while you're doing that, I'll make enquiries about the autopsies on the bodies found in the plane.'

It took Buchanan twenty minutes to track down someone who could tell him what was happening about the bodies.

'Any luck?' asked Street when she returned to the office.

'Apparently the doctor who examined the bodies said the cause of death was drowning.'

'Are you happy with that?'

'No, I am not. I just got off the phone with Dr Mansell. I've asked him if he would have a look at the bodies and give us a second opinion.'

'Won't that be a bit awkward for him, you know, treading on someone else's turf?'

'I did ask him, but he told me that the local forensics doctor is on leave and the locum was only too happy for another opinion. The locum even suggested that the bodies be moved to Eastbourne.'

'When will he go over and check?'

'Sometime tomorrow.'

'That means we won't get any results till at least Monday at the earliest.'

'Not necessarily so. Andrew's wife has gone off to spend the weekend with her cousin, so he has agreed to work through the weekend to get the autopsy results ready for the coroner. All I need to do is keep him supplied with coffee and doughnuts.'

'You're working as well?'

'Needs must. There's something going on and I haven't a clue what it is.'

'Will you need help?'

'Yes, but not Saturday. Tomorrow morning, Friday, would you get on to forensics and impress on them that this case is now several months old, and we would like to wrap it up as soon as possible. It wouldn't hurt to say the ACC is getting agitated.'

'Is she?'

'Don't know, haven't talked to her in a while. Though, I suppose I should let her know what's going on. In the meantime, I think we've done enough for today, I'll see you tomorrow morning after coroner's court.'

6

Old King Log

'Are you going straight to work today?' asked Karen, as she looked at the kitchen clock.

'No, I'm going in later, I've got coroner's court first thing this morning. I'm hoping to be finally winding up the Barazani case. I also thought I'd pop over to the allotment on my way, the tomato plants need watering if they are going to survive.'

'Does Jill know you'll be late?'

'Yes, I told her yesterday.'

'Has she said anything to you about when she'll be taking maternity leave?'

'No, she hasn't said anything to me, how about you?'

'Is there something wrong? You seem to be a bit preoccupied.'

'Sorry,' he said, shaking his head. 'Although I slept like a log last night, I had the weirdest of dreams again.'

'I told you before, you need to stop watching YouTube before you come to bed. What was the dream?'

'It was a beautiful day; I was lying on a riverbank staring up at the passing clouds when a bunch of frogs came out of the river and climbed onto my chest.'

'You always have had quite an imagination, but I must admit that is a corker.'

'That's not all. A heron landed beside me and ate all the frogs.'

'Mr Buchanan, you need a holiday.'

'No, I'm fine. It's this case, or I'm not actually sure there is a case, and that's the issue. I have all sort of bits and pieces which are meaningless, but when put together in context I'm sure they mean something.'

The Jockey's Wife.

'You really do need a holiday. Thankfully it's only a few weeks till we fly to Dallas for a visit with Poppy's parents – do you think you can hang on till then?'

He smiled at the thought and nodded.

♦

The coroner's court for the Barazani case was over and done in forty minutes. Buchanan had given his evidence, as did Dr Mansell and Harvey Littlejohn, all which was received with praise for its clarity and succinctness.

The coroner, summing up in his best stentorian voice said, 'This inquest returns a verdict, in the case of the female victim, of accidental death and, in the case of the male victim, unlawful killing.'

'Hi, how did it go?' said Street, answering Buchanan's call.

'Fine. Verdict of unlawful killing and accident. You can close the Barazani file.'

'Good. What's next?'

'I have to give evidence on the Mountjoy case after lunch. I imagine it will be adjourned now we now have an unidentified body involved.'

'Will that mean Pat and Cynthia will not be able to get married next Saturday?'

'I shouldn't think there will be a problem with that, the coroner has already issued a presumption of death certificate. The only issue remaining will be the identity of and the cause of death of the young man found in Du Marchon's plane.'

'I sent Alan Dale's toothbrush off to forensics. I asked if they had been sent a DNA swab from the body found in the plane.'

'What did they say?'

'They had, and as soon as the toothbrush arrived, they'd do a comparison and get back to me.'

'Good work.'

'Will I see you today?'

'Yes, but it might be late. You know what coroners' courts can be like, fastidious bunch.'

'Fine, see you later.'

♦

Buchanan was back in court an hour later giving evidence at the resumption of the Victor Mountjoy and Julian Du Marchon case.

'Inspector, do you have further evidence to present in the case of Mr Julian Du Marchon and Colonel Victor Mountjoy?'

'Yes, sir. Tuesday morning this week, we were apprised of the fact that Mr Du Marchon's plane had been recovered from the English Channel. The fishing boat, the *Myrtle B*, snagged the plane in its net about thirty miles due south-west of the city of Brighton.

'I attended Shoreham harbour and interviewed the master of the vessel. The master informed me that when the plane was brought to the surface one body could be seen seated at the left-hand controls. A second, and as yet unidentified, body was later recovered from the plane when it was landed at Shoreham beach.'

'Where is the wreckage currently?'

'In an aircraft hangar at Shoreham airport.'

'Have you identified the body in the front left-hand seat?'

'Yes. The medical examiner positively identified the body as that of Julian Du Marchon.'

'And the second victim?'

'We're still investigating. We have submitted DNA samples to the forensics lab and should have the results back later today.'

'Do you have a possible identification?'

'Yes. We believe it may be the brother of someone who has come forward with information about another, unrelated matter.'

'And what about the third person involved, Colonel Victor Mountjoy?'

'We visited the wreckage at Shoreham airport, and it is the opinion of the air accident investigators that when the left wingtip of the aircraft contacted the sea, it caused the aircraft to spin violently, ejecting the occupant of the right-hand passenger seat.'

'So, it is your opinion that Colonel Victor Mountjoy was thrown from the aircraft and subsequently drowned?'

'Yes, that is my opinion based on the facts as we know them.'

'Thank you, Inspector, you may stand down.'

Addressing those present in the courtroom the coroner once more postponed final judgement due to the unidentified body being found in the wreckage.

In his winding up statement the coroner said, 'In an effort to avoid arrest, Julian Du Marchon took off from Headcorn airport with the aircraft ill-prepared for the planned journey. Thirty miles out over the channel the plane crashed-landed in the English Channel. Upon impact Julian Du Marchon died, and Victor Mountjoy was thrown from the aircraft and subsequently drowned. This court tasks DCI Buchanan with discovering the identification and cause of death of the unidentified individual recovered from the wreck.'

◆

'How did it go?' asked Street, as Buchanan returned to the office.

'Fine. As soon as we can confirm the identity of the body in the plane as Ashley Dale's brother, the coroner can close the inquest and you and I can relax.'

'Your wait has ended. Just heard from forensics, DNA sample matches body on the plane.'

'So, the body in the plane is that of Alan Dale?'

'That's what forensics say.'

'Anything else?'

'They said it will take a few days to go through all the artefacts in the plane. We should get a full report as soon as possible.'

'Good. I wonder what Ashley Dale will have to say about the news of her brother's death?'

'I imagine she'll be sad; her brother was her only family. Though she didn't seem to be so concerned when we spoke to her earlier.'

'Maybe they weren't as close as she says they were. Do you have her phone number to hand? No, hang on, I think this needs a personal touch. It's not every day that you can tell someone that their loved one's died in a plane crash.'

'Want me to come along?' asked Street. looking at the time on her PC screen.

'I think that would be an excellent idea.'

♦

'I wonder how she'll take the news?' said Street, as Buchanan reached out to ring the doorbell of Ashley Dale's flat.

'We'll soon know,' he said, as the door chime sounded somewhere deep inside the flat.

A few minutes later the sound of a deadbolt being unlocked, and a security chain being slid back preceded the opening of a stout front door and the appearance of a very perplexed Ashley Dale.

'Oh, Inspector, Sergeant.'

'Hello, Ashley, may we come in for a minute?'

'Yes, er.., why? Has something happened?'

Buchanan smiled. 'It might be better if we explained inside.'

'Oh, sure, come in.'

Buchanan followed Street down the hallway behind Ashley and into the sitting room.

'I'm sorry to say we have confirmation that it was Alan's body that was found in the wreckage of Julian Du Marchon's plane,' said Street.

Ashley nodded. 'I figured that would be the case.'

'Do you have someone you can spend time with?'

'No, it's just me.'

'Will you be all right? We have counsellors available to sit with you.'

She shook her head. 'Thanks for caring, I'll be fine. I shed all the tears I'm going to shed for Alan many years ago.'

'Was he a handful growing up?'

'Yes, he certainly was.'

'You raised him yourself?'

'Yes.'

'That must have been difficult for you. Were there no family members that could help you raise Alan?'

'No, none that lived anywhere nearby. Alan was a late baby, the result of a romantic evening that ended up being more than expected. I was just eighteen when Alan was born and working evenings in a pub. The landlady took pity on me and my circumstances and allowed me to bring him to work with me.'

'Ashley, would you happen to have a recent photo of Alan?' asked Buchanan.

'Yes, probably, but why would you want one of those, seeing how he's dead?'

'Just for the record.'

'I'll have a look, but I'm not sure if I am up digging through old family memories right now –it might take some time. Also, he was always a bit camera shy, so there may not be any that are up to date.'

'I'm sorry, Ashley, I'm being a bit insensitive. If you do come across a recent photo, it would be most helpful.'

'I'll see what I can do. Is there anything else?'

'No, that will be all for now.'

◆

'You're up to something, I can tell,' said Street, as they drove back to the station.

Buchanan smiled and said, 'I can see an arm rising, but not out of our pond.'

Street shook her head.

'Have you and Stephen got plans for the weekend?' asked Buchanan, as they entered the office

'Yes. Saturday evening, we are going to visit his grandparents for dinner. Sunday, we have nothing planned. Anything from forensics?'

'Yes, and quite detailed it is,' he said, as he scanned down the report.

'Anything stand out?'

'Not at first glance. The two suitcases contained nothing other than what you would find the typical tourist takes on holiday. The backpack, a change of clothes sufficient for a three-night stay.

'Victim one's trouser pockets contained an unused handkerchief and some loose change to the value of eighty pence. Shirt pocket, two pens, one blue, the other black ink. Jacket, outer pockets empty, inner pocket, a man's wallet containing three credit cards, a UK driving licence in the name of Julian Du Marchon, and four thousand euros in notes.

'Victim two's trouser pockets contained a pocketknife, a used handkerchief, and loose change to the value of thirty-four pence. Rear pocket contained a wallet, containing forty-five pounds, and a flyer for an upcoming rock concert in Fécamp, but no cards or identifying documents.'

'Sounds like he was going to the concert – but how was he getting home and where was his passport?'

'A very good question.'

'What about Victor Mountjoy?'

'I am assuming one of the suitcases was his, and interestingly they found his wallet in the footwell alongside three credit cards in his name.'

'So, he was definitely on the plane?'

'Looks that way.'

7

Doughnuts and Corpses

'Another Saturday and you're working,' said Karen, as she placed Buchanan's plate of scrambled eggs on the table. 'Will you want a sandwich for lunch?'

'I probably won't feel much like eating lunch today. After watching Andrew disembowel two bodies, I doubt I'll feel very hungry.'

'Well, at least take an apple with you, it should help keep your tummy settled and your mouth refreshed.'

Buchanan looked at Karen and smiled. 'I don't know what I'd do without you looking after me.'

'That's what a policeman's wife does in life. She makes his bed, his sandwiches for his lunch and holds him close when he comes home from work shattered by what he's had to deal with during his shift.'

'My, we are waxing philosophical this morning. What's got you on this bent?'

'It's, it's – well, look out the window, the sun is shining for the first time this week, there's a Spooky Halloween Trail on at the castle and…'

'And you think it would be all perfect if I retired, is that it?'

'Well, it might help a bit with our non-social life and, just in case you haven't realised, you haven't been to see your family since we have been down here.' She let out her breath, then continued, 'Sorry, I'm well – it would be nice to spend more time with you. Even when you are home, you're not here. You're usually off down some dark alleyway chasing some elusive clues.'

'Phew, not quite sure what to say to that, but I will think about what you said, and I promise, when I get home this evening, I will give you my undivided attention.'

'I'm sorry, you shouldn't have to start your day with me moaning at you.'

'Mrs Buchanan, if our marriage were a sailboat, you would be the keel and rudder. Without you, when the wind blew, I would just fall over and head off onto some rocky shore. I couldn't possibly go through life without you. I promise I will give thought to what you said.'

'Jack Buchanan, I love you. Now you need to get your skates on, Andrew has a life outside work and I'm sure Katherine would like her man home for at least some of the weekend.'

'She's gone away for the weekend to see her cousin. That's the reason Andrew is working today.'

'You're not actually going to give him a hand, are you?'

'No, of course not, that could be seen as tampering with evidence. My only involvement will be to supply the coffee and doughnuts.'

Karen shook her head, smiled, and began to pick up the breakfast dishes. 'Dinner – I suppose if you're not having something for lunch, you will be hungry for dinner?'

'Yes, I suppose I'll be hungry for dinner. I tell you what, why don't we pop down to The Heron, they have a new menu, and you could give Jill and Stephen a call and see if they want to join us?'

◆

Buchanan stopped at the newsagents and collected his copy of the *Herald*, then on to the garage for the doughnuts and finally, Starbucks, for his and Andrew's coffees. On the way to the hospital and morgue he dropped in at his office to collect his notebook and to leave his copy of the *Herald* on his desk for his ritual Monday morning read.

As he parked his car Buchanan noticed, with the easing of the Covid restrictions, the visitor carpark at the hospital was daily becoming busier. He nodded at the receptionist then made his way down to the morgue.

'Ah, there you are,' said Mansell, 'and, you have the coffee, good.'

'I see you've made a start,' said Buchanan, as he took a mouthful of doughnut.

'Yes, I'm finished with the young lad, just got the other body to look at.'

'What are you doing this afternoon?'

'I'm going sea fishing.'

'I didn't know you had a boat.'

'I don't. I'm booked on a fishing charter out of the marina.'

'In that case, don't let me hold you up.'

'If you are going to help, I suggest you put on a gown, hat, and gloves, they're hanging over there. While you are at it, boots would save your shoes getting spattered with blood.'

Buchanan swallowed the remains of his coffee and changed into surgery clothes, including a pair of white theatre boots.

'You look like a first-year student at his first autopsy, but I forget, this probably is your first,' remarked Mansell. 'Try to relax and feel the part. You won't actually be doing any of the cutting, all I will need you for is to fetch and carry, all right?'

Buchanan nodded and wondered if this was all a good idea. After all, he could have sat in his office and waited for Mansell to call him with the results. 'You big softy', he muttered to himself.

'You say something?' asked Mansell.

'No, just thinking out loud. Are you ready?'

'Yes, as I said I did the lad before you got here, I've still got the bloodwork to do.'

Buchanan watched as Mansell methodically made an external examination of the body, dictating his observations as he progressed. When complete he laid the body flat on the table and commenced to extract the internal organs for examination.

'What's next?' asked Buchanan. 'Can you determine the cause of death from looking at the organs?'

'Not exactly, I have some ideas, but I will need to do some further examination of them to confirm my thoughts.'

'Will you be throwing them up in the air and looking at the mess when they land on the floor?'

'Ah, no; and for your information, it was chicken innards that the Roman priests used for divination. These days we take a much more professional approach.'

'How quickly can you make sense of the cause of death?'

'Had the body been brought in fresh, it wouldn't have taken long to arrive at a preliminary diagnosis, but since it lay in the sea for several months, a little longer.'

'Are you saying you know what the cause of death was?'

Mansell nodded. 'Look, as I open up the stomach,' he said, carefully slicing it open. 'See the colour, bright pink?'

'Yes, what should it look like?'

'Redder than this. Carbon monoxide poisoning turns the tissues a bright pink, and that would be my diagnosis. I could give you a definite diagnosis by the end of next week, but in the meantime, I'd bet my next doughnut on the cause of death being carbon monoxide poisoning.'

'In an aeroplane, that's a tough one to figure out, but it does sort of make sense. But wouldn't one of the occupants of the cabin notice something wrong?'

'I had my suspicions raised when I did the lad, so, before you got here, I did some checking about carbon monoxide sources in aircraft. In fact, there is quite a great deal written about it. I came across an FAA advisory warning about the dangers of carbon monoxide poisoning from the piston engine heat exchanger that could potentially leak carbon monoxide fumes through into the cabin. Do you know if there was a CO monitor on the plane?'

'Sorry, no, I don't. The report on the inspection hasn't come through yet. But what you say makes sense. I can imagine it now, they stopped at Headcorn to top up the fuel tanks, Mountjoy got out to arrange payment, his cards were blocked by Cynthia, he hears the police sirens and jumps back in the plane, and they take off.

'It was late in the day; the sun is setting, and the cabin is cold. Du Marchon puts the heater on full, and unknown to him, there is a leak in the heat exchanger and the cabin slowly fills with carbon monoxide which we know to be a colourless, odourless, tasteless gas. Everyone passes into unconsciousness.

'Mountjoy comes to as they approach sea level, wait – now I see. When he boarded in a hurry, he didn't manage to properly shut the door and, as the plane descended, the oxygen in the air seeping through the partially-open door improved enough for Mountjoy to wake. When he saw Du Marchon slumped over unconscious, Mountjoy made a grab for the controls and caused the plane to crash.'

'That's plausible and fits with the known facts. Have you seen enough to go on with the case?'

'Ample, thanks for letting me watch.'

'Anytime. Now, if we're done here, I need to get this mess cleaned up and off to the harbour for a late afternoon's fishing. I'll send through the full autopsy report later next week.'

8

Disappearing Evidence

As usual, Buchanan was first into the office. He placed his coffee on the desk, took off his jacket and sat down to read the weekend incident report. He saw that there had been an operation in town to go after county lines drug gangs and disrupt their supply and distribution networks. He next turned to the *Herald* and read a report detailing police attempts at stopping anti-social driving on industrial estates and an unsavoury report about a man who had been accused of killing his estranged wife for her money. Just another quiet weekend in sleepy old Eastbourne.

He checked his emails and saw the air accident investigation engineers had emailed him a preliminary report on their findings.

He read through the report and nodded as he read the part about the plane's instruments. There had been no flight data recorder and the transponder had been switched off, but there had been enough fuel to safely complete their stated destination. After testing the cabin heater had been found faulty and, finally, the luggage door lock was also faulty and had been tied closed by a short length of twine.

He put down the paper and decided it was time to go to work. First on the list was to contact Dan O'Shea and find out what had happened to the Golf GTi.

All during the weekend his mind had wrestled with the question about the death of the carpenter. Was it just an accident? If so, why had the lad not hung around to see what had happened to his mate? Now the lad had disappeared and, with the mate dead, the car was all that was left for Buchanan to investigate. He picked up his phone and called Dan O'Shea.

'Dan, hi, it's Jack Buchanan. Do you know where the wrecked Golf GTi was taken after the accident?'

'Yes, it was recovered by Hobbs, not sure what happened to it after they got it.'

'Thanks.'

◆

'Hobbs Recovery.'

'Good morning, DCI Buchanan, Sussex Police. I'm looking for a Golf GTi, recovered from an RTA on the A27 a week ago Saturday.'

'I think that ended up at Ripley's scrapyard in Hailsham.'

'Thanks.'

◆

Buchanan decided to wait for Street to get in before he went to Ripley's, so while he was alone in the office, he thought he would have a look at *Gardeners World* on BBC iPlayer. He was so busy watching Monty Don divide a clump of rhubarb that he didn't notice Street enter the office and sit at her desk.

Being in a cheeky mood she picked up her phone and dialled Buchanan's extension.

It rang five times before he reached to pick it up and as he did so he looked across at Street's desk and saw she was on the phone.

'Buchanan.'

'Good morning, Boss.'

'Who is this?'

'Me,' she said, waving.

'Good morning,' he said, chuckling as he put down the phone.

'How was your weekend?'

'We slept late on Saturday then spent the rest of the day looking for bedroom furniture for the nursery. Yesterday we decorated the baby's room. And you and Karen?'

'Saturday morning, I inspected the innards of Julian Du Marchon and Alan Dale, then in the afternoon I replaced all the broken glass in my greenhouse and gave the inside and out a good wash. After that I did some weeding and finished the day having a bonfire. Sunday, Karen coerced me into going to church with her.'

'Really? How was it?'

'Not bad, and a lot livelier than the services I went to as a child.'

'Talking of children, do they have a children's programme?'

'They must have something like that. When we arrived, everyone was drinking teas and coffees, and there were children running all over the place, yet at one point in the service the children left.'

'Good. Maybe I'll go along and see for myself. You and Karen staying over after the wedding?'

'Yes, we're going to stay for the wedding breakfast. Should be home after lunch on Sunday.'

'So, Doctor Buchanan, did your patient survive his surgery?'

'No, I'm afraid he was too far gone by the time I got to him.'

'What was the prognosis?'

'According to Dr Mansell, he drowned but was also suffering from severe carbon monoxide poisoning which we surmised caused him to lose control of the plane.'

'What about Alan Dale?'

'Same diagnosis.'

'And you still think Victor Mountjoy was thrown from the plane?'

'Until other evidence shows up, that's what I will put in my report to the coroner.'

'Do you need me this morning?'

'I don't think there's anything, why?'

'I was going to have a chat to Lazarus about the bike thefts. There was another theft from a bike shop on Saturday.'

'That's fine. I'm going to pop over to Ripley's and have a look at the Golf.'

'The one that nearly ran you over?'

'That's the one.'

The Jockey's Wife.

♦

Buchanan parked outside Ripley's and walked into their office while watching out for forklifts and lorries delivering scrap.

'Good morning. DCI Buchanan. I'm looking for a wrecked Golf GTi.'

'Any particular one?'

'Yes. It would have been brought in by Hobbs one day last week, possibly Tuesday.'

'Hang on a minute,' said the receptionist as he scrolled though the screen on his computer. 'Was it a 07 black GTi?'

'Yes, that sounds like it.'

'The car has gone, sold for parts.'

'Who to?'

'I don't know.'

'You must have a record of who it was sold to? It's the law'

'Let me have a look at the records. Ah, here it is, a 07 GTi, sold to a Jason Locke for cash.'

'Do you have an address for him?'

'Of course, it's written down right here. Sandyford Road, Paisley. That address I believe is somewhere in Glasgow.'

'Thanks. What was he driving?'

'A Range Rover with trailer.'

'What day was this?'

'Last Friday afternoon.'

'Do you know what happened to the contents of the car?'

'Not sure, I'll go and ask. You wait here, you're not allowed out in the yard.'

He was back in ten minutes with a bearded individual. 'This is Theo.'

'You want to know what happened to the contents of the Golf?'

'Yes.'

'The contents were collected by you guys, that's what usually happens. The car was quite a wreck, the front all stoved in like it was.'

'Thanks, Theo.'

'So where are Hardcastle's tools?' wondered Buchanan, as he drove back along Diplocks. Could they be in the evidence store, or still be in the barn?

Buchanan left Hailsham on Station Road on his way to Rickney Lane and the site where Hardcastle met his end. His was the only vehicle on the lane so he slowed to give himself time to think about what might be going on. As he made his way along the lane, he was joined by a farmer in a Land Rover who obviously was in more of a hurry than Buchanan, so at the first opportunity he pulled over and let the Land Rover past.

As the farmer drove off, Buchanan returned to his sedate pace till he reached the turn off for the barn. As he came to a halt, he saw the farmer had pulled off the road fifty yards further on and was staring at something off in the distance. Buchanan got out of his car and noticed the gate to the barn property had been secured with a new chain and padlock and the For Sale sign had been removed.

He climbed over the gate and walked over to the barn, now exposed with the scaffolding gone. He tried the large main doors, but they were shut and locked from the inside. Then he tried the small door on the right – it was unlocked.

The air inside the barn on this October afternoon was cool and musty and took his mind back to the days of childhood and Jock's stables when as a teenager he would spend many happy hours working with the horses.

He took a few minutes to allow his eyes to be accustomed to the light. Here there were no animals, human or otherwise, it was just empty, and that bothered him. He walked over to the area where Hardcastle had breathed his last. Gone was the ladder that Hardcastle supposedly fell from, gone was the blood stain in the dirt, in fact gone were all signs that anything untoward happened. After a fruitless search of the empty barn, he realised that everything associated with Hardcastle's death, including his tools, were gone.

He left the barn, climbed over the gate and got back in his car. As he drove off, he passed the farmer standing beside his Land Rover. As Buchanan passed the farmer, he thought he saw a smile on his face.

He drove back to the office wondering where this investigation was going. Could the carpenter's death simply just be an accident? He parked in the compound and went straight to the evidence store.

'Yes? Can I help?' asked the evidence storeman.

'Yes. I'm looking for some tools that were brought in recently, they were the contents of a Golf GTi that crashed on the A27 a week ago.'

'Do you have a case number?'

Buchanan shook his head. 'Nope. Not one I was working on.'

'Can you describe these tools?'

'Nope, again, but I am assuming they are carpenter's tools, chisels, wood planes, that sort of thing.'

'Hang on, I'll go check.'

He was back in five minutes.

'This is the only tool bag we have in just now.'

'Can I see the contents?'

'Sure. You'll need to put these on first,' he said, handing Buchanan a pair of inspection gloves. 'I'll bring them through to the inspection bench. This is the tool bag that was in the Golf. We quite often find items of value in the wrecks brought in.'

'What usually happens to those items?'

'The car owners eventually come and claim them, providing the items were not used in some sort of crime.'

'Is someone coming for these?' asked Buchanan, as he opened the tool bag.

'I don't know.'

Buchanan put on the gloves, opened the large paper evidence bag and puled the tool bag out. He opened it, removed the tools and laid them on the bench. There was a small wooden-handled backsaw, a well-worn claw hammer, three rust-covered plastic-handled screwdrivers of various lengths and a set of plastic-handled chisels ranging in size from three millimetres up to twenty-five millimetres; the twelve-millimetre chisel was missing.

Buchanan picked up the eighteen-millimetre chisel and inspected the cutting edge. It was sharp enough to shave with, but no sign of blood. But then it would not have, the chisel that killed Hardcastle was in the morgue with his body.

'Is there a problem?' asked the storeman, as he saw the look of puzzlement on Buchanan's face.

'Tell me something, if you were working on building, say a wooden barn, would you have a toolkit like this?' said Buchanan, pointing at the assortment of tools on the bench.

'Sorry, I wouldn't know. I collect stamps as a hobby.'

'That's OK. Are you sure these were all that were in the tool bag?'

'Yep. Not much value, is there?'

'How long will you hold on to them?'

'Who knows? I suppose if they were part of an active investigation, I'd hold on to them till the case was over. But since we are cramped for space, if someone doesn't claim them, they could be sold at auction and the money put to good use.'

'Thanks. Would you let me know if anyone is interested in them?'

Yes, give me your number.'

♦

As Buchanan approached his office door, he could hear his phone ringing, he entered and grabbed it.

'Jack, it's Gus. I said I'd get back to you when I have something.'

'Good, what did you find out?'

'Sorry to have to say this, but all we have on Jamie Gallagher is he's resting six feet under in Cathcart Cemetery; been there for the last eight years. I did find a record for a Andy Jameson that would be about the same age as your young lad, but unfortunately he seems to have made himself scarce.'

'What was his MO?'

'He was very fond of knives.'

'Well, he seems to have surfaced down here working as a carpenter's mate.'

'I might have had more success if I had more to go on, like DNA samples.'

'Hmm. I could get a DNA sample from Hardcastle, his body is currently residing in the morgue, and the tool bag of the young lad is locked in the evidence room here at the station.'

'Fine, just send them through and I'll run the samples through our system and see what turns up.'

◆

Buchanan hung up from talking to Fergusson and called Dr Mansell.

'Andrew, any chance I could have a tissue sample from the dead carpenter for DNA matching?'

'You could if he were here'

'What do you mean: *if he were here?*'

'His body was collected by his sister this morning. She said they were going to have a remembrance service, then have the body cremated directly after the service.'

'That was quick. What about the release paperwork?'

'I wasn't here, but I have seen the paperwork, it all looks fine.'

'So, you have nothing of his?'

'No, sorry.'

'Not even his blood-stained clothing?'

'Sorry, Jack. Everything the next of kin didn't take with them has gone off to be incinerated.'

'Do you have their contact details?'

'They're on the release form.'

'Would you send over a copy of the release papers, please? I'd like to talk to the family.'

'OK, will do.'

Buchanan hung up from his call to Mansell wondering what was going on. He felt he was one step behind someone who was sweeping up the evidence ahead of him. At least he still had the tool bag residing in the evidence storeroom.

He picked up the phone and called the evidence room.

'Evidence.'

'Yes. This is Detective Inspector Buchanan; I was looking at a tool bag a short while ago.'

'I remember.'

'I need you to hold onto that bag for me. Could you tag it?'

'Sure, want me to go and look and make sure it's still there?'

'Yes – wait – why shouldn't it be there?'

'Who knows these days?'

'Please, would you go and check for me?'

Three minutes later the storeman was back. 'Inspector, it's gone. I asked Steve at the front desk, and he said it was given to a guy who bought the wreck from Ripley's. He did have a receipt for it to say the tools were sold along with the car.'

'When was this?'

'Not ten minutes after you looked at it.'

'He signed in, didn't he?'

'Yes, she did.'

'Can I have a photocopy of the of the release receipt?'

'Certainly, I'll memo it to you.'

'Thanks.'

♦

'What's wrong?' Street asked Buchanan.

'Something isn't right, it's all too clean.'

'What do you mean?'

'According to Dr Mansell, the carpenter's sister showed up earlier this morning with a death certificate for Jackson Hardcastle. He and his effects have been incinerated. The lad has been using the name of a baby that died a birth. The Golf GTi was sold for parts to someone calling themselves Jason Locke and the tool bag found in the car has been given away to the person who bought the Golf. The lad who crashed the car will not get away with it though, as soon as he shows up in Glasgow, Ferguson and his men will pick him up.'

'So, the carpenter has been cremated along with his effects, there is no body or materials for DNA testing, and the young driver and his car have disappeared. The car and tools have been sold for cash to someone. In my book that equals case closed,' said Street.

'That's looks like the way it has worked out except for one thing.'

'What's that?'

'The B&B where the carpenter and the lad were staying. That will still be there.'

'And where is there?'

'Wiseley B&B, Pevensey. Shouldn't be too difficult to find.'

'Want company?'

'Yes please. I need something to brighten up my day.'

'This is interesting,' said Street, 'the Wiseley B&B is a few doors down the road from the Smugglers Inn, just before you get to the traffic lights. Want me to drive?'

◆

The discrete sign fastened to the low brick wall in front of the building said Wiseley B&B with the phone number below. The Wiseley lived up to its name. The front garden would have not looked out of place at the Chelsea flower show.

Buchanan pressed the doorbell. A few minutes later the door opened.

'Yes, can I help?'

'Good afternoon. Mrs…?'

'It's Miss Dunbar.'

'Miss Dunbar, Detective Chief Inspector Buchanan and Detective Sergeant Street,' said Buchanan, showing his warrant card. 'We're looking into the unfortunate death of one of your recent guests, a Jackson Hardcastle.'

'Oh, I already told the investigator all I know about Mr Hardcastle.'

'What about the young lad staying with him?'

'What is there to know? Andy came home Saturday morning, said there had been a terrible accident and Mr Hardcastle had died. He paid the bill for their accommodation, packed his bags Sunday morning early, and left. He said since Mr Hardcastle was dead there was no more work for him and he was going back home to Glasgow.'

'How did he pay for the room?'

'Cash.'

'Do you still have the cash?'

'No, banked it first thing Monday morning.'

'What about Mr Hardcastle's effects, do you still have them here?'

'No, his sister came and collected them.'

'Do you have an address for him in Glasgow?'

'No, I'm sorry I don't.'

'Had they made a reservation?'

'No. They just knocked on the door.'

'Is that normal?'

'I suppose so. Wiseley is a bed and breakfast, not quite the Dorchester, but just as welcoming.'

'Would you mind if we have a look in his room?'

'I'm sorry, that won't be possible. The room is occupied by a young couple on their honeymoon. I don't think it would be right to intrude.'

'I see. Well, thank you for your time.'

'So, is it case closed?' said Street, as they drove back to the office.

'It annoys me no end, but yes, case closed. Are you still chasing bicycles?'

'Yes. As soon as you drop me off at the office, I am going into town to talk to the bike shop owners, and you?'

'I'm going up to Staveley's Garden Centre in Lower Dicker to have a look at garden tools.'

'Staveley's? Don't you mean Staverton's?'

107

'Yes, Staverton's, I was getting confused with someone else.'

◆

Buchanan returned from lunch to find ACC Helen Markham sitting at his desk.

'You have a comfortable chair,' she said, swinging from side to side. 'I imagine you'd like to keep it?"

'I'm sorry, I don't follow you?'

'How is your case load?' she said, standing and stepping out from behind Buchanan's desk.

'It's fine,' replied Buchanan, wondering what had got her down from the ivory tower of police HQ in Lewes to his humble office.

'I was in town and thought I would pop in and say hello to your partner, Jill. I hear there is a happy event on the horizon.'

'Yes, baby's due sometime in the new year.'

'Where is she?'

'Checking on a spate of bicycle thefts.'

'Good.'

'Would you like a coffee?'

'No thanks, I've tried the canteen coffee before. Are you still frequenting Starbucks?'

'When convenient.'

'Good. Pevensey is on my way back to the office. I've got to see Hanbury about something first, I'll meet you in Starbucks in say, forty minutes, follow me in your car, I don't want to drive back into town.'

◆

'Your usual, Jack?' asked the barista.

'Yes please, Molly.'

'I think there's someone waiting for you, over in the far corner.'

Buchanan looked to where Molly was indicating. Helen Markham was seated with her back to the door, talking on her phone.

'Thanks, Molly. She's my boss.'

'Are you in trouble?'

'Probably,' said Buchanan, smiling as he returned his Starbucks card to his wallet.

He collected his coffee and walked over to the corner table and sat in front of Helen.

She looked up as Buchanan sat in the chair opposite.

'Fine, look I've got to go, my office tomorrow at ten, bye.'

Buchanan sipped on his coffee and waited to hear the real reason of why she felt that only a private meeting would do.

'So, Jack, I've read your report on the Barazani case. The investigation was a bit of a mess at the beginning, but you got there in the end. And talking about the end, I did read between the lines and as long as no one else does, I think we'll just let it drift off into the sunset.'

'Thanks, I did think justice was served.'

'What are you working on just now?'

'Apparently not much. I did think there was a case for further investigation into the death of a carpenter near here. But all I get is closed doors and evidence that keeps getting misplaced.'

'What do you mean?'

'A week ago, Saturday, a carpenter working on a barn restoration fell off his ladder and managed to impale himself on his chisel. Unfortunately, he died before help could get to him.'

'Accidents do happen.'

'I know that. I've had plenty of them in my life.'

'What did the coroner say about it?'

'His verdict was an accident.'

'So, what's bothering you about it?'

'Nothing much, except for the fact that the carpenter's body has been claimed by his sister and removed from the morgue.'

'Where is the issue with that? Sounds like standard procedure.'

'Dr Mansell said it was collected by family and given a farewell service then cremated within hours of being collected.'

'Have you talked to the family?'

'No, not yet. I'm waiting for Dr Mansell to send me a copy of the release certificate, it has the contact details on it.'

'Is that all?'

'The carpenter's mate, who had been driving an unregistered car with cloned plates, has also disappeared. The car has been sold for parts and the tool bag that was in our evidence room has been given to the person who purchased the wreck.'

'I'm not surprised about that.'

'It also was the car, driven by that carpenter's mate that almost ran me down as I went to cross the road.'

Markham put her cup down and leaned back into her chair. 'So, that's what this is all about – you're miffed. Someone driving a stolen car almost ran you down and got away with it. Jack, you should take up writing crime stories, you have a vivid imagination. Don't look at me that way, anyone in your position could make that mistake.'

'But…'

'Jack. You need something to take your mind off this matter. What's this I hear about you taking up gardening?'

'Oh, that. I have taken on an allotment, that's all.'

'Spending every moment and weekend there.'

'Not next weekend. Karen and I are going to a wedding. I'm giving the bride away.'

'Really? Who is the bride?'

'Do you remember the recent case of horserace fixing?'

'That was at Castlewood a few months ago. Didn't one of the owners try and fix the race?'

'Yes, the husband of the bride I'm giving away this Saturday.'

'Wait a minute, how can she get married if she's already married?'

'Her husband died in a plane crash the same day as the horserace.'

'Was that the same plane crash that I read about in last week's *Argus*?'

'Yes. The plane was recovered by a fishing boat.'

'Well then, I think you should concentrate on the upcoming wedding and forget all about missing dead carpenters and a stolen Golf GTi.'

9

Blood in the Sink

As Buchanan locked his car, he looked at the shiny new garden fork and spade he'd collected from Staverton's. Since he'd spent the previous two days writing reports, he hoped to take the afternoon off and spend it at the allotment.

With a lightness in his step, he walked into his office and saw Street was on the phone. 'He's just come in, let me transfer you, please hold.'

'Who is it?' he asked.

'It's a James Hoskins from Ramsdens Property Management. He wants to talk to you about a house in Litlington that they manage for the late Julian Du Marchon.'

'I didn't know he had a house in Litlington' said Buchanan, as he reached for his phone and the speaker button. 'This isn't what I need the day before I actually get time off – DCI Buchanan.'

'Ah, Inspector, my name is James Hoskins. My company has been managing a property in Litlington leased by a Mr Julian Du Marchon, house name Belleview. We have recently been notified by a friend of the family that he has been killed in an aeroplane accident.'

'That is correct.'

'I wasn't sure who to talk to about this, till it was suggested I talk to you.'

'Who was it that suggested you talk to me?'

'Someone calling themselves Ashley Dale, do you know her?'

'We have met.'

'Good, I was worried I had the wrong person.'

'Before we continue, would you tell me what your association is with Ashley Dale?'

'She rents a flat in the marina with us.'

'Thanks. So, what is it you wish to tell me?'

'The house that Mr Du Marchon has been leasing, I think something awful has happened in it.'

'So why would you be calling me?'

'Because there is a lot of dried blood in the bathroom.'

'Why didn't you call 999?'

'I did, but they told me since it was dried blood, I should just report it on 101.'

'A sensible suggestion.'

'I tried that four days ago. If I hadn't given up on the call, I'd probably still be waiting.'

'So, what do you want me to do?'

'Would you please have someone go and look at the mess? I'm sure something terrible has happened there.'

'All right, what's the address?'

'House name is Belleview, it's on The Street in Litlington.'

◆

'Nice house,' said Street as they drove up the driveway and stopped beside a bright blue Bentley Continental GT Speed.

'Nice house,' said Buchanan, 'how about the car? You could buy a flat in Eastbourne for what one of those cost.'

As Buchanan turned off the engine, the driver's door of the Bentley opened.

'Could that be James Hoskins?' said Street. 'Not quite what I imagined when listening to him on the phone.'

'They seldom do. C'mon, the sooner this is over, the sooner I can start my weekend.'

◆

'James Hoskins?' asked Buchanan.

'Yes.'

'Thanks for coming at such short notice.'

'If you'll follow me, I'll show you round.'

Hoskins opened the front door and ushered Buchanan and Street into the small entrance hall. On the floor behind the door were three pairs of shoes, one pair of Nike trainers and two pairs of green wellingtons.

'Through there,' said Hoskins, pointing straight ahead, 'is the sitting room and access out to the garden. Directly to your left is the dining room, and straight ahead the kitchen and larder. This cupboard,' he said, opening a pine door, 'is a cloakroom. If you'll follow me up the stairs, I'll show you the bedrooms and the bathroom in question. Could the blood be from someone cutting themselves while shaving, Inspector?' he asked.

'Possibly, Mr Hoskins. But I think these bloodstains are more than someone cutting themselves while shaving. Jill, would you call Harvey Littlejohn and see if he has someone who could come over and take some samples from the bathroom?'

'Will do.'

'Was I right to call you, Inspector?'

'A bit early to say that Mr Hoskins, and I'm sorry to say we may be here for quite some time.'

'Oh.'

'Jill, when you've called Harvey Littlejohn would you have a snoop around the rest of the house and see what you can find? I'll be downstairs with Mr Hoskins.'

'Fine.'

'While we wait for the CSI team, I wonder if you would tell me about the tenant, Mr Julian Du Marchon?'

'Well, he signed a ten-year lease, that would be about seven years ago, yes, seven years next November,' said Hoskins, consulting a folder.

'What sort of tenant was he? For instance, did he pay the rent on time?'

Hoskins flipped open the folder and flicked through several pages till he got to a single ledger sheet. 'He paid by direct debit on the 5th of every month. As far as I can see, during the previous twelve months, he never missed a payment.'

'Did he live here alone?'

Hoskins once again consulted the folder and said, 'The house has three bedrooms. I'm unaware how many people lived with Mr Du Marchon.'

'That's all right. Have there been any complaints from neighbours?'

'None that I am aware of, this is a quiet neighbourhood. I sure we would have known if there had been any issues with the neighbours. There were no restrictions in the lease on occupancy.'

'What else can you tell me about Mr Du Marchon?'

'Not much I'm afraid. As I said, he always paid his rent on time, except – except for the last month when the bank stopped the direct debit,' he said looking back at the ledger sheet. 'But he did take good care of the property.'

'Didn't you make enquiries as to why he'd stopped making payments, especially since there are several years left to run on the lease?'

'That's what got me started.'

'Do you have a business address for him?'

'The last business address,' he said, once more looking in the folder, 'was an address in Gildredge Road in Eastbourne. I did check the address yesterday and was told that Mr Du Marchon had left the premises quite some time ago and they have since been relet and all his effects had been disposed of.'

'Ah, I better tell Jill, save her chasing after a non-existent office. Is there a swimming pool at the property?'

'Yes, and a hot-tub.'

'Fine. While my sergeant is going through the house, I would be obliged if you would show me round the outside of the property.'

'Certainly. If you'll follow me,' said Hoskins, leading Buchanan through the sitting room and out into the small patio.

'I hadn't expected this,' said Buchanan, as he looked over the large back garden and the fields stretching into the distance and the South Downs Country Park.

'Yes, it is quite special. Fancy trying a bit of that?' said Hoskins, pointing to the paragliders swooping and hovering above the Downs.

'Not for me,' said Buchanan. 'You said there is a swimming pool and hot tub?'

'This way. The previous owners put it behind a hedge, gave them privacy when bathing.'

Hoskins led Buchanan across the expansive lawn to an area behind a tall box hedge. In the middle of it was a narrow opening that led through to the pool and hot tub set low in the ground and surrounded by a wide timber-effect deck.

'That's the changing room,' said Hoskins, pointing to a small timber building at the far end of the swimming pool. Buchanan climbed the three wide steps up onto the decking and walked over to the summer house.

'I don't think it's locked,' said Hoskins.

Buchanan opened the door and looked inside. Immediately on the left was a stack of pale-blue wicker chairs. Facing him was a planked wall with a curtained doorway in the middle. Buchanan stepped in and pulled the curtain back. On the left corner, there was a short bench to enable bathers to dress. In the opposite corner, on the floor, a pile of weathered cushions.

'Is there anything else out here in the garden?'

'A small shed containing gardening tools.'

'Show me, please.'

'It's beside the garage, this way. It's just a shed to keep garden tools in,' said Hoskins, as they made their way across the lawn.

Buchanan tried the door. 'Locked, do you have a key?'

'No, sorry. Probably in the house somewhere, the junk drawer in the kitchen most likely.'

'What would this house sell for if it was on the market?' asked Buchanan, as they walked towards the house.

'Somewhere in the region of three quarters of a million. Why, are you interested?'

'No, not now, I've just purchased a house in the village of Westham. When are the bins emptied?'

'Ah, Westham, an area becoming much in demand. I think the bins are emptied every second Tuesday – why would you want to know that?'

'You'd be surprised if I told you what dustbins can tell a policeman.'

'They're in the carport.'

'So, unless they are pulled out into the street, they remain full of rubbish?'

'I guess so.'

Buchanan walked past the side of the walled-in carport and turned round the end of the wall. There were three bins lined up against the garage doors at the rear of the carport.

'Does the garage get used?'

'It's quite small for modern cars, hence the carport, I think it is only used as a utility room. There is room for the washer and drier, and I seem to remember winter firewood being stored in there as well,' replied Hoskins.

Buchanan entered the carport, walked to the rear, and looked inside the bins. The right-hand one was empty, as was the middle one. The one on the left contained a discarded baseball cap sitting on top of two crumpled newspapers, the *Eastbourne Herald*, and the *Argus*.

Buchanan reached into the bin and removed the cap and newspapers. The *Argus* sported a quarter page photo of Du Marchon's Cessna 320 suspended from a crane being lifted from the river Ardur. The headline blazed: *Crashed plane recovered, all on board perished.*

'This is only a few days old, someone's been here recently,' said Buchanan.

He carried the cap out into the daylight and saw what looked like bloodstains inside on the sweatband.

'Were you looking for something in particular?' asked Hoskins.

'No. I seem to remember you mentioned there's a cloakroom in the hall?' he said, holding the hat away from the bloodstain in one hand, and the newspapers in the other.

'Yes, there is.'

'Good, I'd like to have a look in it.'

They returned to the house and a fruitless search of the cloakroom under the stairs.

'Anything?' asked Street.

Buchanan held up the hat and newspapers. 'Just these, would you bag and tag them, please?'

'What's that on the inside of the cap? Looks like bloodstains?'

Buchanan turned the hat over and nodded. 'I'll leave it for Littlejohn to look at. How about you, find anything?'

'It's confusing. There are signs of occupation, but by who? I looked in the main bedroom, the clothes in the drawers all looked like they belonged to one individual. It was obvious whose room it was, there is a photo of Du Marchon standing beside his plane. Bedroom two, the one at the top of the stairs, had bunkbeds. The dresser drawers were segregated into a his and his sort of arrangement. Going by the size of the waistbands of the underwear I'd say they belonged to two males in their late twenties.'

'What about the third bedroom at the front of the house?'

'Sole occupancy, and by someone quite recent, though I'd say they weren't a regular occupier. Brand new underwear, jeans, socks, and shirt wrappers in the bin, along with a cash sales receipt dated Thursday the 28th of August.'

'That's interesting,' said Buchanan.

'What's interesting?' said Hoskins, who up till this moment had been listening intently to Street and Buchanan's conversation.

'Had it been two months earlier I would have said that it was leftovers from a visit by Colonel Victor Mountjoy, or Julian Du

Marchon, but since they perished in the English Channel on Sunday the 23rd of August it must have been someone else.'

'Are you implying this house was used by people other than Mr Du Marchon?' said Hoskins.

'It is a quiet neighbourhood,' said Street. 'It's not uncommon for rented houses to be used for nefarious purposes.'

'What sort of nefarious purposes?' asked Hoskins, whose face had turned pale.

'It's been known for squatters to settle in abandoned houses, and recently there has been a spate of county line gangs setting up in abandoned houses,' said Buchanan. 'Sometimes, takes months and a fortune in legal fees to get them out.'

'I'm sure that's not what's happening here, Mr Hoskins,' said Street, as she gently elbowed Buchanan in the ribs. 'Probably Mr Du Marchon lent his key to a friend who hadn't heard of his untimely demise.'

'Well, if you are sure.'

'I'm sure it's nothing to worry over,' added Buchanan.

'I'm glad to hear that,' Hoskins said, looking at his watch again.

'Would you like us to return the key to your office when the CSI investigators are done with their work?' asked Buchanan.

'Hmm, yes, why not? I'm sure we can trust the police. So, if there's nothing else you wish to ask me, I'll be off back to the office.'

◆

'We're in the wrong occupation, Jill.'

'Why do you say that?'

'I'm looking at Hoskins reversing his Bentley out of the driveway. Can you imagine how many hours of work it would take to be able to buy one of those?'

'It's probably leased and written off against expenses.'

'Yes, I imagine it's so. Did Littlejohn say how long they would be?'

'Within the hour. He said they were finishing up at another case and would be with us as soon as they could.'

'Can't be soon enough for me, I've got the watering to do at the allotment before we go away for the weekend.'

'You can go if you want, Jack. I could wait for Littlejohn and get a lift back with them.'

'No, no, that wouldn't do.'

'Why are you so interested in Julian Du Marchon? We both know he's dead.'

'Dead in life, but alive in death, on my shadow he treads, wherever I go.'

'How about the other two?'

'I do realise Du Marchon is dead, but there is something, something I can't quite put my finger on. You said there are wrappers from shirts and underwear in the rubbish bin in bedroom three?'

'Yes.'

'Dated two days after we know Julian Du Marchon, Victor Mountjoy and Ashley's brother, Alan, perished in the plane crash.'

'Yes.'

'So, in this little vignette on the life of the rich and the not so rich, instead of a triplet of characters, we have a quartet.'

'So, who is going to be the fourth person?' queried Street. 'Wait a minute – do you think it could be Ashley Dale?'

'I don't think that's very likely. You've met her, can you see her dressing as a man?'

'No, definitely not. So, other than identifying the activity behind the blood in the bathroom and the hat, what does it matter who the fourth actor in your play is?'

'Money, and a great deal of it. So far, we are in possession of a substantial quantity of gilts that were financed by Du Marchon's laundering of cash from the sales of illicit drugs.

Then there's the cash that Victor swindled from investors, that's still to be accounted for. All in all, we are looking at a figure close to a million pounds.'

'Are you thinking the blood in the upstairs bathroom belongs to the fourth person, and they have been living here while trying to figure out where Victor's cash is hidden?'

'That is the conclusion I am coming to.'

'Do you think the cash could be here in the house somewhere?'

'If it is, it could be anywhere, but I think it's extremely unlikely to be here,' said Buchanan. 'Though there is one place we haven't yet looked.'

'Where would that be?'

'The garden shed. It was locked when I tried the door earlier. Hoskins said he didn't know where the key is.'

'It will probably be where all keys are kept,' said Street, 'the junk drawer in the kitchen. Every kitchen has one, usually close to the phone, if there is one.'

'Hoskins said there is a phone, but he wasn't sure if it is still working.'

A search of the junk drawer in the kitchen revealed three pencils all with broken leads, several rubber bands of various sizes and colours, two small notepads, but no keys.

'I was wrong,' said Street. 'The keys aren't in the drawer, they are hanging on the key rack above the radiator. What type of lock are they? There's several keys hanging here.'

'Yale.'

'Here, try these,' she said, passing Buchanan a keyring with six keys, two of them being Yale keys.

'Voilà' said Buchanan, opening the shed door to reveal an old petrol lawnmower, a collection of gardening tools and three sun hats on hooks.

'What do you think, Jill?' he asked, trying on one of the sun hats.

'I can just see you wearing that down at the allotment. Any sign of money?'

'No, just the stuff you'd expect to find in a garden shed.'

'If Mountjoy's money was here at the house,' said Street, 'why did Du Marchon fly to Headcorn instead of Brighton to refuel?'

'A valid point. If Du Marchon was able to land and take off from Castlewood, he could have even landed out there in one of those fields. You said bedroom number two looked like it was shared?'

'Yes, by two men. Do you suppose one was Alan and the other was our mysterious fourth person?'

'We won't know unless we go and look. Let's go and see what we can find.'

'The underwear is in the second drawer,' said Street, as Buchanan followed her into the room.

'I see what you mean, his and his, very neat. Did you look in any other drawers?'

'Yes, lower drawers contain t-shirts, socks and jeans. The top drawers have personal effects, nothing special.'

Buchanan pulled the left-hand drawer out and carefully laid its contents on the bed. Beneath the socks was a small moleskin notebook. He picked it up and slowly flicked through the pages.'

'Anything of interest?'

'Nothing that stands out, mostly notes about grocery shopping and the occasional scribbles about train times and hotels in London.'

He reached the back and saw something in the small pocket on the rear cover. It was a photograph of Ashley standing beside a healthy young man in a camouflage outfit.

'Taken outside by the hot tub I'd say,' said Buchanan, passing the photo to Street. 'Does he remind you of anyone?'

'No, why should he?'

'I don't know, he just looks familiar. Anything written on the back?'

Street turned the photo over. *Me and big sis, summer 2020.* Didn't imagine him being so brawny,' she said, 'I had him as slim built and weedy looking.'

'That's what I imagined. Are there any others?'

'Yes,' said Buchanan, as he handed a second photo to Street.

'Interesting,' she said, looking at a photo of Alan towering a good eight inches over his friend, also in Army fatigues. *'Dan and me at Wiesbaden 2019.* So, now we know what number four in your story looks like. It would be quite easy to tell them apart in a crowd.'

'Anything else?'

'Yes, a weathered photo of Mountjoy and Du Marchon beside the plane.'

'Can you tell where it was taken?'

'No. My knowledge of airports isn't that extensive. Jill, do you remember the description of the unidentified body found in Du Marchon's plane?'

'Yes. A young male in his early thirties, no identifying marks, slim build and five feet six in height. If that was Daniel's body found in the plane, where is Alan?'

'Precisely. Now why would Ashley lie to us? I think we need to have another word with her, did you get her details?'

'Yes, they'll be in my notebook.'

'Good, but that conversation will have to wait till Monday. I'm not having any mystery messing with my weekend off.'

'I'm just wondering about this house,' said Street, 'especially with Julian du Marchon and Victor Mountjoy both dead. Why did Ashley bring it to our attention? She could have said nothing, and we'd never be any the wiser. Do you think she wants us to find something here, something she is afraid to say openly?'

'Then why give us the wrong toothbrush and the gilts, plus falsely identify her brother if not to put us off the scent?

'Without Mountjoy's signature those gilts will be very difficult to cash, so maybe she and her brother are after the cash that

Mountjoy squirreled away before his untimely demise. Anything in the other drawer? Of course, that assumes Alan is still alive,' said Buchanan.

Street closed the left-hand drawer, pulled out the right-hand one and removed the contents.

'Nothing special in here, only clothes,' she said. 'What's this?' She bent down to remove something from the wastebasket. She removed the object, a crumpled piece of yellowed notepaper and handed it to Buchanan.

Buchanan unravelled the paper; it was a piece of hotel notepaper. At the top was the hotel logo, the Crowne Plaza, Heathrow Airport, below was some sort of scribbled letters.

'What does it say?'

'You tell me,' he said, passing it to Street.

'*J and V, I'm here to collect what is owed, I return soon, have it ready, JCB.* 'I suppose J is Julian and V is Victor,' said Street, 'but who is JCB and what is it he was here to collect? Just had a thought, suppose the blood in the bathroom was the result of JCB's failed attempt at collecting?'

'That's a possibility. If they were in the construction industry, I might hazard a guess that JCB refers to backhoes and trench digging. You see them on almost every construction site. But with the names Julian and Victor being mentioned, JCB is more likely someone's initials, some underworld collection thug. If things are quiet tomorrow, would you do a search through the PNC for anyone with those initials?'

'Will do. Shall we have a look in the front bedroom and at the clothes wrappers?'

'M&S, he's got good taste in underwear,' said Buchanan, picking the size tags out of the bin, 'size extra-large - now that presents a problem. What size were the underwear in the drawers in bedroom two?'

'I'll check, back in a minute. Large on the left side of the drawer and medium on the right side.'

'Alan was much larger than Daniel, could he have come back to the house and had to buy new clothes? I'm getting a picture of all four leaving the house, possible because JCB was coming to collect. Victor and Julian went to Castlewood. Alan and Daniel to the squat in town. Alan returned to collect something, possibly the briefcase, and was confronted by JCB. A fight ensued and as a result Alan was gravely injured. There was lots of blood necessitating new clothes, so he took the clothes he had already purchased for going away and used them.'

'That works,' said Street. 'I wonder if we should now be looking for the dead body of JCB buried somewhere on the property?'

Further speculation was interrupted by the sound of the front doorbell ringing.

'That will be Littlejohn,' said Street, 'I'll let him in.'

Buchanan followed Street down the stairs and waited in the hallway for her to open the door for Littlejohn and his team.

'Afternoon Buchanan, where's the washbasin?'

'Upstairs on the left, we'll wait down here. Oh. There is also this,' said Buchanan, taking the baseball hat from the coat hook in the hall and handing it to Littlejohn.'

'Not my size.'

'There's blood on the hatband, would you give it the once over, please? It may or may not be connected to what we are looking into, either way I'd like to eliminate it from our enquiries.'

'Sure,' said Littlejohn, as he led his assistant up the stairs.

'While Littlejohn gives the bathroom the once over, Jill, let's have a look in the kitchen. There isn't room for both of us,' said Buchanan, looking in the narrow galley-style kitchen. 'I'll stand out here in the hall while you go through the kitchen.'

'She's in her element,' he thought, as he watched Street methodically open cupboard after cupboard. 'So, your conclusion of the kitchen's contents, Jill?'

'It's quite confusing. From our perusal of the house, we know four males lived here, but looking at the kitchen and how it is equipped, I'd say it was a woman's domain, probably a mother, or grandmother.'

'Why?'

'Firstly, look at all the cooking utensils, those pots and pans speak of someone who really likes to cook. I had a look in the dining room earlier and the bottom two shelves in the bookcase are mostly well-thumbed cookbooks written by famous female cooks.'

'Why a female kitchen? Television is full of male chefs.'

'Look here,' she said, pointing at a wall plaque, '*Nans like you, are precious and few*, and this one, *It's not the years in your life, it's the life in your years*. Does that sound like something a man would have hanging on the wall? It can only be for either for someone's mother or grandmother.'

Buchanan entered the kitchen and eased himself into a space beside the doorway. He looked at the walls and the wall hangings, '*The best and most beautiful things in life cannot be seen or touched, they must be felt with the heart*. I see what you mean, but that presents a problem. You checked all the bedrooms and found no trace of female occupation?'

'That's correct.'

'Then my conclusion would be that it was originally a female residence and has since been superseded by four males.'

'I wonder who she was?'

'Hoskins said the house is leased, maybe the kitchen utensils were left over from the previous tenant.'

'Houses aren't usually leased complete with cookbooks, kitchen utensils, and those,' said Buchanan, nodding to the plaques hanging on the walls.'

Their discussion was interrupted by Littlejohn coming down the stairs.

'All done?' asked Buchanan.

'Yes, should have the results back to you sometime next week if that suits your needs.'

'You have the hat?'

'Yes. I suppose you want to see if there is a DNA match with the blood in the washbasin?'

'Yes please.'

'Will Tuesday do?'

'Yes, I'm taking tomorrow off.'

'Really? I thought you never rested.'

'Very funny.'

Buchanan followed Littlejohn out of the driveway and watched as they loaded up the van, then left for the office.

◆

'You'll be OK on your own tomorrow?' Buchanan said, as he let Street out of his car at the police compound.'

'Of course, I will. I'm a big girl now, I can even brush my teeth by myself.'

'Sorry, see you Monday.'

◆

Buchanan left the police compound realising he still had the keys to Belleview in his pocket and drove to Ramsdens.

He parked in one of the available slots in Hyde Gardens and climbed the short flight of steps for Ramsdens Property Management.

The reception area was compact with several chairs on the right, with the requisite coffee table replete with a selection of property magazines. The receptionist was seated in a small anteroom behind a sliding glass screen.

'Can I help?'

'Yes, DCI Buchanan. I am returning these keys for the Belleview house.'

'Ah, yes. Mr Hoskins said you'd be by.'

'I wonder if I might have a quick word with Mr Hoskins if he's in?'

'If you'll take a seat, I'll see if he's available.'

Buchanan ignored the selection of chairs and walked over to the window and looked out onto the Hyde Gardens carpark. He smiled to himself as he watched a parking attendant complete his daily ticket quota, including Buchanan's car.

'Inspector, Mr Hoskins can see you now. If you come through, I'll show you to his office.'

There was a click and the intermediate door opened onto a narrow hallway with doors leading off to the right. She stopped at the last door, knocked, and announced Buchanan.

'Inspector, you could have just dropped the keys with Cecily, there was no need to hand them to me personally.'

'Thanks, but I do have one more question for you.'

'What is that?'

'I realise that Belleview was leased to Mr Du Marchon, but can you tell me who owns Belleview, and who the previous tenant was?'

'Interesting questions, Inspector. I would have to check our records, it's not the sort of information I have at the tip of my fingers.'

'I have time.'

'OK,' he said, turning to his computer.

Thirty minutes later, Buchanan removed the parking ticket from his windscreen and climbed into his car furnished with the knowledge of who owned Belleview. According to Hoskins' records Belleview was owned by an investment company called Sovereign Secure Investments, and Buchanan knew from an earlier investigation that Sovereign Secure Investments was a front for Julian Du Marchon's shady money deals. The other interesting fact was the name of the previous tenant, an Andrea Dale.

◆

'How was your day?' asked Karen, as Buchanan undid his tie.

'Interesting, Jill and I went to look at a house in Litlington.'

'They're not thinking of moving, especially this close to her having a baby?'

'No, nothing like that. Just part of an ongoing investigation.'

'You look pleased with yourself, what's happened? No, wait a minute, don't tell me, you have a body?'

He shook his head. 'Sorry, no body. But I do have a mystery to investigate.

'Good, I don't like it when you are in black mood.'

10
The Rehersall

'Jack, you're not going into the office this morning, are you?'

'No. Just going to pop over to the allotment to check the tomatoes in the greenhouse then down to the newsagent for a copy of the *Herald*. If the weather is going to be as warm as it is supposed to be, I can't have the tomatoes and peppers running out of water.'

'OK, don't be too long.'

'I won't, promise.'

On the way to the allotment, he passed three people walking dogs. It caused him to think whether he and Karen should have a dog? If so, what should they have? Of course, the choice was obvious, a policeman should have a police dog, an Alsatian. His grandad had one, it was called Jock.

As he walked up the path, he saw Dave had been picking his King Edwards and had raked the soil flat leaving one row left to pick. Next year he hoped he would be doing the same. Towards the top, he saw that plot 11 was still looking abandoned. This was, according to Tony on plot 6, a travesty, especially since the plot had been rented by the same person for the last two years.

Tomatoes and peppers watered, he left the allotment and walked down the High Street to collect his copy of the *Herald*.

As he opened the front door, he saw that Karen had placed their suitcase on the hall floor. He took the case out to the car and returned to the house.

'Ah, there you are, all sorted at the allotment?'

'Yes, all watered and resting in the warmth of the greenhouse. I put the case in the car. Anything else I can do to help?'

'Thanks,' she said, looking at her watch. 'One last thing, would you check the doors and windows?'

'Would you like a coffee?' said Buchanan, as they drove over Pevensey Haven and approached the A259 roundabout, 'Starbucks is on our way.'

'That sounds good, would you get me a café mocha? Oh, hang on a minute, I'll come with you, I need the toilet.'

Coffees in hand they drove off along Wartling Road towards Battle.

'Jack, just how often do you go to Starbucks? They all seem to know you by name.'

'That's one reason I like going there. Sometimes they make my coffee as they see me drive into the carpark.'

'I'm surprised they don't offer you a job.'

'They did once.'

'Looks like it's going to be a wonderful weekend for Pat and Cynthia's wedding,' said Karen, as they turned off the A21. 'She certainly deserves it after what she's had to put up with. I just don't know why she married Victor. Do you know how long they were married for?'

'Not sure, but I think it was at least twenty years.'

'Do you know much about them?'

'Not much, other than the fact it wasn't a happy relationship.'

'What time is the rehearsal?'

'Cynthia said it was booked for two-fifteen. It's just a formality, I reckon we'll be back by four.'

'How are you? You've been quite distant these past few days.'

'I'm fine. I thought there was something breaking with the carpenter who stabbed himself in the chest with his chisel. But since the coroner has ruled the carpenter's death an accident, and my boss has told me to forget it, I've had to let it go.'

'Sounds just like an episode of *Endeavour*. He always sees things his boss, DCI Friday, doesn't.'

'Yes, but Friday usually hopes Endeavour will keep digging.'

'So, you're not convinced it was an accident?'

'It's not whether I think it was an accident or not, it was something Helen Markham said that bothers me, at least I think it's what I heard her say.'

'What was that?'

'Something about golf.'

'But you don't play golf.'

'I know that. Maybe she was hinting again about me retiring. Things are a bit quiet just now.'

'How quiet is it?'

'We were tidying up the loose ends leftover when Julian Du Marchon's plane crashed in the English Channel.'

'That's the crash where Victor Mountjoy died?'

'Yes. Turns out there is also a very expensive house in Litlington involved. The estate agent handling the property called us yesterday. Jill and I drove over and had a look at it.'

'Did Julian Du Marchon have any relatives?'

'None that we're aware of. But it's a bit more complicated than that. According to the estate agent the house is owned by Julian Du Marchon's investment company, Sovereign Secure Investments, and leased back to Julian Du Marchon.'

'That will be for tax purposes I suppose. Anyone else involved?'

'Victor Mountjoy and two women, one called Andrea Dale, and the other called Ashley Dale. To complicate things further, Ashley Dale's son was supposedly on the plane when it crashed.'

'Is there a relationship between Andrea Dale and Ashley Dale?'

'Only the name at this point. Jill and I are going to go back and talk to Ashley next week.'

'Anything else?'

'There is the matter of a bundle of gilt certificates in the region of half a million pounds.'

'Do you know who they belong to?'

'The paperwork we have for the gilts say they are owned by Julian Du Marchon's investment company. According to Ashley

Dale, her brother was looking after them for Julian and Victor. Ashley said Victor didn't trust Julian, so he had him endorse them all.'

'No love amongst thieves then. So, what will happen to the gilts? You said the coroner has declared Victor dead?'

'I suppose some sort of probate.'

'Where are they now?'

'Securely locked up in the evidence safe at Hammonds Drive.'

'I can now see why you have been so thoughtful these last few days.'

'Thanks, it is a bit of a puzzle.'

◆

'I'm glad you know where you are going,' said Karen, as they drove over the railway line at Paddock Wood.

'Not far now.'

Being the only guests to arrive for the wedding rehearsal, Buchanan had the choice of parking spaces. Over to the left was a large white van, on the side was the company name, Austin's Marquees. As he got out of the car he was greeted by Major, his tail wagging excitedly.

'Hello, boy,' said Buchanan. 'Where's your mistress?'

'Right here,' said Cynthia, as she walked round the corner of the building. 'I heard your tyres on the gravel and figured it would be you. Hello, Karen, thanks for lending your old man for the occasion.'

'Just as long as it's for the occasion, Cynthia.'

'I can assure you it is only for that, I have my own man,' she said, walking forward and kissing Buchanan on the cheek.

'If you'll follow me, I'll show you to your room. It's not the one you stayed in last week, Jack, that's Marjorie's room when she stays here.'

Buchanan and Karen followed Cynthia as she led them across the yard and through the opening in the hedge that divided the yard from the garden. In the middle of the lawn was a large white marquee with sounds of carpets being stapled down. Tables and chairs were stacked up either side of the centre entrance.

'This I didn't expect, Cynthia,' said Karen, 'it's beautiful! Do you look after the garden yourself?'

'When I get time, but I do have a gardener who comes in once a week during the summer months. This way.'

Buchanan and Karen followed Cynthia up the stairs and into their bedroom for the weekend.

'Sorry it's not what you might be used to, but this is the only double available.'

'Cynthia, no need to apologise,' said Karen, 'this is a beautiful room, and the views out of the window are stunning.'

'Thank you. I'll leave you to get unpacked. Normally we would have lunch at one, but since we have the rehearsal at two-fifteen, I'm sorry to say it's everyone for themselves. You'll find a loaf of bread on the cutting board, cheese, sliced ham, tomatoes and whatever else takes your fancy in the fridge. I've just made a pot of coffee.'

'Is there anything I can do to help?' asked Karen. 'I could make up sandwiches for those who wanted them?'

'Are you sure? You're our guest.'

'Sure, I'm sure. I make Jack's sandwiches every morning, have done since he was a constable on the beat in Glasgow.'

'Thanks, that would be a help. I've got the photographer due here in ten minutes and I can't have her see me looking like I am. Pat's with the marquee people sorting out the seating arrangements, and with Marjorie in town chasing up a missed delivery of champagne, I just don't know how I could fit everything in.'

'Great. As soon as I have emptied our case, I'll come down and make lunch for us all. What would you like?'

'Not sure, my tummy is full of butterflies. I'll have whatever you make, see you when you come down.'

'OK.'

The Rehearsall

'Jack,' said Karen, when Cynthia was out of earshot, 'I don't know why Cynthia is apologising for this room, and the bathtub, it's almost big enough to swim in.' She shook off her shoes and sat on the bed. 'The oak beams, the leaded glass windows, it's all so beautiful.'

'You think this room is beautiful, you should see downstairs – the sitting room looks like it could have come right out of a Dickens novel.'

'You know that movie you like to watch, the one with Bruce Willis?'

'*Die Hard*?'

'Yes. You remember the scene at the beginning when he's sitting on the bed in his hotel room, bare feet on the carpet and he's just massaging his toes by curling them into the deep carpet pile? Remember the look of pleasure on his face?'

'Yes, is that what you're doing?'

'Try it, it really works. Come on, take your shoes and socks off and sit with me.'

'Mrs Buchanan, the things you make me do!'

♦

Toes rested, Karen continued with the unpacking while Buchanan went downstairs and out into the yard. As he closed the kitchen door Marjorie walked through the opening in the hedge.

'Hello, Marjorie. Did you manage to track down the missing champagne?'

'Afternoon – it is afternoon?' she said, looking at her watch. 'Oops, not quite – ten more minutes. Stupid delivery driver tried to deliver it to the pub in town. Have you had your lunch?'

'Not yet. Karen is making us sandwiches.'

'Oh, well done. I take it she's in the kitchen?'

'She's just come down from unpacking. I'll introduce you to her.'

'I'd like that.'

'How many guests will there be tomorrow? Cynthia said it would be a quiet affair,' asked Buchanan, as they walked across the lawn.

'Somehow the words quiet and Cynthia don't fit in the same sentence. We are catering for ninety, eighty have been invited, plus the band for after dinner. I guess the caterers will take care of themselves.'

'Hence the need for a marquee.'

'Precisely.'

'Karen, this is Marjorie, Marjorie, this is my wife, Karen.'

'Hi Karen, want some help?'

'Thanks, could you shell the eggs? They're in the pot in the sink cooling off.'

'How about the guys putting up the marquee, are you making them something?'

'How many of them are there?'

'Six, plus Pat.'

'In that case, would you get some more lettuce and tomatoes out of the fridge for me?'

'If you'll excuse me,' said Buchanan, 'I'll just go and see if Pat and the marquee people need any help. It will soon be time for the rehearsal, and we definitely cannot be late for that.'

He walked out onto the lawn and saw two of the men carrying carpet cut-offs out to their van. Entering the marquee he saw that one end had been covered with smooth grey exhibition carpet and the other end had a polished hardwood floor for dancing.

'Hi Pat, thought I'd come and see if you need any help,' said Buchanan, looking at his phone. 'It will soon be time for the rehearsal.'

'Yes, that would be great. Would you put out the chairs, in rows of six down each side of the marquee? Start from the edge of the dance floor and work your way back, please. The blessing and ceremony will be at the dance band end of the marquee. When the ceremony is over it will be time to tighten the girth straps and shorten the reins and get busy rearranging the layout for dinner and dancing.'

'Karen is making sandwiches,' said Buchanan, as he took two chairs from the rack of chairs at the end of the marquee.

'Great, I'm famished.'

'Pat, if I'm giving Cynthia away, who is your best man?'

'My younger brother, Seán. He just called from Gatwick, said not to worry, he's running a bit late but will meet us at the registry office for the rehearsal.'

'Glad to hear that. Chairs are out, is there anything else?'

'No. The caterers will take care of what's left,' she said. looking at her watch. 'Good gracious, is that the time? We need to get a move on, the registry office rehearsal is in an hour.'

♦

'Well, if tomorrow's ceremony goes off as well as today's rehearsal, we can look forward to a wonderful afternoon,' said Cynthia, as Buchanan drove into Appleton Equestrian Centre's carpark.

'It will be a cinch,' said Seán. 'With Jack giving you away, what could go wrong? Relax girl, enjoy the day.'

'Is that your minister?' asked Buchanan, indicating a group of people standing off to the right of the marquee door. 'The chap with the dog collar talking to the young girl?'

'You're not quite correct, Jack. The person taking our wedding tomorrow is Stanley Adebayo, but he is unfortunately unavailable this afternoon, so his friend Michael will be taking us through the rehearsal. The one without the dog collar is Michael, the one with the dog collar must be a friend. The young girl is Sangeya, she is Stanley's daughter, and she is also one of the youngsters who help out at the stables in exchange for riding lessons.'

'Oh, I see.'

'C'mon, let me introduce you.'

Buchanan, Seán, and Marjorie followed Cynthia, her arm linked into Pat's – who was still a bit unsteady on his feet from the previous evening's celebrations – over to Michael and Sangeya.

'Cynthia,' said Michael, 'rehearsal go off, OK?'

'Yes thanks.'

'Cynthia, can I introduce you to an acquaintance of mine, Joshua, he's been staying with us this last week. I'm going to be dropping him off at the station after we're done here.'

'Hello, Joshua,' said Cynthia.

'I was just saying to Joshua it's been a great year for weddings.'

'Any wedding is a great one as long as it's mine. Michael, can I introduce you to the father of the bride, Jack Buchanan? Marjorie you already know.'

'Afternoon Jack, ready to do your duty?'

'Absolutely.'

'Good, we'll run through the blessing ceremony a few times, so we all know what to do tomorrow when Stanley is here.'

Buchanan spent the next hour and a half walking up and down the aisle with Cynthia, while Karen, with Major at her side. stood at the back of the marquee and watched the spectacle. Pat, stood with his brother by his side, while Michael watched as Jack and Cynthia walked up and down the aisle with Marjorie a few steps behind till they could almost do it in the dark.

'Cynthia, I think you'll be fine tomorrow,' said Michael. 'Now if you will excuse me, I need to get Joshua to the station.'

◆

'Well, I think that went OK,' said Pat.

'Let's hope nothing happens tomorrow to spoil the big day, big brother.'

'With Jack, Seán, and Marjorie here, nothing is going to spoil my special day,' said Cynthia. 'Isn't that right, Marjorie?'

'If you say so.'

'Well, look who's waiting for us,' said Cynthia, as they reached the rear of the marquee. 'He's really taken to you, Jack.'

'I like dogs, and they like me.'

'Everything go all right?' asked Karen.

'Perfect,' said Cynthia. 'Horses behaving themselves?'

'Yes. Oh, a man was looking for lessons.'

'Did he say if they were for himself?'

'No, just asked about lessons. I said there was going to be a wedding this weekend and the wedding party were off at the registry office for a rehearsal. I said if he cared to hang on till after the rehearsal, you'd be available and could give him the information he needed.'

'Is he still here?'

'No, he left shortly after and said he'd come back another time. Oh, Major got excited about something, just after he left.'

'What do you mean?'

'I was sitting on the patio reading a magazine when he started barking. I followed him round to the stables but saw nothing out of the ordinary.'

'What did Major do when you got there?'

'Lifted his leg on the fence post.'

'That's Major,' laughed Cynthia. 'Anyone for a drink? It'll soon be time for evening stables.'

◆

'What shall we have for dinner?' asked Marjorie.

'Oh, I can't be bothered with making anything. How about a takeaway?' suggested Cynthia.

'I haven't had curry in a while,' said Pat. 'I may be in training, but I only plan to get married once, so tonight, I'm going to party.'

'Glad to hear that,' said Cynthia.

'OK, curry it is,' said Buchanan. 'What shall I order?'

'How about lamb and chicken tikka dishes with all the trimmings?'

'Will do.'

As Buchanan hung up from ordering dinner, Cynthia said, 'While we wait, there's still evening stables to do.'

They returned from evening stables to find Karen had set the table.

'Dinner has arrived, I've put it in the oven to keep it warm. If you'll take your seats, I'll serve. Be good to have a restful night's sleep before the big day tomorrow.'

'Cynthia, what's up? You're shivering, surely you can't be coming down with a cold at this stage?' said Marjorie.

'I don't know, just felt like someone walked across my grave. It's probably nothing, I'm sure it's just nerves about tomorrow, I'm fine, just need some of that curry to warm me up.'

♦

'That was just what I needed,' said Marjorie, 'but if you'll excuse me, I told Susie I'd call her before she goes to work.'

'Good night, see you tomorrow,' said Cynthia, as Marjorie left the room.

'If you knew Susie, like I knew Susie…'

'Seán,' interrupted Pat. 'Susie is Marjorie's roommate, 'show a little respect, bro.'

'Oops, sorry – blame it on the wine!'

'What does Susie do?' asked Karen.

'She's a pilot for UPS Air-Cargo, she captains a Boeing757 freighter.'

'She must be quite a lady to do that,' said Seán. 'Sorry about the singing.'

'Was that what you call it?' said Pat.

'Tomorrow morning,' said Buchanan, 'how about I do the morning stables?'

'On your own? Not on your nelly, Seán and I will help,' said Pat. 'If we start at six, we'll be done by eight, plenty of time to eat a hearty breakfast then get ready.'

'In that case,' said Karen, 'I'll get breakfast underway while you men are busy in the stables.'

'I can help with that,' said Cynthia,' and I'm sure Marjorie will want to help.'

'Well, that's got the morning sorted,' said Karen. 'Now, early to bed, the lot of you, you've got a big day ahead of you.'

'Are you sure?' said Cynthia.

'Absolutely. There's only the paper plates and a few beer glasses.'

'OK if you're sure, I certainly could do with an early night.'

'I'll give you a hand to clear up,' said Buchanan.

'That's all right, there really isn't much to do.'

'In that case I think a walk round the grounds with Major and locking up the stables for the night also might be a good idea. Get some fresh air before bed.'

♦

'How was the walk?' Karen asked, as Buchanan came in the kitchen door.'

'You know, sometimes I think horses have more sense than humans.'

'What's brought that on?'

'I walked through the stables and listened to them quietly munching on their hay, not a care in the world, not worrying about tomorrow.'

'Are you coming to bed?' asked Karen.

'Not just yet. I'm going to sit and read for a few minutes; I'll be up shortly.'

'OK.'

Buchanan picked up his copy of the *Herald* and saw that, according to a byline by Tony Miasma, the *Herald's* crime reporter, Victor Mountjoy, Julian Du Marchon, and Alan Dale had all died when the plane they were fleeing from the police in ran out of fuel over the English Channel and crashed into the sea.

Not interested in the sports section he put down the paper and picked up the book he'd brought with him – *The Real Taggarts, Glasgow's post-war crime busters*. He never tired of reading about his predecessors and how they tackled crime with what today would be considered primitive methods and equipment.

The Jockey's Wife.

In 1800 the first Master of Police, now referred to as the Chief Constable for the Glasgow police force, was John Stenhouse, with a salary of two hundred pounds a year. Buchanan thought that today that sum might just cover a working lunch for a couple of detectives in the MET. Policemen, then called Watchmen, had only a greatcoat and a four-foot chocolate-coloured stave to protect them.

He reached for his glass and saw he'd already drained it, so he got out of his chair and walked over to the sideboard. He refilled his glass from Cynthia's whisky decanter, added a drop of water and as he returned to his chair by the fire. Major sat up to check Buchanan had returned, sniffed, and growled.

Buchanan was about to pick up his book when Major, ears twitching, barked.

'What is it, boy? What are you hearing?'

Major barked again, then walked over to the outside door and stood growling at something unseen.

Buchanan followed Major to the door, reached for the ever-present flashlight, then opened the outside door to the garden.

Major didn't need any coaxing, he dashed off across the lawn into the dark towards the stables. Buchanan followed at a more cautious pace holding the flashlight out to his side. He once heard about a policeman being shot as he held his flashlight out in front of him, the gunman had used the light as a target.

By the time he arrived in the yard, Major was sniffing along the side of the stable then stopped at the small door. Buchanan walked over to see what had attracted Major's attention. He shone the flashlight on the ground and saw something lying on the ground that shouldn't be there.

'What's this, Major?' said Buchanan, holding a crumpled piece of paper for Major to sniff. 'This wasn't here when we locked up an hour ago. Now, I wonder what it says?' he said, as he unruffled the paper. 'Strange, why would a piece of paper with the address of the Appleton Equestrian Centre be lying on the ground at twelve twenty-five at night and, even more curious, what is the sister of the note I found in Belleview doing here?'

Before returning to the house, Buchanan, with Major at his side, did a search of the grounds. Finding all doors locked, and windows secure, they returned to the house. He turned off the lights and went up the stairs to bed wondering who had left the note, and what were they up to. Then the thought struck him, it was probably discarded by the person looking for riding lessons earlier in the day. So, nothing to worry about; except the fact it was on the same hotel notepaper as the note found at Belleview.

'Why didn't you mention to Cynthia about Belleview and the gilts?' asked Karen, as Buchanan undressed. 'With Victor and Julian both dead, and there being no other family, Cynthia would inherit it all, and I'm sure they could do with the money.'

'It's complicated and I didn't want to create a fuss before Cynthia's wedding. Time enough for that after I have sorted out the mess. Tell me about the person looking for lessons today?'

'Stocky build, about five foot eight tall, well-tanned and black curly hair. He spoke with a Spanish accent.'

'How soon after we left did this person show up?'

'Must have been right after Seán arrived. I heard Major barking and went out to see what caused him to get so excited. There was nothing in the garden, so I went through and there he was, standing in the yard. I don't think he liked dogs.'

'Why do you say that?'

'He had his back to the wall with his hands covering his private parts.'

'You asked him what he wanted?'

'Yes, after I called Major off, he seemed to relax and asked if there was anyone he could ask about riding lessons for his daughter.'

'Seems innocent enough. What did you do?'

'I suggested he called back later in the day.'

'What made you think he was Spanish?'

'His accent.'

11
The Wedding

'I've never done this before,' said Karen, as Buchanan exited from Turpin's box with a bucket of horse droppings. 'You actually enjoy cleaning out horse boxes?'

'Yes, I suppose it reminds me of what I do for a living.'

'Really?'

'No, just joking, I'm reliving childhood memories. We're nearly done here; I can finish off if you want to go and start breakfast.'

'That's all right, I'm sort of enjoying it. What's left to do?'

'Just the hay nets and the horses' water bowls. I can do the hay nets if you check their water bowls.'

'OK, how do I check the water bowls?'

'Make sure they're clean and the water flows when the horse puts its nose in the bowl.'

◆

'How is Pat this morning?' asked Karen, as Cynthia meandered into the kitchen.

'Depends on who's observing,' she said, pulling her dressing gown round her waist and tying it tight. 'He'd be funny on stage as a drunken comedian, but as a prospective groom, he's a bit of a mess. Is there any coffee? He needs something to help him wake up.'

'I made a pot before we started morning stables – should still be hot.'

'Great, I'll take him a cup.'

'Is Marjorie about?'

'I think I heard her in the shower earlier, she's usually an early riser.'

'Will she want breakfast?'

'Probably, but I wouldn't worry too much about it, she usually fends for herself.'

'We can't have that this morning. How about Pat, will he want something to eat? I'm not sure what jockeys eat for breakfast.'

'He usually has a bowl of porridge with some raisins stirred through. Sometimes he also has a small pot of low-fat yoghurt, and of course a large mug of black coffee. Other times he likes poached or scrambled eggs with some crispy bacon.'

'I can make either if you have enough ingredients?'

'Karen, you shouldn't be doing this, you're our guest. It's me who should be looking after you.'

'Nonsense, you should be thinking about yourself, this is your special day.'

'If, you're sure?'

'Of course, I'm sure. Now, take Pat his coffee and I'll get on with breakfast.'

'Karen, you're a treasure. You'll find the eggs in the fridge and there should be a pack of bacon in the freezer, oh, you'll also find the bread in the freezer, keeps longer that way.'

'I got it, now go and get ready. Jack says you need to be out of here by ten if you are going to get to the registry office in time.'

♦

'How are you feeling?' Buchanan asked Pat, as he walked into the kitchen with his empty cup dangling from his finger.

'The last time I felt this bad was two years ago when I fell at the last jump at Plumpton. I'll be fine though,' he said, 'I just need something to eat and another coffee.'

'Karen just made a fresh pot and breakfast is in the food oven keeping warm. Apparently, it's help yourself to breakfast this morning.'

'Good. Thanks for doing the morning stables,' he said, picking up a plate from the table.

'No problem, I'm enjoying myself, I'm reliving childhood memories.'

'Cynthia's in tears, Marjorie and Karen are with her,' he said, scooping up some scrambled eggs out of the bowl.

'Why? She hasn't changed her mind, has she?'

'No. She woke this morning saying she had a bad dream last night.'

'I suppose it's the excitement of starting a new life.'

Pat shook his head. 'You'll understand this, you being a Scot. She said the dream was a premonition of something evil about to happen.'

'What was in the dream?'

'She said in the dream, at the point in the ceremony where the vicar says, *Does anyone know of any reason why this couple should not be joined in holy matrimony?* Victor showed up looking like one of those dead pirates in the *Pirates of the Caribbean* movie. You know, face covered with barnacles and open sores and head draped with seaweed.'

'I suppose it's quite normal to have dreams like that considering the circumstances. She does realise that Victor isn't coming back, he's fish food on the bottom of the English Channel?'

'I'm sure she does, and you're probably right; it's just wedding nerves. I'm sure she will be all right when eleven o'clock comes and we can make it official. I better go and get ready,' said Pat, looking at his watch.

'Ah, yes, so should I. Can't have the father of the bride show up in his everyday clothes.'

♦

'How do I look, Jack?' asked Cynthia.

'Like a bride should.'

'Cynthia,' said Marjorie, 'you're beautiful, Pat's such a lucky man.'

'Of course, I am,' said Pat.

'Of course, you are, my dear,' said Cynthia, 'you're marrying the most beautiful bride in the county.'

The Wedding

'Excuse me,' said Buchanan, 'could I have the mutual admiration group please get in the car? It may only be a thirty-minute drive to the registry office, but there are a shed-load of guests going to be here at one o'clock to toast the health of Mr and Mrs Pat McCall and they won't' be able to do that unless we get you to the registry office, married, and back here to the stables for the blessing ceremony.'

◆

As the stable-yard clock struck one, the first of the guests began to arrive. Buchanan was glad to see Stephen and Jill had decided to car share with Harry and Poppy. That was one less car to find space for in the carpark.'

'Hello, Jack,' said Stephen. 'Ceremony at the registry office go off all right?'

'Yes. Mr and Mrs McCall are now in residence.'

'Are they going to get away for a honeymoon?'

'Yes. That's tomorrow after breakfast.'

'Looks like we're the first to arrive. Do you need help with parking?'

'Yes, and I need to go and do my father of the bride bit again. When guests arrive, make sure they don't block the entrance and see that they are able to leave in an emergency.'

'You're not expecting trouble, are you?'

'No, it's being a policeman all these years, I'm always unconsciously risk-assessing everything.'

'Fine, Harry and I will take care of the parking, you can go and get ready.'

'Is there anything we can do to help?' asked Poppy.

'I don't think so. Cynthia has hired the marquee for the event, and she also arranged for a catering team. They have taken over the kitchen for the day. Marjorie and Karen are helping Cynthia get ready, and Pat's brother, Seán. is helping him. There will be a moment where help will be needed after the ceremony when the marquee will have to be rearranged for the reception and dinner.'

'I thought they were married at the registry office this morning?'

'They were. But according to Cynthia, with the restrictions on numbers in the registry office and the number she had invited, she decided to have an afternoon blessing ceremony. That way, those who couldn't make the registry office would be able to at least see and hear them exchange their vows.'

'Have you met the vicar?'

'No, not yet. I understand he's the father of one of the students who comes here for riding lessons.'

'In that case when everyone is parked, Harry and I will join you,' said Stephen.

'Great. Karen should be in the marquee by now.'

♦

'There you are,' said Karen, as Buchanan with Poppy and Jill worked his way along the row of seats behind the wedding party.

'Sorry, I was chatting to Stephen and Harry,' said Buchanan, 'they're helping get the visitors cars parked. I don't see Marjorie?'

'I think she is helping Cynthia with her makeup.'

'Has anyone seen the vicar?' said Buchanan, looking around. 'Of all the people that could be late, he's the one who mustn't be.'

'Excuse me,' said the person seated in front of Buchanan, 'I believe he is already here; I do not think he has ever been late for an engagement.'

'Glad to hear that. Jack Buchanan, father of the bride, sort of.'

'Reverend Stanley Adebayo, senior pastor for Christ the King in Paddock Wood, the vicar you were so concerned would be late.'

'Glad to meet you, Cynthia has been so looking forward to this day and I for one would feel upset if anything went wrong.'

The Wedding

Stanley smiled and said, 'Why worry? It's the least productive emotion in existence, it never did an honest day's work in its life. The good book says to trust in the Lord with all your heart and lean not on your own understanding; in all your ways submit to him, and he will make your paths straight.'

'Thanks, I'll remember that.'

'You do that.'

As the marquee filled, Stephen and Harry joined them on the second row.

'Jack,' said Stephen, 'Marjorie says it's time for you to come and do your bit.'

'Thanks. See you all shortly.'

'How is she, Marjorie?' asked Buchanan.

'I think she is finally relaxing.'

'How about Pat?'

'Brothers, who'd have them?' laughed Marjorie. 'He and Pat are taking something for their nerves.'

'Well, I just hope they don't overdo it, Seán has the best man speech to give,' said Buchanan.

Buchanan was about to say something when the loudspeaker crackled and the DJ announced, 'Ladies and gentlemen, please be upstanding for the bride.'

As Buchanan, with Cynthia on his arm, stepped into the marquee, heads turned and watched as they walked down the aisle, Buchanan listened to the hushed voices as they passed.

'Doesn't Cynthia look radiant…'

'She looks just like a princess…'

'See, if her father can look smart, why can't you at least give it a try…'

'She should have dumped Victor years ago, look how happy she is…'

They stopped in front of Stanley, who had taken his place in before the bandstand. He waited for the guests to be seated before he began.

'Who gives this woman to be married?'

The Jockey's Wife.

'I do,' said Buchanan.

'Thank you, you may be seated,' said Stanley, as Buchanan stepped back to let Pat step beside his bride to be.

'Cynthia and Pat, you stand in the presence of God as man and wife to dedicate to Him your life together, that He may consecrate your marriage and empower you to keep the covenant and the promise you have solemnly declared.

'The Bible teaches us that marriage is a gift of God in creation and a means of His grace, a holy mystery in which man and woman become one flesh. It is God's purpose that, as husband and wife give themselves to each other in love throughout their lives, they shall be united in that love as Christ is united with his Church.

'Marriage is given, that husband and wife may comfort and help each other, living faithfully together in need and in plenty, in sorrow and in joy. It is given, that with delight and tenderness they may know each other in love, and, through the joy of their bodily union, may strengthen the union of their hearts and lives. It is given as the foundation of family life in which children may be born and nurtured in accordance with God's will, to His praise and glory. This is the meaning of the marriage you have made.

'And now, by the exchanging of rings and this public display of your love for each other and strengthened by the prayers of your friends and family, you may be enabled to fulfil your marriage vows in love and faithfulness. But, before you join your friends to share in this wonderful day, I have a gift for you,' he said, turning to the table behind him and picking up a book.

'This is a Bible. Look upon it as an instruction manual on how to love and live. It comes in handy when the whole family shows up unexpectedly for dinner, or someone suggests you go wilderness camping, and if you have children, it's the go-to-book on how to cope with their growing pains, it even gives advice on fishing. I pray that you will read it together and grow to understand its truths. Pat, in God's eyes, you may now kiss your wife for the first time.'

Pat and Cynthia turned and faced their friends, smiling and nodding as well-wishers came forward to congratulate them.

♦

'That went off well,' said Buchanan to Karen. 'Cynthia's premonition about something going wrong was just wedding nerves. Not even the ghost of Victor could have spoiled today. Cynthia can now start her new life with Pat.'

'I do hope so, she certainly deserves it.'

'Ladies and gentlemen,' said Seán, over the loudspeaker, 'if you will all assemble out on the lawn, please. The marquee needs to be reset for this evening's entertainment. It's a lovely sunny day outside, there's plenty of bubbly, and for those of you who aren't sun worshippers, there is plenty of shade. While you wait, you can watch Mr and Mrs McCall have their photographs taken. As soon as the marquee has been reset, I will call you all back in.

Buchanan followed the guests out and walked over to one of the waiters with a tray of champagne. He took a glass and moved into the shade of one of the numerous fruit trees where several of the guests were chatting.

'Room for one more?' he asked, stepping into the shade.

'Always room for the father of the bride,' said Stanley.

'Oh, I didn't mean to interrupt.'

'Not at all, come in out of the sun.'

'We'll talk to you on Sunday, Stan,' said one of the guests, as the group that had been talking to Stanley shuffled off to replenish their drinks.

'Cynthia told me how you came to meet,' said Stanley.

'Yes, that was a day to remember.'

'She said you are a policeman.'

'For my sins.'

'That's a strange statement coming from a policeman.'

'It's just a figure of speech.'

'None the less, a strange utterance.'

The Jockey's Wife.

Buchanan shrugged. 'It's what I do for a living, and what I hope to continue to do.'

'Looking for sinners?'

'You could put it that way, but isn't that what you do?'

'I only do what the Spirit leads me to do.'

'I follow pace, that tells me what I can do.'

'What is pace?'

'Just another police acronym. It stands for Police and Criminal Evidence act. I suppose it is our version of the ten commandments.'

'It is good to have guidance for what you do. How long have you been a policeman?'

Buchanan smiled. 'If you were to ask my wife she would answer, too long. This will be my thirty-fifth year.'

'You're not from this part of the world?'

'No. I was born and raised in Glasgow. My family worked in the shipyards. It was my dad who steered me away from the yards to becoming a policeman. And yourself?'

'I came to this country twenty-one years ago from Zimbabwe. Just before things in the country became unbearable.'

'Did your family manage to avoid the reign of Mugabe?'

'My immediate family did, but not so my cousins, though they didn't suffer as badly as some of the white farmers.'

'What led you to join the church?'

'It's a long story, my friend, but if you are willing to listen, I will speak.'

'I have time.'

'This all began back in 1984 when the German evangelist, Reinhardt Bonnke, came to Harare on one of his mission trips. They had just come from Cape Town where thousands heard the gospel, and many were saved. Apparently, the forces of evil had tried to stop the crusade by drumming up a terrible storm that ripped the tent to shreds. But that did not stop the preacher, no, he held the meeting in the open air, and it was just as well because the tent could not have held the seventy-five thousand that came to hear the gospel preached.'

'That was a fortunate turn of events.'

'Fortunate turn of events – my friend, can you imagine Moses saying that as he saw the Red Sea parting, or Daniel when he spent the night in the lion's den, unscathed? I think not.

The Wedding

'From Cape Town they moved on to Harare and that is where my father heard the good news and was born again. Next day my father said instead of me becoming a farmer to grow grain to feed a few, I would go to Bible College and feed many with the bread of life. So he enrolled me in Bible College in Harare. In 2001 at the age of twenty-three I left Zimbabwe and came to England to further my training.'

'Do you still have family in Zimbabwe?'

'No. My father died when our village was pillaged by robbers, so I arranged for my mother to come to England and live with us.'

'I'm sorry to hear about the death of your father. You say your mother lives with you?'

'Yes. She lives with my family in Paddock Wood.'

'You are married?'

'Yes, to Preetty. We have one daughter, Sangeya. It is she who introduced us to Cynthia. Sangeya helps out here at the stables in exchange for riding lessons.'

'Is that her talking to Poppy?'

'Yes. Is Poppy your daughter?'

'No. She's the daughter of an American pastor we met a few months ago. She is staying with us while she completes her studies. I see I am confusing you – let me explain. A few months ago, I was taking some time off work and staying at a country club for a week's relaxing and doing a bit of horse riding. That is where I was introduced to her family and Cynthia.'

'So, we do have something, or should I say, someone in common.'

'Cynthia is anything but common, unique would be more accurate a description. Anyway, when I checked in for my week's relaxing, I discovered that on the Saturday there was to be a cross-country horse race. Poppy's father was one of the competitors, as was Cynthia.'

'Did you join the race?'

'For my sins, yes, I did.'

'That's the second time you have used that expression. I could pray for you, and with the help of the Lord all your sins will be forgiven.'

'Ach, it's just a figure of speech, I'm fine.'

'Really, I won't be embarrassed, would you?'

'I've had a lot worse said to me. If it makes you feel good, go ahead.'

'Thanks, but first, tell me, are you working on a case right now?'

The Jockey's Wife.

'Yes.'

'Is it something to do with a river?'

'No, nothing to do with a river, why?'

'As we were talking, the Lord impressed on me a picture of a river. It is on a bend, there are trees on the far side and on the other side, a tall building painted red. There is something in the river, something of great danger to you. Does that mean anything to you?'

'No, nothing.'

'Well, the Lord says you have to be strong and of good courage, not to be afraid nor be dismayed, for He will be with you wherever you go.'

'Not every day one gets a fortune telling like that.'

'Jack, I'm not in the fortune-telling business, I am deadly serious. When the Lord gives a word, it is sure to come to pass.'

'Are you saying God actually speaks to you?'

'Absolutely.'

'You're really serious about this?'

Stanley nodded. 'As sure as I know the sun will rise and set tomorrow.'

'And what you just said, you heard that from God?'

'If He can talk out of a donkey's mouth, He can certainly use me.'

'But why would God be interested in me? I'm just an ordinary bloke who's long past retirement age, doing my job as best as I can.'

'That's what the disciple Peter thought. He was a professional fisherman and had spent the whole night fishing and had not caught a single fish. In the morning he met Jesus on the shore, and Jesus said to try fishing on the other side of the boat. Peter listened and fished from the other side of the boat and caught so many fish the boat almost sank.'

'What's fishing got to do with me being a policeman?'

'You fish for criminals, don't you? And I assume you wouldn't be where you are today if you weren't good at what you do?'

Buchanan nodded. 'But all this is supposing there really is a God.'

'Jack, only a fool in his heart says there is no God. Why don't you ask him? Say, God if you are really there, would you show me?'

'I gave up playing peek-a-boo many years ago.'

'Are you too busy to ask?'

The Wedding

'Maybe,' he said, shrugging. 'I have a lot on my plate just now with an ongoing investigation. I wouldn't have time.'

'Jack, so many people have the wrong idea about what prayer is.'

'So, what is it?'

'You're married, aren't you?'

'Yes.'

'You come home from work, and what do you do?'

'I close the front door behind me and say, I'm home.'

'And?'

'If my wife is in the kitchen, I go in, give her a kiss and tell her how much I love and appreciate her.'

'And what does she do?'

'She usually laughs, asks if I want a drink then tells me what's for dinner.'

'And when you have got your drink, what do you do?'

'We usually chat about what's gone on that day.'

'See, you already know how to pray. Prayer is nothing other than having a conversation with God.'

'But I wouldn't know what to say.'

'Jack, God is not interested in religious words and phrases, or even rituals, he just wants to hear from you, he loves you.'

'I don't know.'

'I tell you what I'm going to do for you. I am going to be praying that God will be real to you in some special way that you and only you will realise. I have no idea what that will be, but I really believe He will show you in a way that you will know He hears you. He may talk to you within the hour, sometime this week, or even next month, but it will be in a way that you will know it is Him.'

'Stanley, what you say sounds fine, but I'm just so busy that sometimes I can't see the wood for the trees.'

'Jack, when Hell is busting out all over, a meeting with the Lord in prayer is like stepping out of the jungle into a clearing with a place to sit and dangle your toes in a stream of cool water.'

'There are times when I could do with a piece of that.'

'Jack, my friend, let's not beat around the bush, I'm going to pray for you right now. Gracious Lord, I stand here with my friend, Jack. He is a defender of justice; he lives with danger and evil nipping at his heels every day. Would you send angels to watch over him and to protect him and his family, and when he asks you to talk to him, will you do it in such a way that he knows inside, in his heart, that you love him so much? Amen.'

Buchanan shrugged. 'I suppose I should say thanks?'

Stanley shook his head. 'You don't have to thank me, it's what *I* do.'

Further talk was prevented by the arrival of Stanley's daughter and Poppy.'

'Dad,' said Sangeya,' you'll never guess what I've found out – oh, were you praying for Mr Buchanan?'

'Yes, but we've finished. Now, tell me what you have found out?'

'Poppy is the daughter of Travis Grant, you know who I mean, I watch him on YouTube.'

'Oh, that Travis Grant, yes I do know who you mean. Hello, Poppy.'

'Hello. That was a lovely sermon you preached at Mrs McCall's wedding.'

'Thank you.

'C'mon, Poppy, let's go look at the horses.'

'Goodbye, Mr Adebayo.'

'Goodbye, Poppy.'

'Do you have children of your own, Jack?'

'My sergeant lost her parents when she was just a young girl. We never managed to have our own children, so we just sort of adopted each other. She is married to another policeman, and they are expecting their first child early next year.'

'Like arrows in the hand of a warrior are the children of one's youth. Blessed is the man who fills his quiver with them! He shall not be put to shame when he speaks with his enemies in the gate. Psalm 127, Jack.'

'I don't know how you vicars remember all those bible verses. All I remember from Sunday school was, Jesus loves me this I know.'

'A lovey verse from a simple but true children's song.'

'Yes, sometimes the simple messages are the best ones.'

'For this reason, Jesus died on the cross and rose again having paid the price of our sins that all men may be reconciled to the Father.'

'You're sounding like my friend Travis; he said the only way society is going to survive is for the church to show leadership.'

The Wedding

'If only. The church has put God in a straight-jacket, worship has become a performance, the Holy Spirit has been muzzled like you would a barking dog. We've taken a wrong turning and have lost our way.'

'Ladies and Gentlemen,' shouted Seán, from the doors to the marquee, 'the tables have been set, the food is ready, and the champagne is on ice. Please come and take your seats – when you enter you will find your table assignment on the list on the easel just inside the door.'

'Which one is our table?' Buchanan asked Karen, as they entered the marquee.

'We're with the bridal party on table one.'

As the last guest was seated, Seán, who'd moved from the marquee door, was now standing by the bandstand. He picked up the microphone and said, 'Ladies and Gentlemen, on behalf of Mr and Mrs McCall, we would like to thank you all for being here today to celebrate my big brother finally getting married and settling down. But before we eat, I would like to call upon Reverend Stanley Adebayo to say grace.'

'Great and gracious Lord, as we assemble here today to celebrate the marriage of Pat and Cynthia, we thank you for this bounteous spread before us. We can rejoice Your cup is ever full to overflowing and running over with good gifts for us. Bless us now as we celebrate by sharing food and drink in the celebration of the marriage of Pat and Cynthia. Amen.'

'You look exhausted,' said Karen to Buchanan.

'I am. I just spent twenty minutes with Stanley. Then earlier it was making sure Cynthia made it to her wedding on time.'

'Well, it's all over, nothing can go wrong now, not even Cynthia's dead husband can spoil the day.'

'Ladies and Gentlemen, if I could have your attention for a moment,' said a slightly tipsy Seán, returning to the microphone. 'So, before we have the speeches, would you please join me in showing your appreciation for the catering staff who have worked so hard to create this wonderful meal.

'Thanks. Now the moment you have all been waiting for, yes, that is correct, it's time for the speeches. So, without further delay, please put your hands together for the father of the bride. For those of you

The Jockey's Wife.

who don't know, Cynthia's father passed away several years ago, so doing an admirable job of standing in is a family friend, Jack Buchanan.'

'Thank you, Seán, for that sterling introduction. Even though I have only known Cynthia a few short months, it feels like a lifetime. We met at Castlewood Country Club, I was there to relax, and she to compete in the Castlewood Cup, a cross country event for non-professional riders. To say she is a whirlwind of excitement is to ignore her wonderful personality and tenacity to get things done even when the odds seem to be stacked against her. It is my hope and prayer that she and Pat will have many happy years growing old together.'

'Thank you, Jack. We have now come to the speech I know a lot of you have been waiting for. I hope your glasses are all full because you know how the Irish love a tale or two. Please welcome my big brother, friend, and Cynthia's husband, Pat.'

'First, I'd like to thank Marjorie for looking after Cynthia and assisting her in getting ready for the big day.

'When I came to work here at Appleton, I was drifting, like a boat on the sea without a rudder. I knew where I wanted to be, but not how I was to get there. Then came the opportunity to work and ride out at Appleton. I – I do not want to speak ill of the dead, but Victor Mountjoy was not a nice man, to me, the horses or to Cynthia. I suppose it was fate that drew Cynthia and I together, that and our love for all things horses. Cynthia at first saw something in me and how I respected horses and they me. I will admit it was more than just the love of horses that drew us together. She said she liked my accent, and me, I loved the twinkle in her eyes and the mischief in her voice. I am so glad that she said yes when I asked her to marry me.'

'Thank you, Pat. I think you have surprised us all there, in all the years I have known you, I don't think you have ever come to the point so quickly! Now, this is the part of the evening I have been looking forward to; I now, for the first time in many years, have my chance to have the last word on my brother, Pat.

'Firstly, I would like to thank Pat for his kind words about the bridesmaid, Marjorie. I must agree that she looks absolutely wonderful, and she did such an excellent job today in assisting Cynthia get ready and to the marquee on time. From what I hear Cynthia put up quite a fight!

'As many of you may know if you have ever had the honour of being the best man, there are many books and websites not to mention people willing to offer advice. Most agree that the best man's main duty is to get the groom to the church on time.

'But they are all wrong, the most important duty is to make sure you bring the rings. There was no way I was going to fail, so I came prepared for every eventuality,' he said, opening his jacket to reveal several rings sewn onto felt and pinned into his jacket.

'When I was putting pen to paper to come up with a few words about Pat, I wrote a list of stories which I would like to tell. I then went through and crossed out any that may get him in trouble with the police, but, most importantly, any stories that may get him in trouble with Cynthia. They all had to go. That doesn't leave a lot to work with. But if anybody would like to buy me a pint of Guinness at the bar later, I may be persuaded to tell a few of them.

'Pat has always been willing to try things himself before reading the instructions, paying a professional, or just buying the correct item. One memory that always sticks in my mind, was about the ancient pony we used to ride. Up to that point we would just use an old rope halter. But that wasn't good enough for Pat, he decided he would repair an old bridle that he picked up at the market. It didn't take long for us to go back to using the old rope halter.

'On a serious note, I am so happy for Pat and Cynthia. I have seen how suited they are for one another over the few short years they have been together.

'Recently I heard something which I think Pat will find to be very true; marriage is a partnership between a man, and a woman who is always right. As with many occasions, no matter how much you want your close family and friends around, not everybody can make it for different reasons. I have taken a selection of cards and messages from several people here, which I would like to read:

'Oh, this one is for Cynthia from her mother, and for your information she is currently recovering from a hip operation. *Hello Cynthia, sorry I am unable to be there for your big day, I'm busy checking to see if any of the donkeys on the beach are missing. Have a great day and see you soon.*

The Jockey's Wife.

'Before I finish up, I would just like to remind you that Pat will be riding Rambler and Turpin next week at Cheltenham. Now it gives me great pleasure to say, Ladies and Gentlemen, please be upstanding to toast the bride and groom – Mr and Mrs Pat McCall.'

Buchanan was about to invite Karen up for a dance when Major, who all evening had been curled up under the top table, sat up and started to growl.

'What is it, Major? What have you heard?' said Buchanan.

With a loud bark, Major dashed between the tables and out the open door. Buchanan followed and as he reached the door a scream from the back of the house almost drowned out the sound of the band.

'What is it?' asked Karen, as Buchanan stood to follow Major.

'I'm not sure, maybe it's your Spaniard come back to book riding lessons. Wait here while I go and have a look.'

'No way, I'm not letting you out of my sight, I know you too well.'

'What can go wrong? Major heard something, probably just a roaming fox.'

'I'm still coming with you.'

'OK, but if I tell you to go back inside, I want you to promise me you will.'

'I will.'

Buchanan and Karen made their way around the dance floor and out the door. They made a circuit of the marquee, saw nothing, then made their way through the opening in the hedge. The PIR for the yard floodlights had operated and the yard was bathed in bright light.

'What's happening over there?' said Karen, pointing at Major who was standing beside one of the catering crew.

'Let's go and see.'

Karen walked a step behind Buchanan as they crunched their way across the stable yard. On the ground, face down, was a body, blood slowly seeping from a gash on the neck. Buchanan instinctively looked at the time on his phone, seven fifty-seven.

'Is it Victor?' asked Cynthia, who'd followed Buchanan and Karen out the door.

'No, definitely not Victor,' said Buchanan, kneeling to feel for a pulse. He didn't have to, the bloody gash halfway across the left side of the neck told him all he needed to know.

'Neck slashed from behind?' said Stephen, who'd followed, wondering what was going on.

'That's what it looks like,' said Buchanan, 'I wonder what happened to the knife?'

'I'll have a look,' said Stephen.

'That's the chap who was here earlier looking for lessons,' said Karen.

'Are you sure?'

'Absolutely.'

'Should I call the police? Oh, you are already here,' said Pat.

'No, go ahead and call,' said Buchanan, 'this is Kent police jurisdiction'.

'Should we cover the body? He looks so cold lying there on the ground,' said Cynthia.

'No, best leave the body for the local police. I think it better if you'd all return to the marquee and wait for the police. Stephen, would you organise that? I'll stay here with Major and wait for the police to arrive, just to make sure no one disturbs the body.'

'Police are on their way,' said Pat, who'd just returned from the house.

'I told you something awful was going to happen,' said Cynthia.

Yes, you did, thought Buchanan.

◆

Buchanan was impressed by the police response: a local squad car and ambulance arrived within fifteen minutes of Pat calling.

'Did you make the report?' asked the constable, who'd just arrived.

'Not me, it was the groom.'

'What do you mean, the groom?'

'There's a wedding reception going on in the marquee.'

'So, that's why there are so many cars at the front of the house. Where's the body?'

'Over there by the stable doors,' said Buchanan, pointing to a dark outline on the gravel.

Buchanan watched as the police constable, with the ambulance crew, walked quickly over to the body to do whatever they could. Buchanan knew that would be to wait for the coroner to declare the body as deceased.

As he observed the spectacle unfolding in front of him, three other police cars arrived, plus one unmarked car.

'That will be the boss, in the unmarked car,' said Buchanan, looking down at Major. 'He'll soon sort this out.'

The three marked police cars parked where they stopped, with the unmarked car behind them. The uniformed officers waited for the occupant of the unmarked car to get out. They stood talking for a minute, then two officers walked around the corner of the barn, presumably to prevent anyone entering or leaving the scene, while the others walked over to the body. The plain clothes policeman saw Buchanan standing by the opening in the hedge and came over.

'Good evening, sir. Detective Inspector Blakey. Did you call in the report?'

'No, that would have been the homeowner.'

'Could I have your name, please?'

'Yes, Jack Buchanan.'

'And what is your relationship with the homeowner?'

'I gave his wife away.'

'You what?'

'I was father of the bride. We're having a wedding reception here this evening.'

'Oh. So, who's the unfortunate guest?'

'I have no idea.'

'Where is the reception being held?'

'In the marquee on the other side of the hedge.'

'Fine, would you please return to the reception and ask everyone to stay where they are?'

'C'mon Major, we have work to do.'

'You,' said Blakey, to one of the uniformed officers, 'go with Mr Buchanan.'

Buchanan walked back to the marquee and returned to his table. The atmosphere, which earlier had been one of gaiety, singing and laughter had descended into hushed whispers. The band, out of respect for the recently departed, were sitting at their table talking to each other.

'What's happening?' asked Cynthia.

'The officer in charge will be arranging for the police surgeon to attend. Then when he, or she, have determined the body as deceased, a search of the area will take place. At a point decided by the SIO, the body will be removed from the scene. I expect shortly we will all have to give an account of our movements this evening.'

As Buchanan was giving his understanding of the steps the Kent Inspector would be taking, he appeared at the door of the marquee and walked slowly over to the head table.

'God evening, may I have your attention? I am Detective Inspector Blakey, Kent Police. Would everyone stay seated at their tables as my men come round and take statements? As soon as we are done, you will all be allowed to leave.'

'It might be helpful if the guests were asked if they saw anyone they didn't recognise at the reception?' said Buchanan. 'You know, maybe they popped outside for a cigarette and saw someone lurking in the bushes?'

'We know what questions to ask, sir,' said Blakey.

'Er, can we help?' said Street.

'No thank you, this is police business.'

Street went to say something, but Buchanan discreetly put his finger to his lips, and shook his head.

'What is it? Why didn't you want me to say something to that policeman?' whispered Street.

'For a start, we're in Kent and Kent is out of our jurisdiction. Besides, I'd like to see how they go about their investigation before I let them know who we are.'

It took the police the best part of two hours to go round the room, letting each table leave as they completed their statements. Finally, it was only the top table, the band and the caterers that were left.

As the caterers began the task of clearing the tables and the band packing away their instruments, the Inspector, carrying a large clear evidence envelope, came over to the head table.

'Sorry to keep you waiting. Since it is your residence, I thought it better to question your guests first so they could get on their way home. Could I have your names, please, starting with yours, sir?'

'Pat McCall.'

'And your reason for being here this evening?'

'I live here.'

'Madam, could I have your name and reason for being here this evening?'

'Cynthia McCall. I also live here, and it is my wedding to Pat that you are interrupting.'

'I'm sorry, but I do need to know who and why everyone is here this evening.'

'I'm Seán McCall, best man. I live in Derry, 57 Heron Way.'

'Marjorie Hollingsworth, bridesmaid. I am temporarily living here while my friend goes off on her honeymoon.'

'Reverend Stanley Adebayo. I married Pat and Cynthia today. I live in Paddock Wood, 43 Station Road, Kent.'

'Preetty Adebayo, same address as my husband and my daughter, Sangeya.'

'Stephen Hunter, you can contact me at 44 Windmill Lane, Polegate, East Sussex.'

'Jill Hunter, same address as Stephen.'

'Jack Buchanan, Finnart, Rattle Road, Westham, East Sussex.'

'Karen Buchanan, same address as my husband.'

'Do any of you know the name of the deceased?'

All heads shook no.

'He was here earlier in the day,' said Karen.

'Did you talk to him?'

'Yes. He said he was looking for riding lessons for his daughter.'

'Did he give his name?'

'No. He said he would call back later.'

'Have any of you anything to add?'

'I found this piece of paper on the ground earlier,' said Buchanan, passing Blakey the paper with the address of the stables written on it.

'Just a scrap of paper, I doubt if it means anything,' Blakely said, placing it on the table.

'If I might ask a question?' said Buchanan.

'Certainly, what do you wish to know?'

'Was he carrying any identification?'

'As a matter of fact, he was.'

'Could I have a look at it?'

'I don't think I can do that. It's evidence in a possible murder case.'

'Suppose I gave you his initials?'

'How would you know that unless you already went through his pockets? If you did, that would be interfering with a police investigation.'

'I didn't go through his pockets; I left that job for you.'

'All right, what do you think his initials are?'

'JCB – am I correct?'

Blakley placed an evidence envelope on the table. Inside was a wallet, a blue biro pen, a black covered notebook, and a mobile phone. He opened the top of the bag and removed the wallet, inside was the deceased's driving licence, a Columbian driving licence. The name on the licence was Juan Carlos Barrera.

'DI Blakely, I am not just Jack Buchanan.'

'No? So what else are you?'

'I am Detective Chief Inspector Buchanan, Sussex CID, and this is my son-in-law PC Hunter and my daughter DS Hunter. This death is part of an ongoing investigation that DS and PC Hunter and I are working on. Would you like me to go through the channels?'

'You talk to one policeman, and you get another two in a row, how odd,' said Blakely. 'No, it's all yours, providing I see some proof you are who you say you are.'

'I like you, Blakely. My warrant card is in my room. If it's all right with you, I'll go and get it.'

'I'm not going anywhere.'

Buchanan was back in under ten minutes with his card.

'Fine, the case is all yours, but I suppose you would like some help calling out the cavalry?'

'I'm assuming by cavalry you are referring to the CSI's?'

'Yes, and I'm sure with you being a DCI, you will know the ropes far better than I.'

'I have investigated a few killings over the years.'

'I'll call control,' he said, reaching for his phone. 'Control, Blakely responding to the stabbing at Appleton Equestrian Centre. We have one male, deceased, could we have the CSI team, please? Also, I am handing the investigation over to DCI Buchanan, Sussex CID.'

Blakely hung up from the call and said to Buchanan, 'Will there be anything else we can help you with, sir?'

'Have all the guests' statements been taken?'

'Yes.'

'How many men do you have here?'

'Just the three.'

'Would you have one of your men stay with the body till the coroner arrives?'

'Already done.'

'Inspector, what is your first name?'

'Harold, sir.'

'Harold, as soon as I get the yard floodlights manually turned on, would you have your men do a sweep of the area? You never know what the killer may have left behind. Leave the immediate area for the CSI's.'

'I'll take care of the lights,' said Pat.

'I'll come with you,' said Street.

'Can I be of any help?' asked Stanley.

'No thanks, Stanley, we have everything in hand. Sorry to have kept you waiting, you and your family are free to go.'

'Thank you, and Jack, anytime you wish to talk, I'm available.'

'I'll see you to your car,' said Seán.'

'What about us?' asked Marjorie. 'This place has lost its charm and in case you haven't noticed, it is getting cold.'

'There's nothing in here for us,' said Buchanan, 'let's adjourn to the house, but please stay away from the area where the police are searching. I'll join you in a minute, just need to let the caterers know what is happening.'

Buchanan, with Major by his side, walked over the caterers and band who were standing in a group by the door. 'Sorry to have messed up your evening. If you are all packed, you are free to leave.'

'Thanks.'

Buchanan turned off the power to the marquee, shut the marquee door and made his way back to the house. As he crossed the yard, he saw the coroner had just arrived. He decided to let them get started, there would be time to talk to them when they had done their preliminary investigation.

'Harry, Poppy, what do you want to do?'

'I have early morning stables at Castlewood,' said Harry.

'I can let myself in,' said Poppy.

'Fine, we'll see you tomorrow, Poppy.'

'Do you need us for anything?' asked Street.

'No, you and Stephen can go home, I'll catch up with you on Monday.'

'I'm off to bed,' said Marjorie, 'I have morning stables.'

'Goodnight, Marjorie,' said Cynthia, 'thanks for all you did today.'

'It was my pleasure, goodnight, all.'

'I'm going to have a word with the coroner,' said Buchanan, 'I shouldn't be long.'

As he crossed the yard, Buchanan could see the three policemen, Blakey and two white-suited individuals standing beside the coroner, who was zipping the body up in a body bag.

'DCI Buchanan. Can you tell me anything about the deceased?'

'Inspector. I am Dr Achmed, standing in for the local pathologist. I have had a cursory look at the body, and I'd have to say the cause of death was due to the deceased bleeding out from a knife wound to the neck. I have seen quite a few knife wounds in my time, but never a throat slashed like that. It must have been someone he knew because to have caused that sort of wound he would have had to be facing the attacker without any indication of what was going to happen. If you were to ask my opinion on how it happened, I'd say he got in some sort of argument with someone, they pulled a knife and slashed him across the throat. There's no way he could have survived a wound like that.'

'Do you have a time of death?'

'About eight pm, give or take ten minutes.'

'That matches. Major barked at about seven fifty-five, I got here at seven fifty-seven and the deceased was on the ground.'

'What sort of knife?'

'I'd say you are looking for a firm-bladed, sharp-edged knife about eighteen-centimetre blade length. The pathologist will be able to tell you more when the body gets to the lab.'

'Good. Could I ask you to liaise with Dr Mansell in Eastbourne? He's our local pathologist?'

'Will do.'

'Is there anything else, sir?' asked Blakey.

'Anything found in the search?'

'We didn't find anything.'

'What about the CSI search? Did you two find anything?'

The taller of the two white-suited individuals said, 'About a metre from where the body was found, there are signs of someone standing by the door. They were patient as the gravel was only slightly disturbed. I think they were waiting for the deceased and were trying not to be seen as that area is in a blind spot for the PIR.'

'That is interesting, though it could have been pure chance. But thanks anyway, that has been especially useful. What about blood spatters?'

'Difficult to see much. He was facing out into the yard; any blood splatters will be mixed in with the gravel. Most of the spilt blood went down his front.'

'Thank you.'

'Do you need us for anything else?' asked Blakey.

'No, I think you've done all that can be done. Could you make sure I get all the guest statements as soon as they have been typed up? Oh, any sign of a mobile phone?'

'In the inside pocket of his jacket.'

'Thanks.'

'My pleasure. It's been good working with you, sir.'

'Same here, Harold, and It's Jack.'

'OK, Jack. Shall I leaver a car here? just in case the killer returns.'

Buchanan nodded, 'An excellent idea.'

'Oh, I've had the crime scene tented, you never know what daylight will show.'

'Good.'

'Well, if your happy with the situation, I'll say Goodnight.'

'Goodnight.'

Buchanan watched as the body was loaded into the ambulance and departed with the police cars, leaving an almost empty carpark.

As he walked back to the house, an idea that had been stuck in the back of his mind was slowly forming into a possible scenario. But without any facts, his idea was just that, an idea. There was no arm rising from a pond holding a sword.

'You look like you could do with some fresh air,' said Karen, as he came into the kitchen.

'In a minute. Where are Pat, Cynthia and Seán?'

'Pat and Cynthia are in the sitting room; Seán has gone to bed. He has an early start in the morning.'

'Where's Seán sleeping tonight? I haven't seen any other bedrooms.'

'There's a small box room with a single bed at the far end of the landing.'

'Ah.'

'Shall we go for that fresh air you were offering?'

'Yes, please.'

'What a strange evening,' said Karen, as they walked across the lawn towards the kitchen. 'Do you remember the evening of our wedding?'

'How can I forget?

'Pity my dad wasn't there to give me away.'

'I suppose that's something Cynthia and you have in common.'

'I suppose it is. But it's not the only thing.'

'What else do you have in common?'

'You were at both our weddings.'

'So I was, how smart of you to notice.'

'Do you think she'll be lucky this time?'

'I think so. Did you see the way Pat was staring into her eyes as they danced?'

'Yes, I did, very romantic.'

'What's very romantic?' asked Cynthia, as she stepped out of the kitchen.

'Your marriage to Pat,' said Karen. 'The two of you looked so perfect on the dance floor.'

'Thanks. Can I borrow Jack for a few minutes? I need to lock up the stables for the night and I'm none too steady on my feet.'

'Certainly.'

'C'mon Jack, we can't stand here all night talking, my husband is waiting for me,' said Cynthia, linking her arm in his. 'How was today for you, not embarrassed about giving me away?'

'No, why should I be?'

'Well, the way I acted when we first met, you do realise I was just flirting?'

'Yes, I did realise.'

'Victor was a real shit, he was always cheating on me, especially when he went overseas.'

'You stayed home?'

'I didn't have a choice. Every time I mentioned going with him, he'd just say that it wasn't possible due to operational circumstances.'

'Did Victor have any family?'

'Not that he ever mentioned.'

'Must have been difficult for you, especially since your mother didn't approve of the relationship.'

'Even though I had the horses, I was quite lonely at times.'

'So, you looked for relationships elsewhere?'

'Yes,' said Cynthia, as she closed and locked the main barn doors. 'When Pat showed up, I realised two could play the game. From then on, I looked forward to Victor going overseas. It wasn't all bad with him. Due to his ambitions of climbing the greasy pole, with every promotion came an increase in income, though there were times he seemed to have quite a lot of free cash. That's what paid for Turpin and Rambler and our previous farm.'

'Did you ever question the money?'

'No, I was naive and just assumed it was what officers were paid.'

'If you don't mind me asking, if your relationship was so rocky why did you get married in the first place?'

'I was two months pregnant.'

'I see.'

'When his CO heard what he'd done he gave Victor no option but to either marry me or see his Army career come to an ignominious end. Victor got compassionate leave so we could get married, I was almost three months pregnant by then.'

'What did you think about that?'

''What could I think? I was pregnant, no prospects for work, I was penniless, and homeless.'

'Homeless. What about your parents?'

'They were strict Catholics, they disowned me, said they would never forgive me for bringing the family name into disrepute. They did say if I gave the child up for adoption and left Victor, things might be all right.'

'What about after you got married, did they forgive you then?'

'Unfortunately, my dad had a weak heart and died before Victor and I got married. My mother blamed me for putting him under so much stress his heart just gave up.'

'Pity she wasn't able to be here today.'

'She would have hated it, she's still a staunch Catholic. Stanley's preaching would have her turning blue. She lives in a retirement home, just had her hip replaced, but isn't well enough yet to travel.'

'What happened to your child?'

'I had a miscarriage a week after we were married.'

'How did Victor take that news?'

'He shrugged and said that was life.'

'That was a callous thing to say.'

'That was Victor. He tried to behave himself when he was home, till one day…'

'What do you mean?'

'There was an incident where he wasn't careful and got a young lady pregnant. She was a barmaid in the NAFFI where he was stationed.'

'What happened to her and the baby?'

'I think he arranged for her to have an abortion.'

'Cynthia, there's something that still bothers me.'

'Poor you, now Victor has gone out of my life, nothing bothers me. What is it?'

'Do you think Victor was planning on running away from the Army? Going absent without leave, I think it's termed?'

She shook her head. 'You remember the night Victor disappeared, Andrew asked you if Victor was arrested, whether he would get the defence he deserved?'

'Yes, I do.'

'Well, on Monday before the race, Andrew called me to say that Victor was about to be charged with falsifying expenses claims. The previous week, someone had provided him with evidence that was incriminating.'

'What was the evidence for such a charge?'

'Over a period of several years, Victor had been claiming for off-base accommodation in London while attending court. A friend of his who runs a small hotel had been providing him with falsified receipts in exchange for a cash backhander. As well as accommodation, Victor claimed for food and a car allowance. It might seem a trivial offence, but when it comes to misappropriation of funds, the Army takes a very dim view.'

'So where was he staying?'

'When he was supposed to be staying in London, he was here at Appleton.'

'Was there much money involved in the scheme to defraud?'

'Andrew said it was in the tens of thousands.'

'Did he confront Victor with the charges?'

'Yes, just before dinner on the Saturday evening that he and Julian took off.'

The Jockey's Wife.

'What did he say to Victor to make him do that?'

'He explained to Victor that he had been provided with incontrovertible evidence of his criminal activities. Andrew told me he was preparing to bring charges against Victor, and if he was found guilty, he would get a jail term, a dishonourable discharge with a reduction of rank and loss of pension.'

'No wonder he decided to try and disappear.'

'C'mon, my new and improved husband is waiting for me.'

12

Headcorn

'Good morning,' said Karen, as Marjorie, her long blonde hair up in a bun, sauntered into the kitchen.

'Is there any coffee?'

'There's fresh coffee in the pot.'

'Thanks, after last night, I definitely need coffee this morning. Are the lovebirds up yet?'

'No. I thought it best to let them sleep on.

'Did Seán get away on time?'

'Yes, the taxi picked him up half an hour ago.'

'Where's Jack?'

'He's gone out to look after the horses.'

'Good, I'll go give him a hand, oh, do you think he'd like a coffee?'

'He took one with him.'

'OK, see you later.'

'Fine, I'll get on with breakfast, full English for you?'

'Yes, please.'

'How would you like your eggs?'

'"Could I have soft yolks, please?'

♦

'Good morning, Jack,' said Marjorie, 'ready to go to work?'

'I already started,' replied Buchanan, setting down a wheelbarrow full of horse manure and staring at the steaming pile.

'What is it?'

'I've just realised, if this lot was a year old, I could use it on my allotment.'

'I bet Karen would just love for you to fill the car with bags of steaming horse manure.'

'I'm sure she'd forgive me if I did. I've done the boarders' bedding, just leaves Cynthia's horses.'

'Fine. I'll start the feeding.'

Returning from the midden with an empty wheelbarrow, Buchanan asked, 'What do you do for a living, Marjorie?'

'I'm a steel erector.'

'You build skyscrapers?'

'Yep, worked on The Shard, currently working on the St Giles Circus Project above Tottenham Court station.'

'How is it, you a woman working in a man's world?'

Marjorie put down her pail and stood up straight. 'I didn't take you for being a misogynist.'

'Oops, sorry. I asked the question wrongly. What I should have asked is, do you find men on the building sites accept you as an equal?'

She nodded and smiled. 'They have to, I have a black CSCS card.'

'What's that when it's at home?'

'CSCS stands for construction skills certification scheme, and they are rated by colour, black being the highest level of skill and competence. The black card is for managers and technical occupations. This advanced level card requires both: technical skill and experience as a manager within the construction industry.'

'I'm suitably impressed.'

'Thanks.'

'Are you married?'

'That depends on what you mean by married. I have a roommate, Susie. We met at a memorial service for our husbands, they died while on patrol in Afghanistan when their Land Rover ran over an IED. We've shared the house for the last seven years.'

'Sorry, I'm doing it again. It's a habit of being a policeman for thirty-five years, sometimes an annoying one Karen tells me.'

'I know what you mean. I have the habit of eyeing-up construction projects as I pass through London. Ninety-nine percent of them have no visible issues, it's just a few of the smaller ones where I see things I would do differently.'

'I understand. When I occasionally watch police shows on television, I cringe at the way they portray police work and how the characters relate to each other. If I treated my team like some TV detectives, they'd have me up in front of the boss before you could say Jack Warner. I'm done shovelling manure, are you done with the feeding?'

'Yes, shall we go in? Despite that magnificent meal last night, I've been thinking of nothing, but the breakfast Karen is making for us.'

'Ah, there you two are,' said Karen. 'Cynthia has been telling me all about their plans for the stables.'

'That's nice, but Cynthia, you should be getting ready, your taxi will be here at ten-twenty,' said Marjorie.

'Thanks, but please don't you worry about us, we're all packed.'

'Good, shall I bring the cases down?'

'No, Pat is doing that.'

'I've set the kitchen table and placed the food, buffet style on the sideboard,' said Karen. 'I thought since time was so short it was the best way to feed you all.'

'Jack, said Cynthia, 'what's going to happen about the dead man? Shouldn't we stay in case the police want to ask us more questions?'

'No, you and Pat go on your honeymoon. I have your mobile number if we need to get in touch, and Marjorie will be here if the local police need to come back to look at anything.'

'Great, said Pat, who'd just come into the kitchen. 'I've left the cases at the front door. Is there any breakfast left for me?'

♦

'It's a pity they couldn't get more time for the honeymoon,' said Karen, as they waved the newlyweds off in the taxi.

"I don't think they could stay away any longer than five days,' said Marjorie. 'Cheltenham is only a couple of weeks away and they need to be prepared for it.'

'Are you sure you will be OK staying here on your own, Marjorie?' asked Buchanan.

'Yes, we'll be fine won't we, Major?' she replied, scratching Major behind the ear.

'Well, if anything happens, you make sure you let us know,' said Karen.

◆

'Karen, do you mind if we take a detour on the way home?' said Buchanan, as they drove out of the stables.

'No, not at all. If it means a nice lunch somewhere in the country I don't mind in the least. Where are you taking me?'

'Headcorn. It's not quite on the way home, but while there I'd like interview the ground staff that handled Du Marchon's arrival and departure if they are there today.'

'And here's me thinking my lovely husband fancies a romantic afternoon in the Kent countryside. Just joking – let's go. Is it far?'

'No, it's only about ten miles, and as for lunch, I've already found an establishment that I think will fit the bill.'

◆

Buchanan turned into Headcorn aerodrome and stopped in the carpark beside a green Range Rover.

'We've never been here before,' said Karen, as they crossed the apron to the hangar.

'My first time as well.'

Out on the grass there was a small high-wing plane being fuelled and a twin-engine plane waiting with one of its engines idling.

'I wonder if that would ever go down well for the motorist?' said Buchanan.

'What would?'

'Imagine having a fuel tanker show up at your house to fill up your car!'

'It might appeal to some, especially those who have the big engine Chelsea Tractors.'

They stood well back and watched while the second plane took on fuel then taxied away towards the end of the grass runway.

'Excuse me, said Buchanan, looking at the name tags on the overalls of the refuelling crew. 'Inspector Buchanan, Sussex CID. I wonder if either of you remember an order to refuel a Cessna 320 a few months back?'

'Is that the one that crashed?' said the one named Chris. 'Yes.'

'About time someone came to investigate. Where have you been all this time?'

'Sorry, we've been busy, just now catching up. Can you remind me what happened?'

'Don't you have records? I reported the theft.'

'I'm not from Kent police, I'm from Sussex,' said Buchanan, taking out his warrant card and showing it to Chris.

'Oh, didn't realise the crime warranted a Detective Chief Inspector.'

'I got the short straw, everyone else is working on something important. Can you go over the events of the evening for me?'

'Well, it was about 20.30 and Becca and I were getting ready to close up for the night. I went into the staff room to get my jacket and found it was gone, along with my wallet. Apparently, whoever stole it also helped themselves to Becca's bottle of whisky.'

'How much money was in your wallet?' asked Buchanan, wondering what the loss of Chris's wallet had to do with the disappearance of Du Marchon and Mountjoy – unless Mountjoy had stolen the wallet meaning to pay for the fuel.

'That was the bad part. I'd just collected cash from our charity raffle and was going to bank the cash on Monday. Really pissed me off, ended up taking the money out of savings to cover it.'

'The bottle of whisky was my winnings,' said Becca.

'What was the brand of whisky?'

'Talisker ten-year single malt.'

Buchanan nodded. 'I can understand your anger.'

'Of course, you would, you're a Scot.'

'How much cash?' Buchanan asked.

'All in, three hundred and seventy pounds.'

'Can I have a description of the jacket?'

'Yes, a dark green bomber jacket with a fur-trimmed hood. On the back was a large image of a Spitfire plane.'

'Thanks, Chris, I'll see what I can do to get your money back for you.'

'Hmm, fat chance of that.'

'But that's not why I'm here.'

'So, why are you here?'

'I would like to know what actually happened that evening, it would have been about seven pm?'

'And you want to know about the incident with the Cessna 320?'

'Yes.'

'We were about to start fuelling but there was an issue about the card one of the passengers wanted to use.'

'What sort of trouble?'

'The bank declined the use of the card.'

'What did the passenger do at that point?'

'He swore profusely, took out his phone and called someone,' said Chris.

'Were you able to hear what was said?'

'No, but after he hung up, he said there had been a mix-up at the bank and it should be sorted within the hour.'

Buchanan smiled as he remembered Cynthia's comments about Victor's credit cards at the club when she hung up from talking to him.

'What happened next?'

'Chaos. We were getting ready to fuel a Piper Cherokee when two police cars, with their lights blazing, arrived,' said Becca.

'I mean, what did the passenger do? Did he get back in the plane?'

'He jumped up on the wing, opened the door, swore profusely, said something to the pilot and threw his wallet in the cabin.'

'What did the pilot of the 320 do?'

'Started up the port side engine and started taxiing towards the end of the runway,' said Chris. 'I tell you, operating a plane on the ground at that speed, he'll never fly here again.'

'What do you mean?'

'Total disregard for others. There is a speed limit when taxiing.'

'What did he do next?'

'I momentarily lost sight of the plane as it taxied behind the skydiving Cessna…'

'Which plane?'

'The red and white Cessna Caravan,' Chris said, pointing, 'and when I looked again, he was halfway into the cabin.'

'How fast was the plane moving by then would you say?'

'Best part of forty miles an hour.'

'Did you see the passenger get all the way back in the cabin?'

'He must have done, when I next looked there was no sign of him and the cabin door was closed.'

'Thanks.'

♦

'Did you find the answer to what you were looking for?' asked Karen, as they drove out of the aerodrome.

'Yes and no.'

'OK, let's start with the yes's, what are they?'

'I now have eye-witness evidence that Victor Mountjoy reboarded Du Marchon's plane.'

'Is that it for the yes's?'

'Yes.'

'What about the no's?'

'Something odd happened shortly after the plane took off. Someone broke into the staff room and stole three hundred and seventy pounds, a bottle of whisky and a green bomber jacket.'

'Why would that be odd?'

'I just don't know, and that is what bothers me.'

'Are we going straight home?'

'Not quite. I've found a lovely place where we can have lunch, it's on the way. It is called The Poacher and Partridge and according to the menu serves everything from poached eggs to sardines.'

'Sounds intriguing, drive on.'

13

Autopsey

'Do you think you will be late home today?' Karen asked Buchanan, as he buttered his toast.

'That depends on whether Andrew has had time to examine the body we found at Cynthia's on Saturday evening.'

'That was quite something. I expected an interesting weekend, but never in a thousand years would I ever imagine I'd be at a murder scene. I still don't know how you do it. If it isn't a shooting, it's a stabbing or something worse, and Saturday evening, you say he had his throat cut?'

'Yes.'

'And the death has a connection with the chap who died in the plane crash?'

Buchanan nodded, as he took a sip of his tea. 'Julian Du Marchon. We found a note at his house that the unfortunate man left for him.'

'Do you think it could it be something to do with drugs? You said the dead man had a Columbian driving licence in his wallet?'

'That's a working hypothesis. But we won't know till we get more information on who he was. I've tasked Jill to dig into his identity to see if he has any kind of criminal record.'

'Would the hotel be able to tell you anything? You said you found a piece of hotel notepaper with Cynthia's address on it.'

'Yes, I did. The piece of paper found at Cynthia's was torn from the same notepad that the note found at the house in Litlington was written on.'

'What did it say?'

'It was some sort of cryptic message about why he was there.'

'Is that what you two will be working on today?'

'Yes, but it won't get done if I sit here and chat with you, my dear. I'm already an hour late for work.'

♦

'Good morning, Jack. How are you feeling this fine day?' asked Street, as Buchanan walked into the office.

'Couldn't feel better.'

'I had such a wonderful weekend,' said Street, 'they were fun people to be around. I must write and thank Cynthia for inviting us.'

'I'm sure she would appreciate that.'

'I like Pat's brother; did you hear his jokes?'

'Yes, and I don't think I will be repeating any of them in public.'

'How was breakfast on Sunday? Did they get away on time?'

'Breakfast was a bit chaotic, but Mr and Mrs McCall got away on time and in style.'

'That statement deserves an explanation.'

'Which part, the breakfast or them getting away?'

'Let us start with the breakfast, then you can tell me about what mischief you got up to with their car.'

'While Karen made breakfast, Marjorie and I did the morning stables. Karen set the breakfast out on the sideboard, buffet style. It was a bit rushed as Pat and Cynthia had slept in. What makes you think I would do something to their car?'

'So, you did do something to the car. Sorry, your face gave you away.'

'Sorry to disappoint you, but they took a taxi to the station.'

'Oh. Pity they can only manage a few days.'

'I think the upcoming Cheltenham races the week after next has put the possibility of a long honeymoon on hold for the present.'

'Do you know where they went?'

'Yes, they have gone to Scarborough to see Cynthia's mum; she lives in a retirement home close to the seafront.'

'That's nice of them to do that, especially since they could have flown off somewhere exotic. Sad her mum wasn't able to come to the wedding.'

'Cynthia told me that after the mess being married to Victor had been, she has taken Pat there to show him off and him being Irish and a Catholic, she hopes he will be more acceptable as a husband.'

'That's nice, hope they have a lovely time.'

'I'm sure they will. Would you call this hotel?' he said, handing her two clear evidence envelopes, one containing the scrap of paper found at Belleview and the other from the stable. See what you can find out about Juan Carlos Barrera.'

'Anything in particular?'

'Just the usual questions, when did he make the reservation, check-in and his check-out dates?'

'How about visitors and messages and room number? Should I contact the local control and have someone go round to the hotel and collect his effects? We don't have his passport.'

'Good idea, these airport hotels can be difficult to get visitor information from. Be better if a uniformed officer asks the questions. We do have Barerra's wallet and little black book though.'

'Anything of interest in the wallet?'

'Just about to look through it.'

'Fine, while you look, I'll call control.'

Buchanan put on a pair of gloves then removed Barrera's wallet from the evidence envelope and emptied its contents onto his desk.

'Anything of interest?' asked Street, who'd just completed her call.

'Disappointingly not. So far all we have are his driving licence and credit cards. There's an American Express credit card, a Columbia Bank card, and an HSBC credit card, all business accounts. A photo of someone called,' he said, turning it over,

'Gabriella, and an inscription in Spanish which says – if my Spanish is any good – *all my love forever.*'

'Forever just came for her. What about the black notebook?'

'Empty. Nothing special about it, sort of thing you buy at W H Smiths. Probably purchased at the airport.'

'Was there a phone with the body?'

'Yes, a Paygo phone with a receipt showing it was purchased from a stall at the airport two days prior to his death – which would have made his arrival sometime on Friday.'

'So, no point in sending it in for analysis, though you could check the call register and see if he managed to make any calls since he got here.'

'Something doesn't fit with our scenario. The note found at Belleview was at least two months old, and the note found at the stables is only a few days old.'

'Then he must have been in the country before and just returned last week. Pity we don't have his passport, then we could see just how often he visits.'

'He could be a courier, but probably not, customs are quite sophisticated these days, not much gets past them. I wonder if he's on a watch list with immigration?'

'I'll add it to my list,' said Street.

'Another item to check will be how did he get to the stables from his hotel? There was no car found abandoned in the area,' said Buchanan. 'Whetsted Road is narrow with narrow grass verges, so he couldn't have parked there. I have DS Blakey's phone number; I'll give him a call and see what he can find for us. The town of Paddock Wood is relatively compact, should be able to find a car that doesn't belong.'

'Suppose he came by train, then got a taxi to the stables?'

'Good point, I'll mention that to Blakey as well. Also, if he came by train, there should be CCTV available from the platform. Have we heard anything from Littlejohn on the search of Du Marchon's house?'

'Not yet.'

'What about Dr Mansell?'

'Yes, he called to say he had your Saturday night body in the fridge, and would you stop by, he has something to show you.'

'Fine, while you chase down the hotel, I'll go and see the good doctor.'

♦

'How went the wedding at the weekend? I know about the body,' said Mansell, pointing to the body bag on the examination table.

'Mr and Mrs McCall are now luxuriating in all the delights that Scarborough has to offer.'

'You were the father of the bride?'

'Yes, enjoyed it no end, in fact I'm getting quite used to the procedure, this was my second time to be the father of the bride.'

'When was the last time?'

'When Jill and Stephen got married. Jill's parents died when she was a teenager.'

'Ah, yes, I remember now you mention it. How did you get to know this lady you were father of the bride to on Saturday?'

'We met at Castlewood a few months ago, I was supposedly taking a week off work to relax. Her former husband drowned in a plane crash in the Channel. She had no other relatives, so she asked me.'

'Was that the plane recovered from the Channel last week, the one I did the autopsies on the pilot and passenger?'

'That's the one. What can you tell me about the cause of death of this one?'

'Want to see?'

'Why not?'

Mansell unzipped the body bag. 'The deceased died from a lack of blood. I found a deep, horizontally placed, long incised neck injury on the lower third of the neck. The left end of the injury started below the ear at lower third of the neck and deepened gradually with severance of the left carotid artery. The right-side end of the injury was at the lower third of the neck with a tail abrasion. The incision went almost all the way to the vertebrae. If you were to ask me how it with the left hand on the forehead and slashed his throat with the knife held in the right hand. The deceased would have died almost instantly. The killer was right-handed and about the same height, 1.8 meters or five foot eleven inches.'

'Would there have been much blood? The CSI's said most of the blood spatters went out onto the gravel.'

'Not as much as you might expect. In my opinion the bloodstains on the clothes are commensurate with him having his throat cut while standing, there are splashes of blood on his shoes.'

'The doctor who attended the scene thought the wound was caused by someone facing him and slashing the neck with a knife.'

Mansell shook his head. 'Definitely attacked from behind. If he had been attacked from the front, the incision would have been deepest at the front of the neck. No, definitely cut from behind.'

'Does it look like he struggled much?'

'Yes. I had a scrape under his fingernails and got some skin tissue that he'd managed to get from the back of his attacker's hand. I've sent the samples off to forensics for DNA matching. I've copied you in on the results.'

'Thanks. As unlikely as it is, could his death have been self-inflicted?'

'A suicide?' he said, shaking his head. 'Where's the knife? A suicidal throat incision would be a more diagonal cut. Though I once read about a man who cut his own throat and had time to clean the scene and get rid of the knife.'

'OK, so it was murder by someone attacking him from behind?'

'Yes, and with a rusty, but sharp, knife.'

'You think the killer sharpened the knife before attacking?'

'It could be it was the only weapon to hand, and they wanted to do a good job of the killing.'

'And cutting someone's throat like that would be a great deal quieter than shooting them.'

'Precisely. Have you talked to the SCI's yet?'

'No, not yet, thought talking to you first was more important. Anything else I should know?'

'He had traces of cocaine in his blood, and his adrenalin levels were high.'

'Sounds like he was worried about the meeting.'

'Or excited.'

'Thanks, Andrew.'

♦

'Oh, good, you're back.'

'What happened?'

'Oh, nothing much, just the blood results from Littlejohn, and we have a visitor.'

'Who is the visitor?'

'The ACC, Helen Markham. She just went down the hall, be back in a minute.'

'Did she say what she wanted?'

'Yes, and you can relax, she came to see me.'

'But why would she want to see you?'

'She stopped by to see how I'm doing, that's all. I'm pregnant and she just wanted to have a chat, and – she brought me these lovely flowers.'

Buchanan let out his breath and went behind his desk and relaxed into his chair as Helen Markham returned.

'Good morning, Helen.'

'Morning, Jack. Jill, have you decided when you will be taking maternity leave?'

'No, still have six months before the baby is due.'

'A spring baby, how nice for you. Well, don't put it off too long. Now, Jack, what are you doing working on a case that should be being dealt with by Kent CID?'

'It is directly connected to another incident here in Sussex,' said Buchanan.

'What case are you referring to? I haven't seen anything about it.'

'The investigation stems from a report from an estate agent about bloodstains found in a washbasin in one of the houses that his firm looks after.'

'Where is this house? It better not be in Kent.'

'No, it's nowhere near Kent, it's in the village of Litlington. During a cursory examination of the house a large quantity of dried blood was discovered in the upstairs bathroom washbasin. I also found a bloodstained baseball type hat disposed of in one of the dustbins. We have since ascertained that the victim found at the scene in Kent has a direct connection to the individuals who are renting the house in Litlington.'

'I'm glad you cleared that up – but is it enough to warrant taking over a murder investigation that happened in Kent? Surely the emphasis should be made from the Kent end? After all that is where the murder took place.'

'I believe it was just a part of an overall crime that has taken place here in Sussex. Let me explain.'

'Please, do.'

'One of the tenants of the house, and his associate, plus one of the guests, perished when the plane they were travelling in crashed into the English Channel.'

'Who were they?'

'The guest's name is Daniel Sanderson, and the two others I recently met at Castlewood.'

'Really? Where, when and who are they?

'The where was Castlewood, when was two months ago at the Castlewood Cup, and the names are Julian Du Marchon and Victor Mountjoy.'

'Du Marchon? Is that the one I read about in the *Argus*?'

'Yes, that's the one.'

'Remind me, who was Mountjoy?'

'The husband of Cynthia, the lady I was father of the bride to last weekend.'

'I think that's clear, but I'm still not sure we should be driving this case.'

'There's more,' said Street.

'Good.'

'According to the blood analysis report from forensics, the bloodstain on the hat matches the blood in the washbasin.'

'Is that it?'

'Not quite,' said Street, looking back at the email from Littlejohn. 'Blood on the hat's sweatband is human and male. It had traces of dead flies, dust, grasses, and human hair. The colour of the hair was brown turning grey. The hair was further examined and contained traces of cocaine. The fragments of flies were from the mosquito family, and the grass samples were a concoction of tall fescue, cocksfoot, timothy and crested dogstail and had been cut by a sharp lawnmower. Littlejohn has created a DNA profile from the blood sample found on the hat for future reference.'

'He got all that from the hatband?'

'Yes, and more. He surmises that the hat belonged to someone other than the person whose blood was found on the hat's sweatband. Apparently, the hat had been worn by more than one person.'

'How many?'

'He says he found three other distinct DNA traces from the sweatband.'

'What about the blood in the washbasin?'

'The report says the DNA of the blood found there matches the blood found on the sweatband and one of the sweat samples on the sweatband. The DNA from the human hair fibres on the hatband is the same DNA as the blood on the hatband.'

'How can anyone make any sense out of that lot? In my mind, it still doesn't connect to the murder in Kent.'

191

'If you'll give me a moment, I believe I can make sense,' said Buchanan.

'All right – let's hear what sort of cake you can make out of the recipe of evidence we have so far.'

'We have an adult male, brown hair with a touch of grey, and he sustained a head injury. The hat, along with a jacket, cash and a bottle of whisky were stolen from the crew cabin at Headcorn. It is possible that the thief cut their head when they broke into the crew cabin. That is when the blood from the injury got on to the hat sweatband. How's that for a scenario?'

'It's a beginning, go on.'

'There are other items we haven't mentioned yet, and those items are what ties the Kent murder to the house in Litlington,' said Buchanan.

'And they are?'

'We found a note, written on a piece of hotel notepaper at the house in Litlington. It was a crude attempt at code, but clearly links the plane crash victims to the dead man.'

'What was in the note?'

'I have it here,' said Buchanan, handing the note in the evidence envelope to Markham.

J and V, I'm here to collect what is owed, I'll return soon, have it ready, JCB. What does it mean?

'We think the initial J refers to Julian Du Marchon, the dead pilot, and the V refers to Victor Mountjoy, the deceased husband of Cynthia Mountjoy, the lady I was father of the bride to last weekend.'

'And JCB?'

'Juan Carlos Barrera, the dead man found in Kent, Jill is still checking into his background. There was a second note found at the scene and written on the same hotel notepaper with the address of the stables where he was killed.'

'That ties it up nicely. What about the blood in the washbasin and the hat you found?'

'The DNA of the blood found on the washbasin and the hatband match. Henry Littlejohn has told us that DNA samples from under the fingernails of Barrera match the DNA of the bloodstains found at Belleview. So, from that we conclude that one of the occupants of the house in Litlington killed Barrera.'

'But how could that be? You just said the occupants of the Belleview house are all dead. They died in the plane crash weeks before Barrera was murdered. You need to explain that.'

'We know that three of the four occupants of the house, Julian Du Marchon, Victor Mountjoy and the young man called Daniel all died before Barrera, so that leaves only one other suspect.'

'Do you have a name?'

'Yes. Alan Dale, brother to another player in this vignette, his sister. Interestingly it was she who contacted us and alerted us to Du Marchon's activities.'

'In what way?'

'She wanted to show us something her brother left with her for safe-keeping.'

'What was that?'

'Several hundred thousand pounds worth of gilt certificates which have only recently matured. Her story is her brother was involved with Du Marchon and Mountjoy and had either been asked to look after the gilts or had purloined them as a form of protection from Du Marchon or Mountjoy.'

'Who do they really belong to?'

'The name on the paperwork says Sovereign Secure Investments. We know this to be a front for Julian Du Marchon's activities.'

'Do you think it's time to involve the NCA?'

'Not just yet, there's more to this. Along with the gilts there is an accompanying sales mandate that only requires the signature of Victor Mountjoy for the gilts to be cashed. But since he also perished in the plane crash, who knows what the disposition of the ownership of the gilts will be?'

'Do you believe the sister when she says she doesn't know where her brother is?'

'Not entirely.'

'What does she stand to gain from what is going on?'

'A possible share of the proceeds of the sale of the gilts.'

'What was the conclusion of the pathologist on the dead man found at the stables?'

'Victim attacked from behind, throat slashed with a rusty blade that had been sharpened just prior to the killing.'

'Doesn't sound like a premeditated killing. If the killer had to sharpen the blade, it must have been a last-minute thought. So, did the killer contact Barrera and invite him to the stables, or did Barrera just show up unexpectedly?'

'I have a print-out of the calls from the victim's mobile,' said Street.

'Were there many calls?' asked Markham.

'No, only three, all to the same mobile number. The last one timed at six forty-seven on Friday evening.'

'So that could have been the one that brought him here. Were you able to trace the call?'

'Yes and no. We were able to get a cell fix on the call to within half a mile of the stables. The cell phone was traced and found in a ditch about half a mile from the stables. There were no fingerprints or DNA. Also, the phone was a Paygo phone, like Barrera's.'

'So, Barrera went there to collect whatever was owing to him, found no one there and before he could leave, was attacked from behind and had his throat slashed,' said Markham.

'Except we have an issue with some of the evidence,' said Buchanan.

'What's that?'

'The two notes we found were written at least two months apart.'

'Well, if anyone can sort that one out, it's you two. Keep me informed of your progress, and Jill, remember what I said,' said Markham, as she stood to leave.

'Thanks, I will, and thanks for the flowers.'

'You're welcome.'

Buchanan stood, walked over to the window, and watched as the ACC got in her car and left the police compound.

'It's a nuisance Ashley tried to trick us with the toothbrush. Jill,' said Buchanan, as he returned to his desk. 'Would you give forensics a call and ask them if they could compare the DNA samples from the hat to the ones from the bodies found in the plane, and while you do that, I'm going to call Blakey.'

♦

'What did they say?' Buchanan asked Street when she hung up from talking to forensics.

'No match, neither Du Marchon nor Daniel have worn the hat, and their DNA doesn't match the bloodstain on the washbasin or the hat. How did you get on with Blakey?'

'He's going to put the word out for abandoned cars, especially in the area where the mobile phone was found.'

'Did forensics say how old the bloodstains were?'

'About three months old.'

'I wonder if it could be Alan's blood? We've not been able to get a sample of his DNA yet.'

'You know, the bloodstains could be a completely innocent occurrence. It could be anyone's. Suppose they had someone working around the house, a handyman, he was replacing a broken pane of glass, he cut himself, washed the blood off in the washbasin and on the way out threw his hat in the rubbish bin.'

'So, why didn't he clean up behind himself? Why leave such a mess for the householder to clean up? I certainly wouldn't want him working in my house.'

'Maybe he couldn't stop the bleeding, got worried and went straight to accident and emergency for treatment.'

'So, my question remains, why didn't someone clean up the blood?'

'If the house was unattended and it was a handyman who had the accident, he would have probably got the key from the agency, and with my scenario, he had the accident and forgot to tell the agency about the mess he left behind.'

'Then why didn't Hoskins figure that out? Why refer the bloodstains to us?'

'Good point.'

'I wonder if Ashley Dale is available?' said Buchanan. 'She has some questions to answer.'

'Shall I call her?'

'No, let's go and surprise her.'

♦

'Do you miss living in the harbour?' asked Street, as they parked on the road across from the harbour lock gates.

'That's not easy to answer. The harbour has its own unique attributes, such as this,' he said, pointing at the view of the boats tied up at their docks. 'Then there's the restaurants and the promenade, all attractive propositions.'

'Granted.'

'Where we currently live in Westham there is peace and quiet. First thing in the morning you can hear the birds singing and the diesel train heading to its rendezvous at Ashford with the Eurostar train to Paris. Then there's the country lanes to wander through.

'For amenities we have a café, a fish and chip shop, a seafood restaurant, a newsagent with a post office, one coffee shop and an excellent tearoom behind the castle. Of course, there is also The Heron pub, great beer with pleasant company.

'If you enjoy getting your hands dirty, there are the allotments. For historical interests there is the castle and Roman fort plus the oldest Norman church in the country that dates to the year 1080, and last, but certainly not least, there's Starbucks by the roundabout.'

'My – you are sounding like a cheerleader for your community.'

'I suppose I am a bit prejudiced when it comes to where I live,' said Buchanan, as he pressed the doorbell for Ashley Dale's flat.'

'That's one of those doorbell cameras,' said Street. 'Stephen showed me some YouTube videos of what they capture.'

'Have you seen the one where a car flies over a roundabout?'

'Yes, but the one that made me laugh is where a woman tries to steal packages from a doorstep and ends up slipping on the lawn and breaks her ankle. Her partner has to get out of the car, pick her up and carry her back to the car.'

Further conversation about YouTube videos were curtailed by the opening of the door by Ashley Dale.

'Ah, Inspector, Sergeant, I didn't expect to see you so again soon. Has something happened?'

'May we come in? There are some questions we need to ask you.'

'Yes, please come in.'

They followed Ashley into the flat and through to the sitting room.

'What is it you wish to ask me?'

'Firstly, do you know someone by the name of Andrea Dale?'

'Yes, she is my aunt on my father's side of the family.'

'Did she live at Belleview in Alciston?'

'Yes.'

'When did she leave?'

'I think it was about five, six, years ago. She sold the house and moved to New Zealand with her husband.'

'Do you know who she sold the house to?'

'No. I think it was someone who buys and rents properties.'

'Did you visit your aunt when she lived at Belleview?'

'Yes.'

'Have you visited since your aunt left?'

'A couple of times, why?'

'Who were you visiting?'

She let out her breath and walked over to the settee and sat. 'I went to see Alan.'

'First you tell me he lived with you in your flat, then you say he lived in a flat rented by Julian Du Marchon, and now you tell me he lived at Belleview, which is it?'

'He lived with me simply to have a postal address but would squat at the flat in town when he wanted to party. When Julian was away for any amount of time Alan would stay at Belleview. The house is quite isolated, and Julian wanted to make sure there was always someone living there. In the end, he ended up spending most of his time living at Belleview.'

'On his own?'

'No, Daniel stayed with him.'

'Is this the same Daniel that was in the Army with Alan?'

'Yes, he and Alan were friends.'

'Were they just friends?'

'I'm not quite sure what you are insinuating, but yes, as far as I know they were just friends, Army buddies.'

'Unfortunately, the body recovered from Julian's plane was too far decomposed for a visual identification. So, the toothbrush you gave us supposedly belonging to Alan for us to do a DNA match led us astray. Where did you get that toothbrush from?'

'I went to my flat and took it from the bathroom.'

'Whose toothbrush was it that you gave to us?'

'Daniel's.'

'How did his toothbrush come to be in your flat?'

'He and Alan sometimes stayed there.'

'Why did you give us Daniel's toothbrush?'

'It was an honest mistake. Both toothbrushes were the same colour.'

'In that case, could we have the other toothbrush, please?'

'Sorry, but I threw it out.'

'When we did a preliminary search of Belleview, we found bunkbeds in one of the bedrooms. Do you know who slept there?'

'Alan and Daniel.'

'How did Alan and Daniel meet?'

'Alan told me he was in a bar in Germany and saw Daniel being pushed around by some locals. Daniel was quite stalky and got picked on a lot for his stature, so Alan stepped in to try and help. Alan said it was a night to remember, between the two of them they put all four locals in hospital and nearly destroyed the bar during the process.'

'What happened to Alan and Daniel?'

'They hightailed it back to barracks. Fortunately, no one was able to identify them. They stayed friends from there on.'

'I'm a bit confused here; you say they were both in the Army?'

'Yes. They were both on short-term engagements. Alan left after four years; I don't know about Daniel.'

'Do you have a surname for Daniel?'

'I think it was Sanderson.'

'Do you still have a key for Belleview?'

'Yes.'

'Did Julian know you had a key?'

She shrugged. 'I suppose so.'

'Did you ever go to Belleview when there were parties?'

'No, those kinds of parties didn't interest me.'

'What kind of parties were they?'

'Pool parties, loud music, lots of booze, and, I imagine, drugs.'

'Did Alan go to these parties?'

'While in the Army, he and Daniel with a couple of friends started a band. When Alan and Daniel left, they used to make money by busking as a guitar and keyboard duo. Alan played guitar, Daniel keyboard, they provided the music for the parties.'

'So, Belleview was really where Alan and Daniel lived?'

'Yes.'

'What was your relationship with Julian?'

'There wasn't one. We met a few times at Belleview, and a couple of times at the flat in town. Look – Julian and Victor were evil brutes.'

'What do you mean? Did they physically hurt Alan and Daniel?'

'No, nothing like that. Alan and Daniel were quite gullible, and I think their naivety was taken advantage of. Julian once got angry with Alan and went to strike him, and Alan told him just what would happen if he did. I think from then on it was a stalemate.'

'What was your purpose for visiting Belleview?'

'I was concerned for Alan, so when they were around, I would try and keep an eye on him by randomly showing up at the house or the flat on some pretext or other.'

'Where is Alan?'

'I don't know.'

'When was the last time you talked to him?'

'Two, three months ago.'

'Do you have a date?'

'The Friday before the horse race. I was going to Brighton to a David Bowie photographic exhibition.'

'And how was Alan?'

'Nervous.'

'Earlier you told us Alan gave you the briefcase at your flat. Where exactly did he give it to you?'

'Belleview on the Friday.'

'Was he alone?'

'Yes. He said Julian had left to check-in to his room at Castlewood.'

'Why did you lie to us?'

'I was afraid something awful was going to happen to Alan.'

'Is that why you gave us Daniel's toothbrush?'

'No, it was definitely a mistake.'

'Have you really thrown out Alan's toothbrush?'

'Yes, sorry.'

'Do you have anything else of Alan's we could use to check his DNA?'

She shook her head.

'And you haven't seen or heard from him since that night?'

'No.'

'What can you tell me about the bloodstains in the bathroom at Belleview?'

'I wasn't aware there were any bloodstains in the bathroom at Belleview.'

'Do the initials JCB mean anything to you?'

'They make tractors, don't they?'

'Yes, they do, but do those initials mean anything else to you?'

'No, sorry.'

'And you're sure you don't know where Alan is?'

'No, I've already told you that.'

'What colour hair does Alan have?'

'Brown, with flecks of grey. I think he took after his dad, he had brown hair.'

'That last night when he gave you the briefcase, how did he look?'

'I suppose he looked a little hyper.'

'Was he wearing a hat, a baseball hat for instance?'

'I've never seen him wear a hat.'

'Can you think of where he might have gone?'

'No, sorry.'

'What did he and Daniel do for Victor and Julian?'

'Whatever they wanted. As I said earlier Alan and Daniel used to provide the music for the parties. They also kept the house and grounds clean and tidy, would make sure everything worked and sometimes look after guests.'

'What do you mean by guests?'

'Alan told me that sometimes Julian would have some of his business acquaintances stay at the house. That way they could have meetings without being disturbed.'

'What kind of meetings were they? Did Alan say?'

'No, but he did say that the people who stayed were usually from either Europe or somewhere in South America.'

'Did he ever mention the names of any of these visitors?'

'If he did, I don't remember.'

'Was he afraid of anyone, enough for him to disappear?'

'Alan said he never could trust Julian, and he could never figure Victor out. He said sometimes, when Victor thought Alan wasn't looking, he would find Victor staring at him with a puzzled look on his face.'

'Ashley, do you have a current photo of Alan?'

'Er, yes, I think so.'

'Could we have a copy, please?'

'OK. I have one on my phone, shall I send it to you?'

'Yes, please.'

Buchanan looked at the photo of Alan on his phone and nodded. It was a more recent one than the one in the drawer at Belleview. This one was a straight head and shoulder shot. 'Thanks, that is perfect, and thank you for your time, Ashley. If you think of anything else that might help, please get in touch.'

♦

'That was interesting,' said Street, as they returned to the office.

'Yes, it was. I'm getting the impression that Du Marchon was using the house in Litlington for more than just somewhere to live. The fact that he had visitors from Europe and South America, and with Juan Carlos Barrera being Columbian, makes me think of drug dealing on a grand scale.'

'Maybe we should be digging deeper into Du Marchon's background, find out who he really was?'

'An excellent idea.'

'What do you know about him? You actually met him. If I remember, I was in France visiting your mother-in-law with Karen?'

'Not much. Though I did have a quick conversation with him while at Castlewood about investing cash from a house sale. Initially when I began investigating him, I found he was involved in drug dealing and money laundering. He had a partner in crime…'

'Victor Mountjoy?'

'Victor Mountjoy had a plan to fix the Castlewood Cup race. I found out what was going on and managed to turn the tables on Victor and his scheme. In the process Du Marchon and Victor tried to kill Harry, the stable manager, by beating him up and leaving for him for dead in one of the horse boxes. He hoped the horse would finish him off.'

'You're right, they do sound like a couple of shits.'

'Du Marchon apparently had contacts in Eastern Europe, and now we find he had contacts in South America as well. I never found out if he had any actual connections with the drug trade, it was just suspicions.'

'So, a dead end, then?'

'Maybe not. Julian and Victor had two accomplices, Lenny and George, both with previous convictions for GBH.'

'Do you know what happened to them?'

'They got eight years apiece for the kidnap and assault on Harry. Not sure which prison they are currently residing in.'

'Shall I check?'

'No, you already have a lot on your plate, I'll do that.'

'Will you interview them?'

'Yes, if doing that would reveal the workings of the Du Marchon operation.'

'You see a definite connection between Du Marchon and Barrera?'

'Yes, but the fact he was found dead at the Mountjoy stables bothers me. Did he know where Victor Mountjoy hid the money he embezzled, or was he meeting someone who did?'

'The only thing that sort of makes sense to me,' said Street, 'would be if Alan had seen the opportunity and taken over the reins of the Du Marchon and Mountjoy operation. Barrera put the squeeze on him to pay some debt that was owed, and Alan decided to rid himself of the obstacle.'

'So, if what you say is true, I still don't see why the meeting was arranged at the stables, unless – unless Alan had found out where Victor had hidden the cash he had embezzled from those betting on his scheme and had decided to pay off what was owed.'

'But how would he know that? Unless Mountjoy had told him, after all he trusted Alan with the gilts. It's just possible when Alan saw how much cash there was, he changed his mind and decided to get rid of Barrera.'

'Or, a slight variation, Jill. Barrera got greedy and tried to extort more than he was entitled to, so Alan decided to get rid of him.'

'But how would Alan know where the stables were?'

'I'm sure that wouldn't be much trouble for him, he probably just asked or listened to Mountjoy during one of his conversations with Du Marchon.'

'Or maybe Victor had arranged for Alan to pick him up at Headcorn and drive him to the stables to collect the money. That Saturday evening at Castlewood, did you notice Victor making any phone calls?'

Buchanan thought for a minute then shook his head. 'It was a very busy evening, and the wine was flowing, sorry, no. Besides Mountjoy wasn't at the dance, he and Du Marchon had already fled the scene.'

'Good, now we have a suspect for the killing of Barrera, and his photo that we can circulate.'

'Yes, and it is a very good photo, and taken quite recently, but I think we'll keep it in-house for a bit, don't want him getting suspicious that we are after him.'

'So, you really believe Ashley when she says she doesn't know where her brother is?'

'For now.'

'You never mentioned what Blakey said.'

'Oh, sorry. He said that it's likely any rental car that's been sitting parked for any amount of time in the area would have been picked up by now. So, he said he will check the CCTV records at the station and forward whatever he finds. How did you do with the hotel?'

'I called the hotel number first that was on the note and got confirmation Barrera was staying there and was unaccompanied. Local control will send a car to collect his effects. I made sure to tell them to collect everything from the room, especially the passport and any other documents or phones. They will send them down with one of their squad cars as soon as they can but not to hold your breath as they are short staffed, as usual.'

'Talking of tomorrow, it's long past dinner time, I'm hungry, shall we reconvene here tomorrow morning?'

'Oh, I forgot to mention, I have a doctor's appointment tomorrow at nine-thirty. It will be a long one so I may not get here till after lunchtime.'

'Is the baby all right, is something wrong?'

'No, nothing is wrong. It seems like there's a baby boom going on right now and the clinic is a bit overwhelmed.'

'In that case, I'll see you when I see you.'

♦

'Tough day?' asked Karen, as Buchanan closed the front door behind him.

'Messy is how I would describe it.'

'Jill still happy to be working?'

The Jockey's Wife.

'Yes. She's got a doctor's appointment in the morning, that's the second in as many weeks. I hope she's not sickening for something.'

'You're just worrying over nothing. Women have been giving birth since the dawn of time. You go and have your dinner, it's keeping warm in the oven, and I'll give Jill a call. Will that put your mind at rest?'

'Yes, thanks. What's for dinner?'

'Typical man, the world could be coming to an end and all he would want is his dinner. Shepherd's pie.'

14

A Suspect

Buchanan slept late, skipped breakfast, grabbed his sandwiches from the fridge and stopped in at Starbucks for coffee and a bacon roll before driving to the office.

He checked for messages and was about to pick up the phone when it rang.

'Buchanan.'

'Jack, it's Blakey, I have the information you requested.'

'That was quick, what have you found out?'

'There have been no reports of abandoned rental cars, but I managed to get CCTV of the victim at Paddock Wood Station. He arrived on the 22:10 from Charing Cross. I contacted the BTP and asked them to check their end. It took a bit of doing but he was seen boarding the 21:15 train. Charing Cross station CCTV showed him walking in fifteen minutes before he boarded the train. He went into WH Smith and purchased a small black notebook and a bar of chocolate.'

'That must have been the notebook we found with him when we searched,' said Buchanan. 'Anything else?'

'Working backwards we managed to pick him up coming out of the Embankment underground station. The BTP traced him back to where he boarded the underground.'

'That would probably be Hounslow West. That's the Piccadilly line. He could have changed for the Circle or District lines at Earls Court for Charing Cross.'

'That's what they found. They also found the taxi that drove him there from his hotel. The timing all checks out, he didn't stop off anywhere on his journey.'

'Thanks Blakey, that's a good job done well.'

'Wait, there's more. We manged to find the taxi that drove him out to the stables, or at least close to the stables. Barrera wasn't quite sure of where the stables were and with his accent, the taxi driver got a bit impatient and was only too happy to drop him off with a nod of the head to indicate he would return when the office was called. As you know, Barrera never made the call. We did find where he was dropped off. One of our eager young constables walked Whetsted Road and found a chocolate wrapper in a layby. I've sent it off to forensics for it to be checked and the results sent to you.'

'Thanks.'

'I wonder if that was where he was supposed to meet his contact?'

'That's possible.'

'Do you have any suspects in the killing?'

'Yes, a young lad, ex-army, though we are not quite sure what the connection might be. I'll send you a recent photo of him.'

'Thanks, I'll circulate it, maybe we'll get lucky.'

'It does happen.'

'I suppose when his contact didn't show up, Barrera made his way along Whetsted Road, saw all the cars parked in the driveway and made his way into the stables to try and find him. It must have come as a surprise to his contact to see him standing in the yard.'

'Yes, it must have been quite a surprise.'

'And on the spur of the moment he decided to get rid of Barrera once and for all. Are you sure you can vouch for the guests at the wedding?'

'Yes, I'm sure. They were all in the marquee watching the bride and groom dance.'

'Fine. Anything else?'

'No, that should do for now.'

'OK, call if you think of anything. In the meantime, I'll circulate the photo of your suspect.'

Buchanan put down the phone and thought back to Saturday evening and to where Pat and Cynthia were when Barrera met his demise. He could remember Pat and Cynthia dancing, but he couldn't remember seeing Marjorie in the marquee. Could she have seen Barrera and slit his throat? She was tough enough, but what would be her reason? Then he remembered her anger directed towards Victor – but would that extend to murdering Barrera? Who knew? He now had two possible killers; how many more would there be by the time the investigation was over?

It was just before eleven-thirty and still no sign of Street, what should he tackle next? He thought of his two possible suspects. Alan Dale, former Army, probably trained in all sorts of martial arts. Then there was Marjorie, steelworker, a cool calculating head in dangerous circumstances. Which of the two would be the most plausible as killers?

But what could their motives be? Alan possibly because he knew Du Marchon and Mountjoy and what they represented, but likewise Marjorie. He made up his mind, he'd investigate them both, but where to start? He didn't know where Alan was, and he didn't even know what Marjorie's surname was.

He decided he would start with Marjorie and get her surname. He picked up the phone and called Karen at home.

'Buchanan residence.'

'Karen, it's me, Jack.'

'Hello, is there something wrong? Is Jill all right?'

'No, nothing is wrong, all is well, I hope. I'm waiting for Jill to arrive; she is still at the doctor's. Listen, I'm in a bit of a hurry, would you check Cynthia's wedding programme for me, I'm looking for Marjorie's surname, she should be listed as chief bridesmaid.'

'OK, hold on … Got your pen handy?' It's Barraclough, got that?'

'Yes, thanks. Got to run, see you at dinnertime.'

Marjorie Barraclough, somehow that name fits, thought Buchanan. Next, it was an online visit to gov.uk to see what he could find out about Alan Dale.

According to the records, Alan sailed through his basic training and went on to successfully complete a combat infantryman's course. Although a suitable candidate, he apparently decided that a career in the Army wasn't what he wanted in life and left at the end of his enlistment. Not the background of a throat-slashing killer, thought Buchanan. But experience had taught him that the love of money was the root of all evil and more than once he'd seen that greed turn law-abiding citizens into murderous criminals and, in this case, there was enough money to make anyone have second thoughts.

He was about to look through the police national computer for signs of Alan when he was interrupted by the arrival of a MET police constable with Juan Carlos Barrera's personal effects.

'Detective Chief Inspector Buchanan?'

'Yes.'

'PC Warner. I have some personal effects for you,' he said, putting down a large blue suitcase. 'There are also these.' He passed Buchanan a large clear evidence envelope. 'Would you mind signing for them, please?'

'Certainly. How was the drive down?' said Buchanan, as he signed for the delivery.

'Fine when I got on the M23, not looking forward to the return drive during commute hours.'

'Neither would I. Thanks for bring these down.'

'You're welcome, so long.'

Buchanan put on a pair of inspection gloves and emptied the contents of the evidence envelope onto his desk. First item to engage his attention was the passport. The latest immigration stamp was for Thursday of the previous week, the time prior to that was two months ago. That matched the known facts. Buchanan scanned through the passport and realised these two entries were the only ones, and further the passport was only five months old. He wondered if it would be worthwhile checking with immigration to see if Barrera had been in the country prior to the entry for two months ago.

A Suspect

He put Barrera's suitcase up on the table and opened it. There was nothing unusual about the socks, underwear, shirts, and slacks or even the contents of the toiletry bag. He wasn't sure if he was disappointed or pleased about the benign contents of Barrera's suitcase: it all looked too new, it had no character. The contents could be the remnants of a clothes shop changing room. All the same he would document the contents and send them down to the evidence store.

His phone rang again. He picked it up. 'Buchanan.'

'Jack. It's Jill, sorry, but the doctor wants me to go and have some blood tests. It looks like I won't make it in to work today.'

'What's wrong?'

'Nothing's wrong, he thinks I might be a bit anaemic, that's all. I'll be back at work tomorrow.'

'OK, see you tomorrow.'

15
Attacked

Next morning, buoyed and refreshed by going to bed early, Buchanan rose and went downstairs to make breakfast. He poured a coffee and walked over to the kitchen window. It was going to be a perfect day; nothing was going to go wrong. On a whim, he looked at the clock, realised that Marjorie would have completed morning stables and called her.

'Appleton Equestrian Centre.'

'Marjorie, it's Jack Buchanan.'

'Oh, I'm so glad you called.'

'Why, what's happened?'

'I was attacked last night.'

'Are you all right?'

'Yes, I'm fine now.'

'Is anyone with you?'

'No, there's no one with me.'

'And you're sure you're alright?'

'Yes.'

'Did you call the police?'

'Yes. I think due to the killing last weekend they had two patrol cars here at the stables within ten minutes. Two more arrived a few minutes later. I told them what had happened, they did a full search of the property but didn't find anyone. At least I had the privilege of feeding George breakfast this morning. He sat up in his patrol car all night in the stable yard.'

'On his own? He didn't have a partner?'

'No, he wasn't alone though, I kept him company till about three, then I went off to bed. The policeman who was in charge last Friday came by a short while ago and said he will leave a patrol car in the carpark for the next few nights, at least till Pat and Cynthia get back.'

'What happened exactly?'

212

Attacked

'I was closing up after evening stables and as I entered the kitchen, I thought I saw someone in the hallway. It was dark, only the upstairs light was on.'

'What did you do?'

'Not what I should, I suppose. I left the kitchen lights off and went into the hallway to see. That was when he grabbed me.'

'You got free?'

'Yes. It's good I've kept up my judo training.'

'I didn't know you did judo.'

'Helps enormously when you're twenty floors up manoeuvring steel girders into place.'

'Who attacked you? Did you see who it was?'

'Just for a fleeting moment.'

'Did you recognise him?'

'No, though he did look a bit familiar. I only saw him briefly in the torch light and that was just a glancing look.'

'Was he young, old, tall, short? Can you remember anything about him?'

'I'd say he was about five foot ten, stocky build, light-grey curly hair.'

'What about the face?'

'It was awful, he had some sort of skin ailment, lots of weeping and bleeding scabs that ran across his face from his right ear down across his nose. He had a broken nose that was bent to the left, and the bleeding scabs ended up below the left side of his chin.'

'Did he say anything?'

'No, though he sorts of made growling sounds. I think the injury on his face made it difficult for him to make sense when speaking.'

'And you weren't hurt?'

'No, though had I not been fit by what I do for a living, things might have turned out much worse.'

'How did you get away from him?'

'It was he who got away from me. Initially he'd tried to grab me from behind, so I elbowed him in the gut and as I turned to grab him and get a better look, he knocked my torch out of my hand and ran off into the night.'

'Would you recognise him if you saw him again?'

'With that face, absolutely.'

'Can I WhatsApp you a photo of someone we are interested in to see if you recognise them?'

'Certainly.'

'I don't have your number.'

'That's all right, I have yours, I'll call you with mine.'

'Hi, got it, photo on the way.'

'I'm not sure, without the scarred-up face he could be,' said Marjorie. 'The only thing I can say is the hair looks right, though there is something about the eyes. Is that helpful, is he the one who attacked me?'

'I can't say at this time. By any chance did you scratch or bite him?'

'I bit his hand – but that won't do you much good, he was wearing gloves.'

'Pity, teeth bites are excellent witnesses to someone being attacked, and you are sure you will be alright?'

'Yes, now stop worrying about me, I've handled worse situations than that on site before and if you'll excuse me, I've got to take George his coffee before it gets cold.'

'Take care. In the meantime, I'll give Blakey a call.'

'Was that Jill you were talking to?' asked Karen, who'd just caught the tail end of the conversation.

'No. It was Marjorie. Someone attacked her when she was locking up last night.'

'Is she alright?'

'Yes. She called 999 but by the time the police got there her attacker was nowhere to be seen. The police left a patrol car there with George to look after her in case her attacker returned.'

'George? Who's he?'

'The policeman who sat up in his police car all night chatting to Marjorie. I'll give Blakey a call when I get into the office'.

'Good. Now, you're not going to work today without breakfast – what would you like?'

♦

'How are you feeling?' Buchanan asked Street, as he entered his office.

'Fine, just a little bit nauseous, doctor gave me something for it. So, want me to check on Alan Dale's Army career?'

'No, that won't be necessary. But we do need to find him urgently.'

'Why, has something happened?'

'Do you remember Cynthia's chief bridesmaid?'

'Marjorie?'

'Yes, that's her. She said someone attacked her last night as she locked up the stables.'

'Is she OK?'

'Yes, apparently so. By the time a patrol car got there her attacker was long gone.'

'Did she get a look at her attacker?'

'Only a partial. I sent her a copy of Alan Dale's photo; she said the hair looked similar.'

'I don't quite understand.'

'She said her attacker had a broken nose and a large weeping wound running diagonally across his face.'

'Could it have been Alan Dale?'

'If it was him, and with Pat and Cynthia on honeymoon and not due back till Saturday morning, I guess he decided this would be the best time to go after whatever cash Mountjoy had stashed away at the stables.'

'What will she do?'

'When I last talked to her, she said she was making breakfast for George, the policeman who sat in his car all night guarding the stables.'

'Sounds like fun.'

'I'll give Blakey a call and make sure all is well.'

'While you do that, I've got a prescription to collect from Tesco's.'

♦

'What did he have to say?' asked Street, as she returned from collecting her prescription.

'He said it was probably some opportunist thief out to pinch saddlery. The thief probably saw mention in the papers that there had been a wedding and the bride and groom had gone off on their honeymoon so assumed that the stables would be unmanned. Blakey has arranged for a stepped-up patrol on the stables, and they'll park a patrol car in the driveway till Pat and Cynthia return.'

'Is that Barrera's effects?'

'Yes.'

'Anything of interest?'

'No and yes. The no is there's nothing to show he's other than just a visitor, and the yes is it's all new, even the suitcase.'

'The airline could have lost his suitcase and he had to go out and buy all new. They sometimes will reimburse travellers when that happens. Are you sure it's all new and not that he has a wife that really cares about how he looks when he travels?'

'Good point, have a look.'

Buchanan picked the suitcase from the floor, laid it on the table and opened it for Street to have a look at its contents.

'I see what you mean, some of them haven't even been worn yet,' she said, lifting out two shirts still in their wrappers. Underneath the shirts was a receipt for a suitcase from the airport duty-free shop dated the day he arrived in the country. Three pairs of socks lay peacefully in a side pocket. Under a pair of slacks was a zippered toilet bag with toothbrush and tube of toothpaste, a comb, and a pair of nail clippers from Boots. 'This doesn't quite make sense to me. Most times when an airline loses your suitcase, you must wait while they search for it. But to get compensated this quickly smells a bit to me.'

'His return ticket shows him flying first class,' said Buchanan.

'Hmm, that's the answer then, the airline protecting its important customers.'

'Do you ever do jigsaw puzzles?'

'Yes.'

'What's the first thing you do?'

'That's easy, you find all the edge pieces, but the most important pieces are the corners.'

'And why do that?'

'Without the corners and edge pieces you can't tell where all the other pieces relate to.'

'Exactly. In this case we have lots of middle pieces and very few edges.'

'When Stephen and I do jigsaw puzzles, we always have the picture of what the puzzle is supposed to be like when we are done.'

'Unfortunately, we don't have that luxury.'

'We could just put the pieces back in the box and put the puzzle away in the cupboard with all the other unsolved puzzles, but then I couldn't sleep not knowing what went on.'

'Me neither. Shall we get back to the business at hand and have a look at what we already know?'

'I'm fine with that.'

'Are you sitting comfortably?'

'Yes.'

'Then I'll begin. Two months ago, Julian Du Marchon, Victor Mountjoy and Daniel Sanderson took off from Castlewood Country Club to fly to France. They stopped at Headcorn to refuel and – it is still conjecture – Victor Mountjoy was going to somehow make his way to the stables and collect his ill-gotten cash that he'd swindled from investors. Pat and Cynthia felt obligated to repay this and by doing so put themselves heavily into debt.

'At the sound of approaching police cars, Victor Mountjoy got back in the plane, but he didn't shut the door completely. They took off - heading for Fécamp in France - but due to a faulty heat exchanger Du Marchon, Daniel Sanderson and Victor Mountjoy succumbed to carbon monoxide poisoning.

'With Du Marchon being unconscious, the plane went into a dive. As it was about to crash, Victor Mountjoy recovered slightly, tried to correct the plane's descent, over-reacted and caused the port wing to hit a wave and the plane to spin and eject him. All three perished in the crash.'

'OK. I'm following you so far,' said Street.

'Two months prior, Juan Carlos Barrera arrives in the country to collect a debt, presumably in cash or something valuable that could be turned into cash. But he left empty-handed. Then, a few weeks ago he returns and makes his way to Appleton to meet with Alan Dale, hopefully to collect what was owed by Julian Du Marchon, but ends up having his throat slashed.'

'But do we have the whole picture?' said Street. 'Let's not forget the part Ashley Dale plays in this case, and there are the gilts and, as you said, Victor Mountjoy's cash.'

'This scenario is based on our assumption that Alan Dale has now got Victor Mountjoy's cash and high-tailed it out of the country. I'm sure Ashley Dale is lying to us and does in fact know where Alan is. But when it comes to the gilts, well, they are possibly worthless without Victor Mountjoy's signature and would probably be tied up in probate for years to come.'

'Want me to do some more digging on Alan Dale?'

'Yes, but first I'm going to call my financial advisor and ask her how gilts get bought and sold.'

While Buchanan made his call. Street looked for any further information on Alan Dale. Her checking returned a surprising file.

'How did you do with your financial advisor?'

'It turns out Gilts, or Bonds as they are sometimes referred to, are far more complex to explain than a phone call can resolve. She's asked for a sample, either a real one or a photocopy. She says when she can see the actual document she can advise further. How about you, did you find anything more on Alan Dale?'

'Did I ever! He's a real bad boy.'

'Really? Tell me more.'

'He was a difficult student at school and was going to be expelled for fighting. So, to save face his sister got him enlisted in the Army. Remember the story his sister told us about Alan and Daniel fighting in a bar in Wiesbaden?'

'Yes, she said he and Daniel got clean away.'

'That's not what the record says. One of the locals had half of his ear lopped off with a knife, Alan got two weeks in the guardhouse for that. For some unknown reason they didn't throw him out. His next appearance was when he stole one of the staff cars and got caught running duty-free booze and cigarettes into the camp. The next and final one is once again for fighting, this time someone almost died. Daniel was drunk at a party and started a fight, apparently Alan threw the other guy out of the second-floor window. If it wasn't for a heavy drift of snow under the window, the other chap could very well have died.'

'Now that is very interesting. Any other reports?'

'No, he seems to have learned to keep his nose clean.'

'Does it mention associates?'

'No, he seems to be a bit of a loner.'

'He did all that during his short time in the Army, but has been clean since coming out?'

'Family influence, you've seen how much big sister goes on about him.'

'If that's the case, why doesn't she know where he is? And why the subterfuge? I don't for one minute believe her story about the toothbrush.'

'Could she be hiding him at her flat in the marina?'

'Who knows? What is Stephen working on just now?'

The Jockey's Wife.

'He and Morris are on duty this weekend. There's a teen tribute music event on Wish Tower Hill late Saturday afternoon and into the night.'

'Do you think they'd miss it if I got them redeployed to watch Ashley's flat in the marina?'

'I think they'd buy you a beer or two in appreciation.'

'Good, will you let them know, and get them photos of Ashley and Alan? I'll call traffic and get them redeployed.'

16

Littlington

'Thanks for the reassignment, Jack,' said Stephen. 'The thought of listening to all those little girls screaming every time the Justin Bieber or whatever tribute band came on stage would have driven me up the proverbial.'

'What did you and Morris discover?'

Stephen took out his notebook and said, 'We started at eighteen-thirty on Friday evening. At nineteen-seventeen, the sister went out. Unfortunately, since there were only two of us, we were limited on how effective we could be in tracking her movements. I left Morris in the car and followed the sister to the Thai Marina. She picked up a take-away meal and returned to the flat. There was no way I could tell if it was for one or two people. That was it for Friday evening. During the remainder of the night Morris and I swapped opportunities to snooze and get something to eat.

'Saturday morning, at seven-thirty, the sister went out for a run, she returned an hour later and stayed in the rest of the day. Sunday morning, she repeated her Saturday run. Both times she was gone for an hour. Sunday evening, she went out in her car, I left Morris watching the flat and I followed the sister into town. She parked in the Arndale, sorry, the Beacon, carpark and went to the cinema. I waited till the cinema closed but there was no sign of her. I checked the carpark, and her car was still there. It was still there this morning. I have asked the carpark attendants to call you when Ashley Dale returns for the car.'

'Well done, and there was no sign of the brother?'

Stephen shook his head.

'Fine, why don't you go get some proper sleep? You look like you need it.'

'Thanks.'

The Jockey's Wife.

'I've cooked some bacon for you before I left for work, Stephen,' said Street. 'It's wrapped in foil in the oven along with a roll.'

'Thanks, love. A bacon sandwich and a large mug of tea is just what I need before I get some much-needed downtime.'

'OK, see you this evening.'

'What do you want to do first?' asked Street.

'This case began in Litlington, so why don't we go and talk to the neighbours there and see what they have to say about the goings on at Belleview? I'll drive.'

'Would you like to live here?' asked Street, as they drove slowly along the road past Belleview.

''What, live in Belleview?'

'No, the village. It's so picturesque and peaceful.'

'If I were retired, maybe. But I am content living where I am. In the meantime let's try the pub.'

'It's a bit early for me.'

'I didn't quite mean for a drink, though a glass of the local brew would go down quite nicely before lunch. You hungry?'

'A bit.'

'Good,' said Buchanan, as he turned off the road and down the lane into the pub carpark. He opened the door for Street and followed her into the pub and over to the bar. There was a man seated at the bar nursing a beer, and seated in the far corner, three women were deep in conversation.

'Yes, sir? What can I get you?'

'Lunch if we're not too early.'

'No, we serve food all day. Would you like to see a menu?'

'Yes, please.'

'Here you are,' she said, passing Street and Buchanan an A4 sheet with the lunch menu. 'Can I get you something to drink?'

'Jill?'

'Could I have a lime and soda, please?'

'And sir?'

'The last time I was here I enjoyed a pint of Longman's best bitter.'

'Certainly.'

'An excellent choice,' said the stranger on the barstool beside Buchanan.

'Rod,' interrupted the barmaid, 'the bitter's off, could you change the barrel for me, please?'

''Certainly, we can't be offering inferior pint to a returning customer, that just wouldn't do.'

'Your bitter will be ready as soon as Rod changes the barrel,' said the barmaid, as she placed Street's lime and soda on the counter. 'When you are ready to order your food just shout.'

'You could try the Long Blond while you wait for me to change the barrel,' said Rod, from the door to the cellar. 'It's a light-coloured golden ale with a distinctive hoppy aroma very smooth, light, and refreshing. Or if you would prefer something with a bit of copper colour and hoppy by nature, you could try the Copper Hop. Of course, if you are thinking of trying something from the barbeque, there's nothing better than a pint of Old Man. This original dark beer has soft malt notes of times gone by.'

'Thanks, for the recommendation, Rod,' said Buchanan, picking up the menu, 'I'd prefer to wait for the bitter.' He winked at Street.

'Have you decided what you want to eat?' asked Street.

'I think I'll have the burger. How about you?'

'Would you order me a Caesar salad, please? I need the loo.'

'Will do. Do you want another lime and soda?' he asked, looking at the almost empty glass.

'Yes, please.'

'Hot weather for the time of the year,' said Buchanan.

'You're not from around here?' asked Rod, who'd just returned from the cellar.

'No, just popping out of the office for a spot of lunch. Thought we'd try further afield from our usual Eastbourne haunts. I was also thinking about moving closer to head office in Lewes. That drive along the A27 in the morning is a bit of a nightmare.'

'Bit out of the way here.'

'But lovely and quiet in the evenings I'll bet?'

'It used to be,' said one of the ladies from the corner seat, who'd just got up to order another round of drinks.

'Seems quite quiet to me,' said Buchanan.

'Hmph, you should be here when they have the parties.'

'When who have parties?'

'The big house down the road.'

'Ah,' said Rod. 'You mean Belleview?'

'That's the one,' she replied, picking up two refilled wine glasses.

'What's wrong with them?' said Buchanan, indicating to the barmaid they were ready to order lunch.

'Not all of us who live at that end of the village are unhappy with the occasional parties,' said one of the other ladies, who'd come up to the bar to order a sandwich. 'I usually got an invitation; I thought that was a very nice gesture for them to invite me.'

'You would, Dot,' said the first lady, 'you're single and your kids are all grown up.'

'You'll get there one day, Nora. You'll see, one day the kids are underfoot, then they will fly the nest and you'll wonder where the time went.'

'What's up?' asked the third lady from the corner table. 'What am I missing?'

'Not much, Alicia,' said Dot. 'This gentleman, sorry – don't know your name?'

'It's Jack, and I'm here for lunch with my daughter, Jill.'

'Ooh,' said Dot. 'Jack and Jill went up the hill to Litlington for lunch, when the food was delivered, Jack and Jill shivered, and asked for a cup of tea as well. Sorry, the best I could do on short notice, I'll work on it.'

'You must excuse Dot,' said Nora, 'she runs the local writers' group and is always coming out with poetic utterances.'

'No need, I thought it was quite good.'

'Thanks.'

'Do they have parties very often?' asked Street.

'It used to be once a month,' said Rod. 'If you are talking about Belleview, you should have seen how many cars showed up, and that's not the worst of it.'

'What is the worst of it?' asked Street.

'Being such a scenic area, a few weeks ago we had the Ramblers show up. They parked their cars nearly blocking the road completely. They then went off for their so-called environmentally friendly walk. You should have heard Dave – he used every swear word under the sun. He had a terrible time getting his tractor along The Street. It was almost as bad as when them at Belleview were having their parties. All those ingrates, no regards for local people.'

'Do you know the homeowner?'

Rod shook his head. 'No, but sometimes I get orders to do a beer delivery for them.'

'Beer delivery?'

'Yes, I know the people at the brewery and sometimes I will do local home deliveries for them.'

'It would have been nice if they'd spent some of that beer money here in the pub,' said the barmaid.

'Is anyone still living at the house?' asked Street.

'Not sure,' said Rod. 'I went past the house a few weeks ago and saw someone in the carport.'

'Was it the owner?'

'No, I don't think so. The owner was tall and thin, looked like a lawyer. No, this one was quite stocky, and he had a large bandage wrapped round his face. I think it was one of the visitors that used to occasionally stay there.'

'You wouldn't remember their hair colour by chance?' asked Buchanan, pointing to the empty glasses on the bar. 'My round.'

'Brown with flecks of grey. Hang on a minute, why would you want to know that?'

'He was supposed to be off work with an injury. It's my job to check that he wasn't up to something and was really not well.'

'Ah, you're one of those insurance investigators —a co-worker of mine got sacked for saying he couldn't come in because he'd strained his back when asked to move a desk at work. He was filmed carrying two chairs and a settee up two floors in an apartment, stupid idiot.'

'It's not only the parties that have stopped these past few weeks,' said Nora. 'I'm not sure if there is a connection, but the planes don't seem to fly over as much. Oh thanks,' she added as the barmaid refilled her glass.

''What do you mean, the planes don't seem to fly over as much?' asked Street.

'Occasionally, and mostly late at night, small planes would fly low over the village.'

'Probably someone learning navigation,' said Rod, looking and smiling at his recently refilled beer glass. 'Thanks, Jack.'

'That will please Reg Brickhill,' said Nora.

'Sorry, said Buchanan, 'being a visitor, I don't know who Reg Brickhill is?'

'He's a retired RAF pilot,' said the barmaid. 'Lives in the village just two houses along the road from Belleview – house's name Buccaneer. He lives there with his dogs.'

'What sort of dogs does he have?' asked Street.

'German shepherds, he breeds them and sometimes he rehomes retired service dogs.'

'Dad, could we go have a look at his dogs, please?'

'We're in the area, so yes, why not? Ah, Jill, I see our table is ready, shall we go and eat before the food gets cold?'

◆

'That was a nice salad,' said Street. 'I didn't know you were interested in dogs.'

'Just thinking about it. But if he's a retired RAF pilot, he may have some ideas about why planes have been flying over the valley at night.'

'I'll bite, what are you thinking?'

'I'm not sure, but could Du Marchon have been flying in illegal aliens?'

'Now that is a possibility, though instead of illegals, how about he could have been running an air taxi service for criminals fleeing the country? There would be a great deal more money in that.'

Buchanan paid for their lunch and the drinks, then followed Street out into the carpark.

'We'll never know, standing here in the Plough and Harrow carpark.'

'OK, let's go talk to a man about a dog.'

'Shall I drive? You've been drinking,' said Street.

♦

Street parked the car in the driveway behind a blue Mercedes 280sl.

'Nice car,' she said, as Buchanan rang the doorbell. The sound of a dog barking behind the front door was followed by a loud male voice telling it to be quiet. The door opened a crack and a brown dog muzzle peeked out and sniffed the air.

'Friend or foe, Jasper?' came a voice from the hallway behind the door.

The dog sniffed again and retreated into the hallway. As he did the door fully opened.

'Yes? What do you want? If you are JW's I've told you a million times you're barking mad.'

'Good afternoon, Mr Brickhill. The barmaid at the Plough and Harrow said you breed German Shepherds.'

'Yes, I do. You should have called first. I don't have any pups available just now, the ones I have are all sold.'

'It's not quite why we're here. I'm Detective Chief Inspector Buchanan and this is Detective Sergeant Street. We've been informed about some low-flying aircraft at night, and we are wondering if you could tell us what you know about them?'

'Well, it certainly wasn't me, I gave that up when I left the RAF. Look come in; we can't stand here jawing at the door.'

Buchanan followed Street as Brickhill led them through the house and out onto the patio.

'It's hot, want something to drink?'

'Just water, please,' said Street.

'Be with you in a minute, while I'm gone Jasper will keep you company.'

'Nice dog,' said Street. 'Pity the person who thought they could try mischief around here.'

'I've taken the liberty of giving you ice and a slice of lemon,' said Brickhill, as he placed a small round tray on the patio table. 'Shall we sit? Bit formal standing round a table.'

'Thanks for the drink, it's quite hot today,' said Street.

'Now, you didn't come here to talk about the weather, you said something about low flying planes?'

'Yes,' said Buchanan. 'One of the patrons in the Plough and Harrow mentioned there's been reports of low-flying planes in the area at night?'

'Bloody nuisance they were. I called the CAA but was told to contact the airport where the plane flew out of and send them the aircraft details. I ask you, how was I supposed to do that? It was dark, and the plane was flying without navigation lights.'

'Was it always the same plane?'

'Not sure if it was the same plane, but it was always the same type, a Cessna 320.'

'Did you see if it landed anywhere?'

'What, a Cessna 320 land out here? He'd have to be a dammed good pilot to do that, especially without runway illumination. The fields are all small, besides there are too many obstacles like farm buildings, trees, and let's not forget the hills. All say no-go for a night landing.'

'Was there anything peculiar – other than the night flights were with no navigation lights?'

'Yes. Made me think the pilot was practising low-level night flying. We used to practise it in the RAF, but only in authorised areas. He would come in from the south, probably using the river and road as landmarks. As he passed over the village, he would back off the throttle, descend, then bank sharply to starboard, circle once or twice, then climb away under full power in the direction of north-east.'

'How often would this happen?'

'Maybe once a month – but never on a weekend, always mid-week.'

'And there was no way the plane could have landed?'

'If it did, it would have a great deal of difficulty in getting up again. Anything else?'

'Yes, when will you have your next litter of pups available?'

'I presume you mean when will my bitch have her next litter? Not for several months. But since you are here, would you like to see the pups that will soon be leaving for their new homes? You can check out the mother while you are here. If you leave your details, I will get in contact when I have pups available.'

♦

'I was only joking about wanting a dog. I didn't know you were looking for one,' said Street, as they drove back along the A259.

'I thought it would be nice to walk over to the allotment with the dog, and with it curled up beside me, sit in my chair, a cup of tea in my hand, and just watch the vegetables grow.'

'And who would feed and exercise this dog when you are working your regular twelve-hour days?'

'You are sounding just like Karen.'

'Thanks, I'll take that as a compliment. Do you think Pat and Cynthia will be home yet?'

'Not sure, would you give the stables a call and find out, please?'

Street dialled the number for Appleton and listened to the phone ring. She was about to leave a message when Cynthia answered.

'Appleton Equestrian Centre. Cynthia.'

'Cynthia, it's Jack. How are you? How's Pat?'

'We're both fine. Have you caught him yet?'

'Which one? Barrera's killer, or the person who attacked Marjorie?'

'Either will do, the horses are still spooked about something, they won't settle at night.'

'Sorry no, not yet, but we are getting closer.'

'Do you know who he is? I presume it's the same person?'

'That's a bit complicated right now, we still have some more investigating to do.'

'When are you and Karen coming for a visit?'

'I thought you are getting ready to go to Cheltenham this coming weekend?'

'Oh, that, we've been getting ready for that for years. I tell you what, you remember Andrew Jackson, Victor's Army associate?'

'Yes, and I also know just what he thought about Victor. If I remember correctly, you said Andrew was going to throw the book at Victor.'

'Yes, that's correct. But with Victor being declared dead in the plane crash, Andrew has dropped the case. Look, Andrew is coming down a week Friday evening and staying over to tell me what I can expect for a pension from Victor's years in service. Why don't you and Karen come as well?'

'That sounds like a lovely idea, but I need to check with Karen first. I'll let you know, and good luck for the weekend.'

'Thanks.'

'Jack, while you were chatting to Cynthia,' said Street, 'I was thinking about our conversation with Brickhill and his description of the plane and what it did.'

'Yes?'

'Have you been watching the television news lately?'

'The headlines only.'

'Are you aware of the famine in parts of Africa?'

'Yes, indeed I am. Karen's church is raising funds to help feed the children.'

'Well, two nights ago, while I was watching the news, they showed a video clip of relief supplies being delivered from the air. The news clip showed several C130's flying over and dropping bags of grain.'

'I get where you are going with this. You think Du Marchon was using his plane to fly over the house and push bags of drugs out the window.'

'Probably not the window, maybe the same door Victor Mountjoy exited the plane from in the Channel.'

'If that is the case, where would he have picked up the drugs from?'

'If he was using the plane, then I would say somewhere on the continent.'

'Most likely from the Amsterdam area, that's where a lot of it is imported to these days. I think I will run this past Klaus Biermann – we are going to his wedding this weekend; he's getting married to Irene Adler.'

'I remember her, we thought her husband had killed her.'

'Yes, that's her.'

'What's the point, though? Du Marchon is dead and whatever distribution network he established will have either been wound up or taken over by someone else. You remember the adage – nature hates a vacuum.'

'Regardless of what happened,' said Buchanan, as they drove into the police compound, 'I think we should find out where Du Marchon hangared his plane, and there is still the matter of who killed Barrera to sort out.'

'Are we going to be working late this evening?'

Buchanan shook his head as Street got out of the car. 'No, you can go home and have an early night, I have some thinking to do.'

'OK, good night.'

How blessed he was, he thought, as he parked his car in the Starbucks carpark, he had an excellent partner and a daughter to work alongside. He ordered a large Americano and took a seat in the corner to do some undisturbed thinking. First thought was to call Harry Carstairs.

'Harry, it's Jack Buchanan. Just wondering about the wrecked plane in your hangar, is it normally based there in Brighton?'

'I doubt it, I would remember seeing it if it were.'

'Thanks.'

'Listen, if you are trying to find out who was the owner and where the plane was registered, you could try the CAA website. They have a search page where you key in the plane's registration number, I think you leave off the G –, it will give you all the relevant info on the plane. Any problems call me back, I'm working late this evening.'

'Thanks, Harry.'

Buchanan googled the CAA website, found the relevant search page, and searched for Du Marchon's plane. He wasn't surprised to find the plane was registered to Sovereign Secure Investments and the registered address was at Headcorn. Tomorrow he and Street would go to Headcorn and see if anyone could expand on their knowledge of Du Marchon and his plane.

Of course, there remained the unanswered question of just where Alan Dale was and his place in this puzzle. It was now obvious that the plan on that Saturday evening was for Du Marchon to fly to Headcorn and to top up the fuel for the cross-channel flight. A memory of a conversation with Nathan Greyspear – or was it something he'd read about the necessity of arriving aircraft landing with minimum take-off fuel as the Castlewood strip was quite short. Yet, the mechanic at

Shoreham airfield, now Brighton Airport, had told them that there was sufficient fuel to safely make the Channel crossing to Fécamp.

If that was the case, it meant that Victor had probably planned to get to Appleton Equestrian Centre to collect his ill-gotten cash. If that was the case, how was he going to quickly make the round trip of what must be about twenty miles? As Buchanan sipped his coffee, he googled the train schedule between the two locations and saw there was a fast, efficient direct train service of fifteen minutes in each direction. But that was between stations, Victor would still need to get to and from the station at each end. So, an alternative would be a round-trip in a taxi, which would require booking, and that could be a problem if the taxi were late. So, that left the option of having someone waiting for him to do the round trip and the best candidate for that position was Alan Dale.

If so, that would resolve the issues of why Alan Dale wasn't seen at Castlewood the night of the party or wasn't on the plane when it crashed. There was also the possibility he collected the cash and when he saw how much money there was, he simply decided to keep it and go on an extended holiday.

Buchanan drained his cup, now resolved to return to Headcorn the next day and see if anyone could confirm or deny the presence of a car waiting for the arrival of the plane, and to talk with anyone who knew Du Marchon or what he did with the plane.

◆

'Hello, tough day?' asked Karen, as Buchanan closed the front door.

'A bit.'

'You look bushed, come here,' she said, reaching out to him, arms open wide.

'My cuddle buddy,' he said, wrapping his arms round her and holding her tight.

She kissed him on the cheek and said, 'Why don't you go and put your slippers on? Dinner is almost ready. Would you like something to drink while you wait?'

'A cup of tea would be nice.'

'How are you getting on with the case?' she asked, placing his cup of tea on the coffee table.

'We have another visit to Headcorn tomorrow, but I believe the case is drawing to a close.'

'It won't prevent us going to Amsterdam for the weekend, will it?'

'No, I shouldn't think so. Train to Gatwick, fly to Amsterdam and relax.'

'I'll believe that when I experience it.'

17

Stranger

'You're up early this morning,' said Karen.

'I've got a return visit to Headcorn today.'

'Oh, that's right, you did mention it. Will you be late?'

'Shouldn't think so.'

'Good, I'll finish packing tomorrow, I won't have time Saturday morning. Will we have time for breakfast at the airport?'

'I hope so.'

'Good, see you at teatime.'

◆

'Ready?' said Buchanan, to Street.

'Yes, just finished checking messages.'

'Anything of interest?'

'Did you know that at three months, a baby in the womb has fingers and toes?'

'No, I did not know that.'

'Isn't life wonderful?'

'Yes, indeed it is. Shall we get going?'

◆

'Why are we going to Headcorn?' asked Street.

'I have an idea that Alan Dale was waiting with a car for Du Marchon to land and then drive Victor Mountjoy to the stables to collect his hidden cash, then return him to Headcorn for their flight to France.'

'If that worked, Alan Dale would have then have known where the stables were?'

'Yes, he would, but as far as we know, Victor Mountjoy never actually left Headcorn.'

'Suppose he'd arranged for Alan Dale to go the stables and collect the cash then drive it to Headcorn to meet up with Du Marchon and Mountjoy when they landed to refuel?'

'That's one of the theories I am working on. Remember, Pat and Cynthia were absent with their horses, so the stables would have been unattended except for Marjorie and the temporary help that comes in to make sure all is well with the boarders.'

♦

'Where shall we start?' said Street, as they drove into Headcorn airfield.

'I plan to reinterview the ground staff.'

Street followed Buchanan as he walked over to the staff canteen. Buchanan opened the door and stood for a minute.

'What are you doing?' asked Street.

'I'm looking for Chris, the person who had his jacket and wallet stolen. Excuse me,' he said tapping a blue-overalled seated individual on the shoulder.

'Yes? Oh, sorry, this staff only, the visitor café is over by the viewing area.'

'We're police, we're looking for Chris.'

'He's in the can.'

'Fine, we'll wait.'

'Tea and coffee over there,' he said, pointing at a counter over a fridge with a kettle and mugs.'

'Shall I?' said Street.

'Yes, please.'

Buchanan chose a small table by a window and sat to wait the arrival of Chris from his mid-morning ablutions. Street brought two cups of tea and placed them on the table as Chris exited the toilet. Buchanan stood and waved him over.

'Inspector, are you here to tell me you've found my jacket and wallet?'

Buchanan indicated Chris to sit. 'I'm sorry, Chris, but no.'

'Then why are you here?'

'We are following a particular line of enquiry and need to go back over what happened that evening the Cessna 320 landed for fuel.'

'But we've told you all we know.'

'I realise that, but sometimes on reflection little details are remembered, little details that can unlock a mystery.'

'Go ahead then.'

'When you arrived to fuel the plane, how many passengers were there on board?'

'Three.'

'Were they all inside the cabin?'

'Yes.'

'When the plane stopped, how many passengers got out?'

'Just the one. The pilot was still at the controls.'

'What about the passenger in the back seat, what was he doing?'

'He was sleeping, slumped to the side, head on the window.'

'Did he wake while the plane was stationary?'

'I don't remember.'

'What exactly do you remember?'

'Like I said the last time we talked, as the plane came to a rest, the front seat passenger climbed out and started barking orders to hurry up and refuel the plane.'

'What did you do?'

'Well, I met his sort when in the RAF, so I told him he needed to pay for the fuel before any of it went into the tanks. You should have seen his face when his cards were declined.'

'What did he do after that?'

'He stood on the wing, like some lord of the manor surveying his estate and phoned someone. They must have told him something, because he hung up the call and climbed down from the wing.'

'Did he go anywhere?'

'No.'

'Did he talk to anyone?'

'No, but he did look like he was waiting for someone.'

'Did anyone show up?'

'Not that I'm aware of, besides, when the police arrived, he jumped back up on the wing as the pilot started the port engine and taxied away.'

'With the passenger still on the wing as the plane taxied away?'

'Yes, he was halfway into the cabin.'

'And you didn't see any suspicious cars parked here waiting for anyone?'

'Who could tell? We have a designated carpark, but not everyone uses it.'

'Who would know if there were any abandoned cars in the carpark?'

'Security, they have a portacabin over by the hangar.'

'Thanks.'

'And you haven't found my jacket or wallet?'

'Sorry, no.'

'Police, why do we pay them?'

♦

'He wasn't a happy bunny,' said Street, as they crossed the carpark to the security cabin.

'No, he wasn't.'

The door was open and an individual in blue shirt and blue trousers was seated at a desk in front of a window talking on the phone. There was cockpit voice chatter coming from a handheld radio on the desk, cigarette smoke drifted up from a half-smoked cigarette in an ashtray. Buchanan knocked on the door and waited. The man at the desk turned and looked at him, nodded and pointed at the phone then held up his hand displaying a finger. Buchanan nodded in understanding.

'Sorry for that,' the man said, 'getting a shopping list from the missus. How can I help?'

'DCI Buchanan,' he said, displaying his warrant card. 'We're checking on a Cessna 320 that landed here for refuelling about two months ago.'

'What's to tell? It landed for fuel, there was an issue with payment details, then it took off again. The rest of the story you can find in the newspaper.'

'Were you on duty when it landed?'

'Yes.'

'Did you actually see the incident?'

'No, I would have been making my rounds. Even though this is a public space, you'd be surprised, or maybe not, at the potential number of valuable items there are here attractive to light fingers.'

'I'm looking for a car, not one of the regulars, or one parked in the visitor parking area.'

'There was one, parked like it was in a hurry to leave.'

'What do you mean?'

'It wasn't parked against the fence like it should be, it was right in the middle of the carpark pointing at the exit, oh, and the engine was running.'

'Did you get a look at the driver?'

'Yes, youngish chap.'

'Description?'

'Tall, well built, greyish hair.'

'What was he wearing?'

'Grey hoodie over a blue t-shirt, jeans and trainers.'

'What made you remember him?'

'He was leaning against the car and eating a sandwich with one hand and trying to talk to someone on his phone with the other.'

'What make of car was it?'

'Dark blue, series seven BMW.'

'What about the registration?'

'It's in my logbook, do you need it?'

'Yes, please.'

'Hold on a minute,' he said, reaching under the desk and retrieving a dog-eared A4 notebook. 'Let me see, that would have been the evening of the twenty-second of August, yes, here we are.' He passed the notebook to Buchanan.

'Did you see him leave?'

'No, but he must have been in a hurry.'

'How do you know?'

'He dropped his phone.'

'Did he come back for it?'

'Nope.'

'Where is the phone now?'

'Probably in the office, that's where all lost property goes.'

'Would you show us where the office is, please?'

'Certainly, follow me.'

Buchanan and Street followed the security officer across the carpark and into the office.

'Jane, this is DCI Buchanan, he's looking for a lost phone. Do you still have that Samsung I handed in a couple of months ago?'

'Hi. Hang on, I'll check in the cupboard.'

She returned a few minutes later with a Ziplock bag containing a black Samsung smart phone.

'This must be it, there haven't been any others handed in.'

'May I have it? I think I know who the owner is.'

'Good luck. The battery is probably flat, and we weren't able to unlock it to find out who owned it.'

'That's all right, we have someone who can do that.'

'Would you just sign the log to say you have taken it, and your contact details as well?' asked Jane. 'Just in case the owner does show up for it.'

'Jane, before we go, would there be anyone here who would remember the pilot of the Cessna 320 that crashed in the Channel a couple of months ago?'

'I do, a bit of a cad. Wouldn't trust him with the time of day. He used to give occasional flying and navigation lessons, but I think he was more interested in getting up in the air with vulnerable young women.'

'Jill,' said Buchanan, as they left Headcorn, 'as soon as we get back to the office, would you get that phone off for fingerprints, DNA, and a log of the phone calls?'

'What will you be working on?'

'I'm going to pay a visit to the A&E. Our man Alan needed medical care, maybe someone will remember him.'

'So, where did he get injured? The security guard at Headcorn said he looked in good health when waiting at the aerodrome.'

'Who knows?' said Buchanan, pushing his hair back. 'This investigation has more twists and turns than a bucket of snakes.'

'It does begin to make sense though. Victor Mountjoy must have realised that he wouldn't have time to get a taxi and train to the stables to collect his cash, so probably called Alan and told him to meet at Headcorn.'

'I agree. But, when and where did he get injured? Rod in the Plough and Harrow said he saw Alan a couple of weeks after the plane crash with a bandage round his head and that, coupled with Littlejohn's report on the bloodstains at Belleview, means he must have been injured sometime between Headcorn and Litlington.'

'Will you try A&E at the DGH?'

'Yes. Oh, before you go home for the day, put a rush on with the phone, will you?'

'Will do.'

♦

Buchanan parked in the visitor carpark and walked into the A&E department. He had to stand in line while a young lad in football kit was being triaged for a possible broken ankle, followed by a young woman with a crying baby. Finally, it was his turn.

'Yes, can I help?'

'Yes. Detective Chief Inspector Buchanan. I'm here on official business, I'm trying to find out if this man was treated here. It would have been about two months ago,' said Buchanan, showing the photo of Alan. 'He had a facial injury which extended diagonally right across the face. Oh, he also had a broken nose.'

'I'll ask Jane, she was the nurse practitioner on duty. Take a seat with the walking wounded and hopefully we will find your patient.'

Buchanan bought a coffee from the vending machine, took a seat beside the partition, and looked at the waiting times: five hours, he resigned himself for a long wait.

He was playing his tenth game of solitaire on his phone when he was interrupted by the arrival of the duty nurse practitioner.

'Inspector Buchanan?'

'Yes.'

'Jane Francis, you were asking about someone with a head injury, about two months ago?'

'Yes, it would have been extremely late on the Saturday evening of the twenty-second of August.'

'Facial injuries?'

'Yes.'

'I remember that case. Sandra was on duty, and she asked me to assist.'

'Did he say what caused the injury?'

'Yes. He said he had been riding his motorcycle off-road and ran into a low tree branch.'

'Was it a bad injury?'

'Yes, but I doubt the injury was caused by a tree branch. When I saw him, he was holding a t-shirt over his face. When I cleaned the wound, there was no debris other than some dirt and gravel with a few strands of grass.'

'So you didn't believe his story about the branch?'

'No. It looked to me like he'd more likely fallen off a horse and been dragged backwards through the woods.'

242

'That's interesting. Did you get his name? How old would you say he was?

'Inspector, that was two months ago, do you have any idea as to how many injuries we see here in the A&E each day? There's no way I can remember someone's name from two months ago. You could try reception, give them the date and approximate time and maybe they will be able to help you with his details.'

'Do you remember what he was wearing?'

'Yes, that I do remember. It was a really nice green bomber jacket with an embroidered picture of a Spitfire on the back.'

'Thanks, you've been a great help.'

But had she? Buchanan wondered as he got back in his car. The guard at Headcorn had said he'd seen Alan leaning against his car wearing a grey hoodie and jeans, yet when he turned up at A&E, he was wearing Chris's bomber jacket and a bandage across his face. Of course, he could have been in a crash. Yet Rod from Litlington said he'd seen Alan in the bomber jacket, face all bandaged.

18

A Request

'You will be home on time today?' asked Karen, as Buchanan put on his jacket.

'Yes, shouldn't be a problem, things have gone a bit quiet.'

'Good, I'll see you at the usual time.'

Usual time! Buchanan thought as he climbed into his car. In all his years as a policeman there never had been a usual time. As he was about to start the engine his mobile rang.

'Buchanan.'

'Jack, it's Jill, sorry to do this but I've been up all night sick. I think the medication the doctor prescribed hasn't agreed with me.'

'Have you called the doctor?'

'Not yet, the clinic doesn't open till eight-thirty. Stephen called 111 and they said to drink plenty of water, rest and call the doctor when the clinic opened.'

'The baby, is it all right?'

'Yes, young Jack is fine.'

'Good, go back to bed and I'll take care of things. I was planning on spending the day going through the evidence we've collected on the case so far.'

'Thanks, oh, hope you and Karen have a great weekend.'

'Go to bed.'

'Yes sir, I will – love you.'

'Go to bed.'

◆

Instead of driving straight to the office, Buchanan made a detour to Starbucks for a large latte.

Twenty minutes later he was in his office, sipping his coffee and checking his emails – what there were of them. He logged on to the *Herald* to see if there was anything he needed to be aware of. He smiled as he read the latest missive from the *Herald's* crime reporter, Tony Miasma.

In the report he waxed lyrically on the fact that there hadn't been any murders in Eastbourne during the past month, a credit to the dedication of the local police and especially to one, DCI Jack Buchanan.

Buchanan shook his head and thought he needed to think kindlier towards Mr Tony Miasma. He finished his coffee and left the office for the evidence store and the evidence collected so far in the case.

He began with the list of items found at Belleview by Littlejohn and his team. The clothes wrappers. The underwear and t-shirts were all one size, large. There were a couple of tear-off tags from jeans size 46 x32. Buchanan nodded to himself that unless Alan had let himself go, the size of jeans would be more appropriate for a middle-aged man, not the Alan he had in mind. The baseball hat with the bloodstains found in the bin was a generic one, the small sewn-in label inside said *Made in China*. What wasn't these days, he thought?

The contents of the Belleview kitchen were quite nondescript and could be found in any Sussex kitchen. The only items of interest were the dates on the perishable items. The use-by date on the milk carton was the fourth of October, the low-fat butter spread the seventh. The remainder of the perishable foods were of similar dates and well after the plane crash.

The kitchen swing-bin contents were of more interest. Top layers consisted of several plastic microwave dinner trays, their cardboard sleeves, and scrunched up kitchen roll that had been used as napkins. There was also an empty ketchup bottle, numerous used tea-bags, coffee grounds, a bread wrapper and other expected discarded kitchen items. But it was the items in the bottom of the bin that were the most interesting. A blood-soaked t-shirt and bloodied kitchen roll.

The Jockey's Wife.

Littlejohn had done a sterling job, even listed the types of breakfast cereal, tins of beans, spaghetti, soups etc. There was nothing listed that showed whoever was living there was much of a cook —more of a camper.

Buchanan looked at Littlejohn's report and at the DNA information. DNA from the clothes wrappers, blood samples, food trays, ketchup bottle, all matched the DNA from the bloodstains in the washbasin and on the baseball cap. Many sets of fingerprints were found on site, most of them unidentifiable from records, but two sets were cross-referenceable to some of those found on the crashed plane recovered from the Channel.

The mention of grass clippings had Buchanan scratching his head. Had it just been a single species of grass he would have put it down to someone cutting the grass at Belleview, but four types, that was a puzzler. He took his phone out of his pocket and googled the grass types. The search result made him smile. The four types of grass found on the baseball cap were the same type used for aeroplane grass runways. If this was the case, what was a baseball cap with airport runway grass clippings and bloodstains be doing at Belleview? The answer of course could only be that it was Alan. For some reason he had got injured at Headcorn, possibly he had been the one who had broken into the staff room, injured his face in doing so, stolen the coat and hat then left with the takings from the raffle, plus a bottle of whisky. That added up – but did it? There wasn't any blood found in the staffroom, and there hadn't been any signs of a break-in.

The final items from the bin were copies of the *Herald* and the *Argus*, the *Herald* dated the 28th of August. The headline on the *Herald* was about the plane crash and presumed loss of life of all onboard. There was a short byline by Miasma conjecturing that plane had been trying to escape from the police and had run out of fuel over the English Channel. The *Argus* dated weeks later showed a half-page photo of the wreckage of Du Marchon's plane hanging from the crane.

246

A Request

Buchanan surmised that it had been Alan Dale who had broken into the staffroom and been injured somewhere. He had stopped at the DGH to get treatment for his head injury then driven on to Litlington, possibly stopping somewhere on the way at a Tesco mini-market for provisions.

He was probably planning on staying at Belleview till his injuries had healed and he could go out without his injuries attracting attention. This might have worked had it not been for the arrival of Hoskins checking up on why the last month's rent hadn't been paid. So where had Alan Dale gone to earth?

He looked through his notes, found the registration number for the car the security guard at Headcorn had given him and did an on-line search for its details. All he could find was the name of the company that leased the car, Ashford Holdings, whose main office was in Battersea, London. Buchanan googled the company and found a phone number for them. He dialled the number and was surprised to get an answer by the third ring.

'Ashford Holdings, how may I help?'

'Ah, yes, I am trying to get in touch with the owner of one of the cars your company leases.'

'And may I ask why you are enquiring?'

'The driver ran into my car and then drove off.'

'Did you inform the police?'

Buchanan was about to say he was the police but thought he would see just how far he could get without saying.

'No.'

'May I suggest you direct your enquiries through the proper channels, sir? We only deal with the actual vehicle lease contracts.'

'Thank you, I will do just that,' said Buchanan, hanging up the call. An idea was forming in his mind, and for the first time since this whole mess had spilled into his lap, he could see an arm rising in the pond, the mist was clearing.

Next, he returned to his computer and googled company's house for Ashford Holdings. Nothing out of place, all returns filed on time. Not that it would do any good, but he took a note of the names of the directors.

His next call was to his friend Nathan Greyspear.

'Castlewood Club, how may I direct your call?'

'Yes, Jack Buchanan, is Sir Nathan available?'

'Do you have an appointment?'

'No, I'm a friend.'

'Oh, sorry, Mr Buchanan, I didn't recognise you. If you'll hold on a minute, I'll see if he is free.'

The sound of *sailing by* floated down the telephone line.

'Jack, how are you? What's up?'

'Why would something be up?'

'I know you, my friend.'

'Well, as a matter of fact there is a small favour I need to ask of you.'

'Why not come over and ask in person? Have you had lunch yet? The restaurant is quiet at this time of day.'

'Well, now you mention it….'

'Good, that's settled, I'll have André set a table for us. See you in thirty.'

Buchanan wondered if his friend Nathan would be quite so enthusiastic when he explained why he needed his help.

Before he left the office for Castlewood, he called Karen to say he was having a late lunch with Nathan Greyspear.

'I suppose you won't be hungry for dinner?'

'Probably not.'

'Fine, see you when I see you, don't be too late, we have an early start in the morning.'

◆

Buchanan parked in the visitor area of the club and went into the reception.

'Yes, sir, how may I help?'

'Jack Buchanan to see Sir Nathan.'

'One moment, please,' said the receptionist, tapping on his keyboard. 'Sir Nathan, I have Mr Buchanan in reception for you. OK.'

Looking back up at Buchanan he said, 'Sir Nathan says to go through to his office. I understand you already know where it is?'

'Yes, I do, thank you.'

Buchanan walked behind the reception desk and down the corridor to Greyspear's office. He knocked and entered.

'Jack, good to see you. Table will be ready in ten minutes. In the meantime, care for something to drink?'

Buchanan thought for a minute then said, 'Whisky and water, please.'

Greyspear pressed a button on his phone. A voice answered, 'Yes, Sir Nathan?'

'Could I have a Lagavulin with water and a large Prosecco in my office, please?'

'Yes Sir.'

'Well Jack, I presume this visit is more than just a social one?'

'I'm afraid it is. I'm stuck on a part of the investigation and wondered if you could help?'

'Try me.'

'It concerns a former soldier that we are eager to talk to.'

'Is he dangerous?' asked Greyspear.

'If he's the one responsible for the death of the Columbian drug-gang enforcer, I'd say yes, a very dangerous young man.'

'Shall we go through? Our table is ready,' said Greyspear, looking at a message on his desk phone.

'I'm ready,' said Buchanan.

◆

'I've put you in your private booth, Sir Nathan, the lunch menu is on the table'.

'Thank you, André.'

'Shall I bring the wine list?'

'Jack?'

Buchanan shook his head. 'I'm working, but a small glass of red is supposed to help with digestion.'

'We'll let you know when we're ready to order, André.'

'Certainly.'

'So, you think he is dangerous?'

'We suspect he cut someone's throat; the object of his deed was a suspected drug runner.'

'Was that the killing that happened at Appleton Equestrian Centre?'

'Yes, and I was a mere hundred feet away when it happened.'

'And you think it was this ex-Army lad? What's his name?'

'Alan Dale.'

'How could I help? I've been out of the services for several years.'

'I realise that, but you must have contacts, people you could ask?'

'Maybe, but who would I be asking and what would I be asking?'

'The person of interest did a four-year engagement, came out and seemed to just wander from place to place with no apparent form of income.'

'Does he have any family you could ask of his whereabouts?'

'There is an older sister who says she is concerned for his safety but doesn't quite show the requisite emotions for that.'

'What is the backstory?'

'Do you remember Colonel Victor Mountjoy?'

'How could I forget? Made a right ass of himself. Didn't I read something about him dying in a plane crash with the pilot, Du something or other?'

'That's him. The lad I am after, Alan Dale, was one of Victor's cohorts and we think he is vying to take over whatever fiefdom Du Marchon was operating, even to the point of murdering a Columbian drug-gang enforcer.'

'I'm sorry, Jack, but I don't see how I can help?'

A Request

'Earlier today, I tried to track Alan Dale down using the known registration of the car he was driving. It was a leased car, so I called the leasing agency and had the most bizarre phone call I have ever had.'

'I've had my share of them as well.'

'I got the impression that Ashford Holdings was a front for something.'

'Jack, you see conspiracies under every table. When will you ever relax?'

'When I'm six feet under.'

'That's one way. How far have you got with the investigation?'

'Our forensics team scoured the house where he'd been staying, not a trace, not even a partial fingerprint. Yet everyone else who stayed in the house left plenty of fingerprints and ample amounts of DNA.'

The conversation was interrupted by the arrival of André.'

'Are you ready to order, Sir?'

'Jack?'

'Could I have the duck with a side salad, please?'

'I'll have the same, and would you bring a bottle of the twenty-fifteen Lafite.'

'Yes, Sir.'

'Jack, you were saying?'

'It seems like everywhere this lad has gone he leaves no trace, he's a virtual invisible man.'

'And you think I can help you make him visible?'

'If you wouldn't mind, just a whisper in the relevant ear. I need to catch this individual before he starts a one-man war.'

'I'll do what I can and hope I'm not opening a can of worms.'

'If you do, I'll bury them on my allotment.

19

Amsterdam

Buchanan pulled the front door closed, put the key in the deadlock and turned the key. Satisfied the house was secure, he and Karen started walking towards the station and the train to Gatwick for their flight to Amsterdam. He was still thinking about yesterday's conversation with Nathan Greyspear, and his friend's reaction to what he said. Was he opening a can of worms, would he be burying something or someone before the case was over?

'C'mon, Jack, stop your daydreaming, we've a train to catch.'

The train at six forty-eight on a Saturday morning was near empty and they arrived at Gatwick in plenty of time to have breakfast before the short flight to Amsterdam.

By the time the plane had reached cruising altitude, Buchanan had drifted off into a deep sleep. The bump as the wheels touched the Amsterdam runway woke him.

'We've landed.'

'Yes. How was your nap?'

'Strange, I was riding a horse and it jumped into a river. When we got out there was a stranger on the shore, I recognised him but couldn't remember his name – he had a letter for me.'

'Did you read it?'

'Yes, but the only thing I remember is that the information contained in the letter was secret and if revealed could endanger the life of the person who handed it to me.'

'You silly pudding, don't you realise what the dream was about?'

'No.'

'Do you remember what you were watching on television a few nights ago? You remember, you said, *he was fit?*'

'Of course, the John Le Carré television mini-series, *The Night Manager*.'

'Good, now we have that settled, maybe you will join me for Klaus and Irene's wedding.'

They walked down the aisle behind the other travellers, through the arrivals hall to the luggage carousel and their suitcase.

As they stood in line for the hotel shuttle, Buchanan asked, 'What time is the wedding set for?'

'We need to be at the hall for two o'clock, and don't forget we are an hour ahead here in Amsterdam.'

'Then we need to get our skates on. Shall we just get a taxi to the hotel?'

'That's fine by me.'

◆

'Welcome, Mr and Mrs Buchanan. Have you stayed with us before?'

'Two years ago,' said Karen, 'we were here with Viking River Cruises.'

'Was that the Tulip and Windmill cruise?'

'Yes, it was.'

'But you're not with Viking this time?'

'No, we're here for a wedding.'

'And it's just for this evening?'

'Yes, unfortunately my husband is busy at work and can't afford to take time off just now.'

'Well, I hope you will come back and stay with us soon. Here are your room keys? Your room is on the fifth floor, the elevator is just across the lobby.'

'One thing,' said Buchanan, 'could you arrange for a taxi for us? We need to be at the wedding venue by no later than half past one.'

'Certainly, if you give me the address of the venue, I will arrange that for you.'

◆

The Jockey's Wife.

'I'm glad you thought to book a taxi,' said Karen, as they entered the country barn and were greeted by a uniformed policeman.

'Goedemorgen meneer en mevrouw.'

'Good morning, Sergeant.'

'Ah, you must be Inspector Buchanan?'

'Ja – yes, we're friends of Klaus and Irene.'

'Hello, let me show you to your seat.'

'That must be their children,' said Karen, nodding to two young girls in the front row.

'Yes, my how they've grown.'

The ceremony was a simple one, exchange of vows, a blessing from the pastor and a cheer from the assembled guests.

Klaus and Irene, along with their children, stood outside in the sunshine for the photos while the barn was reset for the celebration meal.

Buchanan waited till the photos had been taken, family and friends said their congratulations and the children had gone off to play with their friends before he took Karen over to meet the bride and groom.

'Klaus, Irene, what a glorious day for you both.'

'Yes, it is,' said Irene, 'and under much better circumstances for us. Hello Karen, thanks for coming.'

'Thanks for inviting us. Klaus's daughters look lovely in their bridesmaids' dresses.'

'Don't they just! I made the dresses for them, adapting ones we purchased in the shops.'

'Really? They do look wonderful.'

'Thanks.'

'How are you finding living in Amsterdam?'

'It's a bit of a change from Eastbourne, but I must admit I love the shopping and all the restaurants and cafés. What is there not to like? You must come and stay with us; I'll show you round the shops.'

'I'd love that, but Jack might put up a protest.'

'Oh, you don't have to worry about me, I'd find something to keep my mind occupied.'

'I'm sure you would,' said Karen. 'You'd probably be down the station helping Klaus find criminals.'

'She knows me too well, Klaus. How are you doing?'

'Wonderful, it's been chaotic these last few weeks getting ready, but now the day has arrived we relax. And you? How are you, working on anything back home?'

'Klaus, you said you'd behave and not talk shop,' said Irene.

'That's all right, Irene. I did have a question for Klaus, but that can wait for later.'

'Quite so,' said Karen.

'Will you be going away for a honeymoon, Irene?' asked Karen.'

'No, the girls have school and Klaus is busy with work. We felt that since we've both been married before, a traditional honeymoon wasn't quite right. But we will get away for a week later in the year.'

'I'm glad to hear that.'

'I was wondering,' said Irene, 'since we are not having a formal wedding meal, would you and Jack like to join us for a late lunch?'

'Certainly, what time?'

'One-thirty, I'll give you directions to the restaurant.'

◆

By two o'clock most of the guests had left and Klaus, seeing Buchanan standing on the bridge over the canal looking at the plethora of padlocks fastened to the side netting, wandered over to have a chat.

'So, Jack, you had a question for me?'

'Is it safe, will our wives find us talking and tell us off?'

'I doubt it. The last I saw of them Karen was reading to the girls while Irene was writing directions for Karen to find the freshest tulip bulbs.'

The Jockey's Wife.

'In that case, I was wondering if Amsterdam and Rotterdam were still the drug import destinations of choice?'

'Unfortunately, yes. Though recently we have seen a rise in alternative means of transportation. You may have read of two recent cases of sailing yachts being apprehended in the Atlantic Ocean off the Portuguese coast. Total value of both hauls was in excess of one hundred and fifty million Euros.'

'How about incoming airfreight?'

'Not any amount that we are aware of. Why the interest?'

'I have a suspicion that I have uncovered a fledgling drug-smuggling route using small aircraft to dropship significant quantities of drugs into the UK.'

'How far have you got with the investigation?'

'That depends on the scope of the operation. My involvement began when a Columbian enforcement agent called Juan Carlos Barrera was found with his throat cut at the stables owned by one of the cohorts in the smuggling operation. Though the suspect only played a minor role in the smuggling operation.'

'Have you arrested him? I assume the suspect is a male?'

'Oh, yes, ex-Army. He's currently on the run, but I believe he's staying somewhere local.'

'That would account for the method used in dispatching the Columbian.'

'That is what I had reasoned.'

'Yes, that does make sense. But I see my lovely wife pointing at her watch which means she wants to go. I think she promised the girls a trip on a water taxi before lunch.'

'Fine, we'll catch up later at the restaurant.'

◆

'Penny for your thoughts,' said Buchanan, looking at Karen across the breakfast table.

'Oh, just thinking how different it is here, not just that we are in Amsterdam, it's the hustle and bustle of city life, so different from where we live. The busiest our village gets is with the morning school run to Pevensey and Westham Primary School and the occasional noisy maintenance train.'

'Would you prefer to live here?'

'No,' she said, shaking her head. 'I do enjoy visiting cities like Amsterdam, London and of course Glasgow, but I love where we live – it's home.'

'Talking of home, are we still going to look for tulip bulbs before we leave?'

'Yes, Irene said there are lots of places to look alongside the canals and there are coffee shops if you wish to sit and think while I wander.'

'In that case, we can leave our suitcase with left luggage in the hotel and collect it when we come back for the courtesy bus to the airport.'

◆

As they were crossing the arrivals' hall, Karen's mobile rang.

'Hello? Oh, Jill, wait a minute, I'll put you on speaker – OK, Jack's listening.'

'Sorry to do this, but the doctor said I need to rest for a few days.'

'Is the baby all right?' asked Karen.

'Yes, baby's doing fine. It's just my body is taking time to adjust. The new medication the doctor prescribed is starting to work and I should be back at work by the end of the week.'

'Jill,' said Buchanan, 'take whatever time off is necessary. It's going to be a quiet week; I'll manage on my own.'

'Are you sure?'

'Yes, I'm sure.'

'OK, thanks.'

20

Castlewood Surprise

Monday morning, Buchanan was seated in his office drinking his first coffee of the day. He'd just dropped his car off at Eastbourne Tyres to have a slow puncture repaired. He looked across at the empty desk where Street usually sat and once again wondered how he would get on without her to bounce ideas off. Then another thought hit him: suppose the powers that be decided he needed a replacement, what would he get? Probably some cadet straight out of university, full of knowledge and zero experience.

When Buchanan joined the police, he learned the hard way, walking the beat, through the night in all weathers. He shrugged and picked up Friday's *Herald*. He'd tried looking at it on-line, but found he ended up reading pop-up adverts thinking it was part of the article.

A street fight where a young man suffered head wounds. A family worried about scratching and squeaking sounds coming from a cavity wall in their rented accommodation had them calling pest control. On page six he saw that a car had driven into the plate-glass window of his local Tesco store; apparently this was not the first time this had happened.

On a good note, a local charity, Bramber Bakehouse, a charity that helped survivors of human trafficking, had been awarded the Queens Award for Voluntary Service.

By nine-fifteen he had read enough of the *Herald* and decided it was time to get on with his report about the killing of Barrera, but first he needed to go and collect his car.

◆

'Excuse me, sir, I have a message for you,' said the desk sergeant, as Buchanan returned to the police station.

'And the message is?'

'Would you contact Sir Nathan Greyspear at your earliest convenience?'

'Thanks. When was it received?'

'The message was phoned in about five minutes ago.'

'Thank you, I'll call him from my office.'

Buchanan entered his office wondering why Nathan hadn't called him on his mobile, then he saw why: his mobile was still sitting on his desk where he had left it. He picked it up and saw he had three missed calls. But before he could return Nathan's call, his phone rang.

'Buchanan. Oh, hello Karen – he did, when was this? – I just got back from taking my car in to get the slow puncture in the front tyre fixed – yes, there was a message at the front desk for me to call him – OK, see you at dinner time.'

Nathan answered at first ring. 'Jack, glad you called. Any chance you could stop by? There's someone here who would like to have a word with you.'

'Is this anything to do with what we discussed on Friday?'

'Yes.'

'Can't they come to the phone?'

'They could, but it would be better if you spoke with them in person.'

'At the club?'

'Yes.'

'Give me thirty minutes and I'll be with you.'

♦

At nine-thirty on Monday morning the club carpark was almost devoid of cars. As Buchanan turned into a parking slot, he noticed a familiar registration number, HEL1N, the ACC's car.

'Good morning, Inspector,' said the receptionist, as Buchanan approached the reservation desk, 'Sir Nathan said for you to go straight through to the library.'

'Thanks, I know the way.'

Buchanan retraced his steps, passed the grand staircase, turned left, and walked along the photo gallery to the doors to the library, wondering why his boss, Helen Markham, would be here on a Monday morning.

A sign on the library door said it was closed for a private function. He opened the door and went in. A fleeting memory of the first time he met Cynthia surfaced. He was seated in front of the fire, reading. She walked into the library, busy chatting on the phone to – was it Marjorie? He didn't remember, but he did remember the whirlwind that was Cynthia Mountjoy, now Mrs McCall.

No Cynthia this time, just his friend Nathan Greyspear, standing with his back to the fireplace, coffee mug in hand, talking to an individual seated in the Chesterfield armchair on the left, Buchanan could only see the crossed legs. There was another individual seated in the righthand Chesterfield. Nathan Greyspear certainly was the lord of his manor.

As Buchanan walked across the library floor Nathan looked away from his companion and said, 'Jack, come in, sorry to drag you away from your busy day, but I felt in the circumstances it was necessary.'

As he got closer, the occupant of the seat on the left leaned forward and smiled at Buchanan. 'Good morning, Jack, thanks for coming at such short notice.'

'All in a day's work for a policeman.'

Just what was she doing here, wondered Buchanan and who was the other individual, still seated with his face concealed by the wings on the Chesterfield.

'Good morning, Helen.'

'Something to drink, Jack?'

'Coffee would be fine,' said Buchanan, as he turned to look at the third member of the party. It was Alan Dale.

Buchanan was confused. Up till this moment he'd been under the impression that Alan Dale had been the one Rod at Litlington had seen at Belleview, complete with a bandaged face. But no, here was Alan Dale looking healthy without a scar on his face. So, who was the bandaged individual? And why did

Alan Dale look so familiar, could it have been the fact that Buchanan had been staring at his photo so often? No, it was something else, but what was it?

'What, why are you looking at me like that?' queried Alan Dale looking down at his shirt buttons.

'You realise I've been looking for you?' said Buchanan. 'I've chased your car's registration all the way from Headcorn to Litlington and back'.

'Yes, and it's been difficult keeping one step ahead of you. I was told you were good; I didn't realise just how good. I've had to change my car thanks to you plastering my description everywhere.'

'This really takes the cake, Nathan. I ask you to make discrete enquiries about his background and you not only find him, but here he is!'

'Jack,' began Greyspear, 'Alan is here by permission of his superiors with the understanding that what he has to say will not be divulged to anyone outside this room.'

Buchanan shook his head. 'Has he been granted immunity from prosecution?'

'That won't be necessary,' said Helen Markham.

'If you let me, I can explain,' said Alan, 'and why are you looking at me like that, you want to fight?'

'I expected you to have your face in bandages, and there's something else, something I can't quite put my finger on. Has your sister been providing you with a safe place to hide?'

'No, she doesn't need to.'

'Jack, it's not what you think,' said Markham.

'Can you give me one good reason why I shouldn't arrest you for the murder of Juan Carlos Barrera?' said Buchanan, as he stood in front of the seated Alan.

'Yes. I simply didn't do it.'

Buchanan's next question was prevented by a knock at the library door.

'I'll get it,' said Greyspear, 'it will be our drinks.'

Buchanan was puzzled. Neither Greyspear nor Markham appeared to be concerned that they may have a cold-blooded murderer sitting not ten feet from them.

'I'm not a murderer, and I did not kill Barrera,' said Alan Dale, as he reached over to the tray for his drink. 'In fact, his death has caused me a problem, yes a very big problem,'

'You have me totally confused,' said Buchanan,

'I can explain.'

'So, enlighten me, take me right back to the beginning. How did you become part of Du Marchon's organisation?'

'I never really was part of Du Marchon's organisation. It all began during my last year's engagement with the Army. I had a look around for what I could do in Civy Street but didn't find anything that took my fancy.

'In the Army you don't get to watch much television, or go to many movies, so I read a lot. One of my favourite authors was John Le Carré, but it wasn't till I was home on leave at my sister's, that I saw the television series based on his book, *The Night Manager*. That was when I got the idea of leaving the Army to work in some sort of capacity in the security industry. I talked to the discharge advisor, and he suggested I try the National Crime Agency.

'It took a while, there was an aptitude test, interviews, background checks, I'm sure with you being a policeman you will know about those sorts of things. Well, anyway, I applied but it was suggested that I might like to work undercover for the National Crime Agency instead. I thought, why not? I was given specialist training and sent out to do the will of my masters.'

'Do you work alone, or part of a team?'

'I've been part of a team following Barrera to find out just how widespread his network was.'

'And Colonel Mountjoy?'

'That was easy. I was still in the Army at the time and was transferred to the Adjutant General's office. My orders were to keep an eye on Colonel Victor Mountjoy. My cover was to be his driver.'

'And what did you observe the Colonel get up to?'

'Not a lot really. He had a routine of going regularly to London on business. Due to his rank, he was permitted to stay in hotels and eat out while attending court. But instead of staying in one hotel, he would dash off home on the train and book his expenses of staying in a hotel. He had a friend from way back who worked as a barman in one of the more upmarket hotels who would supply him with falsified receipts in exchange for cash backhanders.'

'But that would only amount to chicken feed, a few thousand pounds a year at most.'

'I also observed him selling fairly large quantities of cocaine to known dealers on more than one occasion.'

'Do you know where got the cocaine from?'

'That took a bit of doing. Towards the end of my stint as Mountjoy's driver, I told him that I would soon be leaving the service and was looking for something to do to make money. I said I wasn't interested in an office job or working in a factory, nor was I fussy where the money came from.'

'What did he say?'

'Nothing, at least nothing for a couple of weeks. Then, I think it was a Tuesday morning and we were stuck in traffic on the M25, he wanted to know if I still played music and was I interested in managing a guest house that he and a friend ran.'

'What did you say to that offer?'

'I shrugged and asked for more information?'

'What did he tell you?'

'He said the guest house was in the quiet secluded village of Litlington. My duties would be to maintain the house and keep the rooms fresh for the occasional guests who came to stay. He already knew about Daniel and me playing live music as a duo. He asked, if in exchange for full board, free booze, and women, would we like to be the resident musicians? He sweetened the deal by saying we would be paid in cash.'

'Did you accept?'

'I played it cool, I said I wasn't sure if I should get Daniel involved, so I said I'd get back to him. I tell you; he wasn't very impressed with that answer. I think he expected I'd jump at the opportunity; He gave me the impression he didn't like it when people didn't immediately say yes to him. Well, I talked it over with Daniel and he said why not? I still feel bad that I involved Daniel in the scheme.'

'Daniel didn't know you were working for the NCA?'

'No.'

'So, what happened next?'

'Victor had me drive him down to Litlington and that was when I was introduced to Julian Du Marchon.'

'What were you and Daniel expected to do during the time you weren't playing music for the guests at the parties?'

'Keep the house and garden tidy. Always make sure the bedrooms were available to visitors.'

'Were there many visitors?'

'No, on average, maybe one a month.'

'Same person each time?'

'No.'

'How about nationality?'

'Mostly European and Central American.'

'How often did Barrera visit?'

'I saw him there three times during my stay.'

'Do you know what the purpose of his visits were?'

'He was an enforcer for one of the Columbian drug gangs.'

'What was meant by the message, *J and V, I'm here to collect what is owed, I'll return soon, have it ready, JCB*?'

'Barrera showed up at the house, said he hadn't been paid for the previous two shipments.'

'When was this?'

'Just before Victor and Julian had planned to do their disappearing act.'

'What was the plan?'

'Victor and Julian had gone to Castlewood Country Club to take place in a horse race. He called me and said I was to bring his briefcase and meet them at Headcorn aerodrome. I was then to drive him to his house to collect a case that he'd left behind, then return to Headcorn.'

'What was in the briefcase you left with your sister?'

'It was gilts that he and Julian had purchased to launder their drug money. It was obvious to me that even though they were involved jointly in their criminal enterprise, they didn't trust one another. Victor had Julian sign the gilts, requiring only Victor's signature to cash them. Julian then locked them away in the briefcase then gave them to me to keep safe.'

'What happened to the briefcase?'

'I gave it to my sister. I told her as long as neither Victor, nor Julian, knew she had them, I would be safe, I said it was my security.'

'What did she do with the briefcase?'

'I believe she still has it somewhere in her flat.'

'The security guard at Headcorn said you were observed standing beside your car the night Julian, Victor and Daniel landed for refuelling. You were there to collect Victor?'

'That's correct, but he never showed up. Apparently when the police arrived, Julian and Victor took off again, and I suppose you know the rest.'

'Were you aware that Daniel was in the plane with Julian and Victor?'

'Yes, it was a shame what happened to him. Daniel had talent as a keyboard player. I used to tell him to get away from Julian and Victor, I said they were no good for him.'

'In what way? I thought you said when there were parties at Belleview you two supplied the music?'

'Oh yes we sure did, and as I also said, we got paid handsomely for it. Problem was Daniel got hooked on cocaine, and Julian knew it. Daniel was trapped, death would have come calling for him sooner or later.'

'You never touched it?'

'No, never, booze was the worst thing I ever indulged in.'

'Where did the cocaine come from?'

'That was what I was working on. I'd got as far as finding out Julian used to teach air navigation in his Cessna, sometimes at night. His cover was, he would fly to Amsterdam late in the afternoon with a student, then fly back using instruments as the sun was setting. He had several legitimate students who he was teaching, then when there was a drug drop to do, he would take Daniel with him.'

'What part did Daniel play in the operation?' asked Buchanan.

'He would take the packages of drugs from whoever delivered it, sit in the back passenger seat and when the plane was over Belleview, Daniel would open the luggage door and push the drugs out. Julian would do a couple of low-level circuits round the house and when Victor radioed that the package had been picked up, Julian would then fly on to Headcorn where I would pick him up and drive him back to the house.'

'The night Julian and Victor tried to do their disappearing act, did you break into the Headcorn staffroom and steal a jacket, cash, and a bottle of whisky?

'No, why would you think I would do that?'

'You were in a hurry; you dropped your phone.'

'Is that what happened to it?'

'Yes. I had it examined, sim card calls listed, and DNA samples taken. Did you know how valuable DNA can be in police work?'

'Yes, I am aware of that.'

'As part of our investigation into the death of Barrera, we took many DNA samples, including your sister's.'

'And you're about to tell me Ashley isn't my sister, is that it?'

'Correct.'

'So, who do you think she is?'

'I think you already know the answer to that; and there is something else I know that you don't.'

'So, we all have our little secrets? All right, Ashley isn't my sister, she's actually my mother. She told me that a long time ago, but since everyone knew us as brother and sister, we just let them go on thinking that.'

'Did she say who your father was?'

'She told me she wasn't really sure; she only said it was a soldier she met at a party. Well actually, she said it could have been any one of three soldiers.'

'And you never tried to find out who your father was?'

'How could I? Ashley refused to talk about it any further.'

'Thank you for being so open about it.'

'So, I've told you who I work for, and my side of the events, how about you fill me in with your side of the story?'

'Coffee anyone?' interrupted Greyspear.

'Good idea,' said Markham, 'and I could do with a break.'

◆

The waiter brought the coffee, placed the tray on the table then closed the library door behind him.

'Are you ready, Jack?' asked Markham, as Buchanan put his cup down on the table. He nodded.

'On Saturday the twenty-second of August, on the night of the Castlewood ball, Du Marchon, Mountjoy and Sanderson took off from Castlewood. As you already told us, Victor had previously arranged for you to pick him up at Headcorn, and you were to drive him the short distance to the stables at Paddock Wood so he could collect the cash he had embezzled from his investors. He wasn't able to meet up with you – which means it is probably still somewhere at Appleton.

The Jockey's Wife.

'Du Marchon landed at Headcorn, but unknown to Victor, Cynthia Mountjoy had cancelled all his credit and debit cards. On top of that I had arranged with the Kent police to go and meet the plane and arrest Du Marchon and Victor and anyone else in the plane when it landed.

'Du Marchon taxied the plane up to be refuelled, Victor got out and was told he had to get the payment for fuel pre-authorised, and that was when he found out that his cards were no use. So, at the sound of the approaching police, Du Marchon got spooked, started the port engine, and commenced to taxi at speed out to the runway.'

'Well, in that case, who do you think cut Barrera's throat?'

'A very good question, Alan. Initially I had you down as the slasher, but now, listening to your side of the story, I'm quite content that you had nothing to do with Barrera's death. But can you think of who the bandaged individual was who was seen at Belleview?'

'No, sorry.'

'From interview statements and evidence gathered, this individual was also at Headcorn the same night. He is suspected of stealing a green bomber jacket, a bottle of whisky, a large amount of cash and a baseball cap. The baseball cap is the only item we have been able to recover. With your investigations, Alan, can you think of anyone who would fit the bill?'

'No. Julian and Victor ran the operation by themselves.'

'What about the name Andrew Jackson? Do you know him? He's a major in the Adjutant General's office.'

Alan shook his head, and laughed. 'I report directly to him, Andrew Jackson is my boss.'

'I thought he was a lawyer?'

'He is – amongst other things.'

'So, who the hell is the bandaged man?' said Buchanan. 'Alan, you said there were other visitors to Belleview, can you describe them for me? I'm particularly interested in a male, thick set, about five foot eleven, grey-brown hair?'

'Hmm, that could describe any number of individuals that come from Central America. Did you check to see if Barrera came with anyone else on his last trip?'

'We're sure he came alone.'

'Satisfied, Jack?' asked Markham.

'I suppose I'll have to be.'

'Before you go,' said Markham, 'you'll need to sign this.' She placed a sheet of paper in front of him.

'What's this?' he said, picking it up to look at it. 'The Official Secrets Act?'

'Yes, Alan has shared information that could be prejudicial to the case he is working on.'

'Well, I suppose there has to be a first time for everything.'

◆

Instead of driving straight home, Buchanan drove to the marina to have further words with Ashley Dale.

He rang the doorbell and as he waited he wondered if Alan had called Ashley to say that Buchanan might come back to ask questions. His ponderings were interrupted by the sounds of the locks being undone on the front door.

'Oh, Inspector Buchanan, I didn't expect to see you back so soon. Is everything all right?'

'Yes, all is well. Could I come in for a minute?'

'Yes, certainly.'

Buchanan followed her through into the sitting room.

'Can I get you something to drink?'

'A coffee would be nice.'

'How do you take it?'

'Just black.'

'Fine, take a seat.'

While he waited for his coffee, Buchanan formulated the line of questioning he was going to take.

'Your coffee. I wasn't sure if you wanted a biscuit – so I brought some anyway.'

'Thanks. Ashley, when was the last time you saw your brother Alan?'

'A couple of months ago, but I have already told you this.'

'Can you be more specific?'

Buchanan watched her eyes as she contemplated her answer, she was searching for just the right words.

'Yes, it was a Saturday – not sure of the date. Alan arrived about nine o'clock in the evening with the small briefcase.'

'And you haven't heard from him since?'

'No.'

'What kind of car does Alan drive?'

'I think it's a BMW.'

'Model and colour?' said Buchanan, taking out his notebook.

'It's a blue two-door model. I don't know anything about the engine or the model number.'

'You said you don't remember the date of the last time you saw him. How about phone calls? When was the last time he phoned you, or you phoned him?'

She sighed and her shoulders dropped. 'He called me this evening, just before you got here.'

'What did he say?'

'He said he was still trying to keep safe and that he'd mentioned to you that I was his mother and to expect a visit from you.'

'Has he been staying here with you?'

'No, and that's the truth.'

'Thank you for being frank, Ashley. Now, would you like to tell me the name of Alan's father?'

'I think you already know that.'

'Nonetheless, I'd like to hear it from you.'

'Victor Mountjoy. But how did you know?'

'I didn't till I saw Alan's face and his hair. I expect if we had something of Victor's, something he had touched, DNA would confirm the relationship. Of course, I would also require something of Alan's as well.'

'I can get you those if it would help Alan.'

'What do you have?'

'Alan's toothbrush – the real one – and a letter Victor sent just before he ran out on me.'

'That would work.'

'Wait here, I'll go and get them.'

Finally, thought Buchanan. The penultimate piece of the jigsaw was about to be placed on the table.

'Here, will this do?' she said, handing Buchanan a well-used toothbrush and an envelope with her name and address handwritten on the front with a German postage stamp. 'As soon as he heard I was pregnant he got himself transferred to Germany, the letter was supposed to be some kind of sop. Go on, you can read it.'

'Before I do, do you have a couple of Ziplock bags to put them in?'

'Certainly, but why? Both our DNA will be on the envelope and toothbrush.'

'Forensics already has mine; they will simply note that in their report. When you get the Ziplock bags, would you take an unused one and place it in its own bag, that way we have a definite sample of yours.'

As Ashley left to get the Ziplock bags, Buchanan carefully extracted the letter from its envelope. The contents consisted of a single sheet of A5 paper with a regimental crest on the top and two five-hundred Euro notes. Buchanan could just make out the handwriting in the note,

Ashley, I've been posted, here's some money to take care of the issue, Victor.

'He expected me to have an abortion,' said Ashley, handing Buchanan a Ziplock plastic bag for the letter.'

'Does Alan know who his father was?'

'I never said, but I think he had a friend in the Army do some checking for him.'

'So, he does know about Victor being his father?'

'Yes, I think he does.'

'Why didn't you ever contact Victor for some sort of support? It couldn't be easy to raise a child on barmaid wages.'

'You read the letter. He didn't want to know, and I didn't want to have anything to do with him after that. Besides, shortly after Alan was born, my parents died. They were quite well off and I inherited their house and some investment income.'

'The gilts. Is that why you gave them to me to keep safe for Alan, so that one day the father who abandoned him would make financial restitution?'

'Yes.'

'I'm not sure it will be that simple.'

'Why?'

'I can see several reasons, the first being that Victor was married at the time of his death and the widow will probably have a claim on them. Then there is the Proceeds of Crime Act. If the National Crime Agency decides that those gilts were purchased as a result of crime, the gilts could be confiscated.'

'Oh, I didn't realise that. But it was years ago, surely there has to be some sort of statute of limitations that covers the confiscation of money like this?'

'I can't answer that, but I do know someone who possibly could.'

'Would you talk to them, please?'

'I will, but in the meantime, I need to get these samples of to the lab for testing.'

♦

'A good day?' asked Karen, as Buchanan stepped out onto the patio.

'Yes, I do believe it was.'

'Getting anywhere with the case?'

'Yes, but there is still the issue of who killed Barrera, and where they fit into the puzzle.'

'I thought you had a suspect for his killing?'

'That's what I thought up till this afternoon.'

'What happened?'

'Do you remember me telling you about Ashley Dale?'

'Yes, the sister of the person you thought killed Barrera.'

'That's the one. Well, it turns out she's not his sister.'

'So, who is she?'

'She is his mother.'

'Do you remember the evening of Cynthia's wedding she took me away for a chat?'

'Yes.'

'Well, Cynthia told me when she and Victor were in their early years of marriage Victor got a barmaid pregnant and tried to get her to have an abortion.'

'Are you saying that barmaid was Ashley Dale, and Alan Dale is her and Victor's son?'

'Yes.'

'I wonder what Cynthia will have to say about that. Will you tell her?'

'I don't see what would be gained by it at this time. There may come a time when it becomes necessary.'

'Well, how about the gilts? With Victor being dead, Cynthia is the next of kin and should by all rights inherit them. Or at least half of them if what you say about Alan Dale is true. Does he know about the gilts?'

'Yes. Victor gave the gilts to Alan for safekeeping, and he gave them to Ashley, who subsequently passed them to me hoping that eventually Alan would inherit them from his dead father's estate. But there is a problem with the provenance of the gilts. If they were the result of criminal activity, the government could step in and confiscate them as part of the Proceeds of Crime Act.'

'Oh, that's a pity for young Alan.'

'It's life, Karen.'

'Well, since you mentioned Cynthia's name, she called earlier.'

'Did she say how they did at Cheltenham?'

'Yes, and that was part of the reason for her calling. She's invited us to come over for the weekend. She has also invited a cross-country expert to run a workshop on the Saturday afternoon.'

'Did she say who?'

'Someone called Monica Verdi.'

'Really? She's one of the top cross-country riders in the country.'

'That's Cynthia, only the best. You should feel right at home with some the other guests.'

'Oh, really, who are these other guests?'

'Marjorie and the Jacksons.'

'Andrew Jackson – the one we met at Castlewood?'

'Yes, that Andrew Jackson. Shall I call and accept?'

'By all means. I want to have a word with Major Andrew Jackson, but I will have to go into the office first thing tomorrow, I'm waiting for some DNA tests. Have you heard from Jill?'

'Yes, talked to her just before you got in. She said she is feeling much better and following the doctor's instruction to rest. She said not to worry she'll be at work on Monday morning.'

21
Cynthia's Dream.

'You won't be long, will you?' said Karen, as Buchanan left for the office.

'I'll be as quick as I can.'

He stopped at the newsagents for his copy of the *Herald* then went on to Starbucks. At seven o'clock in the morning, Buchanan was first in line for his coffee. He declined to purchase a cinnamon roll and left for the office feeling Karen would be pleased about his denying himself a Saturday morning treat.

He placed his folded copy of the *Herald* in the in-tray for reading on Monday and turned on his computer. The email from Henry Littlejohn, head of forensics, was there waiting for him. Attached was a message, *Call me when you get this missive, and I'll translate it for you.*

Buchanan looked at the time and called Littlejohn.

'Henry, it's Jack, just got your message.'

'Want me to come by? I'm in my office?

'That would be helpful.'

'See you in twenty minutes.'

While he waited for Littlejohn, Buchanan sipped on his coffee and googled the name Monica Verdi. He was impressed, Monica Verdi was not only a multiple medal and trophy winner; she also ran workshops for professional and amateur riders plus special workshops for disadvantaged children.

The sound of footsteps in the hall announced the arrival of Littlejohn. Buchanan smiled when Littlejohn entered the office, he was holding a coffee in his right hand and a bag of fresh doughnuts in his left.

'Ah, a man after my own heart,' said Buchanan, realising his no treat on Saturday resolve was dissolving.

'I stopped for petrol and saw them at the checkout stand.'

'Jam, my favourite,' said Buchanan, looking at the label on the doughnut bag.

'I see you've printed a copy of the email; anything make sense to you?'

'Bits, but I'd appreciate if you'd explain it in more detail, especially the spreadsheet.'

'Sure, be delighted to,' he said, licking the last of the jam from his fingers. 'I've put all the details into an Excel spreadsheet. In the left-hand column, in alphabetical order, I've listed names of individuals. Across the top, I've put items such as newspapers, items of clothing, and personal bits and pieces. This will enable you to track where people have been and who has been at the same place or touched the same item. For instance, the two Dales, Ashley and Alan, have their DNA show up at the house Belleview, on the gilt sample you gave me, and the toothbrush.'

'Pity it doesn't tell when they last touched them.'

'Maybe someday DNA testing will give us those details.'

'That would be good.'

'I have also done a relationship comparison of the DNA samples from the letter and toothbrush and the gilt you gave me, and very interesting it was. Did you realise they would be related?'

'Yes, I just needed the proof.'

'Mother, father and son, why are you interested in them?'

'The mother is Ashley Dale; the son is Alan Dale, and the father was Colonel Victor Mountjoy.'

'Mountjoy, didn't I read something in the *Herald* about him drowning in the Channel when the plane he was in crashed?'

'The very same.'

'What a way to go.'

'Now this is very interesting, 'said Buchanan. 'If the plane Victor Mountjoy was a passenger in crashed on the 22nd of August, how come his DNA was found on a copy of the *Herald* the Friday after the plane crashed? Where else does his DNA show up?' he asked, scanning the spreadsheet.

'Just follow his name across the spreadsheet.'

'You've certainly made my job easier with this. We may not know when the DNA was deposited, but we can work out a rough guide by dating the items touched.'

'So, if what you say is true, and I have explicit trust in the DNA testing, your Colonel wasn't on the plane when it crashed.'

'It does look like that. With the Colonel's DNA showing up on a newspaper weeks after he was supposed to have died in a plane crash, it now puts him in first place for killing the Columbian, Barrera.'

'So, you say when Barrera was grabbed from behind and had his throat slashed, he gouged skin from the back of the hands of his killer?'

'Yes, that was what Dr Mansell surmised when he scraped the undersides of Barrera's fingernails.'

'Well done, Andrew.'

'Are you available to take swabs of Barrera's body for further DNA testing, just to be sure?'

'Absolutely. It's not often I get to work on a live investigation, most times it's just cardboard boxes full of random detritus of someone's life.'

'I'll give Andrew a call.'

♦

'Well, you have your killer,' said Littlejohn, as they exited the forensics lab. 'The DNA evidence taken from under Barrera's fingernails is a definite DNA match with Victor Mountjoy. I also found traces of eschar in the deceased's hair and its DNA matched the DNA sample of Colonel Mountjoy. I'd say they came from a wound on the Colonel's face.'

'What's an eschar?'

'Scab. Do you know if he'd been injured?'

'Ah, this is now becoming clearer. The witness at Headcorn saw Victor Mountjoy standing on the wing trying to get back

into the cabin as it taxied away towards the end of the runway.
I'm now assuming Victor Mountjoy didn't make it all the way
back into the plane but fell off as it taxied, incurring the facial
wound.'

'What will you do now?'

'I suppose an arrest warrant for Victor Mountjoy, then see if
we can figure out where he has gone to earth. By now he is
running out of safe houses and resources.'

◆

Buchanan said goodbye to Littlejohn and drove home with a
lightness in his spirit that he hadn't felt since the beginning of
the case: he now had a suspect, a quarry to run to earth. As he
opened the front door, he saw Karen already had placed their
overnight bag by the front door in readiness to be loaded into
the car.

'Sorry I'm late, but something came up and I needed to deal
with it before I left.'

'You look like the cat that got the cream.'

'I feel it.'

'So, was Henry able to help?'

'In spades.'

'C'mon then, we're running late, you can tell me all about it in
the car.'

'Coffee? We go past Starbucks.'

'Do you get paid to advertise Starbucks?'

'No, why should I?'

'Because you seem to spend a lot of time and money there.'

'It's convenient for me. Also, it is a great place for a meeting
away from the office.'

'OK, I'll have a Frappuccino.'

◆

As they made their way back out onto the A259, Buchanan said,
'Victor Mountjoy is alive.'

'You mean his legacy lives on?'

'No, he really is alive. He never got back on the plane,' he said, shaking his head. 'Why I never saw that coming, I don't know. Maybe I should just give up and grow potatoes.'

'Jack, stop walking your dog.'

'You know me so well, don't you?'

'Thirty-six years next month.'

'Where have they gone? One minute we were walking hand in hand down Field Road to the Equis Café, and look at us now, off to see someone about a horse.'

'That's life. How about we celebrate next month when we go to Dallas to stay with Travis and Shelly?'

'Mrs Buchanan, we shall do just that.'

'So, tell me more about the case that's put the smile back on your face.'

'From our investigations it looks quite certain that Victor Mountjoy is alive. Our theory is, as Du Marchon taxied his plane out to the end of the runway, Victor, who was still struggling to get back into the cabin, fell off the wing. If Littlejohn is correct in his summation, Victor was hit in the face by the tail wing and ended up unconscious on the grass. Which neatly answers two questions.'

'Which are?'

'Firstly, the grass clippings in the blood sample, they were a specific combination used for aerodrome grass runways.'

'And the second one?'

'The second is the reason why Alan Dale left Headcorn without collecting Victor.'

'Why would Alan be waiting for Victor?'

'According to Alan, the arrangement he made with Victor was, while Du Marchon was refuelling, Alan was to drive Victor to Appleton Equestrian Centre and collect the cash he had stored away then return him to Headcorn.'

'Does Alan know his father is Victor Mountjoy?'

'Yes. I talked with Ashley Dale last night and she confirmed it.'

'Oh, dear. What will Cynthia and Pat do when they find out their marriage is bigamous? Do you think they will get in trouble over it?'

'I doubt it, especially if you consider the fact that it was the coroner who declared Victor dead.'

'So, what will happen? Cynthia can't be married to two men at the same time.'

'I imagine her marriage to Pat will be annulled till a divorce from Victor can be arranged, then they can get married again.'

'What a mess! He should have just stayed dead.'

'My sentiments exactly.'

'Do you have any idea where Victor is now?'

'If I had my way it would be behind bars; but no, I've no idea other than he has to be fairly close to Appleton stables.'

'I think it is inevitable you will have to tell Cynthia and Pat.'

'At some point I suppose I will have to, but not right now. I will have a chat with Andrew Jackson first, he's going to be there this weekend. If you remember he is a lawyer and a Major in the Adjutant General's office.'

'If what you say is true, and Victor is in fact alive, do you think he killed Juan Carlos Barrera?'

'Yes. Littlejohn found samples of Victor's DNA on the dead Columbian's body.'

'I wonder how Cynthia will take that bit of news?'

'Who can tell?'

'Will you ride today?'

'No, my dear, we don't own a horse.'

'What about Mercury? Nathan said you could ride him anytime you wanted.'

'Yes, he did, but getting Mercury to Appleton and back would be too much for him, and besides we neither have a horse trailer nor a hitch on the car.'

'Surely Cynthia would have let you ride one of theirs?'

'There is that possibility.'

'And if Cynthia insists on you going for a ride?'

'My dear, there is only one woman in my life that I will allow to insist on what I do.'

'I wonder who that might be?' she said, smiling at him.

'Besides, I'm not sure if I am up to it, I don't know if I could concentrate on what was being said. With all what's going on just now I need to keep my mind sharp on tracking down where Victor Mountjoy has gone to earth before he kills again.'

'You think it's likely that he will kill again?'

'It's a possibility, especially if he gets cornered and sees killing as his only way out. There's no death penalty in this country anymore, so life for killing one person is the same as if if you kill ten.'

'You think he might get that desperate?'

'There is the lure of all that cash, half a million would buy him a new identity and a place somewhere out of the limelight, ready to start over again.'

'Who is Monica Verdi?'

'Apparently, she has more medals and trophies than Steve Davis has potted centuries.'

'Steve Davis?'

'Snooker player,' said Buchanan, as he turned off Whetsted Road into the Appleton carpark.

'Wow, look at all those horseboxes, Monica Verdi must have quite a reputation to attract all these riders.'

'All the more reason for me to stay out of the saddle.'

'Don't put yourself down, you're a very good rider. The trophy for coming fourth in the Castlewood Cup on the mantelpiece proves that.'

'I wonder what old Jock would make of that?'

'Is he still around? He must be well into his seventies by now if he is still alive.'

'Yes, he is, and he's still got the stables in Busby. In fact, Nathan recently bought a horse from him. Shall we go and find Cynthia and Pat?'

The Jockey's Wife.

Buchanan removed their overnight bag from the boot and followed Karen round to the kitchen door. The kitchen was empty except for a young girl sitting at the counter eating a bowl of cereal and staring at an anatomy textbook. She was wearing headphones and humming along to a tune on her phone.

She looked away from her book, slid her headphones off her ear and said, 'They're all out in the barn waiting for Monica to wind up her lecture.'

'Thanks, but we're not here for the workshop,' said Karen.

'Oh, neither am I.'

'You're not interested in horses?'

'Monica is my grandmother; I've heard it all before, besides, I'm studying to become a nurse.'

'Lots of exams I bet.'

'I'm a first-year adult nursing student and this year we have one essay, then, we have an anatomy and physiology exam which is mostly multiple choice. Next, there's a practical exam where you must demonstrate different clinical skills. Finally, when we are on placement, we get graded on how well we got on. It really depends on the university.'

'Sounds like you have your work cut out for you.'

'I'll manage.'

'In that case, we shall leave you to get on with your studies.'

'Oh, wait a minute, are you the Buchanans?'

'Yes, why?' asked Karen.

'Cynthia said to let you know you are staying in the room you stayed in the last time you were here.'

'Thanks.'

'See you,' she said, sliding the headphone back over her ear.

'She'll go far,' said Buchanan, as they made their way up the stairs to their room.

'I'm sure you are right. Especially with the attitude she has. You go on, I'd like to freshen up first,' said Karen. 'I'll see you downstairs in a minute.'

'Fine, I'll go find Cynthia and let her know we've arrived.'

282

The barn doors were wide open, the riders attending the workshop were chatting while drinking coffee. Just inside the door of the barn there was a trestle table with plates of sandwiches and a large coffee urn. The chatter descended into a quiet murmur as their attention diverted to the person who'd just climbed up onto a low dais: Monica Verdi, thought Buchanan.

'Ladies and gentlemen, if I could have your attention, please? Jenny, can you please bring Candy back here to the ring? Thanks. Before I begin the final session, I'd like to thank you for your most interesting questions and attention this morning. I realise that starting at seven on a Saturday can be a bit daunting but, being associated with horses, early mornings are I'm sure something not uncommon for all of us.

'Before we head out to the exercise ring to put into practice what we have learned, I'd like to take a few moments to sum up what we have discussed this morning.

'The first event of the season is probably the most important one, and that goes for your horse as well. Over the years, I have found that during the off season, it is extremely helpful if you have kept active. If you have a dog, going for regularly walks is an excellent way of remaining fit. Another method of keeping fit is running, I knew one young mother who, to keep fit, pushed her baby in a pram round the local park every morning. Of course, if you can afford it, membership at a health club is probably one of the best ways to stay in shape.

'In the field I often hear the sound of horses making their way round the course and I can hear the sound of laboured breathing – and it's not the horse I hear. So, my advice to you is to get out there, regardless of the weather, and do some hill work, make your horse work off their winter lethargy.

'If you are fortunate to live anywhere near hills, you should have done some hill work, both up and down. Jumping a few low hedges, just enough at the beginning, helps your horse to remember what it learned the previous season.

'If your horse is really eager, he'll probably get fit quite easily and you'll probably want to teach him to settle, so fitness is important for both of you.

'One of the things I find when I get back on the horse at the beginning of the season, whether I've ridden during the winter or not, is that winter riding is a little bit sort of sterile and you and your horse may feel a little bit lethargic.

'Then when you come out onto the open and you start to jump cross-country you can feel a bit vulnerable and – who knows –– maybe our horses feel a bit the same. So, you really need to get stuck in and think of those three jobs that you as a rider have: the engine, the line, and the balance. Given the chance to really to see the fences, sit back and let your horse work his way out how he's going to jump.

'As I said earlier, you want to start with quite small fences, and gradually, you, the rider, will feel the cobwebs blow free and your head will clear. Your muscle memory with return and you will feel invincible, of course, you will need to help your horse feel this way as well. So now, let's go outside and put into practice what you've learned this morning.'

Buchanan stood back from the doors as the riders filed out and walked over to the exercise ring where their horses were patiently waiting for them.

'Are you sure you wouldn't like to be out there with them?' asked Karen, who'd just joined Buchanan.

'Castlewood was a one-off, my dear. If I do decide to ride again, it will be strictly for pleasure.'

'If you're sure.'

'I am. Now,' he said, looking at the time and the leftover food on the trestle tables, 'it's just gone one-thirty and I would like to sample some of that leftover food from the workshop and a cup of coffee. Or maybe sample some of Cynthia's whisky.'

'How about we take the food inside and wait for the workshop to be over?'

'Suits me.'

♦

Buchanan had just settled into the chair in the sitting room when a commotion coming from the kitchen had him returning to investigate. It was Marjorie, she was being helped onto a stool in the kitchen by two of the students.

'What happened? Is Marjorie all right?' asked Buchanan.

'Is she your wife?' asked one of the students.

'No, just someone I know, she's a friend of Cynthia, the owner of the stables – how is she?'

'She'll be all right, fell at the fifth fence, bumped her head on the top rail.'

'What happened?' asked Marjorie, as she blinked and felt for the pain in her neck.

'Apparently you fell off your horse,' replied Buchanan.

'How is he?'

'The horse?'

'Who else?'

'Cynthia collected him and put him in a stall,' said the other student. 'He's fine, just a bit startled to see his rider pass before his eyes. Are you sure you are all right?'

'Yes, I'm fine. I think I'll just go up to my room and lie down for a while.'

'I'll see you up the stairs,' said Karen.

As Marjorie, aided by Karen, made her way out of the kitchen, the student said, 'I think she should be fine after a rest; her helmet took most of the blow.'

'Thanks, we'll keep an eye on her.'

'OK, be seeing you.'

Alone in the kitchen, Buchanan returned to the coffee pot.

'Hello, Jack,' said Andrew Jackson, 'didn't see you at the workshop?'

'Oh, hello. No, you wouldn't have. We were invited for dinner to hear all about the honeymoon and Pat's debut ride at Cheltenham.'

'Good. Are you going to be riding today?'

'I may later – if Cynthia has her way. How was the workshop?'

'Brilliant, it's not every day one gets to be taught by one of the world's top cross-country teachers. Pity about the rider whose horse threw her, I wonder how she is?'

'Marjorie thinks she's fine. Karen has helped her up to her room. She's a friend of Cynthia's. She stays here at the stables when Pat and Cynthia are away.'

'Good.'

'Andrew, there's something I need to discuss with you, it is quite urgent.'

'OK – but can it wait till after I change?'

'Yes, of course it can wait, are you staying over as well?'

'Just this evening and for the workshop.'

'Perfect, I'll meet you here in the kitchen when you've changed.'

'How is she?' Buchanan asked, as Karen returned to the kitchen.

'As I left the room, she was resting with her eyes partially open and singing softly to herself.'

'What was she singing?'

'*Fly me to the moon.* I gave her a glass of water and two paracetamol tablets. I'll check back on her in twenty minutes. Are you sure you wouldn't have liked to have been involved in the workshop?'

'Under normal circumstances maybe, but with Victor running around the county I can't concentrate on anything else.'

'Suppose he's hiding somewhere local? You can't go knocking on doors asking if Victor Mountjoy is staying there.'

'I'm going to call Blakey and bring him up to date on my findings. I think we will need the services of his men to scour the area.'

'So, you think Victor is in this area, sleeping under the stars?'

'As long as he hasn't been able to get his hands on the cash he squirreled away, then my bet is he's possibly staying at a B&B, or under a hedge if his cash has been used up.'

'Is there any coffee left?' asked Andrew, as he returned to the kitchen.

'Yes,' said Karen. 'I'm just making a fresh pot; shall I pour you a cup when ready?'

'Yes please, just black, no sugar.'

'OK.'

'Where shall we go for this secret meeting you want, Jack?' asked Andrew.

'The barbeque area, there's no one there just now and it's quite a private area.'

'Fine, let's go before Pat and Cynthia return from saying goodbye to Monica.'

'Now, Jack,' said Andrew, as they walked towards the barbeque. 'What is it that we need to meet so clandestinely?'

'It's about Victor Mountjoy.'

'He's dead, drowned in the English Channel.'

'I'm afraid not. I received DNA evidence this morning that proves he was still alive a week after the plane crash.'

'So, what is your reason for telling me this?'

'He is also the father of Alan Dale.'

'Ah, that could be an issue.'

'I talked to Alan yesterday at Castlewood, my ACC was also there, along with Nathan Greyspear.'

'What did Alan have to say?'

'I'm not at liberty to say, I had to sign the Official Secrets Act,' said Buchanan, smiling. 'But I'm sure by now you know as much as I do.'

'So, what can I do to help?'

The Jockey's Wife.

'I need to catch Victor before he kills again. I believe Victor slashed Barrera's throat here at the stables last week, and I think he may be in the area attempting to recover a large quantity of cash he hid somewhere on the premises.'

'The killing is your department; the cash might be something of interest to the NCA if it involves drugs.'

'I think the cash is the result of Victor embezzling investors with bad advice, plus his share of the sale of illicit drugs.'

'So, what do you think happened if he didn't die in the plane crash?'

'That's an easy one to answer. It was dusk and at that moment there was a flock of police cars driving into the aerodrome with sirens blaring. He probably fell off the wing somewhere between the apron and the end of Headcorn runway, bleeding profusely from an injury when his head hit the tailplane.'

'He's lucky he didn't die falling off the plane like those unfortunate Afghans did when the Americans pulled out of Kabul.'

'Might have saved us a lot of trouble if he had. I have subsequently found out that Victor Mountjoy was to rendezvous with Alan, who was to drive him to his stables to collect a substantial quantity of cash that he'd embezzled.'

'That matches what Alan told me.'

'While Du Marchon was flying across the Kent and Sussex airspace, it is my conjecture that Victor came to, and made his way back to the aerodrome buildings. He probably thought, despite his injuries, he was quite fortunate not to have fallen off while the plane was in the air. As he walked across the airfield in the dusk, he would have been wondering if Alan would still be waiting for him to drive to the stables so he could collect the cash. But unknown to Victor at this moment Alan had seen the plane take off and decided, when he saw the police cars arrive, he would make himself scarce.'

'Part of his training, stay out of the limelight.'

'Victor, when he finally managed to get to where he was supposed to meet up with Alan, realised he would have to find somewhere to lie low till things quietened down so he could return and collect his cash from the stables.'

'I suppose that makes sense, especially if there was a lot of money involved.'

'There was, we estimated the sum was somewhere in the region of half a million pounds. So, while the police are the centre of attraction at the aerodrome, Victor breaks into the staffroom, steals a jacket, hat, whisky and cash, then makes himself scarce. He probably found the free taxi phone and called for a taxi to take him to the station.

'At Headcorn station he buys a ticket to Eastbourne. By the time he gets to Eastbourne, his wounds are bleeding again, and he decides to get a taxi to the DGH. At the DGH he tells the nurse that he had a motorcycle accident and hit a low branch on a tree. He gets fixed up then gets a taxi to take him to Belleview in Litlington.'

'A very resourceful individual.'

'Or a desperate one. He stays there till one day, we think the first of October, he left Belleview and made his way back to the squat in Eastbourne. There the trail goes cold.

'At some point, he contacted Barrera and arranged to meet at the stables on the tenth. He figured the noise of the wedding would give him sufficient cover to take care of Barrera and recover the cash from its hiding place.'

'So, a question. How did he know about the wedding?'

'He might have heard about it in a pub or read about it in the local newspaper. Or he could have talked to someone who was involved with the wedding.'

'Have Pat and Cynthia located the cash that Victor hid?'

'No, but not from lack of effort looking for it. Unfortunately for Victor, the night of the wedding reception, Cynthia's dog, Major, must have sensed something was wrong and scared him off.

'Having dealt with Barrera, Victor goes to earth once more. We're not quite sure where he was hiding. On the thirteenth, during his attempt at recovering his money, he attacked Marjorie. She was fortunate, she is a tough steel worker and was able to get the better of him.'

'Thanks for this information, Jack. It fills in quite a few blanks in our end of the investigation. Will you let me have sight of your report prior to you submitting it to your superiors?'

'Why?'

'Because I may have to ask you to redact sensitive information.'

'I see.'

'Now, I hadn't realised how far you'd got with your investigation, and I hope I haven't trodden on your toes over this, but I asked Alan to bring Ashley here this afternoon.'

'Why?'

'I am here to advise Pat and Cynthia's of their financial situation. But now, with what you have told me about Victor being alive, and his involvement with Ashley, I will have to rethink the advice I was about to render to them.'

'That makes sense.'

'Oh, there you are,' said Karen. 'Cynthia was wondering where you two have got to, they're in the sitting room.'

'In that case, shall we join them and tell them their news, Andrew?'

'Yes, let's get it over with.'

◆

'Cynthia, Pat, I have some disturbing news that I have to tell you,' said Buchanan.

'You're retiring and going to open a riding stable?'

'No, nothing like that, Cynthia. This has got to do with you and Pat both.'

'I don't like the sound of this. What are you up to, Jack?'

'Cynthia,' said Andrew. 'I'm sorry to say that Victor is alive.'

'But – but how can he be? He died in a plane crash.'

'Apparently not. According to what Jack has just told me Victor was here at the stables a week ago Saturday.'

'At the party?'

'No, not at the party,' said Buchanan, 'but here at the stables. We believe he arranged to meet Barrera here, possibly on the pretext to pay off an old debt. But instead he lured him here to kill him.'

'You think that was Victor? But does that mean Pat and I aren't married, or worse, we're bigamists?'

'I'll let Andrew answer that.'

'Pat and Cynthia, let me reassure you, you haven't broken any laws, and the way I look at it, you have not committed bigamy either. It may be necessary to temporarily annul your marriage to Pat, just until we arrange the divorce with Victor, which in my opinion will be a straightforward procedure.'

'What a mess. When I heard the news he'd died, I thought the worst was over,' said Cynthia.

'I'm afraid there's yet another act in this little drama,' said Buchanan.

'What more can there be? You've just told me my once dead husband is alive and running around slitting people's throats. Oh, my dream – don't tell me it's coming true?'

'Cynthia,' said Buchanan, 'do you remember the story you told me the evening of the party, the one about the early days of your marriage to Victor?'

'The story about the girl he got pregnant, the one he paid for to get an abortion?'

'That's the one.'

'So, what's she got to do with this situation?'

'She didn't get an abortion, her son is alive and healthy, and she would like to talk to you.'

'I suppose she wants compensation for raising his child, is that it?'

'No, nothing like that,' said Andrew.

'I don't know about that; I think I'm going to be too busy for the foreseeable future.'

'That's a pity.'

'Cynthia,' said Pat, 'it might be better to hear what she has to say.'

'Oh, all right, tell her to call and make an appointment.'

'That won't be necessary,' said Andrew. 'I've asked her son to drive her here this evening.'

'Just what mischief have you two been cooking up?'

'Cynthia,' said Andrew, 'I thought that it would only be fair to invite her and her son to be here so I could explain the possible outcome of the disposition of the gilts.'

'What gilts?' asked Cynthia.

'Ah, you're not aware of that side of the story. There is more to this meeting than just getting acquainted. There is the small matter of about half a million pounds worth of gilts that Victor and his partner in crime, Julian Du Marchon, were planning to skip the country with. The gilts only required Victor's signature to have them turned into cash.'

'Half a million? Now I get it, she wants her share, is that it?'

'Not necessarily,' said Andrew. 'If Victor purchased them with the proceeds of criminal activity, the government may decide to confiscate them under the Proceeds of Crime Act.'

'So, the jerk has one last slap in the face for me.'

'There's also the fact that had Victor been dead, his son and you could have been in line to inherit the gilts.'

'When will they be here?'

Andrew looked at his watch. 'Any time now.'

'That makes eight for dinner. I'd better set a place at the table then.'

'I'll check in on Marjorie, then come and give you a hand,' said Karen.

'Anyone for a refill?' asked Pat.

Pat had just finished topping up Buchanan and Andrew's glasses when Major started growling.

'That will be Ashley and Alan,' said Buchanan. 'I'll go and let them in.'

'Bring them through to the sitting room,' said Pat. 'I'll let Cynthia know they have arrived.'

'Why are we here?' Ashley asked Alan, as Buchanan closed the front door behind them. 'Whose house is this?'

'It is owned by a Mr and Mrs McCall,' said Buchanan.

'Never heard of them.'

'They're involved in the horse world.'

'Oh. And who's the bossy britches who invited us?'

'He's sort of my boss,' said Alan.

'Your boss? I thought you just took care of Belleview?'

'I do, but that is just part of what I do. I also work for bossy britches.'

'This way,' said Buchanan, leading them into the sitting room.

'Ah, Alan, and this must be Ashley?' said Andrew, 'thank you for coming.'

'Why have you got us here?' asked Ashley.

'All will be made clear in a moment,' said Andrew. 'First, let me introduce you to Pat McCall, it's his house we are meeting in. Would either of you care for a drink?'

'Is there any beer?' asked Alan.

'Yes,' replied Pat, staring at Alan. He shrugged then went over to the sideboard to get Alan's beer. 'Ashley, can I get you something to drink?'

'Gin and tonic, please. Where's your wife?'

'She's setting a place at the table for you both, she'll be with us shortly.'

'I don't think this is such a good idea. Alan, would you take me home, please?' asked Ashley.

'I think it's time to explain,' said Buchanan. 'Pat, would you go and ask Cynthia and Karen to join us, please?'

'Will do.'

'What's going on?' asked Cynthia. 'The chicken is almost ready.'

'This shouldn't take long,' said Buchanan, who'd taken residence with his back to the fire.

'OK, but if dinner gets ruined it won't be my fault.'

'Cynthia, can I introduce you to Ashley Dale?'

'Hi.'

'Ashley, this is Cynthia McCall, Pat's wife.'

'Hello.'

'The reason I wanted you two to meet is you both have something, or should I say, someone, in common.'

'Common isn't the word I would use,' said Cynthia. 'Conman would be more apt.'

'As I said, I wanted you two to meet and I'm glad Andrew asked Alan to be here. I have already told Cynthia, and I thought it only right to tell you both.'

'Tell us what?' asked Ashley. 'Please come to the point.'

'When I began this investigation, it was simply to tidy up the loose ends on a previous case where a felon died in a plane crash while trying to escape. One of those felons was Victor Mountjoy. Subsequently I have discovered two interesting facts. The first being Victor is in fact alive and currently being pursued for the murder of a Columbian drug dealer called Juan Carlos Barrera. The second fact was Victor has a son, one he tried to prevent from being born. This son is with us this evening.'

'You're Victor's bastard son?' said Cynthia, staring at Alan.

'Steady on,' said Alan, 'I didn't choose who my parents were going to be, and besides his only claim to fatherhood is purely a biological one.'

'Well I never!' said Pat. 'Who'd have thought the old sod had it in him?'

'So, where does this fine mess leave us?' asked Cynthia.

'Exactly where we were a short minute ago,' said Buchanan. 'Between you four, there is the ownership of a potentially large sum of money to be resolved.'

'How much?' enquired Pat.

'Somewhere close to a million pounds,' replied Buchanan. 'But I think Andrew would be better to advise on the disposition of the money.'

'Now that is good news,' said Cynthia.

'We know what happened to the passengers in the plane,' said Andrew, 'they succumbed to carbon monoxide poisoning and crashed into the Channel. Victor, on the other hand, never managed to reboard the plane and is now seeking the cash. Jack has the gilts, which are unfortunately minus Victor's signature, and may just be useless bits of paper.'

'I don't understand,' said Cynthia. 'What exactly are gilts?'

'Gilts are government bonds; they are the equivalent of U.S. Treasury securities. The term gilt is often used informally to describe any bond that has a very low risk of default and a correspondingly low rate of return. They are called gilts because the original certificates issued by the British government had gilded edges.'

'So, where are these gilts?' asked Cynthia.

'I gave them to Ashley,' said Alan.

'And I passed them on to Inspector Buchanan,' said Ashley. 'The last thing I wanted was for someone to come looking for them.'

'Wait a minute,' said Buchanan. 'Who do you think would come looking for them?'

'I don't know who, I just didn't like having them in my possession.'

'I see.'

'That night at Headcorn,' said Alan, 'the night I waited for Victor to show up, something didn't seem quite right to me. And when I later heard about the plane crash and it only having two male occupants, I became suspicious. As part of my job,' he said, looking at Andrew who nodded his assent to what Alan was about to say. 'As part of my job of keeping an eye on Victor, I did some snooping. I began to wonder if Victor hadn't been on the plane when it crashed, if he was skint, what would he do? Get to somewhere he could be safe as soon as he could I reasoned.

'I didn't know you had spiked his cards, Cynthia. If I had known, it would have made my job a lot easier. So, a week later I returned to Headcorn and found out about the robbery. I put two and two together and realised Victor was skint. So, I went and checked local taxi companies and found a driver who took a passenger from the aerodrome to the station.

'The taxi driver told me that his passenger had a bad wound to the face and explained he'd had an accident on his motorcycle and run into a low branch on a tree.'

'I wish I'd been holding that branch,' said Cynthia, 'if I had, he wouldn't have been in any state to get in a taxi.'

'Of course,' continued Alan, 'with these days of automation there wasn't anyone at the station I could ask. So, I got on to the Transport Police and had them check CCTV for passengers on that night about the time the taxi dropped off their passenger. There I hit paydirt, Transport Police were able to track Victor all the way to Eastbourne station. From there it was a simple job to check the taxi rank till I found a driver who said he'd driven someone with a facial injury to the DGH.

'It took several hours of enquiring before I was able to talk to the nurse who treated him and confirmed the story about the motorcycle accident.'

'What about after the DGH, were you able to follow his tracks?'

'Yes, I returned to the taxi rank and found he'd been driven out to Litlington and Belleview.'

'So,' said Buchanan, 'why didn't you let us know what you were doing? It would have maybe saved Barrera from having his throat cut.'

'I wouldn't let him,' said Andrew. 'We were after much bigger fish than Victor, he was only a bit player in the overall scheme of things. It's a pity about Barrera getting his throat cut, makes our job of tracing his connections more difficult.'

'The drug smuggling enterprise?' said Buchanan.

'Precisely, there was also the money laundering trail.'

'What was that?' asked Cynthia.

'Each time Du Marchon flew out across the channel he was flying out with the cash to pay for the drugs he was bringing back. We estimate his share of the drug sales was in the multiple thousands. I won't go into what happened to the cash, as this is still part of an ongoing investigation.'

'He and Victor were very stupid though,' added Alan.

'Why?' asked Cynthia.

'Because they were also skimming the returns. That's why Barrera was here in the country.'

'So, where are the gilts now?' asked Cynthia.

'I have brought them with me for Andrew to look at and determine if they are cashable,' said Buchanan.

'I'll have a look at them later,' said Andrew, 'but in the meantime I could do with some fresh air.'

'Why would I be interested in the gilts?' asked Ashley.

'I was thinking about Alan, since Victor is dead and Alan is his son, he may be eligible for an inheritance of some sort.'

'No thanks, I had nothing from him during his life, I want nothing from his death. Mum and Cynthia can have it all,' said Alan.

'All the same, I'll let you both know what transpires.'

'Fine with me,' said Ashley.

'Good idea,' said Cynthia. 'Why don't all you men go out and do evening stables? There's still time before dinner.'

'A brilliant idea,' said Andrew. 'All this talk of drugs and money has given me a desire to get on a horse.'

'Fine, while you men are out enjoying yourselves, I'll make sure there's enough food for us all.'

'I'll check on Marjorie,' said Karen.

'Er...' said Alan, 'what about me? I don't know anything about horses.'

'That's not a problem,' said Cynthia, 'Andrew can teach you when you go for a ride with him.'

'Me ride a horse? No way.'

'Don't be a chicken, Alan,' said Andrew. 'It's just like riding a bike. You climb onboard and sit on the saddle, and it only has one horsepower to deal with, see, simple.'

'How's Marjorie?' asked Buchanan.

'I just checked in on her and she was reading,' said Karen. 'She said she would stay in bed a little longer then come down when it's dinner time.'

'Good.'

22
Double, Double, Toil and trouble

'Standing here talking isn't getting dinner ready,' said Cynthia, 'and if we are going to eat this evening, someone has to do the preparation.'

'C'mon, lads,' said Pat, 'let's leave the women to do the dinner, we'll go for a ride.'

'Pat,' said Cynthia, as he was about to leave the room.

'What?'

'Mind how you go.'

'What a woman,' said Pat, as they crossed the yard to the stables. 'How can one man be so fortunate to land a beauty like her?'

'Fate smiles on whom it choses, rhyme or reason not. So, either live for something, or die and rot.'

'You're a bit of a poet,' said Andrew.

'Not really,' replied Buchanan, as he opened the barn door.

♦

'I needed that,' said Andrew, as he walked Turpin into the barn. 'How about you, Alan?'

'As my first time riding a horse, it wasn't that bad. Though I'd rather have been out on my Triumph triple.'

'Same for me,' said Pat. 'Sometimes it's just nice to get on a horse and go where the hell you want. No starting gates, no pacing the other riders, just pure fun to go for a ride. How about you, Jack? You spend your life behind a steering wheel.'

Buchanan's answer was interrupted by Cynthia hurrying into the barn.

'Pat?'

'What's up, Cynthia?'

'Is Marjorie here?'

'No. We've just returned. I thought she was going to rest till dinner time. Did you check her room?'

'That's what we thought. Karen just went up to see her but she's not there.'

'Did you check the bathroom?'

'Of course we did. We've checked every room in the house, she's nowhere to be found.'

'Calm down and start again.'

'Cynthia, Ashley and I had to pop into town for some more food,' said Karen, 'but beforehand, I went up to her room and Marjorie was fast asleep. That would have been about an hour ago, just after I heard you go out riding.'

'When we checked her room just now,' said Cynthia, 'she wasn't there, and the room is in a right mess.'

'What mess?'

'The mess on the floor.'

'I'm not following you.'

'You know the trap door to the loft in her room?'

'Yes, it's been painted shut for as long as I can remember.'

'It's not shut anymore.'

'You think Marjorie opened it up? That doesn't make any sense.'

'Pat, we need to do something, I think Marjorie is in some sort of trouble.'

'Right, let me put Turpin in his box and I'll come and see what you are talking about.'

As Pat slid the bolt in Turpin's box, Major growled as a piercing scream came from the loft.

'That sounds like Marjorie,' said Cynthia.

'Remind me, what's up there?' said Buchanan, pointing to the wooden staircase at the far end of the stables.

'The loft flat. That's where the new stable lad will be living when he starts work next month.'

'A flat? Why would Marjorie have gone up there?'

'How should I know? It's just used for storage, been empty for years, no one goes up there.'

'I would like everyone to stay here,' said Buchanan, 'keep talking like you never heard the scream.'

'What are you going to do, Jack?' asked Karen. 'I hope you are not going to do what I think you are about to do.'

'I'll be fine, I'll take Major with me. It was probably just the wind.'

'If you believe that, I have a bridge I can sell you.'

'We'll be fine, won't we, Major?' said Buchanan, scratching the side of Major's neck. 'Cynthia, would you put Doxy in the stall for me, please?'

'Sure. But, Jack, I don't like the idea of you going up to the loft either.'

'It's my job, it's what I'm paid to do. Besides, I'm not going alone, I'm going with Major, we're both trained for this sort of scenario.'

'But...'

'Needs must, Cynthia.'

'Be careful then.'

'I always am. Let's go, Major,' said Buchanan, as he walked towards the set of stairs at the end of the barn.

As Buchanan climbed the steps with Major at his heels, he glanced down at the treads and saw two sets of footprints in the dust. A large set of footprints and a much smaller set, the larger set on top of the smaller set.

'Here I go again, Major,' said Buchanan quietly. 'Once more into the lions' den.'

He made his way up the stairs, treading quietly while staring up into the gloom of the unlit loft.

He reached the top of the stairs, eyes staring, ears straining for any indications that someone was waiting for him. All was quiet, there was no one waiting to bash his head in.

'What do you think, Major?' he whispered, just before he climbed the final step, 'Anything evil lurking in the dark?' He took no response as a positive sign. He looked back down at the seven faces staring up at him. He smiled, put his finger to his lips, then gave a curt salute and climbed the final steps up into the loft.

As he waited for his eyes to become accustomed to the gloom, he realised it wasn't completely dark. There was a small window set in the gable wall behind him. As his eyes adjusted to the low level of light, he saw he was standing on a small landing with a view of a narrow corridor that ran the full length of the barn. The low left corridor wall had a single cupboard door. The right-hand full height wall had several doors, presumably to the rooms that made up the flat.

He stood for a minute, trying to catch any sounds that would indicate a menace waiting further down the hall. All was quiet, save for the murmured voices coming from the stables below. Gradually his hearing tuned into the ambient sounds of the loft. His strengthening vision caught the sight of long tendrils of a spider's web waving in the draughty corridor.

He moved away from the top of the stairs and approached the first door. He wished he had a torch with him, but then realised its light beam would draw attention to his position. Buchanan inclined his head to the door and listened: no sound. He carefully reached for the doorknob and turned it. Slowly pushing the door, he found it opened into a small room, lit by a dusty skylight and bereft of any furniture. The room only contained cardboard shipping boxes from a time long ago when the Mountjoys moved into the house with their personal effects.

'OK, boy. Go check out the room.'

Buchanan watched as Major sniffed his way round the room, then he retraced his steps to the hallway and gently closed the door behind him. He made his way further along the passageway and realised there was an open door wedged back on his right, probably the actual front door to the flat he reasoned.

Just beyond the flat's front door, there was another door on the right and, like the others, shut. He repeated the process and, when he opened the door, he saw this room also was lit by a dusty skylight. In the far corner, under the skylight was a metal-framed bed, with a mattress and a pile of bedclothes. Just inside the door on the right was a small chest of drawers, and on the left a small open-front wardrobe. Major repeated his search, but this time became agitated while sniffing at a pile of discarded clothes.

'We're getting warm, boy. C'mon, let's try the next room.'

Working along the passageway he found the next room to be a small washroom and toilet. He crept in and had a quick look around. The wastepaper bin was half-full of discarded bandages and the toilet needed flushing.

The door to the final room was also closed. What to do he wondered? Should he just open the door and rush in? No, that wouldn't do, fools rush in where angels fear to tread. But suppose that scream had been Marjorie hurting herself? Maybe she was lying on the floor bleeding to death. Was this a risk Buchanan was prepared to take? He decided the angels were on his side and he'd take it. He hammered on the door with his fist while shouting, 'Marjorie, it's Jack! Are you alright?'

He got no response and was about to hammer on the door again when the door partially opened onto the sitting room. Buchanan waited to see if the door would open fully. It stayed partially open, blocking the view into the room. He held onto Major's collar as he listened to the distinct sound of shuffling footsteps as though someone was being forced to go where they didn't want to.

Buchanan counted to sixty then pushed the door open with his foot. He scanned the room looking for places of refuge in case Marjorie was able to break free from Victor.

There was a small table with two chairs on the left. On the right, there was a two-seater settee with small coffee table in front. Beside the table was another door which Buchanan reasoned led through to the kitchen and was the probable source of the scream and the location of the person responsible for the opening of the door.

'You can come out, Victor, and please let Marjorie go, she can't help you. Victor, I know you are in there, let Marjorie go and come out.'

'Stay away from the door.'

'I am away from the door, Victor. I'm standing in the passageway.'

'Make sure you stay there.'

Buchanan stood in the passageway continuing to hold Major's collar. He reasoned Victor's only options were to either hold out in the kitchen with Marjorie as a hostage and bargaining chip, or come out and try bluffing his way to freedom. He opted for coming out.

'Don't try anything stupid,' said Victor, as Marjorie crept out of the kitchen with him two feet behind, dragging a large rucksack. He stopped Marjorie three feet from the passageway door and said, 'You see the pistol?'

'Yes, Victor, I see your pistol, is that your service weapon?'

'Yes, a Glock, just like the police. If fired from this range it would spread Marjorie's brains all over you. Now back off, all the way down the passageway.'

'I suppose the stolen money is in the rucksack – is this where you hid it?'

'No. I came up here to get my stuff, this stupid bitch woke as I was in the room.'

'So where did you hide the money?'

'That, my friend, is none of your business.'

'In the loft in the room where I stay when visiting,' said Marjorie.

'Ah, eureka!' said Buchanan. 'Now it all makes sense. Every time Pat and Cynthia are away, you stay in that room preventing Victor getting to the money he hid in the loft.'

'Smart boy. Now you know the truth, get moving.'

Buchanan walked backwards towards the staircase as Victor, rucksack over on his shoulder, his Glock pointing directly at Marjorie's head, came steadily forward.

At the top of the stairs Buchanan stopped and said, 'Victor, you do realise this is futile? Even if you manage to get away from the stables here at Appleton, there will be a hue and cry for you. Within minutes all roads will be blocked, police helicopters will be up scouring the countryside for you. Shooting Marjorie and me will be just another wasted gesture.'

Victor stopped and moved his pistol away from being aimed at Marjorie's head and pointed it straight at Buchanan. 'Get down the stairs.'

'No,' said Buchanan, 'I can't let you get away to kill again.'

'Move out of my way or I'll shoot you where you stand.'

'No, you shall not pass. Give up, throw down the gun and let Marjorie go.'

'If you want it, here have it,' he said, throwing his pistol at Buchanan's face.'

'Thanks,' said Buchanan, catching the errant pistol. 'Empty, I see, just like your threats. C'mon, Victor, you must by now realise it's all over, you have no hope of getting away.'

'I still have this,' Victor said, grabbing Marjorie by the hair and placing the edge of his knife blade against her throat. 'The gun may have been empty, but this blade still works.'

'Is that the knife you used to kill Barrera?'

Victor smiled and said, 'You recognise it? Good, then you'll realise I'm not afraid to use it. Now, back off down the stairs. When I get to the bottom, I don't want to see either of you anywhere near the door.'

Buchanan made his way backwards down the stairs while looking at Victor standing at the top. He was now standing behind Marjorie holding the knife to her throat.

'Victor, you're alive!' said Cynthia.

'Not according to the coroner.'

'Victor,' said Andrew, 'don't make it any worse for yourself. Put the knife down and let Marjorie go.'

'It's no use, Victor,' said Buchanan, 'listen to good advice, it's all over, time to give up and face the consequences.'

'Not while I hold the winning hand.'

'We know all about what you've been up to, how you fell off Du Marchon's plane, made your way to Eastbourne, the DGH and then on to Litlington. About how your partner, Du Marchon, flew out the cash and flew in the drugs; and how you turned your ill-gotten gains into gilts.'

'So?'

'We have the gilts, all of them.'

'How thoughtful of you. Place them by the door and I will pick them up on the way out. Oh, also the Rover, bring it round, there's a good boy, Pat.'

'Victor, give up now, don't make things worse for yourself,' repeated Buchanan.

'Shut up. Move away from the stairs and no one will get hurt and stop trying to change the subject. Leave the Rover keys and the gilts by the door and Marjorie will live to tell the tale.'

'Like Barrera, did you give him a chance to move away?'

'He was a fool; thought he could muscle in on my territory.'

'Your territory? I thought Du Marchon was running the show?'

'Him, what a laugh! The Rover keys and the gilts by the door. *Now!*'

'Victor, please,' said Alan, 'give up, don't make it any worse than it is.'

'Who the hell are you to tell me what to do? You're nothing more than a glorified pool-boy.'

'My friends know me as Alan Dale; but my birth certificate says my birth name is Alan Mountjoy. You can deny it all you want, but the fact remains, you are my father.'

'I have no son.'

'In the true sense of the word you are correct. The only link between you and me is our DNA.'

'You're just making it up. Want to cut in on the money, is that it?'

'If you were a real father, you would…'

'Would what? Wipe your snivelling nose, you're no son of mine.'

'Yes, he is,' said Ashley. 'Alan is your biological son.'

'What is this, Saturday night charades?'

'You don't remember me, do you? The pretty little NAFFI barmaid, the one who you got pregnant and tried to buy off with a thousand Euros and told to have an abortion?'

'That was you? You stupid bitch, you should have taken the money and got rid of the kid.'

'Is that the jacket you stole from Headcorn?' said Buchanan. 'The owner would like it back,'

'This? You can have it,' he said, momentarily forgetting he had his knife at Marjorie's throat and raised his arm to give Buchanan a one-finger salute. As he did, Marjorie sneezed, snapped forward and threw Victor over her shoulder. He tumbled down the stairs and then lay face down in the dirt of the stable floor.

Buchanan was the first to reach the prone body. He reached down, and gently turned Victor over onto his side. The knife that was moments before millimetres from Marjorie's jugular vein, was now sticking out of Victor's chest.

'Is he – is he – dead?' asked Cynthia.

Buchanan felt for a pulse,

'Is he dead?' repeated Cynthia.

'No, not yet. Would someone call for an ambulance?'

'How bad is it?' said Ashley, as Andrew carefully undid Victor's shirt.

'Pretty bad, his pulse is weak, and he is losing a lot of blood.'

'Here,' said Cynthia, handing Andrew a large gauze pad from a first-aid box by the barn door. 'First time we've had to use it.'

'What? Aargh…'

'He's coming to,' said Andrew. 'Easy, Victor, you've fallen down the stairs.'

'Ambulance is on its way,' said Karen. 'I told them the patient was bleeding heavily from a knife wound.'

'Lie still, Victor,' said Buchanan. 'You've had an accident and you're bleeding badly. Lie still, please, there's an ambulance on its way.'

'Karen, Ashley,' said Andrew, 'would you go with Cynthia and make some tea for us all?. Pat, would you and Alan go out to the road and watch for the ambulance?'

Andrew carefully held the gauze pad over Victor's wound and managed to stem the flow of blood while Buchanan found a feed sack to put under his head.

The ambulance, along with a police car, arrived within minutes of the emergency call. Pat led the ambulance crew and police round to the barn.

'Where is the injured party?' asked one of the paramedics.'

'Over here,' said Andrew.

'Did you see what happened?' the sergeant asked Buchanan.

'Yes.'

'Who else saw what happened?'

'Everyone did.'

'Where is everyone?'

'In the kitchen,' said Andrew, 'I thought it best if they kept the area clear.'

'Would you show me to the kitchen, please?'

'Certainly.'

'Good evening, I am Sergeant Stevens. I didn't think we would be back here again under the same circumstances; can someone tell me what happened this evening?'

'I think I can,' said Andrew. 'Major Andrew Jackson, I work for the Adjutant General's Office,' he said, presenting his identity card. 'We are here this evening as dinner guests of Mr and Mrs McCall. Mrs McCall's former husband – the chap whose life the paramedics are trying to save – broke into the house, apparently looking for some money he said was owing to him. He appeared at the top of the stairs brandishing a knife. He was asked to put it away and leave, but unfortunately tripped on the top step and fell down the stairs injuring himself.'

'Is that what happened? Anyone see anything differently?'

No one spoke.

'Where were you when this accident happened, er... Mr?'

'Detective Chief Inspector Buchanan. I was at the bottom of the stairs pleading with the victim to put the knife away.'

'DCI Buchanan. Are you the same DCI that DI Blakey was working with on the previous killing here at the stables?'

'Yes, strange that.'

'I'd call it more than strange, sir. Where was everyone else while this little drama was unfolding?'

'Everyone was standing at the bottom of the stairs pleading with him to put his knife away,' said Andrew.

'Did he find the money he was here to collect?'

'We have no idea.'

'Which one of you is Mr McCall?'

'I am,' said Pat.

'Did you invite – what is the injured man's name?'

'Victor Mountjoy.'

'Did you invite Mr Mountjoy to the house?'

'How could I? He was dead.'

'I don't follow you on that.'

'Mr Mountjoy was reported as having died in a plane crash a couple of months ago.'

'And the same question, where were you when the accident happened?'

'Same as the Major, and everyone else, at the bottom of the stairs.'

'Thank you. And your name, sir?'

'Alan Dale, a friend of the Mr and Mrs McCall, also invited here for dinner, and before you ask, also standing at the foot of the stairs.'

'Inspector, Major, Mr McCall, would you follow me back to the barn, please? Do any of you know why Mr Mountjoy would find it necessary to use a knife in his discussion?' asked the sergeant as they crossed to the barn.

'Mr Mountjoy is the former husband of the present Mrs McCall,' said Buchanan.

'Top of those stairs?' the sergeant said, pointing 'Is that where the injured man fell from?'

'Yes,' replied Buchanan.

'I think I'll wait for the ambulance crew to do their stuff. Mr McCall, can you tell if anything has gone missing?'

'No. Until Mr Mountjoy has been taken away to the hospital, we can't get up the stairs to check.'

'What's up there?' he asked, nodding at the stairs.

'Just storage. It used to be a flat for the stable lad, now it's just full of stuff we no longer use but don't want to throw out.'

'Fine.'

'Would you like a coffee or tea?' asked Cynthia, who'd joined them in the barn. As she asked, she nodded to Buchanan regarding the rucksack sitting on the floor at the top of the stairs. 'The kettle has just boiled.'

'Ah, yes, nothing beats a nice cup of tea.'

'I think we could all do with something to take our mind off the evening's events,' said Cynthia.

'What happens here at Appleton, Mrs McCall?' asked the sergeant.

'Appleton is an Equestrian Centre and we also board horses for their owners. Do you ride, Sergeant?'

'A bicycle only.'

'OK if we transport, Sergeant?' asked one of the paramedics.

'How is he?'

'Not good.'

'Where are you taking him to?'

'Maidstone and Tunbridge Wells.'

'Thanks.'

'The kitchen's this way.' said Cynthia, nodding discreetly at Buchanan.

While the sergeant and his constable sipped on their coffees, Buchanan slipped out of the kitchen, over to the barn up the stairs. He picked up the rucksack, returned to his bedroom and placed the rucksack on the floor beside their overnight case. He took a moment to unzip the top and look inside, it was full of bundles of fifty, twenty and ten-pound notes. He smiled and returned to the kitchen.

The sergeant and constable were chatting to Cynthia and Pat. Andrew and Alan were huddled together in quiet conversation and Karen was sitting opposite Marjorie, holding her hands and praying quietly.

'Everything OK, Jack?' asked Cynthia.

'Everything is fine.'

'Well, I think we'll be off,' said the sergeant, putting their empty cups on the table.

'I'll see you to the door,' said Pat.

Pat returned with a smile on his face.

'Well, Jack, was the rucksack what I thought it was?'

'I do believe it is. I put it in our bedroom on the floor beside our case. I didn't think it would be of use to the sergeant's investigation, it would just cloud the issue.'

'Good, I'll go and get it and bring it down.'

Forty minutes later the kitchen table stood resplendent with four hundred and forty-eight thousand pounds in stacks of fifty, twenty, and ten-pound notes.

'I have never seen so much cash in all my life,' said Cynthia. 'Is it ours, Andrew, or does it belong to the government?'

'That all depends, and I must warn you, even though I am a lawyer I am unable to give you a definitive reply to that question. You said you repaid all the money that Victor swindled?'

'Yes. We had to take out a second mortgage on the farm to do it, but everyone had every penny returned.'

'How much did you have to borrow?'

'Three hundred and seventy-three thousand, four hundred and fifty-two pounds,' said Pat.

'Hmm, if it were up to me, I'd say just keep the cash. Doing a quick calculation in my head, if you subtract the cash, you are out of pocket with compensating Victor's victims, plus the interest and expenses involved with the refinancing of the farm's mortgage, as far as I'm concerned, it's all yours.'

'Really?'

'Yes, but the bank will require you to show that the money has been legally acquired and is not from the proceeds of crime.'

'Oh, how will we do that?'

'I'll have a chat with a colleague at the office and come back to you with an answer.'

'Thank you, Andrew, but what about Victor? If he survives won't he want a share, or something?'

'I don't think you need worry about that. If he survives his injury, he will have a great deal more to worry about than attempting to lay claim to any of this money.'

'But will that be so?' said Marjorie.

'Oh, sorry Marjorie, I forgot to ask,' said Cynthia, 'how are you feeling?

'I'm fine, Cynthia, thanks for asking.'

'First you get thrown by your horse, then you are throwing my dead husband around like he was a sack of potatoes.'

'If only he were that useful.'

'Is anyone still hungry?' asked Cynthia.

'Surprisingly, yes,' said Pat.

'OK, ladies, let's leave the men to feed and water the horses and we can go and set the table.'

◆

The four of them worked quickly and within the hour the horses had their stalls cleaned, bedding prepared and all were fed and watered.

'Dinner is ready,' said Cynthia, from the kitchen door.

Buchanan followed Andrew, Alan, and Pat through to the dining room.

'How is Marjorie?' Buchanan asked, as Cynthia returned from upstairs.

'She's just gone upstairs.'

'Is she coming down for dinner?'

'Yes, she said she will be down shortly after she has a shower.'

'That smells great, what's for dinner, love?' asked Pat.

'Chicken madras.'

'Ooh, can't beat a good curry,' said Pat. 'It's not every day I get to eat and enjoy it.'

'It's also low fat so shouldn't mess up your training schedule. If you'll all take your seats, I'll serve.'

'How was the honeymoon, Cynthia?' asked Karen.

'It was wonderful. I was concerned that my mother would be funny about Pat, but they hit it off right from the start. Pat charmed mother with his tales of old Ireland and his upbringing in the country. We have invited mother to come and live with us. We will convert one of the unused offices into a small self-contained unit for her. She won't be on her own though, there will be an adjoining door at the end of the hall so she can come through and take meals and sit with us.'

'Did you see much of the area while you were there?' asked Buchanan.

'Not really. With mother recovering from surgery, we spent most of the time with her.'

'I hear you rode at Cheltenham, Pat?' said Andrew.

'Yes, two races, rode Rambler on Friday and Turpin on Saturday.'

'How did you do?'

The Jockey's Wife.

'Third place on Rambler and a well-deserved second place riding Turpin,' said Cynthia.

'Well done, Pat,' said Buchanan. 'When's your next ride?'

'Back to Cheltenham the weekend the 12th to 14th of November. Fancy coming along?'

'I don't think we will be able to,' said Karen. 'We'll be getting ready to fly to Dallas that week.'

'What's in Dallas?' asked Cynthia.

'Do you remember Travis and Shelly Grant?'

'The John Wayne character?' said Pat.

'That's him. Well, his daughter has been staying with us these last few months while she attends Brighton University. She has invited us to go over with her to spend Thanksgiving with her parents.'

'Isn't she engaged to Nathan's stable manager?' asked Cynthia.

'The very same.'

'Has he got a new manager to replace – what's the lad's name?'

'Harry. I'm not sure.'

'Andrew,' said Cynthia, 'I'm a bit confused about the gilts, how and where did Du Marchon and Victor get them from?'

'Cash from drug deals and cash syphoned from the businesses that Du Marchon acted as consultant for. I'll have a better idea how he went about robbing companies when we go through their tax returns and whatever paperwork we can dig up. We at the NCA have been tracking Du Marchon for several months. A few years ago, there was a scam running where unscrupulous company directors would rob the assets of a company and invest it in another, bankrupting the donor company. Quite often these assets would include unpaid taxes, pension payments and money owed to suppliers. What's really bad about Du Marchon was since he wasn't a director, he was free to repeat the process.'

'But that's immoral,' objected Karen.

'Yes, it certainly is. Du Marchon pulled this trick several times and we estimated the total money embezzled come to several hundred thousand pounds.'

'Is that where the money to purchase the gilts came from?' asked Cynthia.

'In part, there was also cash from drug sales.'

'This news makes Victor sound like just a bit player,' said Pat.

'My conclusion as well. But there is one thing that comes to mind and that was what Victor said about Barrera trying to muscle in.'

'Are you referring to the other week when the Columbian was murdered?' said Cynthia.

'That and other events.'

'Of course,' said Cynthia, 'I am sorry, Marjorie, how tactless of me. You were the target of those incidents. Oh, Jack, do you suppose it could have been Victor who attacked Marjorie and killed the Columbian?'

'Quite likely.'

'Where were you in the yard when you were attacked, Marjorie?' asked Buchanan.

'Just outside the stable doors.'

'And Blakey's men didn't find anyone?'

'No.'

'What about footprints?'

'They did a thorough search of the grounds in the morning but found nothing untoward.'

'One thing that puzzles me,' said Buchanan, 'when you do the rounds in the evening, do you take Major with you?'

'Yes, it's part of his daily routine.'

'What did he do when you were attacked?'

'I don't remember, he might have been in the stables. He likes to say goodnight to the horses.'

'And he didn't bark, or growl?'

'Not that I remember. Why?'

'The fact he didn't bark makes me sure it was Victor who attacked you.'

Now, if you will excuse me, I think I've had enough excitement for one day,' said Marjorie, 'see you all in the morning.'

As the table was being cleared, Buchanan's phone rang.

'DCI Buchanan – he did – no, I'll take care of that, I'm with them now, thanks for letting me know.'

'Was that the hospital?' asked Cynthia.

'Yes.'

'How is Victor?'

'They said Victor didn't survive the drive to the hospital.'

'He's finally out of my life.'

'Yes, he's finally out of your life. For it is written, for all who take the sword will perish by the sword.'

The End.

Lightning Source UK Ltd.
Milton Keynes UK
UKHW021812200222
398942UK00009B/170